GREAT MODEL ESSAYS

SHORT
MODEL
ESSAYS

ANN M. TAYLOR
SALEM STATE COLLEGE

Little, Brown and Company
BOSTON   TORONTO

for Frank

808.0427
Sh8
125397
June 1983

Library of Congress Catalog Card No. 80-83779

ISBN 0-316-833584

9 8 7 6 5 4 3 2 1

MV

Published simultaneously in Canada
by Little, Brown & Company (Canada) Limited

Printed in the United States of America

For the Instructor

The oftrepeated student question, "Can you give me some idea of what you want?" is the major motivation for this book. In spite of detailed explanations and in spite of some lively discussions about "great" essays, my students continued to have difficulties deciding what I did want in my composition course. So I decided to show rather than tell them. I collected sample student essays that fulfilled most of my expectations for a freshman assignment, and I combed through published material gathering the most readable and imitable examples I could find. This collection has grown out of that very practical effort.

My main intention is that students immediately begin to see themselves as writers, not as inmates working out a one-year sentence. So I have chosen essays and other prose pieces that are complete, simply structured, and imitable in both content and method. Each one is, for the most part, short enough to be read closely in a single class. Because writing benefits from close reading, I have tried to include major essayists who reward such scrutiny, but the subject and structure of the essay were ultimately more important considerations than the reputation of the writer.

My intention is not to reduce writing to the commonplace or to limit it with rigid structural definitions, but simply to provide beginning writers first with the basic pattern for the whole essay and then with some of the countless ways of working with it. Each essay in the first section, including several student models, contains an introduction with a clearly recognizable thesis statement, body paragraphs that develop this thesis, and a separate conclusion. In the later sections the essays become more complex, providing developments, variations, combinations, and elaborations of the basic pattern.

This progression from a simple to a more complex structure is intended as a convenient order for study and imitation, but you might easily adapt later models in the book to the simpler plans of the earlier assignments. Within each section I have also arranged the models in the order of increasing difficulty, and in the last section, I have included examples of other writing assignments students are likely to encounter. Ideally, these models will be starting points for the students' own creative efforts.

At the beginning of each chapter, I have introduced the structural patterns to be noticed in the subsequent group of examples, and before each model I have called attention to the distinguishing characteristics. To prevent unnecessary stalling at possibly unfamiliar references, I have included footnotes where I thought necessary. After each selection, I have listed vocabulary words to be looked up by the student, plus questions on content and method to encourage study of those aspects of writing that can move the essay from exercise to art. Finally and most importantly, I have made suggestions for writing, some on analysis of topics or techniques, but most based specifically on the approach of the model.

Although the questions on method after each essay will often bring up major rhetorical principles, these principles are treated more systematically in the "Checklist for Readers and Writers" in the appendix. My students have found this list helpful for both reading the models and writing their own essays. Also included in the appendix is a discussion of the checklist questions, illustrated in a short piece by Kenneth Tynan, "The Difficulty of Being Dull." In the *Instructor's Manual* are suggestions for using the checklist in the course. For those who prefer an alternative approach or who may want to focus on particular rhetorical elements, the *Instructor's Manual* also contains a "Thematic Index" and a "Rhetorical Index."

My hope is that your students will become as eager to write as some of mine have when inspired by a model. As one freshman said, "It really helps to see what someone else did first."

I would like to acknowledge the help and support of students at Salem State College, who continued to ask the right questions; teachers, colleagues, and friends—Raymond Blois, Ellen Vellela, Philip de Palma, Judith Saunders, Raymond Perry, William Mahaney, Francis Devlin, Guy Rotella, and Alicia Nitecki—and my husband, Francis C. Blessington. I would also like to thank the staff of Little, Brown—particularly Charles H. Christensen, Joan Feinberg, Jane Muse, and Elizabeth Philipps.

A.M.T.

For the Student

All of the essays in this collection have been chosen as models for your own papers, as patterns for you to imitate while you are learning the basics of good writing. Ideally, when you read one of these models you will say to yourself, "I think I can do that!" and run for your paper and pen. If the effect is not quite so dramatic, I hope that you will at least see some possibilities in the essays that will become more obvious as you study them closely. They all have something to teach. You will not be expected to duplicate these examples, but to mine them for ideas and inspirations that will help you to clarify your own thoughts and feelings for expression in prose.

In Part I you will study the basic pattern, the most simple structure for an essay and, in later parts, you will be looking at some of the many ways of working with this pattern. The subjects cover a wide variety of areas—memories, everyday life, the modern world, people, places, sports, writing, the natural world, and values. Some essays are personal, some objective, some simple, some complex; but they are all chosen because of their interest and value for you. The purpose is that with each new essay you will gain new ideas about writing. The introductions to the parts of the book and to each essay, plus the questions on content and method following each essay, are designed to help you do just this.

To get the most out of a model, read it through once without stopping at all. Read it again, this time looking up the words you do not know and answering the questions. Finally, read it at least once more in order to "put it back together again." Analysis is only one step in the process of appreciation but it is an indispensable one—especially for a reader who wants to become a writer. After you learn as much as you can from a model, the suggestion for writing following each one will give you a chance to try it on your own.

As an additional help for reading the models and writing your own papers, I have included in the appendix a "Check-list for Readers and Writers." This is a list of questions I wrote when students asked for a summary of things I considered important for every essay. Also included there is a discussion of the main points in the checklist, illustrated with a short, published essay.

With all these things on your mind, you may at first feel like a tripped-up beginner on a ski slope or a novice pianist trying to coordinate chords, keys, and pedals. Just remember that with understanding and practice, writing gets easier, as do skiing and piano playing. Try focusing on one assignment at a time and doing the best job you can so you will be learning new skills, not just repeating old, familiar errors. Be patient, write often, and keep a sense of humor—your progress will be faster. As the English poet Alexander Pope wrote, "True ease in writing comes from art, not chance,/As those move easiest who have learn'd to dance."

A.M.T.

Contents

III · Variations   83

In this section, writers vary the basic pattern by implying the thesis, by interrupting the march from one topic to another, or by absorbing the introduction or the conclusion into the body of the essay.

IV · Combinations   137

Here the departure from the basic pattern becomes more variable by combining a thesis with a "sub-thesis," using more than one method of variation, or developing sub-topics and interruptions more fully.

V · Elaborations   189

This section contains a great variety of approaches, since some subjects call for more complex patterns.

VI · Applications   291

This last section is a collection of models for typical college writing assignments. Their close connection to earlier assignments in this book will be apparent.

APPENDIX

I · The Basic Pattern

*In everything we learn to do there is emulation.
But if we make good on our imitation we soon begin to try wrinkles of our own. Possibilities suddenly appear, as chickadees and juncoes do when
seeds are scattered on the snow. . . . Sidney Cox*

All complete essays do three things—introduce the subject, develop it, and conclude it. No matter how elaborate
or idiosyncratic the pattern may become, these three basic
elements are always present. In Part I, the three essentials
and their arrangement in the basic pattern are most
clearly visible.

The purpose of this part is that you read and then
attempt to write a basic and well-organized essay. In all
of the following selections, however simple or complex
their subject matter and however personal or impersonal
their approach, the introduction provides a clear statement of the thesis; the controlling idea governs the topics
of all the body paragraphs, which are linked to one another by smooth transitions; and the conclusion (a separate paragraph) develops logically from the entire piece
and ends it. It is out of this very simple pattern that all
well-written essays grow.

Now read the following student essay. Look closely
for the thesis, the controlling idea, the transitions and
topic sentences. Be sure you understand the relationship
of each paragraph to the introduction and the purpose of
the conclusion. After you finish reading, you might try
to write your own essay on embarrassing situations that
you can remember. Be sure to think of tone. How do you
feel about these experiences now?

CAROLINE CURLEY (student)

Embarrassments at a Safe Distance

When I think of my years at St. Clement's School, many memories return: the joy of buying a blue chiffon dress and having my hair decorated with baby's breath for my first prom, trying to stay awake after three A.M. for an "Algebra I" test, sharing the sadness of graduation with old friends who soon headed to the dorms of different colleges all over the country. But, outstanding as these memories are, none are as memorable as the embarrassing situations I got myself into at St. Clem's.

One such embarrassment was caused indirectly by my school uniform. One day I was hurrying across the crowded cafeteria trying to make a volleyball practice, but I got only half way when I saw students pointing at me and giggling. It didn't take me long to find out that I had forgotten to button up my skirt as I hurried from my locker and that now it was draped somewhere between my knees and my ankles. Though I snatched it up immediately, the damage had been done. It doesn't seem like such a big deal now, but when things like that happen to a twelve-year old, they have a way of sticking in the memory. I'm still very careful of my buttons.

Getting laughed at at age twelve by a group of kids looking for a joke was bad enough, but flunking a sex education test in the junior year of high school was even worse. Sex education is a quick course at St. Clem's. The nuns mention it for one day during the junior year and never bring it up again. During our day, we got a special class taught by a hired teacher "from the outside" and supported by our parents. At the beginning of the class, this teacher passed out a questionnaire to see how much we knew. I flunked. I thought an IUD was an abbreviation for a youth organization; I won't mention some of the other things I thought. Needless to say, I learned a lot from the class

1

2

3

that followed, after I got over the horror of passing my answers in.

But neither the skirt nor the test were as bad as my disastrous role as a tooth in a skit on health. I was called "Bicuspid," a rotten, unbrushed tooth. In the play, a boy was brought to court and charged with neglect of his health. The fruit, milk, vegetables and toothbrush made their cases against him, but I was the main evidence of his shameful neglect. My costume, however, realistic as it was, was not easy to get around in. Made from a cardboard box and draped with an old, partly-blackened white sheet, my tooth outfit tripped me up as I ran out to make my charge against the untidy boy. I fell flat on my back and couldn't get up. I felt like a flipped-over turtle. By the time I did manage to roll over, crawl to a bench a few feet away, and struggle to my feet, the audience was alive with laughter, not with disapproval of my cavities. They didn't learn much about brushing bicuspids, but they did have a good time—at my expense.

And I too have fun—now. When I get together with my old friends, I can look back at these embarrassments, happy that they are so far behind me and able to see how funny they actually were. After some good laughs at the silly things we all did, I inconspicuously check the button on my skirt and rush on to whatever new disasters might lie in store.

TINA MOSTACCI (student)

So Little to Do in So Much Time

*In this essay, a student evaluates her most recent vaca-
tion—in this case, the Christmas break. Again, the structure is clearly based on the thesis—ways in which she
wasted her time—and each paragraph develops details
about her "nothing" vacation. Being concrete and honest
can add a good deal of life to a potentially dull "What I
Did on My Recent Vacation" paper.*

During my first semester, my days were extremely full. In 1
addition to the work for six courses, I also had my work at a
mens' formal wear shop. When I wasn't memorizing the anatomy of a frog or learning the four forms of discourse or re-
learning my high school French, I was helping to measure jit-
tery grooms for their June weddings or planning wardrobes
for local proms and Atlantic cruises. Busy I was. But when
the Christmas break came along, everything changed. My
courses were over, my hours at the shop were cut from twenty-
five to six a week, and I was fast becoming a poverty case. So,
what did I do? Nothing. At least nothing that I'm proud of.

For one thing, I took up knitting. I didn't have the money 2
to buy Christmas presents for my mother, two brothers, two
sisters, one grandmother, eleven cousins, and two bosses. So I
began to knit. For ten dollars, I bought ten skeins of yarn and
began to "knit one, purl two" my way through hours of cute
tube socks. I could picture my grandmother out "boogie-ing"
while I was being creatively monotonous at home. Maybe it
was a "labor of love," as my mother said, but I really got worried when I started to feel happy as another striped leg-
warmer took shape.

This didn't last forever, however. Soon the thrill of knit- 3
ting was done and I was forced to find another pastime. I did.

Eating. For two weeks after Christmas, I ate leftover lasagne for breakfast. Then I became a walnut addict. By New Year's Day, I was ready to resolve on a diet, but not before I downed the traditional Chinese food stuffed into our refrigerator. I ate it hot and cold for about a week into 1980. My little body metamorphosed into a chubby little body. I was so disgusted with myself that I didn't want to be seen outside of the house; all I really wanted to do was sleep.

So I went to bed at midnight (often without shaking the   4
crumbs from my last piece of cake off the spread) and got up at one the next day. My thin dreams battled with my fat ones. I would appear at one time a slinky size ten, but then I'd start cheating on my diet and having visions of my next meal. I slept so much that I felt as if my brains were stuck to the back of my skull. But there really was nothing to be awake for, ex- cept maybe television.

When I did finally wake up, I tuned in the "Twenty Thou-   5
sand Dollar Pyramid," and then, well-stocked with peanut butter, marshmallow and crackers, I settled in for my afternoon soap operas. I liked "As the World Turns" and "One Life to Live," but "Another World" (what an appropriate title) was my favorite—an hour and a half soap. What a treat! I began to worry if Janice would really poison Mack, or if they would ever discover Kit's true identity. Big problems.

The boredom began to get to me. I knew I had to get out   6
of the house, but I did even better than that. I got out of the state. Going to New York to visit my sister was the best move I made during my whole vacation. I got up by eight A.M., I ate a balanced diet, I hiked all over the city, and I didn't care a bit what happened to Janice, Mack, or Kit. By the time I got home, I was ten pounds thinner, a lot more awake and ready to go. Back at the tuxedo shop for twenty-five hours a week and back in school, I'm busy again. So much to do in so little time.

Vocabulary

discourse (1), metamorphosed (3)

Questions

1. Did the student enjoy her vacation?
2. How did she escape from the boredom?

3. What is the thesis?
4. What is the controlling idea?
5. What is the tone?
6. What is the topic of each body paragraph?
7. How does the conclusion relate to the body of the essay?
8. Select two details that seem particularly effective and explain how they work in the essay.
9. How do the paragraphs link to one another? Explain the transitions.
10. Which is the best paragraph in the essay?
11. Do you like this essay? Why? Do you see any way it might be improved?

Suggestion for Writing

(Sorry.) Write an essay on how you spent your recent vacation. Consider what your *real* attitude was during the time off, not just what you might think a teacher wants to hear. If you enjoyed yourself, help the reader to feel the enjoyment. If you were miserable, illustrate the misery. Try to be as honest as you can.

BILL FRANCIS (student)

The Holloway Huns

In this essay, a student discusses his not very successful experience with a local football team. Notice the detail and the tone. How seriously does he take the failure?

It is time to put my shoulder pads, hip pads and cleats into 1
their wooden milk box in the cellar and hope they keep from
mold until next fall. Any mold that gathers would be appropriate, however, because this year we managed not only to
lose every game—we've done that most years—but this year we
did not even score a touchdown. We are easily the worst team
in football.

If you saw the Mary Holloway field you would probably 2
blame the field: a dust bowl with little scraps of grass struggling
up only to be uprooted by iron and plastic cleats. In the summer, the dust blows and piles up against the twenty foot cement
wall crowned with a chainlink fence that surrounds home
plate. It looks like the remains of a prison yard after a big
break. At the back of the park, a series of small hills lope
sharply up to another fence as if they were running away from
the dinginess. One night Sid Lyons drove his motorcycle up
there and put himself in the hospital for several months. He
still can't get insured.

Each night during the late summer and fall we meet in this 3
desert for practice under the solitary light bulb that the city
affords us. When Charlie gets out of work, he comes over to
coach us and we begin. Or almost begin. The problem is that
the team is so depressed that almost no one shows up. The first
time I went, Charlie was so put out that so few had turned out
for practice that he demonstrated illicit blocking by picking

me up off the ground by my sweatshirt and throwing me backwards on the ground. Charlie is a decent guy, but he gets little thanks for his work as I expect most sandlot coaches do.

Attendance is never good, and even when people do show 4 up, they are usually nursing some injury so they can't practice. Zeke has had a sore finger for two years and his brother, the Gimp, has had such a variety of ailments, no one even bothers to ask him what's wrong anymore. Others make sure they have on neat clothes so they can't roll in the field or they'll ruin them. (Later, they play cards or drink beer to develop their masculinity.) I am one of the faithful, so I get to be fullback; due to the lack of numbers, all we ever can rehearse is the backfield. Joe Finn is the quarterback because he is one of the few who can remember the plays which consist of matching the number of the back with the hole in the line (a hole which never shows up).

The reason it never shows up is that the Park League put 5 us, the Huns of Holloway Park, in a league above us. This in itself seems to make practicers scarce, but somehow enough players always appear for the Sunday game—usually after Charlie's urgent, last minute telephoning. We do have an ex-marine to run the ball for us occasionally and our secret weapon is Fang, a big kid who has a ferocious broken tooth and an unbreakable head. Nevertheless, we never win. The semi-pro monsters we play against are too big, too experienced, and not yet too old, though they're getting there. It's a commonplace to go to the hospital; you don't have to continue the game then. Right now, Billy Lovett has a broken wrist and earlier this year, I broke a few ribs. I almost didn't go to the hospital since Ronny Grant is still playing with a black bulge on his heroic side. There were also a few mild concussions.

Sometimes we end in a fight with the other team, but only 6 when we have a majority of spectators on our side. After the forty second brawl, the cops always slowly get out of the cruiser and suggest that the game be called. At least we don't lose all the time.

Vocabulary

illicit (3), concussions (5)

Questions

1. What is the thesis?
2. What is the topic of each paragraph? Pay close attention to paragraph 4.
3. What is the writer's tone? How serious is he?
4. How does the conclusion relate to the introduction and to the body of the essay?
5. Select and discuss two details that contribute to the effect of the essay.
6. Which sentence do you like best? Why?
7. Which do you think is the best paragraph? Why?
8. Do you see any way to improve the essay? How?
9. Do you like the essay? Why?

Suggestions for Writing

1. Write an essay on any club (fraternity, 4H, Rainbow), team (athletic, drill, chess), or group (family), to which you belong. Make a judgment about it and then illustrate with examples—"We are/were the ____ team ____."
2. Write an essay on an activity or pastime with which you are frequently involved. Consider how you would describe it and how you really feel about it.

KIMBERLEY ORDWAY (student)

Mistaken Ideas about College

After some experience, this writer compares her old ideas with her new ideas about college. Notice that she bases her paper on the idea of change—the change from old ideas to new ones. Rather than divide her paper into two halves (as in the history examination answer on p. 315), she makes each paragraph into a small comparison of a past idea with a present one, mistaken expectation and reality.

Before I came to college, I was sure I knew all about it. I had 1
talked to guidance counselors, I had met some college students, I had looked at some catalogues, and I had seen more than my share of old "college" movies where the heroes belonged to "jock" fraternities and the heroines to sophisticated sororities. I knew all about it. Or so I thought. But, now, after one semester as a college student, many of my old ideas have changed completely.

I used to imagine bossy upper-classmen, for example. I 2
thought they would be know-it-all rulers of the campus who got their kicks from harassing freshmen. I pictured being directed to the wrong classrooms, being snubbed because I was too young, and eating lunch standing up because older students wouldn't allow me at their tables. But, in fact, the upper-classmen (when I could tell them from the freshmen) turned out to be quite civilized. They didn't even notice me, but if I did need help, they were willing to give it. In the beginning, more experienced students helped me to choose my professors and courses and to find my rooms, and later they encouraged me to stick with my tough courses (even calculus) and they tried (unsuccessfully) to teach me how to stay cool during examinations. No harassment here.

The upper-classmen weren't the only ones I worried about. 3
I was also concerned about the other freshmen. I was afraid
they might think I was too fat, too shy, too ugly, too cowardly, or
even too dumb to bother with. I thought their backgrounds and
interests would be much more exciting than mine; I wondered
who would care about a small-town girl whose typical pastime
was strolling to the corner store for penny candy, popsicles,
and Pepsi. And, most of all, I was afraid of being alone, with
my old friends far away and no new ones here. Again, I was
wrong. When I finally got to college, I discovered that most
students felt exactly as I did. They were as uneasy with me as I
was with them, and as we started to open up, we began to trust
one another. We began to become curious about each others'
backgrounds and interests; the differences among us actually
became attractions. We laughed, for example, at our comparative pronunciations of "car" as "cah" or "car," and I learned
that "Get down" means "Feel good" in Boston. And no one
seemed to think that I was fat, shy, ugly, cowardly, or dumb!

These weren't all of my worries, though. I was also fright- 4
ened by the classes and especially by the teachers. I imagined
myself lost in a two-hundred seat lecture hall, desperately
scratching down pieces of notes preached from a great distance
by a tiny, inaudible male professor with white hair and little
gold-rimmed glasses. I was convinced he'd have no patience
with my stupid questions, so I'd be perpetually lost. Wrong
here too. Most of my classes had only thirty to forty students
(some were smaller) and the professors, male and female,
looked downright ordinary. One teacher had prematurely grey
hair and none of them had gold-rimmed glasses. I did find myself desperately scratching down notes, but I also had plenty
of chances to ask questions and even to take part in discussions. In the one-to-one meetings after class, I came to appreciate the teachers even more. They were actually interested in
teaching me!

I changed my mind about other things too. I had expected 5
homework to be a book-filled nightmare as I burned the midnight oil until two A.M., fighting off a headache which would
keep me from meeting due dates and eventually send me back
to the corner store. Actually, I got most of my homework done
well before midnight and I met all my due dates. And even

the examinations were not a total disaster. They were not three-hour tests crammed into one hour, nor were they made up of many pages of single-spaced typed questions exclusively on details I had overlooked. Oh yes, I did have some awful tests; I did break out in a clammy sweat, develop a stomach upset and a gigantic headache; and I did spend finals week on Pepto-Bismol, but contrary to expectations, I passed all of my exams with good grades.

I've always been a pessimist. Then if the worst happens,   6 I'm ready for it. For at least three and a half more years, I plan to live by this philosophy, but even with this, I know I won't be as negative as I was before I got to college. Not all schools would be the same, but this one turned out to be much better than I thought it would be—a good lesson in not jumping to conclusions. And, being a pessimist, I had the extra fun of discovering just how much better it could be. No doubt my attitude toward college will shift still more as I go on, but I know I'll never be as far off as I was before I got here.

Vocabulary

harassing (2), pessimist (6)

Questions

1. What mistakes did this student make when thinking about college?
2. Where did she get her ideas about college?
3. How did the upper-classmen actually behave?
4. What kind of background does the writer have?
5. What is the writer like? Can you tell anything about her personality by reading her essay?
6. What is the thesis?
7. What is the controlling idea?
8. What is the tone?
9. What is the basic pattern of organization?
10. How does the introduction prepare the readers for what comes afterward?
11. How is each paragraph developed?
12. Select two details that seem particularly effective and explain how they work in the essay.

13. Which is the best paragraph in the essay? Why? Which one do you like least? Why?
14. How does the conclusion relate to the body of the essay?
15. What do you think of the whole essay? Can you think of any way of improving it? Is the student too optimistic?

Suggestion for Writing

Write an essay in which you compare the ideas you had about college before you came with the ones you have now. Base your essay on your own expectations and realities. If you got what you expected, show that. If you were disappointed, give the reasons why.

EUGENE J. WALTER, JR.

Why Do They Do What They Do?

*Eugene J. Walter, Jr. is curator of publications for the
New York Zoological Society and editor of the magazine,
Animal Kingdom. This selection is the complete answer
to a question, "Do Animals Really Play?" taken from a
larger article on animal behavior. Notice that, as in the
student essays, the writer argues the thesis stated in the
first paragraph, giving examples of "serious" play among
animals. In each paragraph, he gives a description of the
play among the animals and then discusses the lesson.*

Do animals really "play"? Yes, and sometimes it's nothing 1
more than fun and games, as when a monkey swings from a
vine and tosses a stick, or when polar bears amuse themselves
with stones, which they sometimes balance on their heads.
Often, though, the seemingly frivolous antics we interpret as
"play" are serious.

Play can be viewed as a pleasurable way of developing sur- 2
vival skills. The next time you're at a zoo, watch how the lion
cubs frolic. One will crouch low against the ground, stalk
slowly toward its littermate and then pounce on the surprised
"victim." That usually touches off a knockabout wrestling
match, with the cubs cuffing each other harmlessly. Such rough-
house sessions occur frequently among most carnivores such as
wolves, tigers, cheetahs, raccoons, and coyotes. As they play,
these young develop the abilities they need to become efficient
predators.

Among monkeys and apes, playing helps lay the foundation 3
for social order—a requirement for the survival of primate
communities. Through play-fighting, a young monkey learns—

in a harmless way—where it stands among its peers. The individuals that are most often victorious in the "matches" of infancy are most likely to assume a dominant role when they mature. Others that are lower on the social ladder learn their places early in life. This reduces more violent clashes among the monkeys as adults.

Many hoofed mammals engage in play, too. In herds of Mongolian wild horses, the breeding stallion will play-fight with his offspring, thereby helping the youngsters develop the agility they will need when confronted by predators or other stallions. 4

It appears that even whales play. A calf will perform all sorts of acrobatic gyrations on and around its mother, sliding over her tail, standing on its head or slapping its tail or flipper against the water's surface. It's possible that such play helps cement the bond between mother and offspring. 5

And what of birds—do they play? Some ornithologists are convinced that a few of the brainier ones do. The subject needs further inquiry. At this point, it's the mammals who appear to dominate the animal playground. 6

Vocabulary

frivolous (1), carnivores (2), predators (2), gyrations (5)

Questions

1. Do animals really play?
2. Which animals does Walter discuss?
3. Do birds play?
4. What is the thesis? the controlling idea?
5. What is Walter's main purpose?
6. What is the tone?
7. How does the introduction prepare the reader for the body of the paper?
8. Why does Walter mention the games that are simply play?
9. What is the topic of each body paragraph?
10. What do you think of the conclusion?
11. Do you like this discussion? Why? Do you see any way it could be improved?
12. Which examples do you find most interesting? Why?

Suggestions for Writing

1. Do you know any children's games that have a serious side? In the African country of Zaire, for example, children hunt grasshoppers, rats, and birds for fun, but they must make their own bows and arrows, a valuable skill for later life. Write an essay on children's games with which you are familiar and point out lessons they teach. In each paragraph, give an example of a game and the lesson it teaches.

2. Write a paper on any game—football, hide-and-go-seek, Simon Says—that may have a variety of lessons. Make the lessons the subjects of your paragraphs.

3. Consider adult games. Do they too have a serious side? Write a paper in which you discuss the lessons that might be derived from "Monopoly" or "Mastermind," for example.

4. Describe and comment on the play of a pet animal or possibly of an animal at a zoo. Be sure your observation of the behavior is detailed enough for the reader to understand and give your explanations for this behavior.

JAN MORRIS

A Passion for Cities

Jan Morris, born in 1926 in England, writes on travel, history, and personal reminiscence. She now lives in Wales, at times writing a steady 2,000 words a day. Her books include Coronation Everest *(1958),* Venice *(1960),* The Presence of Spain *(1964),* Oxford *(1965),* Pax Britannica *(1968),* Farewell the Trumpets *(1978),* The Oxford Book of Oxford *(1978), and* Destinations *(1980). In this discussion of a variety of cities, Morris does not simply list places she has enjoyed, but divides them into categories. Notice the use of details that illustrate the topic sentence of each paragraph.*

Love apart, and perhaps wine, more than anything else I 1
enjoy looking at cities—not looking at them methodically, or
even analytically, but just as E. M. Forster recommended long
ago, "wandering aimlessly around." [1] The pleasure they have
given me has been varied, ranging from the delight of sheer
serendipity to the satisfaction of knowledge gained or anticipa-
tions fulfilled, and now that I have visited (with one single
exception) all the incontestably great cities of the earth. I find
myself sorting my favorites not just by degrees of enjoyment,
but by category.

For example, nobody could seriously deny that the most 2
beautiful of all cities is Venice: the Shakespeare of cities, as it
was once called, all on its own, water-lapped, shadow-dappled,
tower-crowned, gilded and flagged and marvelously chim-
neyed, stacked so subtly beside its lagoon that as you sail past

Reprinted by permission of Julian Bach Literary Agency, Inc. Copyright
© 1979 by Jan Morris. First published in *Travel and Leisure*, July 1979.
1 E. M. Forster: see note on p. 129.

its palaces in your long black gondola its layers seem to be moving, building behind building like a marble ballet.

On the other hand, for intricacy of interest nowhere can 3 match London, the most richly experienced, adaptable, devious and cynical of capitals. London is a theater. Nothing is unpremeditated there, almost nothing is altogether frank, from the astonishing permutation of royalty (clank of cavalry down the Mall, billow of golden ensign above the Palace) to the infinite sense of gentlemanly cunning that informs the financial quarter of The City.

For stimulus and rejuvenation, for staying up late and 4 dancing in the park—well, hackneyed though the judgment seems, it can only be New York. I am always more than myself in New York: partly because of its architectural intensity, that masonry thicket of Manhattan, partly because of its climatic extremes, but chiefly because nearly everybody I know there is cleverer (if not necessarily wiser) than I am.

Mind you, for majesty, for tremendousness, I think another 5 American city beats it. Charles Dickens was told by his train conductor, when he first went to Chicago, that he was entering "the boss city of the universe." It is hardly that, but all the same no other city so impresses me with the scale of the human potential. That magnificent lakefront, those terrific windy boulevards, that stupendous Sears skyscraper, like a slab of living rock left standing when the rest of a precipice was quarried away—Chicago is a city fit for giants.

I suppose one must grant that Paris is the most elegant of 6 cities still, but I have never really responded to it. I prefer a more spontaneous kind of stylishness, and I find it preeminently in Rio de Janeiro. Rio is urbane and squalid cheek by jowl, but its overwhelming characteristic is charm. Set there on its lovely bays, serenely supervised by its hilltop figure of Christ, it seems designed to soothe the cares away. More than any other city I know it possesses what the Arabs call *baraka,* the gift of being blessed, and of bestowing blessings, both at the same time.

I detested Sydney when I first went there, but it has grown 7 on me—partly no doubt because I have matured, but partly because it has blossomed miraculously during the twenty years I have known it. Now, if I were asked to name the *jolliest* city, I think my mind would spring at once to the good-natured bustle of the Circular Quay, the shambled bonhomie of Kings Cross, the mordancy of the Sydney taxi drivers and the inimitable Sydney humor.

The city where I really grew up, where I experienced I suppose the most formative years of my young adulthood, was Cairo, and it remains for me in many ways the grandest of them all. As Charles Doughty observed of the Arabs,[2] it has its feet in a sewer but its brow touches heaven. As old as the Sphinx, as brash as television, with its incomparable medieval center, the desert that hems it in and the benign old Nile that flows through the middle of it, it is truly the greatheart of towns, addled by poverty, inefficiency and bad luck, but ennobled always by human sympathy. 8

And there remains one more category of city than enthralls me: the tantalizing city, the mysterious, the beckoning, the never-quite-understood. Of all the supreme cities of the earth, for me the most tantalizing is Peking, because that's the one I've never been to. 9

Vocabulary

serendipity (1), incontestibly (1), category (1), dappled (2), permutation (3), ensign (3), rejuvenation (4), hackneyed (4), preeminently (6), urbane (6), squalid (6), shambled (7), mordancy (7), inimitable (7), benign (8), enthralls (9), tantalizing (9)

Questions

1. Why does Morris like New York?
2. What does she think of Sydney?
3. Where does she hope to go soon?
4. What is the thesis of this essay?
5. For what readers was the essay written?
6. How does Morris avoid simply listing cities she has liked?
7. What possible method for organizing the essay is mentioned and then broadened?
8. Why does Morris quote the train conductor's description of Chicago?

---

[2] Charles Doughty (1843–1926): English poet and traveler.

9. What is Morris' favorite city? Why?
10. What is the tone?
11. What does the use of the first person contribute to the essay?
12. What is the effect of Morris' comparisons—"Shakespeare of cities," "like a marble ballet"?

Suggestions for Writing

1. Write an essay on several places that you have visited and that may be placed in the same category—campgrounds, schools, cities, sports arenas, states. How do these (campgrounds, for example) compare to one another? What is your opinion about them?
2. When you evaluate a city or a town, what characteristics are most important to you? What do you look for first?

DWIGHT MACDONALD

Too Big

Dwight Macdonald, born in 1906, has long been a commentator on American life, constantly criticizing the dominance of mass culture, which thrives not on merit but on marketability. He also disapproves of what he calls "mid-cult," which also thrives on false values (the appearance of appreciating culture while actually debasing it). A critic of literature and film as well as of society, he has been a staff writer for the New Yorker, *has edited* Parodies: An Anthology from Chaucer to Beerbohm—and After *(1960), and written* Against the Grain: Essays in Mass Culture *(1962),* Discriminations: Essays and Afterthoughts 1938–1974 *(1974), and* Memoirs of a Revolutionist *(1957), from which this essay is taken. Notice that he states his thesis emphatically at the end of the first paragraph and then offers four concrete examples to support his point. He does not simply refer to these incidents; he recounts them with enough detail for the reader to envision what happened. Consider the movement toward a climax and also the special effect of the conclusion.*

The trouble is everything is too big. There are too many 1
people, for example, in the city I live in. In walking along
the street, one passes scores of other people every minute; any
response to them as human beings is impossible; they must be
passed by as indifferently as ants pass each other in the corridors of the anthill. A style of behavior which refuses to recognize the human existence of the others has grown up of

necessity. Just the scale on which people congregate in such a city breaks down human solidarity, alienates people from each other. There are so many people that there aren't any people; 7,000,000 becomes 0; too big.

Some episodes:

(1) A friend was going home in the subway at about ten 2 o'clock one night. About half the seats in his car were filled. Opposite him two men were sitting on either side of a third, who was very drunk. Without any attempt at concealment, they were going through the drunk's pockets and taking his watch, money, etc. A dozen people watched the performance from their seats, but no one, including my friend, did anything, and at the next station the two men let the drunk slide to the floor and got off the train.

(2) An elderly woman I know slipped going down the stairs 3 in an "El" station and fell all the way to the bottom, where she lay stunned and gasping. A crowd of people—it was the rush hour—were waiting on the platform at the foot of the stairs. Some of them stared at her but no one moved to help her. She told me that she lay there several minutes, too shaken up even to speak; several people remarked "she must be drunk." Finally, a man did come forward and helped her to her feet. She was frightened by the incident. She had lived in New York all her life without realizing she was living among strangers.

(3) I was told a similar story about another person—the 4 friend of a friend. He was knocked down on a mid-town street by a car late at night. The car didn't stop and no one saw the accident. He lay in the gutter, badly hurt and only half conscious, for five or six hours. There must have been scores, probably hundreds of people who passed by, saw him, thought "must be drunk" (the formula by which, in the city, one denies human recognition) and went on their way. Finally, the next morning, a policeman investigated and called an ambulance. (The policeman is the only person in a big city who is professionally required to see people as people, to break the shell of apartness that encases each human being.)

(4) The wife of a friend of mine last year became psychotic 5 and is now being treated in an institution. She had been acting "queerly" for some time, but the first big outburst came about

ten o'clock one night as they were returning home after visiting friends in Brooklyn. The wife suddenly began to accuse her husband of attempting to poison her; she became increasingly violent and suddenly broke away and began running down the street screaming "Help! Help! He's trying to kill me!" She ran along thus for several blocks, shouting, before he could overtake her and try to calm her. Although most of the houses showed lighted windows, for it was still early, not a door opened, not a window went up, no one paid the slightest attention. When he finally got his wife back to their apartment building, she broke away again as he was unlocking the door, and rushed into the hallway screaming for help. This lasted at least ten minutes, he told me, and again not a door opened, no one appeared although her cries and screams echoed all through the building. Finally a youth came downstairs in his bathrobe and shouted: "Shut up! We're trying to sleep!" He disappeared again immediately. A half hour later, after my friend had persuaded his wife to go inside, he received the first help since the nightmare had begun: Again in the form of a policeman, who had been sent for by some of the neighbors. (When people are forced to see others as human beings, they make contact vicariously through the police. What a "style" of communal relations!)

But he, desiring to justify himself, said unto Jesus: "And 6 *who is my neighbor?" Jesus made answer and said: "A certain man was going down from Jerusalem to Jericho; and he fell among robbers, who stripped him and beat him, and departed, leaving him half dead. And by chance a certain priest was going down that way; and when he saw him, he passed by on the other side. And in like manner, a Levite also, when he came to the place and saw him, passed by on the other side. But a certain Samaritan, as he journeyed, came where he was; and when he saw him he was moved with compassion, and came to him, and bound up his wounds, pouring on them oil and wine; and he set him on his own beast and brought him to an inn and took care of him. And on the morrow he took out two shillings, and gave them to the host, and said: 'Take care of him, and whatsoever thou spendest more, I, when I come back again, will repay.' Which of these three, thinkest thou, proved neigh-*

bor to him that fell among the robbers?" And he said, "He that showed mercy on him." And Jesus said unto him, "Go, and do thou likewise." [1]

Vocabulary

scores (1), congregate (1), alienates (1), psychotic (5), vicariously (5), communal (5)

Questions

1. What is "too big"?
2. What is the effect of the comparison "as ants pass each other in the corridors of the anthill"? (1)
3. Compare the first and last sentences of paragraph 1. Why does Macdonald word them the way he does?
4. What is the controlling idea of the essay?
5. What is the tone of the essay?
6. Why do you think Macdonald chose a parable from the Bible for his concluding paragraph? What is the connection to the body of the essay?
7. What is the purpose of the essay?
8. Why does he include direct quotation?
9. For what readers is the essay written?
10. What words seem well chosen to support the meaning of the essay? Select two and explain your choice.
11. What is the effect of the comments Macdonald places in parentheses?
12. Is there any irony in paragraph 1?
13. How does Macdonald view himself? Does he see himself as separate from the overcrowded society?

Suggestions for Writing

1. It is interesting and sobering to realize that this essay was written in 1946, eighteen years before the famous case in New York City, in which a young woman, Kitty Genovese, escaped her assailants once, only to be caught and killed later by them because no one would answer her cries for help. Write an essay illustrating

---

[1] Luke 10: 29–39, The Parable of the Good Samaritan.

such behavior with which you might be familiar. Be sure examples are vivid and to the point.

2. Write an essay on other, possibly more attractive, human behavior. Do you see the city as a friendly place? Whatever virtue or vice you choose, make specific examples the basis of your essay.

3. Write an essay on anything in your life that seems either "too big" or "too small" to you—your family, your school, your hometown, etc. Again, base your essay on concrete examples, as Macdonald does.

4. Choose a parable or tale from the Bible, the lesson of which might be valuable for our time. (See, for example, "The Parable of the Sower," "The Prodigal Son," "The Story of Ruth.") Give illustrations of its possible relevance.

J. B. PRIESTLEY

On Travel by Train

J. B. Priestley, born in 1894 in Yorkshire, England, is a novelist, short story writer, playwright, literary historian, biographer, writer on the arts, and prolific essayist. He served in the infantry in World War I and attended Cambridge University where he wrote essays, criticism, and reviews. His many novels include The Good Companions *(1929) and* Angel Pavement *(1930), and among his plays are* I Have Been Here Before *(1938),* When We Are Married *(1938), and* An Inspector Calls *(1945). His essay collections include such titles as* Papers from Lilliput *(1922),* I for One *(1923),* Open House *(1927),* Apes and Angels *(1928), and* The Balconinny *(1929). In this essay from* Papers from Lilliput, *he classifies types of railway passengers he has encountered. His categories are drawn from personal experience and his details from close observation of human behavior. Notice his careful choice of words to suggest the precise meaning.*

Remove an Englishman from his hearth and home, his [1] centre of corporal life, and he becomes a very different creature, one capable of sudden furies and roaring passions, a deep sea of strong emotions churning beneath his frozen exterior. I can pass, at all times, for a quiet, neighbourly fellow, yet have I sat, more than once, in a railway carriage with black murder in my heart. At the mere sight of some probably inoffensive fellow-passenger my whole being will be invaded by a million devils of wrath, and I "could do such bitter business as the day would quake to look on." [1]

Reprinted by permission of A. D. Peters & Co. Ltd. From *Papers From Lilliput* by J. B. Priestley.

[1] *Hamlet,* III, ii, 409–10.

There is one type of traveller that never fails to rouse my 2
quick hatred. She is a large, middle-aged woman, with a rasping
voice and a face of brass. Above all things, she loves to invade
smoking compartments that are already comfortably filled with
a quiet company of smokers; she will come bustling in, shouting over her shoulder at her last victim, a prostrate porter, and,
laden with packages of all maddening shapes and sizes, she will
glare defiantly about her until some unfortunate has given up
his seat. She is often accompanied by some sort of contemptible,
whining cur that is only one degree less offensive than its mis-
tress. From the moment that she has wedged herself in there
will be no more peace in the carriage, but simmering hatred,
and everywhere dark looks and muttered threats. But every one
knows her. Courtesy and modesty perished in the world of
travel on the day when she took her first journey; but it will
not be long before she is in hourly danger of extinction, for
there are strong men in our midst.

There are other types of railway travellers, not so offensive 3
as the above, which combines all the bad qualities, but still an-
noying in a varying degree to most of us; and of these others
I will enumerate one or two of the commonest. First, there are
those who, when they would go on a journey, take all their
odd chattels and household utensils and parcel them up in
brown paper, disdaining such things as boxes and trunks;
furthermore, when such eccentrics have loaded themselves up
with queer-shaped packages they will cast about for baskets
of fruit and bunches of flowers to add to their own and other
people's misery. Then there are the simple folks who are forever eating and drinking in railway carriages. No sooner are
they settled in their seats but they are passing each other
tattered sandwiches and mournful scraps of pastry, and talking with their mouths full, and scattering crumbs over the
trousers of fastidious old gentlemen. Sometimes they will peel
and eat bananas with such rapidity that nervous onlookers are
compelled to seek another compartment.

Some children do not make good travelling companions, 4
for they will do nothing but whimper and howl throughout
a journey, or they will spend all their time daubing their faces
with chocolate or trying to climb out of the window. And the
cranks are always with us; on the bleakest day, they it is who

insist on all the windows being open, but in the sultriest season they go about in mortal fear of draughts, and will not allow a window to be touched.

More to my taste are the innocents who always find them- 5 selves in the wrong train. They have not the understanding necessary to fathom the time-tables, nor will they ask the rail- way officials for advice, so they climb into the first train that comes, and trust to luck. When they are being hurtled towards Edinburgh, they will suddenly look around the carriage and ask, with a mild touch of pathos, if they are in the right train for Bristol. And then, puzzled and disillusioned, they have to be bundled out at the next station, and we see them no more. I have often wondered if these simple voyagers ever reach their destinations, for it is not outside probability that they may be shot from station to station, line to line, until there is nothing mortal left of them.

Above all other railway travellers, I envy the mighty sleep- 6 ers, descendants of the Seven of Ephesus.[2] How often, on a long, uninteresting journey, have I envied their sweet oblivion. With Lethe [3] at their command, no dull, empty train journey, by day or night, has any terrors for them. Knowing the length of time they have to spend in the train, they compose themselves and are off to sleep in a moment, probably enjoying the gor- geous adventures of dream while the rest of us are looking blankly out of the window or counting our fingers. Two minutes from their destination they stir, rub their eyes, stretch themselves, collect their baggage, and, peering out of the win- dow, murmur: "My station, I think." A moment later they go out, alert and refreshed, Lords of Travel, leaving us to our boredom.

Seafaring men make good companions on a railway journey. 7 They are always ready for a pipe and a crack with any man, and there is usually some entertaining matter in their talk. But they are not often met with away from the coast towns. Nor do we often come across the confidential stranger in an English railway carriage, though his company is inevitable on the

---

[2] Seven legendary young noblemen who hid in a cave to escape persecu- tion (A.D. 250) and slept for at least 230 years.

[3] The mythical river of Hades, a drink of which produces forgetfulness.

Continent, and, I believe, in America. When the confidential stranger does make an appearance here, he is usually a very dull dog, who compels us to yawn through the interminable story of his life, and rides some wretched old hobbyhorse to death.

There is one more type of traveller that must be mentioned   8 here, if only for the guidance of the young and simple. He is usually an elderly man, neatly dressed, but a little tobacco-stained, always seated in a corner, and he opens the conversation by pulling out a gold hunter and remarking that the train is at least three minutes behind time. Then, with the slightest encouragement, he will begin to talk, and his talk will be all of trains. As some men discuss their acquaintances, or others speak of violins or roses, so he talks of trains, their history, their quality, their destiny. All his days and nights seem to have been passed in railway carriages, all his reading seems to have been in time-tables. He will tell you of the 12.35 from this place and the 3.49 from the other place, and how the 10.18 ran from So-and-So to So-and-So in such a time, and how the 8.26 was taken off and the 5.10 was put on; and the greatness of his subject moves him to eloquence, and there is passion and mastery in his voice, now wailing over a missed connection or a departed hero of trains, now exultantly proclaiming the glories of a non-stop express or a wonderful run to time. However dead you were to the passion, the splendour, the pathos, in this matter of trains, before he has done with you you will be ready to weep over the 7.37 and cry out in ecstasy at the sight of the 2.52.

Beware of the elderly man who sits in the corner of the   9 carriage and says that the train is two minutes behind time, for he is the Ancient Mariner [4] of railway travellers, and will hold you with his glittering eye.

Vocabulary

corporal (1), inoffensive (1), prostrate (2), cur (2), chattels (3), disdaining (3), tattered (3), fastidious (3), sultriest (4), draughts (4),

---

[4] In Coleridge's (1772–1834) "Rime of the Ancient Mariner," the old seaman tells his guilty tale of killing the sacred bird, the albatross, to an unfortunate wedding guest, whom he holds "with his glittering eye."

fathom (5), hurtled (5), pathos (5), oblivion (6), interminable (7), hobbyhorse (7), hunter (8), eloquence (8)

Questions

1. Which travelers does Priestley envy?
2. What are the thesis and the controlling idea of the essay?
3. What is the basic pattern of organization?
4. Does the essay rise to a climax?
5. Why does Priestley mention the "whining cur" in paragraph 2 or the "fastidious old gentleman" in paragraph 3?
6. What does the reference to the "Seven of Ephesus" have to do with the essay?
7. For what readers is the essay intended?
8. What does this sentence contribute to the essay: "I can pass, at all times, for a quiet, neighbourly fellow, yet have I sat, more than once, in a railway carriage with black murder in my heart"?
9. Why would Priestley like to have Lethe at his command?
10. What is the tone of this essay?
11. Why does he use exaggeration and humor?

Suggestions for Writing

1. You may or may not be familiar with your own categories of travelers on the railroad, but no doubt you have had occasion to classify people according to type—the early morning riders on the subway, drivers on the highway, types of students or roommates, types of bosses or customers, types of teachers. Write an essay in which you make these categories the topics of your paragraphs. Simple listing will have no life, so be sure to include enough details, incidents, possibly quotations, and carefully chosen words, so that the reader may bring them vividly to mind. Decide if your presentation is to be simply objective or if you wish to express an attitude toward them as Priestley does with his railway passengers who can produce "black murder" in his heart.
2. Early in Priestley's career as an essayist, he was strongly influenced by the graceful prose of the early twentieth century in England. In this essay, do you see any evidence of the formality of style and diction characteristic of the "Edwardian" essay? You might compare it to a very modern American essay, "The Women's Movement" by Joan Didion (p. 257), for example. Write an analysis of those characteristics which make it seem different from the American writing of our time. Do you see any similarities?

3. E. B. White says that the essayist is "sustained by the childish belief that everything he thinks about, everything that happens to him is of general interest." Discuss in relation to this essay (and others, if you wish).

JAMES THURBER

There's an Owl in My Room

*James Thurber (1894–1961) was born in Columbus, Ohio.
He spent most of his professional career as a writer for
the* New Yorker, *chiefly for the "Talk of the Town" column. Also well known as a cartoonist, teller of fables, and
essayist, he published a volume,* Is Sex Necessary? *(1929)
with E. B. White, an autobiography,* My Life and Hard
Times *(1933), and other works including* The Middle-
Aged Man on the Flying Trapeze *(1935),* Let Your Mind
Alone *(1937),* Fables for Our Time *(1940), and* The Thirteen Clocks *(1950). In an interview, Thurber said that he
wrote as many as seven drafts for his essays, "For me it's
mostly a question of re-writing. It's part of a constant attempt on my part to make the finished version smooth,
to make it seem effortless."*

I saw Gertrude Stein on the screen of a newsreel theater one   1
afternoon and I heard her read that famous passage of hers
about pigeons on the grass, alas (the sorrow is, as you know,
Miss Stein's).[1] After reading about the pigeons on the grass alas,
Miss Stein said, "This is a simple description of a landscape I
have seen many times." I don't really believe that that is true.
Pigeons on the grass alas may be a simple description of Miss
Stein's own consciousness, but it is not a simple description
of a plot of grass on which pigeons have alighted, are alighting, or are going to alight. A truly simple description of the

[1] Gertrude Stein: American poet, novelist, travel writer, expatriate resident of Paris (1874–1946).

pigeons alighting on the grass of the Luxembourg Gardens (which, I believe, is where the pigeons alighted) would say of the pigeons alighting there only that they were pigeons alighting. Pigeons that alight anywhere are neither sad pigeons nor gay pigeons, they are simply pigeons.

It is neither just nor accurate to connect the word alas with pigeons. Pigeons are definitely not alas. They have nothing to do with alas and they have nothing to do with hooray (not even when you tie red, white, and blue ribbons on them and let them loose at band concerts); they have nothing to do with mercy me or isn't that fine, either. White rabbits, yes, and Scotch terriers, and bluejays, and even hippopotamuses, but not pigeons. I happen to have studied pigeons very closely and carefully, and I have studied the effect, or rather the lack of effect, of pigeons very carefully. A number of pigeons alight from time to time on the sill of my hotel window when I am eating breakfast and staring out the window. They never alas me, they never make me feel alas; they never make me feel anything.   2

Nobody and no animal and no other bird can play a scene so far down as a pigeon can. For instance, when a pigeon on my window ledge becomes aware of me sitting there in a chair in my blue polka-dot dressing-gown, worrying, he pokes his head far out from his shoulders and peers sideways at me, for all the world (Miss Stein might surmise) like a timid man peering around the corner of a building trying to ascertain whether he is being followed by some hoofed fiend or only by the echo of his own footsteps. And yet it is *not* for all the world like a timid man peering around the corner of a building trying to ascertain whether he is being followed by a hoofed fiend or only by the echo of his own footsteps, at all. And that is because there is no emotion in the pigeon and no power to arouse emotion. A pigeon looking is just a pigeon looking. When it comes to emotion, a fish, compared to a pigeon, is practically beside himself.   3

A pigeon peering at me doesn't make me sad or glad or apprehensive or hopeful. With a horse or a cow or a dog it would be different. It would be especially different with a dog. Some dogs peer at me as if I had just gone completely crazy or as if they had just gone completely crazy. I can go so far as to say   4 that most dogs peer at me that way. This creates in the consciousness of both me and the dog a feeling of alarm or downright terror and legitimately permits me to work into a description of the landscape, in which the dog and myself are figures, a note of emotion. Thus I should not have minded if Miss Stein had written: dogs on the grass, look out, dogs on the grass, look out, look out, dogs on the grass, look out Alice. That would be a simple description of dogs on the grass. But when any writer pretends that a pigeon makes him sad, or makes him anything else, I must instantly protest that this is a highly specialized fantastic impression created in an individual consciousness and that therefore it cannot fairly be presented as a simple description of what actually was to be seen.

People who do not understand pigeons—and pigeons can 5 be understood only when you understand that there is nothing to understand about them—should not go around describing pigeons or the effect of pigeons. Pigeons come closer to a zero of impingement than any other birds. Hens embarrass me the way my old Aunt Hattie used to when I was twelve and she still insisted I wasn't big enough to bathe myself; owls disturb me; if I am with an eagle I always pretend that I am not with an eagle; and so on down to swallows at twilight who scare the hell out of me. But pigeons have absolutely no effect on me. They have absolutely no effect on anybody. They couldn't even startle a child. That is why they are selected from among all birds to be let loose, with colored ribbons attached to them, at band concerts, library dedications, and christenings of new dirigibles. If any body let loose a lot of owls on such an occasion there would be rioting and catcalls and whistling and fainting spells and throwing of chairs and the Lord only knows what else.

From where I am sitting now I can look out the window and 6 see a pigeon being a pigeon on the roof of the Harvard Club. No other thing can be less what it is not than a pigeon can, and Miss Stein, of all people, should understand that simple fact. Behind the pigeon I am looking at, a blank wall of tired gray bricks is stolidly trying to sleep off oblivion; underneath the pigeon the cloistered windows of the Harvard Club are staring in horrified bewilderment at something they have seen across the street. The pigeon is just there on the roof being a pigeon, having been, and being, a pigeon and, what is more, always going to be, too. Nothing could be simpler than that. If you read that sentence aloud you will instantly see what I mean. It is a simple description of a pigeon on a roof. It is only with an effort that I am conscious of the pigeon, but I am acutely aware of a great sulky red iron pipe that is creeping up the side of the building intent on sneaking up on a slightly tipsy chimney which is shouting its head off.

There is nothing a pigeon can do or be that would make me   7
feel sorry for it or for myself or for the people in the world, just as there is nothing I could do or be that would make a pigeon feel sorry for itself. Even if I plucked his feathers out it would not make him feel sorry for himself and it would not make me feel sorry for myself or for him. But try plucking the quills out of a porcupine or even plucking the fur out of a jackrabbit. There is nothing a pigeon could be, or can be, rather, which could get into my consciousness like a fumbling hand in a bureau drawer and disarrange my mind or pull anything out of it. I bar nothing at all. You could dress up a pigeon in a tiny suit of evening clothes and put a tiny silk hat on his head and a tiny gold-headed cane under his wing and send him walking into my room at night. It would make no impression on me. I would not shout, "Good god almighty, the birds are in charge!" But you could send an owl into my room, dressed only in the feathers it was born with, and no monkey business, and I would pull the covers over my head and scream.

No other thing in the world falls so far short of being able   8
to do what it cannot do as a pigeon does. Of being *unable* to do what it *can* do, too, as far as that goes.

Vocabulary

alighted (1), impingement (5), dirigibles (5), stolidly (6), cloistered (6), bewilderment (6)

Questions

1. What does Thurber think of pigeons?
2. Why does he mention the quotation from Gertrude Stein?

3. What is his thesis?
4. What is the purpose of the essay?
5. What is the tone?
6. What two sentences would you choose as most effective in the essay? Why?
7. What is the effect of repetition in this essay?
8. How would you describe the pace of the essay? Does it move along quickly or is the reader invited to stop and ponder each point? Compare it with Macdonald's "Too Big."
9. Why does he so often repeat the word "pigeon"?
10. Do you see any distortion of facts or any exaggeration for the sake of effect? Where?
11. Does the essay seem effortless as Thurber says he wants his essays to seem? If so, what is it that makes it seem effortless?
12. What does the title have to do with the essay?
13. Do you like it? Why?

Suggestions for Writing

1. This essay is a humorous attempt to strip pigeons of the special quality implied by Gertrude Stein's "alas" in her description of them. Write an essay on anything that you feel has been notoriously overrated, something that you feel deserves to be put back in its less exalted place—a certain hockey team, a public holiday, a type of vacation, for example. Be sure to make the undeserving qualities the topics of your paragraphs and develop these observations with details to prove it. Your subject will help you to determine your tone.
2. This model too can be inverted. You might, for example, argue in a similar pattern for something usually degraded, which in your estimation does not receive the proper respect—pigeons, maybe, or possibly an entertainer not often appreciated, or a type of car.
3. About humor Thurber says, "With humor you have to look out for traps. You're likely to be very gleeful with what you've put down, and you think it's fine, very funny. One reason to go over it is to make the piece sound less as if you were having a lot of fun with it yourself. You try to play it down. In fact, if there's such a thing as a *New Yorker* style, that would be it—playing it down." [2] In this essay do you see any evidence for Thurber's playing it down? Might he be talking about literature or some other subject as well as about pigeons?

[2] Charles S. Holmes (ed.), *Thurber* (Prentice-Hall, 1974), pp. 108–109.

LAWRENCE DURRELL

Thinking about "Smartie"

Lawrence Durrell, born in India in 1912, is a well-known British poet, novelist, humorist, literary critic, playwright, translator, and travel writer. Educated in India and En-gland, he has spent most of his life in Egypt, Greece, Italy, and in France where he was a member of the foreign ser-vice and now a permanent resident. Perhaps best known for his tetralogy of novels, The Alexandria Quartet *(1957–60) set in Egypt, Durrell has written many books set in the Mediterranean world, including* Spirit of Place: Let-ters and Essays on Travel *(1969) and* Greek Islands *(1978). This brief essay is from a set of memorial pieces, "Walter Smart by Some of His Friends," done in honor of "Smartie," who was the Oriental Councillor at the British Embassy in Cairo during World War II. In the early part of the essay Durrell looks back to wartime Cairo, when it was one of the few safe large cities of the old world and when poets, novelists, and painters gathered to practice their art. "Smartie," according to Durrell, greatly admired many of these young artists. Later, after the war, "Smartie" moved to Gadincourt in Normandy, which Durrell also recalls. The personality of the main character remains the same throughout, however. Notice that each paragraph is an illustration, drawn from per-sonal experience, of the central point mentioned at the end of paragraph 1.*

Despite the eminence of his official rank nobody in the Cairo 1
Embassy ever succeeded in thinking of him as anything but

From *Spirit of Place* by Lawrence Durrell, edited by Alan G. Thomas.
Copyright © 1969, 1966, 1965, 1964, 1963, 1962, 1960, 1959, 1958 by Lawrence
Durrell. Reprinted by permission of the publishers, E. P. Dutton and Faber
and Faber Ltd.

"Smartie"—even down to the secretaries and typists. Where the nickname came from I do not know but it imposed itself on us all and carried with it a concrete image of this lovable, whimsical, curious and delightful man. Perhaps the most endearing of his many qualities was that he was afflicted by one of the intellectual pieties which one finds more often among Frenchmen than Englishmen: he was an "artist-cherisher."

This was brought home to me during my first week as a   2 junior in the Press Department of the Cairo Embassy. I was late for the office one afternoon (I had been lunching with an Egyptian poet), and when I arrived I heard, with sinking heart, that my Oriental Councillor had been looking for me: had, indeed, actually dropped into my office. This was unheard of— for normally juniors were summoned, not *visited*. I immediately concluded that Smartie was a low-down dog who had been testing my punctuality and general efficiency by a surprise visit. (I was rather weak in both qualities.) I picked up the phone and rang his office; immediately his voice came over the wire, warm and reassuring. "I wanted to talk to you about your new book of poems which Amy and I got yesterday," he said. He sounded almost apologetic for troubling such a great man!

Talk we did, later that evening, in his beautiful Cairo house,   3 with its great army of books, on a terrace overlooking a shady garden and my timidity melted almost as swiftly as the ice cubes in my glass. I had discovered (as everyone did) The Smarts. The house itself was a fitting frame for a life which might be described as one of pure intellectual curiosity—it was crammed with books, paintings, manuscripts, pamphlets in a number of languages. But it was not merely the house of a great collector, or an antiquary, or a patron of the arts. There was a continuous and *purposeful* life being lived there among its treasures which included several big grave thoughtful paintings by Smartie's wife Amy Nimr. And so many books! Persian, French, Arabic, Greek . . . The house of the Smarts was a hinge between a dozen cultures; their world was completely international and the house reflected it. It smelt of Paris, Damascus, Jerusalem, Istanbul, Cairo, London and New York. I became (as everyone did) a frequent visitor. If one were invited to tea one never knew whom one would meet—a soldier just back from India or Ethiopia, a parachutist-poet like Patrick Leigh Fermor or Xan

Fielding, a Persian poet, a mystic, a scholar of international renown, or perhaps even a pure eccentric deeply cherished by Smartie and Amy for a wayward habit of life or a singular theory about the Holy Ghost.

Smartie's first anecdote fully illustrated this physiological 4 predisposition towards the arts and sciences; he told me, with that delightful self-deprecating ruefulness with which he always gave point to a story against himself, just how as a junior accredited to Cairo he had committed the worst of all sins by forgetting, not only to sign the book, but even to present himself for duty for a number of days. The reason for this lapse was that someone had given him an introduction to a then completely unknown Greek poet called C. P. Cavafy [1] who lived over a brothel in Alexandria. Smartie had been impelled to visit him and spend several days talking literature with him. It was well worth the reprimand, he added.

But if Smartie adored and cherished artists he never used 5 them for copy, so to speak; he savoured and enjoyed them, derived amusement and self-instruction from them, but would never have dreamed of publishing anything about them. He was like a Persian monarch in his attitude to his artists. An English poet once said: "Smartie is so refreshing because he always makes art seem worth while." And it was something more than a *boutade* [2] when someone else coined the phrase, "Art for Smartie's sake."

After the war, and after Suez, [3] the axis shifted though not 6 the central preoccupation; for the lovely Norman house belonging to the Smarts took over the role of the now sequestrated Cairo one. Poets, writers, painters converged on Gadencourt to gladden Smartie's heart with their banter and their theories, while for his part he delighted in building log fires and stoking the Aga [4] against the mammoth meals which were put before them.

Physically he was very tall and thin; he had a sort of head 7 which made sculptors feel hungry. A long wide slanting nose

---

[1] C. P. Cavafy (1863–1933).

[2] A flash of wit.

[3] In 1956, Egypt nationalized the Suez Canal after seventy-four years of British control.

[4] Aga: a coal- or coke-burning stove.

which gave his face sometimes (in repose) a slight resemblance to Wellington,[5] but more often to some Norman knight of the past. There was always the suggestion of a smile—and indeed one cannot think of Smartie's smile without instantly hearing the small and wicked chuckle with which he always greeted a jest. The general impression he created was one of gentle singularity, while the lively eager flow of his questions held always a hint of ingenuousness. Something in him remained fresh and unspoiled, like a child bubbling over with youthfulness; and I cannot recall ever meeting a happier man. And, of course, happiness is infectious. With Smartie everything became a treat, even a bus ride across Paris, even walking to the corner to post a letter. The whole world held a sort of pristine freshness for him—it was always newly born, curious, variegated and utterly absorbing. And, of course, after a few moments with him one began to see it through his eyes rather than through one's own. There was inspiration to be gained this way and encouragement—as necessary to artists as oxygen.

I dare not mourn his passing—the memory of his chuckle 8 inhibits me. Besides, he himself once told me wistfully that he would have given almost anything to have a chance of discussing poetic theory with the Sufi poet Jalaluddin Rumi—"if only one could reach the brute." Perhaps he has. At any rate I seem to hear the quiet laughter and conversation of their shades as I write.

Vocabulary

eminence (1), whimsical (1), pieties (1), cherisher (1), timidity (3), antiquary (3), anecdote (4), physiological (4), predisposition (4), deprecating (4), ruefulness (4), accredited (4), impelled (4), savoured (5), sequestrated (6), mammoth (6), singularity (7), ingenuousness (7), infectious (7), pristine (7), variegated (7), inhibits (8), wistfully (8), shades (8)

Questions

1. How did Durrell first react when Smartie "dropped in" to his office?

---

[5] Arthur Wellesley, First Duke of Wellington (1769–1852): British general and statesman, called "The Iron Duke."

2. What was the Smarts' house in Cairo like? Why does Durrell describe it?
3. What was Smartie's "mistake" when he first arrived in Cairo?
4. How would you describe Durrell's attitude toward the subject of the essay?
5. Why was the essay written?
6. How much does Durrell assume his readers would know about his subject?
7. What does the description of Smartie in paragraph 7 have to do with the rest of the essay?
8. How does the conclusion relate to the essay? How has Durrell prepared the reader for this ending?
9. Why does Durrell say, "But if Smartie adored and cherished artists," at the opening of paragraph 5?
10. What would you select as the detail that most helps the reader to understand Smartie's character?
11. How does Durrell avoid sentimentality?

Suggestions for Writing

1. Write a "memorial piece" in honor of someone you have admired. Try to focus on a dominant impression and on situations where this trait was evident.
2. Write your own "obituary"—an essay on yourself in which you attempt to illustrate the outstanding trait or traits for which you would be most remembered. Consider tone.
3. Both suggestions 1 and 2 may be adapted to living subjects. You might consider a person you know well and select a dominating characteristic for which you have several pieces of evidence (e.g., "My brother is easy to trick"; "My friend, Joan, can't stand to throw anything away"; or "My father is a full-time sports fan."). Consider your feelings about this trait, as Durrell does when discussing Smartie's affection for artists. Or you might write on your own "ruling passion," giving specific and lively evidence for this judgment.
4. Write an essay on a famous person of the past—Abraham Lincoln, Martin Luther King, Marilyn Monroe, etc. Do some research in order to understand the character.
5. Are you in any way a "cherisher"? If so, write an essay on "I am a/an ____ cherisher," and give examples to illustrate. You might also write this essay on someone else who is a "cherisher," as Durrell does.

II · Developments

There are as many kinds of essays as there are human attitudes or poses, as many essay flavors as there are Howard Johnson ice creams. . . . E. B. White

The model essays in this part use more than one paragraph for introducing, developing an idea, or concluding —one of the most obvious ways of modifying the basic pattern studied in Part I. The structure remains clear and straightforward, but the essay may need room for additional introductory information, a single topic may break down into two or more parts, or the conclusion might require fuller discussion than a one-paragraph wrap-up will allow. A single essay might even need all of these things.

This multiplication of parts does not, however, dismiss the basic pattern as the underlying support for the essay. It simply puts additional weight on some parts as it moves through the discussion. The advantage is that the writer is not forced to compress two or three parts of a complex idea artificially into a single paragraph. The dangers are that the essay will be choppy, if ideas are split that could be logically combined under a larger topic, or sketchy, if separate thoughts are not adequately developed.

Because of the limitations of columns of print and the speed of the reader hurrying down the page, journalistic style is often broken down in this way. For college papers and formal essays, it is best to develop full paragraphs rather than to fragment thoughts into smaller units. But, as you will see in the following examples, it is possible to elaborate on relevant ideas without squeezing them, like Cinderella's stepsisters' big feet, into a space too small for them.

LAWRENCE WITCHEL

A Pepsi Person in the Perrier Generation

*Lawrence Witchel is a Group Vice President at Har-
court Brace Jovanovich Publications. Although he has
spent most of his life as an executive, he has written many
articles for such publications as* Skiing Magazine, New
York Magazine, New West Magazine, The New York
Times, *and* Travel and Leisure. *This model is a "confession"—in this case of the gourmet writer's previously hidden yearning for fast foods. (It is a light subject, no aspect
of which could bear extended analysis.) Pay attention to
the tone and the pace of the essay.*

Not another moment can I bear the duplicity. I must con- 1
fess all. I once wrote that the *faisan braisé au Porto* at Maxim's
in Paris was much too dry to be taken seriously. At the same
time I thought, but would never have said aloud, that the
greatest culinary creation of the 20th century was possibly a
Whopper. A Burger King Whopper. Worse: at an important
wine tasting during which some of the finest palates in America
had gathered to greet the first shipment of Beaujolais *nouveau,*
I with immense arrogance stated that as far as I was concerned,
Beaujolais *nouveau* was always so full of tannin, it made my
mouth feel as if it had swallowed a cashmere sweater. Two days
later, without telling a soul, I drove 20 miles to the only place
I know that makes a green pistachio soft ice cream.

It isn't that I don't know better. I do. I can unhesitatingly 2
name every ingredient in a classic veal Prince Orloff, but I can
also name nine of the 11 secret herbs and spices in Kentucky
Fried Chicken. Call me schizophrenic. I don't care. I am tired of

From *Travel and Leisure,* September 1979. Reprinted by permission.

hiding. I love fast foods, and while I can wax romantic about the glories of a *gâteau* Saint-Honoré just as well as the next critic, I truly believe there is a place in life for—well, for Twinkies.

My double culinary life began in childhood. My grand- 3 mother, who was Hungarian, turned out the world's flakiest strudels, creamiest pickled herrings and the tangiest sweet and sour stuffed cabbage. But I was a child. What did I know? I preferred Nathan's. Their hot dogs were so full of garlic that two of them could keep vampires away for a month. Nathan's still exists in the New York and Miami areas, and while they are no longer what they used to be (what is these days?), they are in my opinion the best fast-food restaurant in the United States.

This pattern has continued throughout my life. In New 4 Orleans, I took a business associate to lunch at the Caribbean Room in the Hotel Pontchartrain, which surely makes the greatest oysters Bienville in the South. But where did I eat dinner? At Takee-Outee. Takee-Outee, a chain of Oriental stands on Bourbon Street, has marvelous skewers of battered, fried chunks of pork that land in the stomach with a most satisfying thud. There is also a chicken chain in New Orleans called Popeyes which is the best of all the fried chicken chains. The breading is soft and spicy, and you get little cups of hot sauce for dunking.

The same thing happened in Atlanta. After crêpes Fitzgerald 5 at Brennan's at noon I had fried pies at the Varsity drive-in (the world's largest fast-food restaurant) at night. The Varsity fried pies are half-moon shaped and filled with apples or peaches, similar to the ones you get at McDonald's, only at the Varsity, the crust is flaky, the filling sweet and the fruit fresh enough to still have some crunch left. It's as good a way as I know to OD on a dessert.

Obviously, I would think Los Angeles is nirvana. It was 6 there that I had my first Taco Bell taco. It was so crisp it crumbled in my hand and ruined a perfectly decent Turnbull and Asser tie. But I didn't mind. I was 35 years old at the time and had no idea that a fried tortilla filled with chopped meat, cheese, shredded lettuce and hot sauce could be so delicious. When I found out that there were hundreds of Taco Bells all over the country, I knew what Scarlett O'Hara meant when

she held up the radish and cried, "I'll never be hungry again!"[1]
At least not for Mexican food.

One of my favorite places is a small chain in L.A. called 7
El Toro. The *chiles rellenos,* although frozen and reconstituted, are puffy and crisp. Lest you think I am indiscriminate,
let me warn you to keep out of Kosher Burritos on Hollywood
Boulevard; their creation filled with pastrami is abysmal.

Whether or not you share my enthusiasm, the fact is, fast 8
food is fast closing in on us. There are more than 70,000 fast-
food restaurants in America and they sell $20 billion worth of
food annually. Even you, who know the difference between
beluga and sevruga, will one day pull your Mercedes into the
parking lot of a Pizza Hut and send the chauffeur in for a slice.
On that day, I will no longer have to sneak off in the dark of
night just to get a Whopper, and if I meet you in Jack in the
Box, I won't have to say, "I'm here because of my kids."

Vocabulary

duplicity (1), culinary (1), palates (1), tannin (1), schizophrenic (2),
strudels (3), nirvana (6), reconstituted (7), indiscriminate (7),
abysmal (7)

Questions

1. What is the significance of the title?
2. The thesis is implied in paragraph 1. Where is it actually stated?
   Why?
3. What audience does Witchel have in mind?
4. Why was the essay written?
5. What is Witchel's tone? Where do you find it expressed? Is he
   amused?
6. How does the topic for each paragraph relate to the controlling
   idea?
7. Which paragraph seems the most successful? Why?
8. What do you think is the most outstanding characteristic of the
   essay?
9. Why does he mention so many exotic dishes?

---

[1] Scarlett O'Hara: heroine of Margaret Mitchell's novel, *Gone with the
Wind* (1936).

10. Why does he use the foreign terms?

11. What is the major variation from the basic pattern in Part I?

Suggestions for Writing

1. Write your own "confession," making the different occasions for your "crimes" the subjects of each paragraph. Maybe you are a closet "junk food junkie," a reader of "unsavory" literature, a "creature features" addict, or a soap opera fan. Are you a "chicken" at heart or a person plagued by shyness? Remember to consider your tone and your audience. Are you basically amused by your folly or seriously guilt-ridden? How would you expect your readers to react to your essay?

2. Write an "appearance and reality" essay. "I may appear to be a ____, but I am actually a ____." Once you have the contrast set up, it is not necessary to use these exact words, but remember that your paper is based on contrast—one proof for each paragraph.

BILL SURFACE

Referee: Roughest Role in Sports

Bill Surface, born in 1935 in Louisville, Kentucky, has been a professional writer since age eighteen. He has often written about sports, publishing a book with Dick Groat, The World Championship Pittsburgh Pirates *(1961), and several articles for such magazines as* Life, Look, McCall's, Sport, *and* Saturday Evening Post. *He has also written about the war in Viet Nam. Here Surface discusses the responsibilities of a job—in this case, the difficulties that make being a referee the "roughest role" in sports. Notice the illustrations drawn from actual experiences of referees.*

The scene: Boston Garden, tightly packed for the fifth game 1
in the 1976 National Basketball Association (NBA) championship series. A high-leaping Boston Celtic player swishes the ball through the basket, and the buzzer sounds to end the second overtime period—and the game. Bedlam erupts as the hometown fans cheer a Celtic victory over the Phoenix Suns.

But a sweat-drenched referee, Richie Powers, views the game 2
more precisely. The timekeeper, he notices, failed to stop the clock after the goal, so Powers rules that there is one second left in the game. When the clock starts again, the score is 112–110 in favor of Boston, but in that one second the Suns tie the game and send it into a third overtime period. Now, the hometown .fans feel like killing Powers. One woman throws her purse at him and screams: "You ain't even human!"

"In this job," Powers retorts, "that helps." 3

Indeed, it takes a special breed of man to excel at the most 4
difficult job in all of professional basketball, baseball, football

---

and hockey: officiating the game. Expertise is not enough. Simply no one in sports endures more pressure—and needs greater discipline—than the plucky, perceptive autocrats wearing "prison stripes" or "mortician's blue," depending on the sport.

Whether he's called referee, umpire or official, such a man 5 must be superbly skilled in his job in order to instantly interpret as many as 100 pages of complex rules. And an official often needs to outhustle the players to gain a strategic view of every frenzied battle for the ball or puck to detect player violations.

An official also has to be something of a detective to notice 6 players' varied ruses to get opponents penalized for supposedly fouling them. Referees often foil these plots swiftly—as when hockey's Lloyd Gilmour simply ignored a crafty Chicago Black Hawk who pretended that he had been tripped so viciously that he somersaulted across the ice. The faker got up and fumed, "What's it take to get a penalty on that killer?" Gilmour replied: "Better acting."

Far different techniques are needed to detect players who 7 conceal their violations more adroitly. Basketball players, for example, will position their bodies to keep a referee from seeing when they clutch, rather than legally touch, opponents. But referees learn through watching slow-motion films that the position of a player's arms or body tells, without fail, when he is holding an opponent.

All officials need superior vision. Consider the baseball um- 8 pire's task. Bent in a fatiguing crouch behind the catcher, he determines where the blurred, aspirin-sized image spinning toward him at up to 100 m.p.h. unpredictably drops, rises or curves. During 1/60 of a second, the umpire decides if the slightest part of the ball crossed the plate while traveling on a plane between the batter's armpits and knees. Even when the ball misses the strike zone, an umpire must also judge if the player—though he has drawn his bat back almost instantly—has made a swing for a strike. Likewise, an umpire needs the savvy to tell if the ball dropped suddenly because it had been illegally dampened with a pitcher's hair oil, saliva or perspiration; or because a sharpened thumbnail had cut a hole in the ball.

Referees must retain their composure while absorbing al- 9

most unbelievable psychological and verbal punishment. A referee, *always* working before unfriendly crowds which are apt to jeer at the first sight of him, has orders to exude poise under the most testing circumstances—no matter if pelted by ice, frankfurters, and even bottles. Tougher yet, an official must resist both teams' attempts to unnerve him and gain more favorable decisions.

Still, a referee cannot be too rigid. Since league authorities 10 rarely overrule his judgment, an official must also function as the sport's supreme court and thus deliberate if he, as the district judge, might have erred. Though never swayed by how loudly a fiery coach protests, a good official will change decisions when additional evidence appears.

Even when a referee's instant call is correct, he's still got 11 to face the anger that smolders long, long after a game. Sometimes that anger takes on an ominous tone, as it did in the 1975 World Series. Umpire Larry Barnett's disputed ruling that a batter did not obstruct the catcher brought him a letter warning that if he did not make up a $10,000 bet loss, the sender would "put a .38-caliber bullet in your head." Yet, as one official reasons, "An umpire's really in trouble—not in making 'bad' calls—but when his decisions bring nice mail and nice smiles."

A referee must be strong physically and shrug off frequent 12 pain. Occupational hazards include torn muscles, being cut by punches and spiked shoes when breaking up fights, being stunned by frozen pucks rocketing at 120 m.p.h. Baseballs, which often travel almost as fast as hockey pucks, have snapped the steel bars of umpires' face-masks, then knocked out teeth and broken jaws. In football, even an agile referee can be knocked down by gargantuan athletes charging full speed.

To get into superb shape, each sport official must report to 13 pre-season training camps at a stipulated weight. There he stretches, sprints, lifts weights, does calisthenics and other exercises needed especially for his sport. Hockey's officials, for instance, must run a mile in no more than seven minutes, do 80 sit-ups within two minutes, and skate in relay races for two hours. Then, to stretch and strengthen their leg muscles, they practice alternate squatting and standing on skates. Next comes the hand-wrestling needed to separate brawling players.

In an average pro-basketball game, a referee sprints some 14
six miles on a hardwood court and loses up to ten pounds.
Yet basketball's referees must satisfy a supervisor that their
facial expressions show "firmness and confidence"—and that
their whistle's short blast always has the requisite "sharp,
crisp tone." Baseball's umpires holler "ball" and "strike" from
deep in their chests to develop such a booming, authoritative
voice that they seldom can ever speak in a normal tone.

Pre-season study sessions are equally strenuous for football 15
officials. They plunge into a daily, 14-hour program that includes a 200-question rules examination and a concentrated
film study of all the major calls made by each of the 84 officials
during the previous season.

Referees have demonstrated their spunk long before they 16
finally reach a major league. Combining a fondness for sports
and a need for extra income, most start officiating for as little
as $2 a game in small arenas. A "take-charge" referee may be
noticed by scouts as he doggedly advances to college games, to
umpiring schools or league try-out camps. Even so, the grittiest
ones who impress major leagues may wait for the few available
jobs that, like those in pro basketball and hockey, eventually
pay around $43,000 a season (plus another $8000 if selected for
championship playoffs).

Football's weekend referees—mostly coaches, teachers and 17
executives—wait still longer before they can hope to officiate
pro football for up to $575 a game ($1500 for the Super Bowl).
The National Football League (NFL) considers only men with
records proving that they have officiated for at least ten years
(including five years in college games) and have a lifelong dedication to the game. Nonetheless, of 150 such men found qualified to officiate, the NFL hires no more than six new ones each
season.

Referees in all sports are evaluated by scouts, supervisors 18
and often by wide-angle cameras focused on them. After poring
over films, the supervisors rate officials and notify them of the
conclusions. At season's end, usually from one to six officials in
each sport who are considered unsatisfactory are quietly dis-
missed.

Even the best referees find themselves under growing scru- 19
tiny. Television's slow-motion instant replays of close decisions

foster demands by angry fans that such cameras be used to overrule, or even replace, officials. But in fact TV replays pinpoint only a few dozen of pro-football officials 41,000 split-second decisions during a season that are genuinely arguable or wrong. As a result, many athletes are *against* cameras replacing referees. Instant replay, says one, eliminates a common alibi for the mistake that cost his team a victory: "The ref missed it."

The members of this exclusive breed of men are proud of   20
their oft-scorned, but indispensable, role. Such pride was perhaps best characterized in a baseball game when umpire Nestor Chylak carefully brushed home plate, then "discovered" that he needed to be resupplied with baseballs—a kindly intended ploy to enable the catcher to shake off some pain caused by a wild pitch earlier. Minutes later, the ungrateful catcher grumbled loudly and waved his arms wildly over the final call ending the game. Chylak was loudly jeered on leaving the field.

"Is it worth fighting off the world this way every day?"   21
Chylak was asked later. He beamed, then said, "What other guy can walk away from a game feeling he's a winner—*every* time?"

Vocabulary

mortician (4), strategic (5), frenzied (5), ruses (6), foil (6), fatiguing (8), savvy (8), exudes (9), erred (10), obstruct (11), agile (12), gargantuan (12), stipulated (13), requisite (14), strenuous (15), doggedly (15), poring (18), scrutiny (19)

Questions

1. What are the important skills for a referee to have?
2. Why is it the "roughest role," according to Surface?
3. Why is there opposition to instant replay?
4. How does the introduction differ from those in Part I?
5. What is the thesis?
6. What part does the title play?
7. What is the topic of paragraphs 12 and 13?
8. Discuss the conclusion. Does it have any connection to paragraph 9?
9. Why does Surface include direct quotation?
10. Do you like this analysis of the referee's job? Why?

Suggestions for Writing

1. What are the characteristics necessary for a job or a sport with which you are familiar. Use as many illustrative details as you can.
2. What do you think is the "roughest role" in sports (or in the household, in government, at the supermarket, etc.)? What is the "softest" role?

JAMES THURBER

How to Get through the Day

*Although slightly longer than most of the essays in this
collection, Thurber's essay has a structure that is clear
and easy to follow. Notice how some of the topics are
expanded to more than one paragraph. (See introduction
to the writer on p. 32.)*

"How do you get through the day?" a woman out in Iowa 1
has asked me in a letter. I can't tell whether she wants help in
getting through her own day, or whether she has made a wager
with somebody that I don't get through my own day at all, but
somehow contrive to get *around* it. The truth is that I do get
through the day and, if it will benefit anybody, I shall be glad
to state how I manage it. It might be simpler to put my method
in the form of rules.

One: Never answer a telephone that rings before breakfast. 2
It is sure to be one of three types of persons that is calling: a
strange man in Minneapolis who has been up all night and is
phoning collect; a salesman who wants to come over and dem-
onstrate a new, patented combination Dictaphone and music
box that also cleans rugs; or a woman out of one's past. Just let
the phone ring. The woman would be sure to say:

"This is Thelma Terwilliger. What are you going to *do* 3
about me?" If you talk to her before your orange juice and coffee, or even afterward, for that matter, you will never get
through the day. Professors Radnor and Grube, in their monu-
mentally depressing treatise *The Female of the Species,* list a
total 1,113 possible involvements with a woman, all but eight
of them ranging from the untoward to the inextricable.

Two: If you want to keep your breakfast down, do not read 4

the front page, or any page, of the morning newspaper. Fifteen years ago the late Professor Herman Allen Miller of Ohio State University wrote me that, out there, no news was the only good news. He would be saddened, but not surprised, to learn that nowadays no news is the only good news anywhere. It is better to dip into *The Last Days of Pompeii* than to peruse the morning paper at breakfast,[1] but what I do is turn on WQXR for classical or semi-classical music, or WPAT for popular music out of the late lamented American past—such songs, for example, as "Whispering," "Sleepy Time Gal," "Sunny," and "Honey, Honey, Bless Your Heart." (If you have been foolish enough to talk with Thelma, the last two songs will probably become "Money," and "Money, Money, Bless Your Heart.") One morning, by mistake, I got another station than WPAT and listened, relaxed, to a recording of "People Will Say We're in Love," sung by Alfred Drake and Joan Roberts, when suddenly it terminated and a young detergent voice began yelling:

"Don't knock rock 'n' roll, it's a rockin' good way to mess   5
around and fall in love." What have we done to deserve this? Or should I say, what have we done not to deserve it?

Three: Avoid the ten-o'clock news on the radio, at all costs.   6
It is always confined to disasters—automobile accidents involving seventeen cars, the fatal stabbing of a fourteen-year-old girl by her twelve-year-old sweetheart, attacks on young mothers in Brooklyn basements, and riotous demonstrations by fifteen thousand students in Graustark. It is comforting, in a vaguely uneasy way, to realize that American students do not engage in political demonstrations, but reserve their passions for panty raids, jazz festivals, and the hanging of football coaches in effigy.

Four: Do not open the morning mail when it arrives if you   7
are alone in the house. If I am alone when my mail arrives, around eleven o'clock, I wait for my wife to get back from the hairdresser. If she says, "God!" or "Oh, no!" after glancing at a letter, I hastily tell her to send it on to our lawyer or our agent, without reading it to me. I now get about twelve letters every morning, and she is happy if not more than two of them

---

[1] *The Last Days of Pompeii:* a novel by Edward Bulwer-Lytton (1803–73).

call for wedding presents. About seven of the twelve always call for something, and you ought to consider yourself lucky that you are not me. I am asked to read something, to write something, to send something, to do something, to explain something, or to go somewhere. These letters invariably begin like this: "I realize that you are a very busy man, but . . ." and they always end: "Thanks for your time and trouble." I am pleased to report that at least two letters every day are intelligent, warm, and even humorous, and that they almost invariably come from American wives and mothers unknown to me, who frequently say, "I love you." This cheers me up enormously, until I begin thinking about Thelma Terwilliger again.

Five: Some years ago a distinguished American woman 8 physician recommended "a nap after lunch and a nip before dinner." I myself do not recommend the nap after lunch, except for infants. My researchers among those who have tried it show that 80 per cent of the males and 100 per cent of the females just lie there wide-eyed, strumming the headboard with their fingers and/or, as the lawyers say, moaning low. Among the thoughts that keep Americans awake are—but why should I list them, sleepless reader, when you know what they are as well as I do?

As for the nip before dinner, I'm all for it, unless it leads to 9 a nipping that doesn't end until after three o'clock in the morning. Speaking of tranquillizers, which everybody always is, I do not turn to Miltown, but to Milton, and to some of the other bards sublime, and a few of the humbler poets. Because of the distressing process of mental association, however, poetry is not always a help. The other morning, for example, I got to Edna St. Vincent Millay's "There isn't a train I wouldn't take, no matter where it's going" when it suddenly turned into "There isn't a train that I can take, no matter where I'm going." [2] This disturbing paraphrase grew out of a seven-week period of travel in the Middle West last winter, during which I had to be driven by car from Columbus, Ohio, to Detroit because the only train out of the Ohio capital for the great Michigan city leaves at 4 A.M. I also found it simpler to be driven from

---

[2] Edna St. Vincent Millay (1892–1950): American poet.

Detroit to Cleveland, since railroad transportation in the
Middle West has regressed to about where it was at the time of
Custer's Last Stand.

The trouble with turning to verse while nipping before 10
dinner, especially in a public place like the lobby of the Hotel
Algonquin, is that one is likely to grow irritable, or even bitter,
instead of leaning back and relaxing in one's chair. A playwright I know, who tried repeating lines of Longfellow to himself in the Algonquin lobby at six o'clock one evening, was
abruptly impelled, while nipping his fourth martini, to accost
a strange lady and proclaim, "*I* say the struggle naught availeth, madam," [3] after which he turned to a male stranger and
snarled, "Life is but an empty dream, Mac." [4] He then returned
to his own chair. All of a sudden he spotted a poet across the
lobby, and he was upon him in a moment, saying, "Hell with
thee, blythe spirit, bard thou never wert." [5] When the rude
fellow later told me, proudly, what he had said, I could only
snarl, on my own fourth nip before dinner, "I am glad you did
not once see Shelley plain, and did not stop and talk to him." [6]

Six: This brings us to the dinner hour and the problem of 11
getting through *that*. Here everybody has to work out his own
system of getting his dinner down, and keeping it down.
Dinner-table conversation should be selected with great care
nowadays since the first seventeen subjects that spring to mind
are likely to be gloomy, running from the muddle-fuddle of
international relations to the dangers of cholesterol and di-
ester stilvesterol, and if you don't know what they are, I'm not
going to tell you. My wife and I, Monday through Friday,
usually dine in our own home with thirteen and a half million
and one Americans, the thirteen and a half million members of
the C.I.O.-A.F. of L. who sponsor the commentator Edward P.

---

[3] The quotations here are distortions of lines from poetry, illustrating
effects of turning to verse while nipping before dinner. Arthur Hugh Clough
(1819–61) wrote, "Say not, the struggle naught availeth," in a poem of the
same title.

[4] Henry Wadsworth Longfellow (1807–82) wrote, "Tell me not in mournful numbers/Life is but an empty dream," in "A Psalm of Life."

[5] Percy Bysshe Shelley (1792–1822) wrote, "Hail to thee blithe spirit/
Bird thou never wert," in "To a Skylark."

[6] Robert Browning (1812–89) wrote, "Ah, did you once see Shelley plain/
And did he stop and speak to you," in "Memorabilia, I."

Morgan on WABC at seven P.M., and Mr. Morgan himself.
The good strong voice of Elmer Davis is no longer heard in the
land, but Mr. Morgan carries on ably in his stead, with the
same intelligence, devotion to American ideals, courage, and
wit. One night, during Christmas week of 1959, he discussed
the lavish, expensive, and empty celebration of Holy Week and
said, "We seem to forget that Christ was born in a manger and
not in the Bethlehem-Hilton." It is a thought to remember.

Seven: Tender is the night no more,[7] as we all know, espe-   12
cially the summer night, and when it falls, I always think of
Robert Benchley's provocative title, "What to Do When It
Gets Dark." Most married couples, I have found out, totter to
the television set and turn it on, but I would rather read something restful instead, like *The Naked and the Dead*.[8] It is perhaps enough to say of the Westerns, that endless series of mor-
bid discharges, that they inspired a certain little girl's definition of a hung jury as "twelve men hanging from a tree." As
for the police bang-bangs, they seem more and more given over
to the theory that most killers in our society are women, so that
as soon as a demure wife or ex-wife appears on the scene, you
can be pretty sure that she did it. She usually confesses, at the
end, in a quiet voice, saying, simply, "Yes, Lieutenant, I killed
him."

This may not give *you* the creeps but it gives *me* the creeps.   13

Eight: This brings us to beddy-bye. Well, good night, and I   14
pray the Lord your soul to keep. My own nocturnal problem in
the summertime consists of flying creatures, great big June
bugs, or bang-sashes. One of them banged the sash of the window nearest my bed around midnight in July, and I leaped
out of sleep and out of bed. "It's just a bat," said my wife re-
assuringly, and I sighed with relief. "Thank God for that," I
said. "I thought it was a human being."

Vocabulary

contrive (1), untoward (3), inextricable (3), effigy (6), invariably
(7), bands (9), regressed (9), demure (12)

---

[7] From John Keats' (1795–1821), "Ode to a Nightingale," where he writes,
"Already with thee! tender is the night."

[8] Novel about World War II by American author, Norman Mailer, born
in 1923.

Questions

1. How does Thurber introduce his subject?
2. Why does he mention Thelma Terwilliger so often?
3. Why does he mention *The Last Days of Pompeii* and *The Naked and the Dead?*
4. What is the tone? Is it serious?
5. What is the purpose of the essay?
6. Which details seem particularly well chosen for his purposes? Discuss three.
7. What is the meaning of the last sentence?
8. Why does he misquote Browning in paragraph 10?
9. For what audience is Thurber's essay intended?
10. Are there any suggestions of satire in this essay?
11. Does this essay seem "effortless," as Thurber says he wants?
12. How is narration used in the essay?

Suggestions for Writing

1. Write your own essay on "how to get through the day," setting up and discussing a series of rules. Be sure to illustrate each rule and to consider how you feel about the larger question of simply "getting through the day." Do you have as many "do nots" as Thurber does, for example?
2. A *New York Times* reviewer commented on Thurber, "But he is not only a humorist; he is also a satirist who can toss a bomb while he appears to be tipping his hat." Discuss this comment in relation to "How to Get through the Day."
3. How do you see a day? Is it something to be gotten through?

GILBERT HIGHET

Go and Catch a Falling Remark

Gilbert Highet (1906–78) was born in Glasgow, Scotland, and graduated from Glasgow University and Oxford. Married to novelist Helen Clark MacInnes, Highet was professor of Greek and Latin at Columbia for most of his teaching career. He became an American citizen in 1951. His many publications include The Classical Tradition: Greek and Roman Influence on Western Literature *(1949),* The Art of Teaching *(1950),* Talents and Geniuses *(1957), and* The Anatomy of Satire *(1962). His wife once remarked, "Gilbert reads all the time; even when he's putting on his socks he's got a book propped on the table." In "Go and Catch a Falling Remark," Highet is in one of his lighter moments (of which there were many), offering a specific suggestion on how to pass time. Every paragraph is fully developed with a variety of details—argumentative, descriptive, narrative.*

Most people love wandering through strange cities: Paris 1 is my own favorite, and San Francisco, if only for its superb situation, comes next. Some people, though not very many, enjoy roaming through unfamiliar parts of their home towns. At one time or another I have idled along nearly every street in Manhattan, constantly finding something curious or diverting—a shop selling love-potions and magical equipment, the headquarters of an organization investigating unidentified flying objects, a group of Albanian stores and eating houses. It is a pleasant way to pass time.

But what do you do when you journey day after day along 2 the same streets? Subway to office; office to restaurant for lunch;

© 1973 American Heritage Publishing Company, Inc. Reprinted by permission from *Horizon* (Summer 1973).

restaurant to bank and back to office; office to subway. . . .
Well, if you don't mind spending a few extra minutes, it is an
excellent idea to try to vary your route every day: zigzag or
make detours. Most people, however, prefer the shortest line
between two points, and then what do they do? The men look
at the girls; the girls look at the girls; all look at the shop-
windows; and nearly all stare at the occasional kooks and
freaks, loping along in fancy dress like Dr. Falke in *Die Fledermaus,*[1] who walked home from a ball in broad daylight dressed
as a gigantic bat, "to the delight of all the street urchins."

I have devised a new pastime for—one can't say "street-   3
walkers," "strollers" now means vehicles for transporting small
children, and the French *flâneurs,* which is exactly right,
sounds affected outside of France. Anyhow, a new pastime,
harmless and costfree. Instead of looking at other people, listen
to them. Of course, I do not mean put them under surveillance or eavesdrop on an entire conversation. Far from it. The
point of this game is to catch a single fleeting remark, a floating
fragment of dialogue, and then let it flutter around in your
imagination. People in the streets talk freely to one another,
with no idea that they can be overheard. Therefore they will
say the most absurd and memorable things, and as you pass you
can often pick up just a few meaningless but meaningful words.

The other day I stopped on Madison Avenue in the fifties,   4
waiting for the green light. Two men came up on one side of
me, two girls on the other. Thinking of something else, I did
not even try to listen. But just as the light changed, one of the
men said very earnestly, "We can get the second million from
Switzerland," while one of the girls, giggling remarked, "And
then she married the *other* one!" You fill in the rest. Again,
on Park Avenue at 49th Street a fat man said (almost in my
ear), "Hundreds of thousands of dollars of insurance, and not
worth a nickel!" while a moment later a pretty but rather
harried-looking woman bent over a little boy of five and answered him, "But, darling, *both* your daddies love you!" Now
and then these flying splinters are a little more pointed. In a
voice like a load of gravel sliding into an excavation, "Illegal it

---

[1]Operetta by Johann Strauss (1825–99) in which Dr. Falke, disguised as
a bat (hence the title) is left asleep at a carnival and forced to find his way
home in broad daylight — still in disguise.

may be; impossible it's not" (Sixth Avenue and 47th). With an accent as smooth as Jello, "Leather underwear, for Godsake, looked like a scuba diver!" (Third and 52nd).

People who speak a foreign language usually assume that no 5 one can understand them in a strange country. I know a lady, born and brought up in Argentina, who gave up traveling on the New York subway because she could not endure the comments made about her face and figure by men who thought she knew no Spanish. Walking near the United Nations one Sunday, I saw an elegant couple in their early forties approaching: handsomely dressed, with an air that stamped them as members of the diplomatic world. They looked serenely self-possessed, strolling along in untroubled silence. However, just as they reached me, the man turned to the woman and said, almost spat out, "*¡Dinero! ¡Dinero! ¡Siempre dinero!*"—"Money! Money! Always money!" She did not even tilt her head.

Once you get your ear accustomed to picking up scraps, you 6 can play the game almost anywhere. Wandering through working-class London, I went into a pub. As I pushed open the swinging doors there was a great burst of laughter, and then, just before I ordered my pint of mild-and-bitter, a great voice said, "Old Sam! What a card 'e was! Walked dahn Covent Garden wiv nuffin on 'im but 'is truss!"

It is difficult, but rewarding, to try this kind of phrase- 7 grabbing at cocktail parties. As well as the fluent and energetic conversation of the woman I have just been unintelligibly introduced to, I usually get four or five broken messages from behind and from both sides. Thus, she will be telling me what is fundamentally wrong with Lincoln Center, and at the same time I hear ". . . he told her he would kill her and he damn near did . . ." and ". . . owes money to everybody in the publishing business . . ."

One of Homer's immortal clichés is "winged words." Phrases 8 like these are winged words. They fly around like butterflies, and it is fun to snag them as they pass. Some of the butterflies may have a sting, but it is not meant for you.

Vocabulary

diverting (1), surveillance (3), harried (4), fluent (7), unintelligibly (7)

Questions

1. What line is echoed in the title?
2. This essay has a three-paragraph introduction. Why?
3. Try to reduce the introduction to one paragraph. What happens?
4. Do you see any examples of figurative language? Explain one.
5. What does Highet mean by "meaningless but meaningful words"?
6. Evaluate the conclusion. Do you think it is an appropriate ending for this essay? Why?
7. Which "falling remark" did you like best? Why?
8. What is the tone of the essay?
9. Which descriptive details seem particularly well chosen?
10. What is the purpose of the reference to Dr. Falke in "Die Fledermaus"?
11. Do you like the essay? Explain your reaction.

Suggestions for Writing

1. Write an essay on what you see as a valuable way to pass time—however unusual. Be sure to include examples of the pastime in operation and make it lively with description and possibly quotation. Remember, you are arguing in favor of this activity.
2. Write your own essay on "falling remarks" you have heard, making examples of each the subjects of your paragraphs.
3. Do you enjoy strolling in the streets? Have you developed a pastime to keep you alert and entertained while strolling? Write an essay on your own "street pastime." What do you see or hear as you hike the streets (city or country)?
4. How much time do we allow ourselves for pastimes nowadays? In *Life without Principle,* Thoreau says, "There is no more fatal blunderer than he who consumes the great part of his life getting his living." Comment.

SYLVIA WRIGHT

Quit it *Ompremitywise*

Sylvia Wright (b. 1917), whose "first substantial work was a verse play about the nine Muses," written when she was nine, has worked for a publishing company, for the Office of War Information in New York and overseas, for the United States Information Service, and for the magazines McCall's, Vogue, *and* Harper's. *Her other publications include books,* A Shark-Infested Rice Pudding *(1969) and* Get Away from Me with Those Christmas Gifts *(1957), from which "Quit It Ompremitywise" was taken. Here she discusses one of the techniques of advertising about which she feels intolerant. Notice that she defines her term and then gives specific examples of its use.*

I feel tolerant about advertising, but there is one device of the advertisers that I would like to call their attention to. I think it may get them into trouble. 1

I am calling this device Omitted Premise Superiority, and, since I am a real American, advertised at regularly, in the flow, the swim, and the drink of our national life, and not an outsider, I am going to be like the advertising copywriters and hereinafter (a word I have always wanted to use) call this device Ompremity. 2

Here is an example of Ompremity: Gallo wine; picture of lush grapes. "These grapes are only squeezed *once*." 3

What, I want to know, is wrong with squeezing grapes twice, or three times, or as many times as it takes to get every bit of juice out of them? There may be a perfectly good reason, such as that if you go on squeezing, you get crushed seeds in your 4 wine. But I want to be told. I don't automatically know why squeezing grapes once is superior.

"The only mustard made with two kinds of specially grown mustard seed." Why are two kinds of mustard seed better than one? You could sell me just as badly if you said, "The only mustard made with only one specially grown mustard seed." 5

"The only cereal with two whole grains." Do all the other cereals have one whole and one half grain? If the bulk were the same, mightn't half grains be easier to chew and not stick in the teeth as much? I'm not questioning the veracity of the statement. I simply want that omitted premise. 6

Ompremity, as you see, is often associated with the word "only." It is also often associated with a made-up word, as in "the only tooth paste that contains 'Gardol.' " Gardol and Irium and such don't irritate me quite as much, because by their very vagueness they give my busy little mind something to work on. I can picture to myself some extraordinary substance, a great technical advance, developed in our clean, modern laboratories by a new process, which could certainly do whatever they say it does. My only quarrel with these words is that they aren't alluring. I am told not to buy a chicken unless it is acronized. Does this make my mouth water? Am I yummyized? I'm not, because acronized does not sound like what I would want done to a chicken. It sounds like what I would want done to a hot-water bottle. 7

Pillsbury tells me that if I use their Hot Roll Mix, I will have the "excitement of working with living dough." What is living dough? Is all dough but Pillsbury's dead? Who's that there in Pillsbury's dough, trying to get out? 8

If you are not alert, Ompremity can trick you into belief. There is a deodorant which is better because it rolls on. At first reading, this seemed to me obvious: of course a deodorant that rolls on is better than one that—well, what?—scrunches in? But mightn't scrunching in be more thorough? 9

"Roto-roasting" is the "secret that brings out all the golden goodness of the peanuts" used in Big Top peanut butter. (By the way, why is goodness always golden? What about bisque goodness, as in lobster bisque, or chartreuse goodness, as in chartreuse?) Roto comes from the Latin, rota, a wheel. Because of having a dictionary, I can get a little further with this 10

Ompremity than with most, but I can't get very far. The implication is that these peanuts are roasted on all sides. How do you suppose they do this? Do they spit each peanut on a fine sewing needle?

The point is that, if they don't watch it, the advertisers will 11 be hoist with their own Ompremity. I am thinking of the face powder which is proofed against moisture discoloration because it is triple-creamed. I am, as I mentioned above, a regular American, and I have been advertised at to the point where I take it for granted that I am entitled to the very best. Why should I be satisfied with face powder that is only triple-creamed? I want face powder that is at least quintuple-creamed; and now that I think of the very delicate skin I have, I think I should have face powder that is centuple-creamed.

In this country one person is just as special as the next one, 12 except that I am more so. I have just written the *only* article than contains Ompremity.

Vocabulary

premise (2), hereinafter (2), acronized (7), bisque (10), chartreuse (10), implication (10), hoist with (11)

Questions

1. Explain the meaning of the word "ompremity."
2. What is implied by the title?
3. Why are so many of the paragraphs, including the conclusion, short? Try to combine some of them. Can it be done without hurting the essay?
4. Why, in paragraph 1, does Wright suggest that she hopes to call advertisers' attention to ompremity? Who is the audience for this essay?
5. Which paragraph do you think is the most effective? Why?
6. Which sentence is the most effective for developing the thesis?
7. Which individual vocabulary words are most valuable for her main point?
8. Do you like the tone?
9. How does she use the techniques of advertising against it?

Suggestions for Writing

1. Write an essay in which you give examples of an advertising technique that you find irritating. If possible, give it a name, define it, and then give specific examples of its use. Or, following the same model, write an essay in which you give examples of an appealing technique of advertising. In either case, remember to consider whether your technique is widely used or limited to a specific medium—TV, radio, print, highway signs—or to a specific season, for example. Also remember tone. How do you really feel about this approach?

2. In an essay called "Morals" (in *Speaking of Advertising*, ed. John S. Wright and Daniel S. Warner), Walter Toplin explains, "When we use the word "advertising" we understand it to include the commendation of goods, the emphasizing of their more attractive features, and the frequent use of hyperbole. . . . To condemn advertising because it attempts to persuade, it would be necessary to prove that persuasion was always directed to bad ends." Discuss "morals" in advertising, basing your judgments on your own experience (or on research, if the project would be appropriate).

3. A *New York Herald Tribune* (Oct. 27, 1957) reviewer of Wright's book commented, "Her writing is a deceptively innocent and gentle weapon not intended to rip great holes in things, but merely to expose those insidious bits of nonsense that have been drummed into us for so long that we no longer realize they are ridiculous." Write an essay in which you expose something you consider an "insidious bit of nonsense" (possibly sending cards for every occasion in the yearly calendar or wearing "Smiley Face" pins?)

ROBERT BENCHLEY

Why I Am Pale

*Robert Benchley (1889–1945) was born in Worcester,
Massachusetts, and educated at Philips Exeter Academy.
There he wrote a paper, "How to Embalm a Corpse,"
when told to write an exposition on how to do something
practical. Later he wrote a study of a Newfoundland
Fisheries dispute—from the point of view of the fish. He
graduated from Harvard where he was president of the*
Lampoon *and a chorus girl in a Hasty Pudding show. He
was also a radio and film performer and a prolific essayist, whose collections include* Twenty Thousand Leagues
under the Sea or David Copperfield *(1928),* My Ten Years
in a Quandary *(1936), and* Inside Benchley *(1941). Travel
pamphlets would have us believe that there is nothing
to be compared to the joys of basking in the tanning sun,
but Benchley felt otherwise. This essay, using two paragraphs for introducing, is a very simple account of a very
personal dilemma, typical of Benchley's approach. Pay
particular attention to the use of detail that helps the
reader "feel" the discomfort. Also, notice that the tone is
appropriate to the lightness of the subject.*

One of the reasons (in case you give a darn) for that unreasonable pallor of mine in mid-Summer, is that I can seem
to find no comfortable position in which to lie in the sun. A
couple of minutes on my elbows, a couple of minutes on my
back, and then the cramping sets in and I have to scramble to
my feet. And you can't get very tanned in four minutes.

I see other people, especially women (who must be made of

From *The Benchley Roundup* edited by Nathaniel Benchley. Copyright
1933 by The Hearst Corporation, New York Mirror Division. Reprinted by
permission of Harper & Row, Publishers, Inc.

rubber), taking books to the beach or up on the roof for a whole day of lolling about in the sun in various attitudes of relaxation, hardly moving from one position over a period of hours. I have even tried it myself.

But after arranging myself in what I take, for the moment, 3 to be a comfortable posture, with vast areas of my skin exposed to the actinic rays and the book in a shadow so that I do not blind myself, I find that my elbows are beginning to dig their way into the sand, or that they are acquiring "sheet-burns" from the mattress; that the small of my back is sinking in as far as my abdomen will allow, and that both knees are bending backward, with considerable tugging at the ligaments.

This is obviously not the way for me to lie. So I roll over 4 on my back, holding the book up in the air between my eyes and the sun. I am not even deluding myself by this maneuver. I know that it won't work for long. So, as soon as paralysis of the arms sets in, I drop the book on my chest (without having read more than three consecutive words), thinking that perhaps I may catch a little doze.

But sun shining on closed eyelids (on *my* closed eyelids) soon 5 induces large purple azaleas whirling against a yellow background, and the sand at the back of my neck starts crawling. (I can be stark naked and still have something at the back of my neck for sand to get in under.) So it is a matter of perhaps a minute and a half before I am over on my stomach again with a grunt, this time with the sand in my lips.

There are several positions in which I may arrange my arms, 6 all of them wrong. Under my head, to keep the sand or mattress out of my mouth; down straight at my sides, or stretched out like a cross; no matter which, they soon develop unmistakable symptoms of arthritis and have to be shifted, also with grunting.

Lying on one hip, with one elbow supporting the head, is 7 no better, as both joints soon start swelling and aching, with every indication of becoming infected, and often I have to be assisted to my feet from this position.

Once on my feet, I try to bask standing up in various postures, but this results only in a sunburn on the top of my forehead and the entire surface of my nose, with occasional painful blisters on the tops of my shoulders. So gradually, trying to look as if I were just ambling aimlessly about, I edge my way toward the clubhouse, where a good comfortable chair and a long, cooling drink soon put an end to all this monkey-business.

I am afraid that I am more the pale type, and should defi- 9 nitely give up trying to look rugged.

Vocabulary

actinic (3), deluding (4), maneuver (4)

Questions

1. Why does Benchley go to the beach in the first place?
2. What is the thesis?
3. For what purpose was this essay written?
4. How does he introduce his subject?
5. Why is paragraph 2 included in the essay? Why mention the "other people"?
6. Select two details that you find particularly effective and explain why.
7. How does the conclusion relate to the essay?
8. Do you see any exaggeration? If so, can you suggest some reasons for it?
9. Why does he mention "monkey business" in paragraph 8?
10. List ten words chosen primarily for their physical qualities.
11. Compare this essay with Priestley's "On Travel by Train," p. 26.

Suggestions for Writing

1. This model focuses on a physical sensation—in this case, discomfort at the beach. Write an essay on a situation in which you feel particular discomfort, making various aspects of this feeling the topics of your paragraphs—sitting in a classroom, riding in a car pool, babysitting, going on a first date, etc.
2. Use this model for an essay on another physical sensation—comfort, heat, chill, sleepiness, for example. Why do you feel comfortable in a certain place, or what is the sequence of events as sleepiness overcomes you during a late-night conversation?
3. Would you like to lounge in a sun that sleeps only after you go to bed, as a travel advertisement might offer, or would you share Benchley's attitude? Write an essay on the pros and cons of a day at the beach or argue against it. Remember to make it lively and interesting with details drawn from your own experience.

FRANCIS BLESSINGTON

Roots

Francis Blessington was born in Boston in 1942, educated at Boston Latin School, Boston College, Northeastern University, and Brown, and teaches English at Northeastern University. He has published several articles on Milton, a book, Paradise Lost and the Classical Epic *(1979), and poems in a variety of journals. Here is a brief essay in which he recalls his attitude toward a summer job on the roofs with his father. Notice that the thesis has two sides and that he takes two paragraphs to discuss the reaction of fear.*

Most of my friends had well-grounded first jobs—they delivered groceries or newspapers or tried to sell lemonade (which nobody wanted even in the summer) on an empty orange crate on the sidewalk. If you came to our supermarket, my cousin Jimmie would have offered to swipe down your Packard while you shopped. We knew all of the *75 [Dull] Ways for Boys to Make Money,* but I had the mixed blessing of a 76th; I helped my father work on roofs. 1

It was a perverse God who sent me, born afraid of heights, to a father who seemed to have magnetic feet and who wanted me to work with him. I told him I did not need extra money for anything, but when he asked me to help him, it would have been ungrateful, not to say unmanly, to refuse. So with ice cubes in my feet, I agreed to go—all the time remembering how Eddie would climb up the red maple and then up and over Mrs. Greene's slanted roof and how Joey was in bed for two weeks with a face like a raccoon from falling down only ten feet from the same tree. I had always managed to do better than Joey, but Eddie's fearlessness made me dizzy. 2

I was never excessively afraid of heights, at least not until I 3 felt the squeak of the cracked ladder rungs and felt the ladder sway in towards the house like one of Tarzan's vines. Pale, aged wood groaned even worse in the rickety, though perfectly safe, staging boards barely stretching across two ladders. These tired boards seemed to call out to me not to hurt them, like the damned souls who called out to Dante in Hell.[1]

This premonition of Hell was intensified by the blistering 4 summer heat of the roof and by the melting pitch that stuck to my hands from the undersides of the shingles we were laying down. When I looked below, I could see my corpse splattered on the driveway beneath me and mused about clowns rushing out with large firemen's nets for me to jump into, as I had seen trapeze artists do in the circus. In fact, I had my own juggling act of keeping tar paper, shingles, nails, and a hammer in the right position while looking down most of the time.

What made matters somehow better was the nonchalance of 5 my father. He would bend over as casually as a sleepwalker and attach a gutter by driving in nails with one or two blows of a hammer while he puffed on a cigarette. He was a model of concentration and of balancing forces. It was nerve-wracking but assuring to know that he had fired one of his men because he tossed his tools down onto the grass rather than carry them down the ladder, saying "You can't work on a roof with a fool like that."

As my juggling hands calmed, I became more accustomed to 6 the roof, though I never stayed there a moment longer than I had to. I even perversely began to enjoy my own fear when the staging dipped and bounced. My world had become enlarged. I could watch the little people below who would superstitiously worry for a few seconds about whether to pass under our ladders—maybe they knew about my father's short-time helper. Above, the sky opened like a parachute above the shrinking houses, and, now and then, I would flush a bird from a rotting board, or a bat, that would snap away to freedom. I had a feeling of earned transcendence, balanced by a strong sense of reality from the smell of the tar and the echo of our hammers off the roofs. It was the world of fearful but enticing dreams and the world of hammer and nails.

Later I was excused from the job because of increasing 7

---

[1] For example, Inferno, VIII.

homework. Looking back, or rather up, I still could not follow
Eddie over Mrs. Greene's, but, given a choice of jobs, I
wouldn't take the rag away from Jimmie either.

Vocabulary

perverse (2), premonition (4), pitch (4), nonchalance (5), transcendence (6), enticing (6)

Questions

1. What did Blessington dislike about working on the roof?
2. What did he like?
3. What is the purpose of the sentence, "What made matters somehow better was the nonchalance of my father?"
4. What is the thesis? the controlling idea?
5. What is the tone?
6. Which two details seem to contribute most to the meaning of the
   essay?
7. How does the conclusion relate to the body of the essay and to
   the introduction?
8. Are there any examples of figurative language?
9. What does the title have to do with the meaning?
10. Do you like the essay? Why?
11. What is the major variation from the basic pattern?

Suggestions for Writing

1. Write an essay on one of your own jobs. Was it a good, bad, or
   mixed experience? Base your paragraphs either on the feelings
   you had about the job or on the things you liked or disliked
   about it.
2. Describe and discuss something that frightens you now or did
   frighten you in childhood.

KENNETH JON ROSE

2001 Space Shuttle

Kenneth Jon Rose, born in 1954, is a freelance science writer. After graduating from the University of Connecticut with a B.A. in psychology, he worked at the Oceanographic Institute, Woods Hole, Massachusetts, studying the behavior of sharks. His articles have appeared in magazines including Natural History, Travel and Leisure, Boy's Life, *and* Omni Magazine. *He has also been a guest on radio talk shows, discussing our technological future. This model shares some characteristics with science fiction in its attempts to envision an as-yet-unknown future and in its use of the journey as a way of portraying that world. Notice the use of two introductory paragraphs rather than one and the careful plotting of the paragraphs along the major stages of shuttle travel in the year 2001.*

When NASA built the first space shuttle and with it the first 1
chance to carry both men and equipment inexpensively into space, it opened the doors to the eventual building and operating of commercial shuttles by private corporations that, possibly within the next generation, may be able to fly us to a space station as routinely as we are flown to Europe.

What follows is a highly speculative look at what it may 2
be like to shuttle through space. However, with space technology changing at the speed of light, today's blueprint will likely be made history by tomorrow's research.

You'll need tickets first. Unlike the NASA shuttle, which 3
launches like a rocket, the future passenger shuttles will take

---

The author's source for much of this article was Dr. Jerry Grey, administrator of technical activities and public policy at the American Institute of Aeronautics and Astronautics.

From *Travel and Leisure,* November 1979. Reprinted by permission.

off the way jets do now, that is, horizontally on a runway. Ticket and reservation counters, as well as the shuttles themselves, most likely will be located at several airports around the world.

The tickets won't be cheap, though. One round-trip fare 4 may cost four times the amount of a flight from New York to Tokyo, or about $4,500. This might seem a lot to pay for a flight that is going to take 30 minutes to get up and the same coming down.

Once you've sat in the cushioned seats and have strapped 5 yourself in (the belt across your shoulders and lap will be needed to keep you in your seat when the shuttle is in weightless space), the large ship—which will be totally controlled by an on-board computer—will fire its engines and rumble down the runway. Before you notice the steadily increasing pressure of the acceleration pushing you gently back, the craft will have already lifted into the air.

Looking out your window, you'll see the earth rapidly fall- 6 ing away, and the light blue sky progressively turning blue-black. You'll now be about 30 miles up, traveling at about 3,000 mph. Within minutes, the sky will appear jet black, and only the fuzzy curve of the earth will be visible. Then, at per-haps 130 miles above the surface of the earth and traveling at greater than 17,000 mph, engines will shut down and—if the shuttle is in orbit with the planet and not accelerating—you'll become weightless.

There are some very strange effects in weightless space. At 7 first you may feel as if you are endlessly falling; soon it will pass. You may notice, too, that the faces of your fellow passen-gers look bloated and puffy and that they can't keep their hair in place. Without gravity to pull down your hair and skin, your features will become distorted. It won't do any harm; it'll just look funny.

Lack of gravity will also affect what you will eat. For in- 8 stance, because zero gravity causes water to form globs which are uncontrollable in confined spaces, you will not find run-ning water anywhere on board. And you probably will also not find food that is apt to crumble for the same reason that tiny crumbs are not kept down by gravity. What you will find are liquids that can be squeezed from a tube into the mouth

as well as foods that are sticky, or at least ones that stick together.

Looking out the window, you will see the best sights of the   9
trip. Because there is no up or down in space, earth may loom
either above or below you, but in any case you'll see the blue
of the oceans covered with swirls and patches of white clouds.
You might even see the brown-green fabric of a continent or
two. And, if the sun goes behind the earth, there will be a billion clear, bright, nonflickering (because there is no distorting
atmosphere in space) stars.

You will realize that the ship is entering the earth's outer   10
atmosphere when, once again, you feel an invisible force pushing you back into your seat. You will still be seated as if the
craft were horizontal and, in fact, it will descend in just that
way. As the shuttle passes through much of the outer atmosphere, the bottom of the craft, covered with special tiles, will
glow red from the air friction. Then the rapid descent begins.
The shuttle slows to five times the speed of sound (3,750 mph).

Meanwhile, the sky turns lighter and layers of clouds pass   11
you like cars on a highway. Minutes later, still sitting upright,
you will see the gray runway in the distance. Then the shuttle
slows to 300 mph and drops its landing gear. Finally, with its
nose up slightly like the Concorde SST and at a speed of about
225 mph, the shuttle will land on the asphalt runway and
slowly come to a halt. The trip into space will be over.

Vocabulary

    shuttle (title), speculative (2)

Questions

1. How does this essay vary from the most basic pattern in Part I?
2. What is the thesis?
3. What does Rose mean by "However, with space technology
   changing at the speed of light, today's blueprint will likely be
   made history by tomorrow's research" (paragraph 2)? Is it a cliché?
4. Why does Rose use the second person ("you") throughout the
   essay?
5. Why does he say that his account is highly speculative?

6. What is echoed in the title?
7. Which details contribute most to the meaning of the essay?
8. Which paragraph is the most effective?
9. Would you like to take this trip?
10. Does Rose assume interest in his subject? Should he?

Suggestions for Writing

1. Choose a particular year in the future and give your own account of an experience in that world — possibly going out to dinner or enjoying an evening's entertainment at home. Let your "futuristic" imagination take over here, but be sure to allow the reader to share your experience by setting up a clear structure for your essay and by using concrete details.
2. Write a "fantasy" in which you describe the world (or some aspect of it) as you would like to see it in the year 2001.
3. In 1857, Thoreau said in *Walden,* "If it is necessary, omit one bridge over the river, go round a little there, and throw one arch at least over the darker gulf of ignorance which surrounds us." Evaluate this comment in the light of your ideas about our twentieth-century "progress." Will we necessarily have progressed when we are able to board our space shuttle 2001?

JOHN HAY

The Musicians

*John Hay, born in New York City in 1915 and edu-
cated at St. Paul's School and Harvard, studied writing
with poet Conrad Aiken. He is president of the Cape Cod
Museum of Natural History, teaches at Dartmouth College, and is the author of* The Run *(1959),* The Great
Beach *(1963), and* Natures' Year: The Seasons of Cape
Cod *(1961), from which this essay is taken. "The Musicians" is an essay on the sounds of an August night. Hay
listens carefully and then records the great variety of
sounds that he had previously ignored, without a "shred
of attention." Notice how he combines his night walk with
a sequential discovery of sounds, how he makes an extended comparison of the sounds of nature with the experience of music, and how he chooses vocabulary words to
help us hear the sounds through words. Here the essay approaches poetry in its use of figurative language and philosophy in its concern for the relationship of humanity to
the natural world.*

Many Augusts, singing loud, have passed me by without my 1
giving them a shred of attention. What made the sound? The
air, or the trees, the month itself, embodied in unknown voices?
I don't think I knew much more than that, although I suppose
I was aware of what a cricket sounded like. Perhaps it is time to
find out more. I know now, as I did then, that at night when
the air is soft and cool, a multitude of separate actions having
died down, and when the earth is relieved of a fire taken to the
stars, a plainsong goes up and the night takes substance in
pulsing sound.

When I listen, I see that in detail the sounding of an August 2 night is not melodious. It is full of clicks, dry rasps, ratchets, reedy, resinous scrapings, and except for countless populations playing on one string, disassociated. There is only one phrase for each species of insect. The overall sound is occasionally reminiscent of telegraph wires, mechanically shrill and tense; but in the context of the night, speckled with stars, it becomes as wide, warm, and luminous as any symphony.

Having heard of using a flashlight to search for these musi- 3 cians, I go out, sometime after eight-thirty, and start training it on sounds, with complete lack of success at first. Either the sound stops, or the animal that makes it is invisible to me. A bat flies overhead, chasing insects. It is known for accuracy, having ears with a receptiveness like radar, tuned to the finest measurements of space, but its flight seems frantic. It beats back and forth, around, over and under. Suddenly it is very close, perhaps a few inches over my head. I duck at the leathery, fluttering sound, something like the rippling folds of a taut chute, despite my knowing that only in lingering myth and hearsay do bats catch in human hair. Then it is off again, with its violent, erratic flight.

The darkness takes deeper hold. It is full of the loud throb- 4 bing, the insistently high-pitched rasping of the insects, with an occasional tree frog sounding a contrapuntal "Ek-ek." Playing my flashlight under the trees shows up a spider web in beautiful detail. The silk strands are clear against the black night, their swoops and whorls all held together by long perfected execution, with the tiny engineer way up on his round span, his semblance of the globe in its vast waters.

In high suspension, in the larger silences of the sky, all rings 5 well in consonance, and the pulse of living instruments is with the massed stars that run out and dive away above all heads, and with the ground, my heart and ear, my blood and bone.

A persistent light racheting makes me concentrate on one 6 bush, where I eventually find a green, well-camouflaged, long-horned grasshopper with orange eyes—a male, since it has no ovipositor on its abdomen. The females are silent, with the honored role of being courted and invited.

The flashlight seems to have no effect on him. The front 7 wings are slightly apart, raised up a little, and vibrating . . . a kind of fast, dry shuddering. The sound is a light "*zzz,*" ending with a rapid "tic-tic-tic." This grasshopper is a waxy green. His antennae, almost twice as long as his body, go up in sweeping curves, and wave, sometimes both together in a semicircle, sometimes singly in both directions, as he stops his playing, and begins to move slightly down a twig. Then I notice a female moving in his direction. Had he increased the tempo of his playing when she came near? Did he sense success?

Still harder to spot—almost impossible by day, and difficult   8
enough at night—are the snowy tree crickets, but they are numerous in this low-treed, shrubby area. Where the long-horned grasshoppers sound at intervals, the combined chorus of snowy tree crickets pulses on. They are slender little creatures, a very pale, almost immaterial, green, but their fragile, transparent, membranous wings, raised higher than those of a long-horned when it plays, make a cry that rises up like peepers in the spring. This is the famous "temperature cricket" whose song speeds up or slows down in response to heat or cold. According to the field manuals, you can divide the number of notes per minute by four and then add forty, which will give you the approximate temperature in degrees Fahrenheit.

So this great scraping and fiddling perpetuates a dance. The   9
first frost will end the lives of most of these musicians. August's high sounding means a coming end, but all of its connections and associations join in sending on the year. This is what the month means, as well as the hum of tourists driving down the Cape and back again. Listen to the chosen string.

There is a miraculous sensitivity in the cricket that slows   10
down when the temperature begins to cool at night, or even when a cloud passes over the sun by day. The male calls to attract the female, though it is apparently not known whether her arrival may not be the result of happenstance. His playing is as much a part of general expression as individual intention or reaction. In any case the eggs are laid, which will stay dormant throughout the winter, to hatch in the spring. The organic cycle continues, making an announcement, sending up a music whose players are so attuned to light and dark, sunlit or clouded skies, warm air or cold, day or night, that their existence depends upon the slightest change.

Vocabulary

shred (1), plainsong (1), pulsing (1), rasps (2), ratchets (2), resinous (2), disassociate (2), reminiscent (2), shrill (2), luminous (2), taut (3), chute (3), erratic (3), contrapuntal (4), swoops (4), whorls (4), execution (4), consonance (5), ovipositor (6), membranous (8)

Questions

1. What did Hay find when he concentrated on one bush?
2. What happens to the cricket when the temperature cools?
3. What is the effect of the two questions in paragraph 1?
4. Why does he compare the sounds to telegraph wires or the rippling folds of a taut chute?
5. What words are derived from music? Explain the special effect of at least one of them.
6. What is the thesis?
7. Which words might be described as "onomatopoeic," chosen to imitate the sound they describe? Explain.
8. Which paragraph seems to be the most vivid? Why?
9. What is the purpose of paragraph 5? What does it contribute to the essay?
10. What is the purpose of paragraph 9?
11. Try to rewrite one of the paragraphs in your own style. Did you lose any effects?

Suggestions for Writing

1. Try this kind of essay yourself. Go outside during a particular time of day or night and carefully record all the sounds that you hear. Write an essay in which you attempt, like Hay, to bring these sounds to life. Vivid, onomatopoeic vocabulary words and comparisons that will help the reader actually hear the sound will strengthen your essay. It is not necessary to choose a set of country sounds, nor is it necessary to be pleased with what you hear. (In a well-known Middle English poem, "The Blacksmiths," the poet complains about his neighbors who keep him awake all night, "Swarte, smekyd smethes, smateryd wyth smoke, / Dryve me to deth wyth den of here dyntes," that is, "Black, smoky smiths, smattered with smoke / Drive me to death with the din of their strokes.")

2. You may also limit your "sound" essay to what you hear inside your house, your dormitory, or the library during a certain hour. Make the physical setting clear and then help the reader to hear the sounds around you. What is your attitude toward them?

III · Variations

Only connect the prose and the passion and both will be exalted. . . . E. M. Forster

As in Parts I and II, the basic pattern is still the foundation beneath these essays, but here the writers "break away" by varying the approach. It is not always necessary, for example, to state a thesis at the end of the introduction, especially if the title of the essay or the entire thrust of the argument makes the main point obvious. Stated or not, however, the thesis should never be in doubt.

Occasionally, too, the writer may wish to interrupt the step-by-step flow of the paragraphs for digression, background information, suggestion of possible meanings, dialogue, transition, etc. At best, such interruptions allow for more complex development of the essay by making the pattern a more accurate reflection of the writer's thought. At worst, they allow for a pointless trip down the byways, leaving the reader wandering in the wood of error, permanently off the main trail. An interruption is literally a "breaking in" (suggesting that there is something to break into), not a coverup for mental drift. The purpose of your "break" should be clear to the reader and the path *back* to the main trail should be clearly marked. Transitions are important.

And, to return to the variations, a writer may occasionally combine the introduction with the first topic or round off the essay in the last paragraph of discussion. Because the reader usually needs and appreciates the orientation of a complete opening and the sense of completeness provided by a separate conclusion, such "absorption" is not usually advisable. But if the subject allows, as in some of the following models, it is preferable to the tedium of spelling out what does not even need saying.

ELIN SCHOEN

Remembrances of People Past

Elin Schoen is a freelance writer and author of Tales of
an All-Night Town *(1979), a factual study of the death of
a town deputy in a shootout. In this piece she discusses
the memories of people recalled by reading names in an
address book and by seeing objects associated with them.
Notice that her introduction also begins discussion of her
first example, thus combining the two purposes, and notice
also that she attempts to interpret these reactions within
the body of the essay, not only at the end.*

J. Cunningham is a tapestry. J. (his first name eludes me) 1
heads the C's in my 1971 address book which turned up recently as I was rattling through the cartons in my closet. For
some reason, J. does not appear in my present address book or,
for that matter, in any of the revised editions since 1971. But
he has never disappeared from my living rooms—and there
have been many of them. The tapestry he gave me, right off the
back of his 15th-century Italian chair, has presided over all my
fireplaces, embodying J. and those long afternoons talking of
things rococo and provincial in his cavernous Seattle store-
house of antiques.

We all have our archival idiosyncracies, our ways of filing 2
friendships. Some people stuff business cards in drawers. Some
people save matchbooks in which they have jotted names and
numbers. I collect miniature address books—my life in zip
codes. Moving right along in the 1971 volume, the little leath-
erette chronicle of people who passed through my personal
cosmos during the college, Kibbutz Lahav, Greece, London,
Monterey and Seattle years, I found Nina. We were so close

that I didn't record her last name. Now I can't recall it. Somehow, after Monterey, Nina became a chili recipe—with no return address. And Anna Hostettler, my favorite college roommate, is now a blue glazed mug, a treasure from her Swiss childhood which went on to hold, at various times, my paper clips, pens and pencils, coffee and several collections of *crayons pour les yeux.*

That I have never dropped this mug, that it has outlived   3
an entire set of Baccarat crystal and countless other valued, but less emotionally charged, vessels is no miracle. A good friend is hard to lose. My paranoia protects the mug and its promise that someday Anna, last heard from in the winter of '75, having assumed a married name and a Massachusetts postmark, will resurface—again.

It is paranoia, too, that explains all those cartons in my   4
closet, boxes of letters (if I keep them long enough, goes the subconscious rap, the senders will become as clear as their signatures); photos of people I can't quite place, but can't throw away, either (I am as devout as a Moslem in connecting the image to its subject); the address books that contain the clues I'll start with should I ever find the time to track down J. Cunningham, Nina and Anna, as well as friends of later vintage, some as recent as today's address book, whose names with the prefix "Call" appear on each succeeding list of "Things to Do" that never get done.

It is hard enough, in the continuing drama of real life, what   5
with remembering to replenish the toilet-paper supply and calculating the Russians' next move, to find time for friends who live upstairs, let alone the ones in abeyance. And then I keep making new friends. They will send me greetings for at least two Christmases in a row. Their greetings will vanish into the cartons in my closet. They will vanish from my immediate thoughts. From time to time, I will excavate their greetings. My life will pass before me like "The March of Time," complete with the apocalyptic sound track. Overcome with remorse, I will vow to drop a line to one and all.

Generally, I get as far as one. This month, it was Edoardo.   6
Edoardo is an olive green, bat-sleeved sweater and about 95 postcards emblazoned with *ricordi di Roma.* Late one night, with tears in my eyes, knocking back the Valpolicella, I scrib-

bled to Edoardo the heartfelt wish that he and the rest of the gang in Rome lived down the block from me. I would have gone on to say the same to the rest of the population of my past, but I absolutely had to take my herring-bone skirt to the tailor and see my shrink (we're working right now on my feelings of rootlessness).

Somehow, though, I managed to call Frances. Frances, 7 during her periodic disappearances from my here-and-now, is a mauve-swirled Nekker vase. Over the phone, we experienced the special thrill that comes only when two friends discover that absence has not dimmed the intensity of their connection. Frances and I have experienced that thrill often. She wanted to take me to lunch to celebrate my birthday and the fact that one of us had finally called the other. At lunch, it was revealed that during the two years since we last got together, Frances has thought of me often. In fact, I occupy an important place in her kitchen. I am a pottery jar labeled "Vibes."

We are all more immortal than we think. 8

Vocabulary

tapestry (1), eludes (1), rococo (1), archival (2), idiosyncracies (2), paranoia (3), abeyance (5), excavate (5), apocalyptic (5), remorse (5), emblazoned (6)

Questions

1. How is this essay organized?
2. For what purpose is this essay written?
3. What is the effect of the opening sentence: "J. Cunningham is a tapestry"?
4. To what does Schoen attribute her saving cartons full of memorabilia?
5. Which objects are associated with specific people?
5. How is she remembered by one of her friends?
7. What is the tone?
8. Write a separate introduction for the essay. Which way do you prefer it?
9. How does the conclusion relate to the body of the essay and to the introduction?

10. Why does she say, "but I absolutely had to take my herring-bone skirt to the tailor . . . and see my shrink (we're working right now on my feelings of rootlessness)"?
11. Does this essay seem sincere?

Suggestions for Writing

1. No doubt your life too is filled with objects that recall specific people and events. Write an essay on three or four of these, discussing the object itself and the person associated with it. Why do you think you save these things?
2. About friendship, Samuel Johnson says, "To let friendship die away by negligence and silence, is certainly not wise. It is voluntarily to throw away one of the greatest comforts of this weary pilgrimage." Discuss.
3. Write an essay on some of the reasons, in addition to negligence and silence, that friendships die away. What does it take to keep friendships alive?
4. Do you agree that "we are all more immortal than we think"?

CHARLES DOSS

A Long Road Ago

Charles Doss, born in Cleaton, Kentucky in 1936, served eight years in the army. He and his Filipino wife have raised five children, four of whom are in college. Now he is a prison writer, sentenced to life for murder; from 1974 to 1977, he was on death row in Arizona State Prison. He devotes his time to writing essays and poems, published in a variety of magazines and newspapers, and some of which have been collected in a book, I Shall Mingle (1979). Here he recalls a journey he took frequently as a child. Notice the variety of methods for developing his paragraphs.

My boyhood was highlighted by an epic adventure that re- 1
occurred once in every two months. This was when Dad and
Mom loaded everything in the car, including me and Pat, our
Boston bull terrier, and set out from Indiana for the distant
country of Kentucky. That's where my folks had roots, and at
least six times a year they were drawn by the old sod just as
surely as moths are drawn to flame.

As we pulled away from home, I settled down in the back 2
seat of the '49 Windsor Chrysler. I was armed with comic books
(Bugs Bunny, Superman, Plastic Man, Captain Midnight and
yes, I should have saved them), potato chips and candy bars.
As the car eased up Fourth Street Hill, which later became
Highway 41 through some sort of miracle, my nose was pressed
against the left window and Pat's against the right. All through
the journey we respected each other's territory except for the
times she snoozed with her head in my lap.

Suddenly the buildings fell away. The Chrysler's fluid drive 3

From *The Christian Science Monitor,* January 29, 1980. Copyright ©
1980 by Charles Doss.

effectuated a smooth change. Gears meshed, the journey was happening. As we crawled over the green countryside, gradually escaping the pull and the rank sweetness of the Wabash, I liked to imagine that I was an intrepid explorer in quest of new lands. I was Balboa or Cortés or DeSoto,[1] looking for oceans or gold or new empires!

But first, of course, we had to get Romney and Crawfords- 4 ville out of the way. Then the journey really began. Suddenly Fincastle fanned out on either side of our ship. To the prosaic eye it was just a little cluster of gas stations and clapboard shacks, but my heart pounded as we sailed through. I knew what it was, if all the rest of the world were ignorant. *It was the point of no return!* Fincastle would yield to Greencastle, and after that: Gosport, Bloomfield, Loogootee (pronounced GOA-Tee) and all those dim lands in the southern latitudes, where probably we would be set on by brigands. Who could guess what we might run up against in Schnellville, if by some chance we made it that far? Shudderingly I drew Pat close, and swore to protect her as she licked my nose.

When fantasies of swashbuckling began to pall, I watched 5 little rain drops that spattered the windshield. They were fat, and exploded with dear little plops. I liked to put out my hand and feel the burgeoning moisture. By the time we reached Spencer (where the weather was warm; I fancied they were prey to tropical storms down there) I was reduced to counting the oncoming cars and being a sportscaster. "It's a '47 Studebaker, folks! Look at that nose, it's really a Studee. That makes the score Chevy 17, Ford 12, Packard 2, Hudson 1, pickup trucks 12, clunkers 8, Dodge 3, Studebaker 1. This game is not over by any means! Ford will never give up!" However, Chevy always won, and I generally gave it up long before we got to Rockport near the Kentucky border.

The Burma-Shave signs were always fun. These were little 6 quips printed on four signs that appeared perhaps a mile apart, whose purpose was to persuade male motorists they ought to be clean shaven. SHE WISHED TO BE HELD/SHE GAVE A

---

[1] Balboa (1475–1517), discoverer of the Pacific Ocean; Cortes (1485–1547), Spanish conqueror of Mexico; DeSoto (1500?–1542), Spanish explorer in America.

WHISTLE/BUT SHE WAS REPELLED/BY HIS AWFUL BRISTLE and then, another mile down the road, the triumphant last sign: BURMA SHAVE! I thought this was great poetry.

And more than Burma Shave signs I remember the people 7 whose images were projected through the windows. These were Indiana folk who flourished in 1948. They were among the first people that I ever observed systematically, though with a boy's eye, and I shall retain their aura for the rest of my life.

There were the farmers. Middle aged men with bib overalls 8 and blue shirts, who stood in their fields and wiped away sweat with the backs of their hands. The corn was tall and straight and waving in the stiff breeze. But the farmers, who were apt to be short and bent, did not bend. Their feet were planted in the ground, and I in my passing ship felt strength exude from their pores along with sweat. Once a farmer waved at me as I was whisked along on Highway 41. I waved back eagerly, and kept him in my field of vision till we rounded the curve. Then for some reason that I didn't know I pretended that part of me stayed with him on the land, and that part of him came with me in the purring Chrysler.

And there were women. They exist this moment just as I 9 first perceived them during these Marco Polo days.[2] Indiana Woman, as I saw her all those decades ago, was brave, implacable, not to be withstood. She was attached to the land as surely as were the gigantic stalks of corn.

Children teemed. In the little towns they rode on Schwinn 10 bicycles, in the fields boys went barefoot or shod in sturdy clodhoppers. I saw a girl my age in Jasper who was wearing a blue frock. Her light brown hair sort of rippled in the warm breeze, and I had no way of understanding that I would pay her the compliment of remembering, all these years afterward, that she was beautiful. There were boys who were digging a well with their father on a tiny farm near Huntingburg. One sat astride a massive plough horse and threw a desultory salute when I waved frantically.

And suddenly the sun was declining to my right. We shot 11 through Rockport and darted across the flatlands toward the

---

[2] Marco Polo (1254?–1324?): Venetian traveler and adventurer.

Ohio River, and Kentucky. There was the country where I was born, and how it tugged at my spirit. Western Kentucky! All these long years afterward, when I have seen so very much of the world, I can't think of that patch of country, with its strip mines and piney woods and steep hills, without a deep stirring that is surely of the soul.

If I close my eyes, it comes to me the way it was at the end 12
of a Marco Polo day. Red clay that stretches from Owensboro to the banks of the Green River. . . . the headlamps of my father's powerful ship burning brightly as we crept cautiously along the narrow snake of a state highway . . . hills and woods, a stream, a few little shacks and sheds known as Punkin Center. At the end of my journey I was utterly untired.

We drew up at Aunt Kate and Uncle Ebb's house, just over 13
the wooden bridge. Hot biscuits and fried chicken waited for us, and fried potatoes and gravy and fried apple pies. Pat leaped and bounded and raced down a ravine. My folks were tired, but happy smiles lit their faces as they felt the caress of the country that spawned them.

In a few moments I was racing down the holler, looking for 14
Dan Jones and Norman Logsden. I wonder where they are today.

Vocabulary

reoccurred (1), effectuated (3), intrepid (3), prosaic (4), brigands (4), burgeoning (5), quips (6), aura (7), exude (8), implacable (9), desultory (10)

Questions

1. Is the thesis implied or stated? How does it vary from the basic pattern?
2. Why does Doss refer so often to specific names of places?
3. What is his attitude toward this journey? How do you know?
4. Why does he refer to Marco Polo in the essay?
5. Why does he refer to his father's "powerful ship" in paragraph 12?
6. What do the allusions to the explorers contribute to the essay?
7. Is this essay sentimental?

Suggestions for Writing

1. Write an essay in which you trace your progress down a well-known route, whether in a car or on foot, either in the past or in the present. Do not simply list the things that catch your eye, but select them for a specific impression and develop paragraphs based on them.

2. In an essay called "Dissolution in Haymarket," J. B. Priestley happily describes his favorite London street, Haymarket, but then realizes how much it has changed over the years: "Everything was changed. The whole cheerful pageant of the street immediately crumbled and collapsed, with all its wavering pattern of light and shade, its heartening sights and sounds, its warm humanity, its suggestion of permanence, and I was left shivering in the middle of a tragedy." Have you experienced changes either in a street or a neighborhood about which you have strong feelings as Priestley does about Haymarket? If so, discuss the changes that are most vivid to you.

NANCY BUBEL

How to Make a Terrarium

Nancy Bubel, a regular contributor to Country Journal *magazine, specializes in the growing and care of plants. She is the author of two books,* Vegetables Money Can't Buy *(1977) and* The Seed Starter's Handbook *(1977), plus two more in collaboration with her husband, Mike,* Working Wood *(1977) and* Root Cellaring *(1977). The Bubels raise most of their own food on their farm in Pennsylvania. Here she discusses how to grow and care for plants in a terrarium. The thesis is strongly implied in the title but never actually stated in the body. Notice the order in which the instructions are given and the use of details that help to clarify them.*

If you need an excuse for a walk in the woods, make a ter- 1
rarium. Gathering terrarium ingredients sharpens one's appreciation of the rich variety of life at boot level. Terrarium
makers see the world in fine. No detail escapes their attention.
A confirmed devotee could probably wander in a redwood
grove with gaze fixed on the ground—looking for moss of just
the right texture, tiny seedling trees, interesting bark chips.
After I made my first terrarium, I found myself gathering tiny
plants, lichens, and pebbles on every walk—and mentally col-
lecting when I was not walking our own land.

Woodland plants are perfect for the terrarium. Most things 2
that grow on the forest floor thrive in cool, moist, partly shady
situations, which are easy to provide under glass. Many house
plants adapt equally well to life in a terrarium. You can even
grow exotics like the Venus flytrap, which requires warmth and

moisture and gets along on soil nutrients when no flies happen by.

Whether you gather the makings of your miniature land- 3
scape on the trail, in a greenhouse, or from among your houseplants, the procedure for assembling the terrarium is the same.
First, you need a container. Any kind of transparent, water-
proof, easily covered container may be used to house a terrarium. Some of the more popular enclosures for these self-contained gardens include brandy snifters, apothecary jars, fish
bowls, rectangular aquarium cases, and large glass carboys.
Wine jugs, large test tubes, butter jars, mason jars, gallon
mayonnaise jars (from restaurants), and even baby-food jars
may also be used. Jean Hersey, the authority on wildflowers,
once constructed a terrarium in the globe of a 150-watt light
bulb with the threaded end broken off.

Wide-mouthed containers are easiest to plant by hand; those 4
with narrow necks are tricky but by no means impossible. You
need a few tools—a planter made of a length of wire coat
hanger straightened out, with a loop on one end to hold the
plant; a tamper, which could be a dowel stuck into a cork, or
whatever you can improvise from materials at hand; a digger,
a long-handled spoon, or any kind of long, thin poker capable
of making a hole in loose soil. A long-handled tweezers is also
useful. Use a rolled-up newspaper as a funnel to direct the
soil to the bottom of the jug.

Begin by putting down a base composed of several layers, as 5
follows, remembering that each layer serves a purpose. First,
put down a mat of moss to absorb moisture and form an attractive lining. Then pour a layer of sand or fine gravel over the
moss to promote drainage and prevent waterlogging. Next
scatter a handful of charcoal pieces over the gravel to prevent
souring of the soil.

Now add the final layer—soil. Bagged sterilized soil is fine, 6
but if you want to mix your own, aim for the following propor-
tions:

2 parts topsoil
1 part sand
1 part leafmold or compost.

Put in a thin layer, just covering the charcoal. Then set the 7 plants in place and firm the remainder of the soil around their roots. Much of this soil will later settle lower around the roots.

Arranging the topography of the terrarium is a matter of taste. You might keep in mind that a variety of leaf textures is usually pleasing, and that plants of different heights and shapes —pyramidal, tall and spiky, short and shrubby, trailing—make the scenery interesting. If your container is large enough you can even make a small hill or a path within its bounded wildness. Color may be provided by including partridge berries, mushrooms, lichens, and stones. No well-made terrarium needs a plastic deer or a china bird, but the woods are full of props that can add local color to your small scene: mossy twigs, weathered pieces of wood, scraps of textured bark, squirrel-gnawed nutshells. A weird craggy stone may be just the boulder you need for a classic gothic scene—a *romantische Landschaft* [1] in miniature.

The pleasure of terrarium building, though, has more to do with the freedom to improvise, collect, seed, play with your materials, arrange a world as *you* would have it, than with conformity to a form. Do with it what you wish. Arrange and rearrange the plants until you are happy with the way they look.

When all the plants are in place, water the soil lightly, using less water than you think you'll need. You can always add more but you can't remove it. Overwatering encourages rot, mold, and fungus.

Covering the terrarium makes it a self-contained system, with its own weather: water vapor condenses on the walls and returns to the soil. Use the cover provided with the vessel or simply place a circle of glass over the top. (Plastic wrap is a more temporary but nonetheless practical cover.) Since each terrarium is a different ecosystem with its own water balance, it is impossible to formulate definite schedules for watering. Observation is the key. If the glass is misty, or if you notice mold anywhere within it, or water pooling on the bottom, the terrarium needs to be ventilated. Uncover it for about a day. Some people ventilate their terrariums routinely once a week.

When should you add water? Seldom, if at all. If the terrarium is too dry, the soil will be lighter in color and the whole

[1] Romantic landscape.

thing will feel lighter than normal when you pick it up. Use an eye dropper to add water—you'll be less likely to overwater.

Terrarium plants need some light, but direct sun will cook 13 them. Indirect light on a table or light from a north window should suit most plant populations. If leaves turn brown, the terrarium is probably too hot. Try putting it in a cooler place.

Those of us accustomed to fertilizing houseplants may tend 14 to include the terrarium in that routine, but it is best to keep terrarium soil on the lean side, lest the plants outgrow the container. Choice of plants influences the length of their stay too, of course. Our first house—a mid-nineteenth-century Philadelphia weaver's cottage—is now guarded by a pine that spent its first two years in a terrarium. When its top hit the cover we planted it in front of the loom shed. Now, twenty years later, it towers over the house. The loom shed is gone, but pine needles fall around its foundation. Everything lasts, we think as we drive by—just in a different form, sometimes.

Vocabulary

devotee (1), carboy (3), improvise (9), ecosystem (11)

Questions

1. Why does Bubel use the second person (you) form of address?
2. Why does she mention the redwood grove in paragraph 1?
3. Which details are valuable for helping the reader to visualize the process of making a terrarium?
4. For what readers is the essay written?
5. How does she develop her paragraphs? Look particularly at paragraphs 3 and 8.
6. What does she include in the essay to keep it from being simply a recipe for building a terrarium? What does she feel about the subject?
7. Evaluate the conclusion.
8. Did Bubel interest you in making a terrarium?
9. Rewrite this essay, removing all but the essential directions. What happens to the essay?

Suggestions for Writing

1. Select a process with which you are very familiar — repairing a muffler, getting a date, making a skirt, studying for an examination—and explain the steps in detail to the reader. Keep in mind that the reader should be able to imitate your actions after finishing your essay, and try to put some feeling into your lesson.
2. Why do people bring pieces of the outdoors into their houses? Why would anyone want to create a "romantische Landschaft" for a coffee table?
3. Write an essay on how to write an essay.

E. V. LUCAS

The Town Week

E. V. Lucas (1868–1938), an English publisher, essayist, and travel writer was on the staff of Punch *and served as chairman of Methuen and Company. He wrote* The Life of Charles Lamb *(1905) and many other books, and edited* The Letters of Charles and Mary Lamb *(1935). For quick reference, he used to travel with a complete* Dictionary of National Biography *at his side; he even had a special case constructed for easy transport. "The Town Week," typical of the selection of subjects which Lucas finds interesting, traces the days of the week from Monday back to Monday and attempts to describe the special character of each day. Notice how Lucas varies the approach in each paragraph in order to keep from simply listing days and traits and notice the use of comparison.*

It is odd that "Mondayish" is the only word which the days 1 of the week have given us; since Monday is not alone in possessing a positive and peculiar character. Why not "Tuesdayish" or "Wednesdayish"? Each word would convey as much meaning to me, "Tuesdayish" in particular, for Monday's cardinal and reprehensible error of beginning the business week seems to me almost a virtue compared with Tuesday's utter flatness. To begin a new week is no fault at all, though tradition has branded it as one. To begin is a noble accomplishment; but to continue dully, to be the tame follower of a courageous beginner, to be the second day in a week of action, as in Tuesday's case—that is deplorable, if you like.

Monday can be flat enough, but in a different way from 2 Tuesday. Monday is flat because one has been idling, perhaps unconsciously absorbing notions of living like the lilies; be-

Reprinted by Books for Libraries Press. Distributed by Arno Press Inc.

cause so many days must pass before the week ends; because yesterday is no more. But Tuesday has the sheer essential flatness of nonentity; Tuesday is nothing. If you would know how absolutely nothing it is, go to a week-end hotel at, say Brighton,[1] and stay on after the Saturday-to-Monday population has flitted. On Tuesday you touch the depths. So does the menu— no *chef* ever exerted himself for a Tuesday guest. Tuesday is also very difficult to spell, many otherwise cultured ladies putting the *e* before the *u:* and why not? What right has Tuesday to any preference?

With all its faults, Monday has a positive character. Monday 3 brings a feeling of revolt; Tuesday, the base craven, reconciles us to the machine. I am not surprised that the recent American revivalists held no meetings on Mondays. It was a mark of their astuteness; they knew that the wear and tear of overcoming the Monday feeling of the greater part of their audience would exhaust them before their magnetism began to have play; while a similarly stubborn difficulty would confront them in the remaining portion sunk in apathy by the thought that to-morrow would be Tuesday. It is this presage of certain tedium which has robbed Monday evening of its "glittering star." Yet since nothing so becomes a flat day as the death of it, Tuesday evening's glittering star (it is Wordsworth's phrase) is of the brightest—for is not the dreary day nearly done, and is not to-morrow Wednesday the bland?

With Wednesday, the week stirs itself, turns over, begins to 4 wake. There are matinées on Wednesday; on Wednesdays some of the more genial weekly papers come out. The very word has a good honest round air—Wednesday. Things, adventures, might happen very naturally on Wednesday; but that nothing ever happened on a Tuesday I am convinced. In summer Wednesday has often close finishes at Lord's, [2] and it is a day on which one's friends are pretty sure to be accessible. On Monday they may not have returned from the country; on Friday they have begun to go out of town again; but on Wednesday they are here, at home—are solid. I am sure it is my favorite day.

---

[1] The most famous seaside resort in England.
[2] Lord's cricket ground in London.

(Even politicians, so slow as a rule to recognize the kindlier, 5
more generous, side of life, realized for many years that Wednesday was a day on which they had no right to conduct their
acrimonious business for more than an hour or so. Much of the
failure of the last Government may be traced to their atheistical
decision no longer to remember Wednesday to keep it holy.)

On Thursday the week falls back a little; the stirring of 6
Wednesday is forgotten; there is a return to the folding of the
hands. I am not sure that Thursday has not become the real
day of rest. That it is a good honest day is the most that can be
said for it. It is certainly not Thor's day any longer—if my reading of the character of the blacksmith-god is true. There is
nothing strong and downright and fine about it. Compared
with Tuesday's small beer, Thursday is almost champagne; but
none the less they are related. One can group them together. If
I were a business man, I should, I am certain, sell my shares at
a loss on Monday and at a profit on Wednesday and Friday, but
on Tuesday and Thursday I should get for them exactly what I
gave.

I group Friday with Wednesday as a day that can be friendly 7
to me, but it has not Wednesday's quality. Wednesday is calm,
assured, urbane; Friday allows itself to be a little flurried and
excited. Wednesday stands alone; Friday to some extent throws
in its lot with Saturday. Friday is too busy. Too many papers
come out, too many bags are packed, on Friday. But herein, of
course, is some of its virtue; it is the beginning of the end, the
forerunner of Saturday and Sunday. If anticipation, as the
moralists say, is better than the realization, Friday is perhaps
the best day of the week, for one spends much of it in thinking
of the morrow and what of good it should bring forth. Friday's
greatest merit is perhaps that it paves the way to Saturday and
the cessation of work. That it ever was really unlucky I greatly
doubt.

And so we come to Saturday and Sunday. But here the ana- 8
lyst falters, for Saturday and Sunday pass from the region of
definable days. Monday and Tuesday, Wednesday and Thursday and Friday, these are days with a character fixed more or
less for all. But Saturday and Sunday are what we individually
make of them. In one family they are friends, associates; in an-

other as ill-assorted as Socrates and Xantippe.[3] For most of us Saturday is not exactly a day at all, it is a collection of hours, part work, part pleasure, and all restlessness. It is a day that we plan for, and therefore it is often a failure. I have no distinct and unvarying impression of Saturday, except that trains are full and late and shops shut too early.

Sunday even more than Saturday is different as people are 9 different. To the godly it is a day of low tones, its minutes go by muffled; to the children of the godly it is eternity. To the ungodly it is a day jeopardized by an interest in barometers that is almost too poignant. To one man it is an interruption of the week; to another it is the week itself, and all the rest of the days are but preparations for it. One cannot analyze Saturday and Sunday.

But Monday? There we are on solid ground again. Monday 10 —but I have discussed Monday already: that is one of its principal characteristics, that it is always coming round again, pretending to be new. It is always the same in reality.

Vocabulary

cardinal (1), reprehensible (1), deplorable (1), notions (2), nonentity (2), craven (3), reconciles (3), revivalists (3), astuteness (3), magnetism (3), presage (3), tedium (3), bland (3), genial (4), accessible (4), acrimonious (5), atheistical (5), urbane (7), flurried (7), anticipation (7), realization (7), morrow (7), cessation (7), analyst (8), definable (8), muffled (9), jeopardized (9), barometers (9), poignant (9)

Questions

1. Discuss the introduction. What purposes does it serve?
2. What is the topic of paragraph 2? How is the idea developed?
3. What is the topic of paragraph 3? How is it developed?
4. What kind of personality emerges from Lucas' discussion? Can we get a sense of his way of life?

---

[3] Socrates (469–399 B.C.), the Greek philosopher; Xantippe, his wife, said to be a bad-tempered nag.

5. What is the purpose of paragraph 5?
6. Why was the essay written?
7. Notice Lucas' extensive use of parallel construction, by which equal elements are given equal importance in the sentences (in the last sentence of paragraph 1, see "To begin . . . to continue . . . to be . . . to be. . . ."). Why does he use this construction so often?
8. Why are there so many "buts" in Lucas' essay?
9. Why does he use so many descriptive adjectives and why so many in lists?
10. Lucas' words are carefully chosen. Select two that seem particularly effective and tell why.
11. What techniques does Lucas use to give each day its character?

Suggestions for Writing

1. Write your own characterization of the days of the week. Remember to give some specific reasons why you see a certain day in a certain way and try to make the judgments more subtle by comparing when it seems valuable. Consider which is the best day, the worst day, the day "in-between," etc. It is not necessary to begin with Monday, of course; the only requirement is that you cover all of them.
2. You might also use the same model for a discussion of the months (or selected months), or for a discussion of the seasons. You might try to write an extended characterization of a single month, explaining why you react to it the way you do.
3. About Lucas, H. N. Wethered explains, "E. V. insisted that in every sentence there is a preordained place for each word; in every sentence there is a place preordained for that part of the sentence which is of the most significance." Do you see any evidence for this attention to placement in "The Town Week"? Limit your discussion to a few sentences and discuss the effect and appropriateness of word order.
4. Write an essay on the day of the week you like most or least. Why do you like or dislike it so much? (Look at Lucas' techniques for giving character to a day.) You might also write a comparison of the best and worst days.

RUSSELL BAKER

No More Orange Motorcycles

Russell Baker, born in 1925 in Virginia, received his B.A. from Johns Hopkins, worked for several years as London Bureau Chief for the Baltimore Sun *and later served on the Washington Bureau of* The New York Times. *His column for the* Times, *the "Observer," is widely syndicated, and articles are published in such magazines as* The Saturday Evening Post, The New York Times Magazine, *and* Sports Illustrated. *In 1972 he published* Poor Russell's Almanac, *and in 1977* The Upside Down Man, *and most recently,* So This Is Depravity, *(1980). He received the Pulitzer Prize for commentary in 1979. In a recent* Esquire *interview he said, "I've had an unhappy life, thank God." "No More Orange Motorcycles" is a typical "Sunday Observer" column. Here he traces the progression of the Christmas gifts he has received from a toy orange motorcycle to a more recent "gift crate of vitamin pills." Notice the tone, a balance of the humorous with the painfully sad.*

One of the first things I ever got for Christmas was an iron 1
motorcycle with a sidecar and an iron policeman mounted on the saddle. Motorcycle, sidecar and policeman were all orange. The policeman could be removed from the motorcycle seat, but he was frozen perpetually in the seated position—arms spread to grasp the handlebars—and looked silly almost everyplace else except on the edge of a pie pan.

Next, I got an ocean liner which looked more or less like 2
the Titanic and sank just as inexorably on every voyage across the bathtub.[1] Time passed, and I got Big Little Books and Oz

---

[1] Titanic: ocean liner sunk April 15, 1912 on its maiden voyage after collision with an iceberg.

books, which I enjoyed because teachers said they would rot my mind.

One year, I discovered the pleasure of standing on Wisen- 3 goff's grocery-store corner and watching girls go by without letting them notice I was watching. For Christmas that year, I got a used bicycle with balloon tires.

Time kept passing, and I got a board game called "Bulls and 4 Bears." You sold short, cornered vanadium and made a killing in utilities. At that time, I still got English walnuts and tangerines for Christmas, too, so that year wasn't a total loss. Still, you could tell something vital was running out.

Christmas marched on. I got two neckties, an Arrow shirt, a 5 large bottle of Vaseline hair tonic and a recording of Ravel's "Boléro," [2] conducted by Andre Kostelanetz.[3]

I became sour and disagreeable as Christmases persisted in 6 recurring every 365 days—except in leap years, when they arrived a day later. This did not stop the getting. I got socks, I got subscriptions to the National Geographic, Collier's and The New Republic, and I got gloves.

Then I got after-shave lotion and a shoeshine kit. 7

One Christmas, I got a scarf, six undershirts, a styptic pencil 8 and a leather-bound book for recording telephone numbers and addresses.

The country began to boom and so did Christmas. In a 9 quick flurry of Christmases, I got a radio, a hi-fi set, the nine symphonies of Beethoven conducted by Leonard Bernstein,[4] a case of beer and a compass to attach to the car's windshield so I could tell what direction I was driving.

The direction was always the same: directly toward another 10 Christmas.

I got a dispatch case, an unabridged dictionary, a camel's 11 hair coat, a Swiss watch, English shoes, an assortment of German sausages, an Italian cookbook and a Japanese cassette player and recorder.

The following Christmas, there was an odd pause. You could 12

---

[2] Boléro: an orchestral work by French composer Ravel (1875–1937).

[3] Andre Kostelanetz (1901–1980): conductor, New York Philharmonic (1952–79).

[4] Leonard Bernstein (b. 1918): American conductor and composer.

sense people thinking, could feel imaginations failing. I got a deerstalker cap.

The next Christmas was even less memorable. I got an assort- 13 ment of Swiss cheeses, gift wrapped.

Several Christmases passed before I noticed that something 14 was different. I first remarked this the Christmas I got a rocking chair and a packet of marvelously treated paper for cleaning bifocals.

Next Christmas, I got a large, handsome jar of hair pomade 15 guaranteed to conceal the gray in less than three weeks.

Then I got an electronic gagdet for changing the television 16 station without getting out of the rocking chair, as well as a case of Geritol and a pair of tickets to the taping of "The Lawrence Welk Show."

Christmas after that was puzzling at first. Bounding out of 17 bed to dash downstairs to see what Santa had brought, I was stopped by one of the children—a huge brute with the odor of Christmas Eve's bibulations still clinging to his beard. "You don't have to use the stairs anymore, Dad," he said. "Look what Santa Claus brought you." It was one of those stair-rail elevators where you sit down, push a button and get a free ride.

I sat down and took the ride. Sitting there in slow descent, 18 I was reminded of a Christmas long ago when I got an iron motorcycle with an iron policeman mounted in its saddle. I did not straighten up at ride's end, but preserving my seated posture, I moved toward the Christmas tree for the annual surprises.

The lad seemed troubled by this strange posture. "Gosh, 19 Dad," he said, "we went to a lot of trouble to get you an autographed copy of 'How To Avoid Probate' this Christmas, but it's not too late to find a wheelchair down at the hospital."

"That won't be necessary," I said. "The edge of a pie pan 20 will do just fine." And I took the gift crate of vitamin pills with a smile, because I was remembering about the Titanic.

Vocabulary

inexorable (2), vanadium (4), utilities (4), styptic (8), dispatch case (11), pomade (15), bibulations (17), probate (19)

Questions

1. What is the major variation from the basic pattern?
2. What is the purpose of paragraph 6?
3. What is the purpose of the sentence, "Still, you could tell something vital was running out?"
4. Why is paragraph 10 included?
5. The transitions in this essay are obvious, providing links for the passage from one Christmas to the next. Why does Baker use them so relentlessly? How does he achieve variety?
6. What is implied by the title?
7. The publication date for this essay was on December 23. Does this fact contribute anything to the essay's effect? Is it possible to appreciate it at any other time, or is it just a Christmas piece?
8. Is this essay humorous?
9. In what ways are the details suggestive?
10. Compare this essay with "Remembrances of People Past" by Schoen, 85.

Suggestions for Writing

1. Write an essay in which you trace the progress of your own gifts up to this point. Try to focus on a single holiday, not necessarily Christmas, and see if you can detect any hidden patterns in the selection of certain gifts for you as Baker traces the growing up and aging process in his gifts.
2. Write an essay on the particular significance of one gift.
3. In an article called "Christmas Ghosts," published on the same day as Russell Baker's article, Paul Theroux says, "And because Christmas celebrates birth, we are nagged by its opposite, that things end. . . ." Do you agree? What is the Christmas spirit? Are you "nagged" at Christmas?
4. Describing his own column, Baker said, "This is daily journalism, not literature." Discuss. Do you agree with Baker? What separates the two?

HARRY STEIN

A Day in the Life: Russell Baker

Harry Stein is a contributing editor and columnist for Esquire *and* Panorama *magazines. He was also the co-founder and co-editor of the* Paris Metro, *an English-language magazine published in Paris. His work has also appeared in* Playboy, New York, The New York Times Magazine, *and* TV Guide. *He writes this "Day in the Life" in the first person, basing it on an interview with Russell Baker, author of the preceding essay. Notice the transitions that call attention to the progress of time throughout the day.*

My job is to write three newspaper columns a week. I do 1
one every Thursday, Sunday, and Monday, and each one takes
me four hours. So basically I'm on a twelve-hour week. Still, I
get a little irritated when people raise their eyebrows and say,
"What, you only work twelve hours a week!" because, of course,
when you write you're doing it all the time. Most of my week
I'm trying to take in this junk, this garbage, that we all swim
in, so I'll have something to put out when I do sit down at the
machine.

I'm a late sleeper. I started out working for a morning paper, 2
the Baltimore *Sun,* from 6:00 P.M. until 2:00 A.M., and I find
those hours very congenial. On this job, I usually get up
around 9:00. Then I begin plodding through the trash of civilization. I start with the *Times,* then go through the *Daily News*
and *The Washington Post.* That kills about an hour and a half.

If it's a day I have to do the column, and I'm in New York, 3
and my wife is getting sick of having me around, I head over to
the *Times* around 11:00—by subway. I feel that taking the subway keeps me in touch with humanity, and also inhumanity.

From *Esquire* magazine, January 30, 1970. Reprinted by permission.

Being in touch with inhumanity is an important part of being a New Yorker.

When I arrive at my office, there's the mail. I can always kill 4 a couple of hours doing the mail. I get a lot of nice mail, but I get a lot of lousy mail too. The worst mail I get is from people who submit their manuscripts and want my comments. There's always a batch of that stuff. They think of their writing as humor. There's an astounding number of people in this country who yearn to be humor writers. God knows why. Writing is Siberia enough in terms of money, but humor writing!

Then, too, there are an extraordinary number of people who 5 have missed the point of something I've said, and they write attacking me for it. An extremely large percentage of these kinds of letters, by the way, are from New York.

When I finish the mail, it's usually lunch hour. Now I don't 6 lunch in the New York sense of lunching. That's one of the world's great time killers. Besides, I don't lunch well. I've always been a third-rate luncher: I never get the right table, and the captain never knows me, and as a result, people I invite to lunch are always embarrassed.

So what I do is trot up one floor to the *Times* cafeteria. 7 They have wonderful Jell-O at the *Times* cafeteria. They make it so tough that if it hit the floor, it would bounce. You've got to chew it. I'm very fond of the Jell-O. It reminds me of the Depression.

Afterward, I go back to my office to work on the column. 8 I never write a piece till I'm on deadline, and then I write the way a bricklayer or a carpenter works, on a fixed schedule, conscientiously. I very rarely have an idea of what I'm going to write before I sit down. I try not to. I've always felt that journalism ought to be a little spontaneous, and I want my stuff, which is a very personal kind of journalism, to reflect how I feel at the moment.

That's why there's so frequent a change of voice from day to 9 day. When I started doing this column, it seemed to me that the vice of most columnists is that they get predictable very quickly, and this was my way of trying to keep people reading after they knew everything about me.

That choice has cost me a lot. People who ride in Cadillacs 10 in this country are the ones who create one character and stick to it. If Groucho Marx had sat down on learned panels and pontificated on the future of mankind, it wouldn't have helped his career a bit. Walter Lippmann didn't make jokes about the state of the nation.

No matter what time I start the column, I finish it at 6:00. 11 It's kind of spooky. I've tried starting it at 8:00 in the morning; I finish at 6:00. If I start at 5:00, I'll still finish at 6:00. Oh, every once in a while I'll get one that goes on till 6:30 or 7:00, but this is very rare—and terrifying. Those are the days when I feel that I'm almost at the end of the line, that the world is coming to an end. I go home and drink.

But assuming I do finish at 6:00, I get back on the subway, 12 get out at Bloomingdale's, walk along Fifty-ninth Street checking out the porn houses, and go home.

I've been married for twenty-eight years. Our children are 13 grown, so we have an oversize apartment, and we knock around in it. I'm not social. We don't go out much.

What I do in the evening is go back to the trash again. Like 14 most writers, I don't read much, at least not good stuff. You can either write or you can read. I thumb through journalism, magazines, quickie books. If I'm home in time, I'll watch the news, always on NBC, because I get good reception on Channel 4 without having to pay for cable.

I realize I should watch prime time to keep up with *that* 15 junk, but it comes on when we have dinner, around 8:00 or 9:00. I'll normally get back to TV around 11:00 to catch the local news and then old movies. I watch until about two thirds of the way through a film, when they begin piling on commercials every three minutes. At that point I usually have a temper tantrum, snap it off, stomp downstairs, and make a drink. Then I return to bed.

Vocabulary

congenial (2), spontaneous (8), predictable (8), pontificated (10)

Questions

1. What is the implied thesis?
2. What is the purpose of paragraphs 9 and 10?

3. Notice the transitions. Which ones contribute most to keeping the day moving?
4. What kind of personality do you discover through this day's events? Refer specifically to paragraphs and lines that led you to your opinion.
5. Which paragraph seems to you the most revealing? What does it reveal?
6. Which sentence is the most telling?
7. How does the introduction set up the subject?
8. It is very easy to forget that Harry Stein composed this piece. Why does he place himself so far in the background by writing about Baker as if Baker himself were the author? Do you get any sense of the writer?

Suggestions for Writing

1. Write your own "Day in the Life" for yourself. Choose activities that will help the reader to get a sense of your daily existence, and try to give an impression of personality and attitudes, not just a list.
2. You may also find it interesting to write a "Day in the Life" for someone else (possibly a student in your class, or a relative), basing it on an interview with that person as Stein did with Baker. Prepare questions ahead of time and take careful notes (or use a tape recorder, with permission) and keep in mind that you are after a character study as well as the sequence of the day's events. Ask about feelings and attitudes. You may write it in the first person as Stein did (but be very careful to quote accurately and not to distort the interviewee's responses), or you may present it in the third person.
3. Baker says, "Being in touch with inhumanity is an important part of being a New Yorker." Do you feel that this is an important part of everyone's life, or should we avoid contact with it as much as possible?
4. About humorists, E. B. White says, "Humorists fatten on trouble . . . there is often a rather fine line between laughing and crying. . . . Humor, like poetry . . . plays close to the big hot fire which is truth." Compare Baker to other humorous writers in this collection—Benchley or Thurber, for example—in the light of White's comment.
5. Does this portrait of Baker seem consistent with the writer of "No More Orange Motorcycles"? Explain.

D. H. LAWRENCE

Dull London

D. H. Lawrence (1885–1930), British playwright, novelist, short story writer, travel writer, poet, and essayist, was the son of a coal miner. His works include Sons and Lovers *(1913),* Women in Love *(1921), and* Lady Chatterley's Lover *(1928), the latter two banned because of what was then seen as a too explicit treatment of sex. He believed strongly in the necessity of following instinctual rather than intellectual responses and opposed the sterility of the industrial world, which seemed to be destroying basic human feelings. This essay, "Dull London," appeared first in the* Evening News, *in 1928. In the eighteenth century Samuel Johnson said, "If a man is tired of London, he is tired of life; for there is in London all that life can afford." Apparently, Lawrence would not agree, at least about the London of his own day. There is little doubt about the thesis of this essay. Like the tolling of a bell, the word "dull" rings throughout—from the title to the last sentence. Pay careful attention to Lawrence's use of repetition and his unembarrassed, almost headlong, building up of sentences and paragraphs to make his point.*

It begins the moment you set foot ashore, the moment you 1 step off the boat's gangway. The heart suddenly, yet vaguely, sinks. It is no lurch of fear. Quite the contrary. It is as if the life-urge failed, and the heart dimly sank. You trail past the benevolent policeman and the inoffensive passport officials, through the fussy and somehow foolish customs—we don't *really* think it matters if somebody smuggles in two pairs of

From *Phoenix II,* edited and collected by Warren Roberts and Harry T. Moore. Copyright © 1959, 1963, 1968 by the Estate of Frieda Lawrence Ravagli. Reprinted by permission of Viking Penguin Inc.

false-silk stockings—and we get into the poky but inoffensive train, with poky but utterly inoffensive people, and we have a cup of inoffensive tea from a nice inoffensive boy, and we run through small, poky but nice and inoffensive country, till we are landed in the big but unexciting station of Victoria, when an inoffensive porter puts us into an inoffensive taxi and we are driven through the crowded yet strangely dull streets of London to the cosy yet strangely poky and dull place where we are going to stay. And the first half-hour in London, after some years abroad, is really a plunge of misery. The strange, the grey and uncanny, almost deathly sense of *dulness* is overwhelming. Of course, you get over it after a while, and admit that you exaggerated. You get into the rhythm of London again, and you tell yourself that it is *not* dull. And yet you are haunted, all the time, sleeping or waking, with the uncanny feeling: It is dull! It is all dull! This life here is one vast complex of dulness! I am dull! I am being dulled! My spirit is being dulled! My life is dulling down to London dulness.

This is the nightmare that haunts you the first few weeks 2 of London. No doubt if you stay longer you get over it, and find London as thrilling as Paris or Rome or New York. But the climate is against me. I cannot stay long enough. With pinched and wondering gaze, the morning of departure, I look out of the taxi upon the strange dulness of London's arousing; a sort of death; and hope and life only return when I get my seat in the boat-train, and hear all the Good-byes! Good-bye! Good-bye! Thank God to say Good-bye!

Now to feel like this about one's native land is terrible. I am 3 sure I am exceptional, or at least an exaggerated case. Yet it seems to me most of my fellow-countrymen have the pinched, slightly pathetic look in their faces, the vague, wondering realization: It is dull! It is always essentially dull! My life is dull!

Of course, England is the easiest country in the world, easy, 4 easy and nice. Everybody is nice, and everybody is easy. The English people on the whole are surely the *nicest* people in the world, and everybody makes everything so easy for everybody else, that there is almost nothing to resist at all. But this very easiness and this very niceness become at last a nightmare. It is as if the whole air were impregnated with chloroform or some other pervasive anaesthetic, that makes everything easy

and nice, and takes the edge off everything, whether nice or
nasty. As you inhale the drug of easiness and niceness, your
vitality begins to sink. Perhaps not your physical vitality, but
something else: the vivid flame of your individual life. England
can afford to be so free and individual because no individual
flame of life is sharp and vivid. It is just mildly warm and safe.
You couldn't burn your fingers at it. Nice, safe, easy: the whole
ideal. And yet under all the easiness is a gnawing uneasiness, as
in a drug-taker.

It used not to be so. Twenty years ago London was to me   5
thrilling, thrilling, thrilling, the vast and roaring heart of all
adventure. It was not only the heart of the world, it was the
heart of the world's living adventure. How wonderful the
Strand, the Bank, Charing Cross at night, Hyde Park in the
morning! [1]

True, I am now twenty years older. Yet I have not lost my   6
sense of adventure. But now all the adventure seems to me
crushed out of London. The traffic is too heavy! It used to be
going somewhere, on an adventure. Now it only rolls massively
and overwhelmingly, going nowhere, only dully and enormously *going*. There is no adventure at the end of the buses'
journey. The bus lapses into an inertia of dulness, then dully
starts again. The traffic of London used to roar with the mystery of man's adventure on the seas of life, like a vast sea-shell,
murmuring a thrilling, half-comprehensible story. Now it
booms like monotonous, far-off guns, in a monotony of crushing something, crushing the earth, crushing out life, crushing
everything dead.

And what does one do, in London? I, not having a job to   7
attend to, lounge round and gaze in bleak wonder on the ceaseless dulness. Or I have luncheons and dinners with friends, and
talk. Now my deepest private dread of London is my dread of
this talk. I spend most of my days abroad, saying little, or with
a bit of chatter and a silence again. But in London I feel like a

---

[1] The Strand, one of the busiest streets in London, site of hotels, shops
and theaters; the Bank, area in central London, near the Bank of England;
Charing Cross, an ancient London road junction, originally the site of a
cross erected in 1291 for Queen Eleanor's funeral procession; Hyde Park,
one of many large London parks, often the site of spontaneous public
speeches.

spider whose thread has been caught by somebody, and is being drawn out of him, so he must spin, spin, spin, and all to no purpose. He is not even spinning his own web, for his own reasons.

So it is in London, at luncheon, dinner, or tea. I don't want 8 to talk. I don't mean to talk. Yet the talk is drawn out of me, endlessly. And the others talk, endlessly also. It is ceaseless, it is intoxicating, it is the only real occupation of us who do not jazz. And it is purely futile. It is quite as bad as ever the Russians were: talk for talk's sake, without the very faintest intention of a result in action. Utter inaction and storms of talk. That again is London to me. And the sense of abject futility in it all only deepens the sense of abject dulness, so all there is to do is to go away.

Vocabulary

dull (title), gangway (1), lurch (1), benevolent (1), inoffensive (1), uncanny (1), impregnated (4), chloroform (4), pervasive (4), anaesthetic (4), vitality (4), inertia (6), comprehensible (6), monotonous (6), bleak (7), jazz (8), futile (8), abject (8), futility (8)

Questions

1. Why does Lawrence use so much repetition? Choose a specific example and explain its effect.
2. Why does he begin his essay with a vague "It" rather than with a specific reference to dullness?
3. Why does he include mitigating statements in his essay?
4. What is the purpose of paragraph 4? of paragraph 5?
5. Discuss the two extended and complex comparisons used to characterize London traffic in paragraph 6.
6. What is the climax of the essay? Does it have one?
7. Attempt to rewrite the conclusion, destroying Lawrence's special effects.

Suggestions for Writing

1. Choose a place about which you have a dominant impression (not necessarily an impression of dullness), and write an essay explaining the situations in which this trait manifests itself most

strongly. Try, if you can, to imitate Lawrence's style as well as his structure.

2. Lawrence called himself a "human bomb." Do you see any evidence for this possibilty in his essay?

3. About repetition, the Latin rhetoric *Ad Herennium* translated by Harry Caplan, says, "the frequent recourse to the same word is not dictated by verbal poverty; rather there inheres in the repetition an elegance which the ear can distinguish more easily than words can explain." Discuss in relation to "Dull London."

EDWIN DIAMOND

The Social Set

Edwin Diamond, born in 1925, has been a reporter, a lecturer at MIT, Harvard, and the University of Chicago, and a science writer. His books include The Media and the Cities *(1966) and* Good News, Bad News *(1978), a study of the news media. "The Social Set" too is about media, in this case television. It is argumentative, an attempt to present his point of view on the social value of television. Notice the extended introduction and conclusion.*

I suppose there are still some intellectuals who denounce 1 television as the boob tube or idiot box. Perhaps some blinkered critics still believe in "audience flow theory"—that is, viewers sit video-tranquilized in front of the television, tuned to one channel through the evening.

The intellectuals and critics, of course, are as behind the 2 times as a black-and-white television set with no remote control or videocassette attachment. Television and the television viewer have changed while the theorists weren't looking. We no longer watch television qua television: we now watch specific programs, and for specific purposes. Television has become a lively part of our social transactions, much like the out-of-town visitor whom we invite our friends to meet, or the late-arriving guest who picks up the party just before it sags.

Not all television, obviously, has grown up to be literate and 3 adult; but enough has changed to warrant a systematic look at the social role of television. The contemporary role of television as social instrument recalls the earliest days of the

Reprinted with permission from the February 1979 issue of *American Film* magazine, © 1979, The American Film Institute, J. F. Kennedy Center, Washington, D.C. 20566.

117

medium: When a family on the block was the first to buy a television set, the rest of us flocked over to marvel at the new technological wonder. No matter that the wonder brought Uncle Miltie's old burlesque routines or primitive two-camera coverage of sports;[1] television viewing was a social occasion. Later the superhype that preceded each Super Bowl drummed up more social television gatherings. Though the game seldom lived up to the advance billing, the occasion was pleasant in itself—a friendly afternoon for nursing a few drinks and noshing.

Special programs have also become occasions for more serious social interaction. Black friends of mine made "Roots" into a family matter, setting their children down in front of the set for each episode. Discussions would follow, and teenage children would check out the Alex Haley book from the library. Jews and their Christian friends watched the "Holocaust" series—usually separately—but met to discuss the programs the next day.

As might be expected, television has become a focus of social life for younger men and women, the under-thirty-five year olds who have grown up with the medium. A twenty-seven-year-old friend of mine recently threw a big Saturday night party with plenty of food, wine, and disco music. At 11:30 everyone sat down to watch "Saturday Night Live." The party didn't die; it shifted into a different gear, and the hostess didn't complain.

Some of my older, more sophisticated friends find television much more of a social experience than, say, going to a Broadway play or to the movies. While no talking is allowed in the theater, social television encourages interaction between audience and set, and among the audience. The viewers can guess at the dialogue and plot of dramas, editorialize on the news, predict the Oscar winners, or single out from the semifinalists the next Miss America. It can be much more fun to talk back to the set than to sit silently in a darkened theater (the product on the screen being equal, naturally).

I am not claiming that social television has brought back the wit and brilliance of the salon to American homes. Social television can't replace real conversation or tête-à-têtes or a good book or a blazing fireplace or solitary thought.

---

[1] "Uncle Miltie": Milton Berle (b. 1908), American television entertainer.

Television has proved, on the whole, to be a good guest in 8
the house, especially when it is not invited to perform too
often. Most of our work and much of our play forces us, as individuals, into specialized roles. Even our reading materials
have become like private languages—father is down at the
Wall Street Journal or looking into his *Fortune;* mother can
be found, or may be lost, in *The Women's Room;* the college
kids are like a *Rolling Stone.*

Television can be a national tongue. At its best, television 9
can provide a common basis for experience, maybe a few
laughs, some information and insight, perhaps the chance to
engage one's intelligence and imagination. In these days of run-
away prices, inflated mediocrities, and deflated hopes in our
public lives, that's not a bad record. Television has a standing
invitation to come to my place.

Vocabulary

tranquilized (1), noshing (3), salon (7), tête-à-tête (7)

Questions

1. What is the implication of the title? Is there a possible double
   meaning implied?
2. Why does Diamond extend both his introduction and his conclusion?
3. Why does he mention the "boob tube" and the "idiot box" in
   paragraph 1?
4. Explain the similes in paragraph 2. What do they imply about
   television? What is the relevance of these comparisons in this
   essay? Supposing television were compared to an uninvited guest
   or to a late-arriving visitor who breaks up the party?
5. What is the purpose of paragraph 7?
6. Do you see any attempts to personify, give human characteristics,
   to the television? If so, explain why Diamond might do this.
7. Were you convinced by this essay? Do you see any faults in the
   argument?

Suggestions for Writing

1. What is the role of television in your household? Is it a welcome
   visitor? Convince the reader of your characterization.

2. Write an essay in which you defend something that is frequently attacked—lowering the drinking age, attending spectator sports, or even watching television (if you have additional arguments in its defense). Or, reverse the approach and criticize something that is usually defended—going to college, traveling, being patient, etc. Be sure to keep the opposition in mind, as Diamond does.

3. Are critics of television as "behind the times" as a "black-and-white television set with no remote control or videocassette attachment"? Daniel Boorstin, in *The Americans: The Democratic Experience,* says, "Before, the desire to share experiences had brought people out of their homes gathering them together (physically as well as spiritually), but television would somehow separate them in the very act of sharing." Discuss.

LANGSTON HUGHES

Salvation

*Langston Hughes (1902–67), black American poet,
short story writer, playwright, lyricist, lecturer, professor
of creative writing, was known as "the poet laureate of
Harlem." Having studied at Columbia University and
graduated from Lincoln University, he traveled widely
and devoted much of his life to bringing black achieve-
ments to the attention of a public who often ignored
them. His works include* The Book of Negro Humor
(1966); The Best Short Stories by Negro Writers *(1967);
autobiographical works,* The Big Sea *(1940) and* I Wonder as I Wander *(1956); a history of the NAACP,* Fight for
Freedom *(1962); and many poems strongly influenced by
jazz and blues. "Salvation" is a recollection of a childhood "coming of age" experience. Notice the contrasts
between what was expected of him and what he actually
felt.*

I was saved from sin when I was going on thirteen. But not 1
really saved. It happened like this. There was a big revival at
my Auntie Reed's church. Every night for weeks there had been
much preaching, singing, praying, and shouting, and some very
hardened sinners had been brought to Christ, and the mem-
bership of the church had grown by leaps and bounds. Then
just before the revival ended, they held a special meeting for
children, "to bring the young lambs to the fold." My aunt
spoke of it for days ahead. That night I was escorted to the
front row and placed on the mourners' bench with all the other
young sinners, who had not yet been brought to Jesus.

My aunt told me that when you were saved you saw a light, 2

From *The Big Sea* by Langston Hughes. Reprinted by permission of
Farrar, Straus & Giroux, Inc.

and something happened to you inside! And Jesus came into your life! And God was with you from then on! She said you could see and hear and feel Jesus in your soul. I believed her. I had heard a great many old people say the same thing and it seemed to me they ought to know. So I sat there calmly in the hot, crowded church, waiting for Jesus to come to me.

The preacher preached a wonderful rhythmical sermon, all 3 moans and shouts and lonely cries and dire pictures of hell, and then he sang a song about the ninety and nine safe in the fold, but one little lamb was left out in the cold. Then he said: "Won't you come? Won't you come to Jesus? Young lambs, won't you come?" And he held out his arms to all us young sinners there on the mourners' bench. And the little girls cried. And some of them jumped up and went to Jesus right away. But most of us just sat there.

A great many old people came and knelt around us and 4 prayed, old women with jet-black faces and braided hair, old men with work-gnarled hands. And the church sang a song about the lower lights are burning, some poor sinners to be saved. And the whole building rocked with prayer and song.

Still I kept waiting to *see* Jesus. 5

Finally all the young people had gone to the altar and were 6 saved, but one boy and me. He was a rounder's son named Westley. Westley and I were surrounded by sisters and deacons praying. It was very hot in the church, and getting late now. Finally Westley said to me in a whisper: "God damn! I'm tired o' sitting here. Let's get up and be saved." So he got up and was saved.

Then I was left all alone on the mourners' bench. My aunt 7 came and knelt at my knees and cried, while prayers and songs swirled all around me in the little church. The whole congregation prayed for me alone, in a mighty wail of moans and voices. And I kept waiting serenely for Jesus, waiting, waiting—but he didn't come. I wanted to see him, but nothing happened to me. Nothing! I wanted something to happen to me, but nothing happened.

I heard the songs and the minister saying: "Why don't you 8 come? My dear child, why don't you come to Jesus? Jesus is waiting for you. He wants you. Why don't you come? Sister Reed, what is this child's name?"

"Langston," my aunt sobbed. 9

"Langston, why don't you come? Why don't you come and 10
be saved? Oh, Lamb of God! Why don't you come?"

Now it was really getting late. I began to be ashamed of my- 11
self, holding everything up so long. I began to wonder what
God thought about Westley, who certainly hadn't seen Jesus
either, but who was now sitting proudly on the platform,
swinging his knickerbockered legs and grinning down at me,
surrounded by deacons and old women on their knees praying. God had not struck Westley dead for taking his name in
vain or for lying in the temple. So I decided that maybe to save
further trouble, I'd better lie, too, and say that Jesus had come,
and get up and be saved.

So I got up. 12

Suddenly the whole room broke into a sea of shouting, as 13
they saw me rise. Waves of rejoicing swept the place. Women
leaped in the air. My aunt threw her arms around me. The
minister took me by the hand and led me to the platform.

When things quieted down, in a hushed silence, punctuated 14
by a few ecstatic "Amens," all the new young lambs were
blessed in the name of God. Then joyous singing filled the
room.

That night, for the last time in my life but one—for I was a 15
big boy twelve years old—I cried. I cried, in bed alone, and
couldn't stop. I buried my head under the quilts, but my aunt
heard me. She woke up and told my uncle I was crying because
the Holy Ghost had come into my life, and because I had seen
Jesus. But I was really crying because I couldn't bear to tell
her that I had lied, that I had deceived everybody in the church,
and I hadn't seen Jesus, and that now I didn't believe there
was a Jesus any more, since he didn't come to help me.

Vocabulary

dire (2), gnarled (4), rounder (6)

Questions

1. How old was Hughes when he experienced his "salvation"?
2. Why is the essay called "Salvation"?

3. Who is Westley? Why is he included in the essay?
4. Discuss the figurative language of paragraph 13.
5. Why wasn't he saved?
6. For what purpose was the essay written?
7. What does Hughes discover about himself and about life?
8. Where is the climax of the essay?

Suggestions for Writing

1. Write an essay about an occasion on which you were required to fake the way you really felt, when you had to act a part rather than show your real feelings. Are there occasions like this now?
2. This may also be a model for a "coming-of-age" experience in which you learned something about adult values that you had not previously recognized. If you can remember such an occasion (or if such an experience has happened recently, discuss the situation and the insight).

CARLL TUCKER

Fear of Dearth

Carll Tucker, a frequent contributor to the "Back Door" column in the Saturday Review, *often comments on contemporary pastimes and values. In "Fear of Dearth," he attempts to give the causes for an already existing effect, jogging. He moves from the personal to the smaller explanations of others, to the larger, more inclusive explanations, and finally back to the personal—a very effective circular pattern with much development along the way.*

I hate jogging. Every dawn, as I thud around New York 1
City's Central Park reservoir, I am reminded of how much I
hate it. It's so tedious. Some claim jogging is thought conducive; others insist the scenery relieves the monotony. For me,
the pace is wrong for contemplation of either ideas or vistas.
While jogging, all I can think about is jogging—or nothing.
One advantage of jogging around a reservoir is that there's
no dry shortcut home.

From the listless looks of some fellow trotters, I gather I am 2
not alone in my unenthusiasm: Bill-paying, it seems, would be
about as diverting. Nonetheless, we continue to jog; more, we
continue to *choose* to jog. From a practically infinite array of
opportunities, we select one that we don't enjoy and can't wait
to have done with. Why?

For any trend, there are as many reasons as there are par- 3
ticipants. This person runs to lower his blood pressure. That
person runs to escape the telephone or a cranky spouse or a
filthy household. Another person runs to avoid doing anything
else, to dodge a decision about how to lead his life or a reali-

zation that his life is leading nowhere. Each of us has his carrot and stick. In my case, the stick is my slackening physical condition, which keeps me from beating opponents at tennis whom I overwhelmed two years ago. My carrot is to win.

Beyond these disparate reasons, however, lies a deeper cause. 4 It is no accident that now, in the last third of the 20th century, personal fitness and health have suddenly become a popular obsession. True, modern man likes to feel good, but that hardly distinguishes him from his predecessors.

With zany myopia, economists like to claim that the deeper 5 cause of everything is economic. Delightfully, there seems no marketplace explanation for jogging. True, jogging is cheap, but then not jogging is cheaper. And the scant and skimpy equipment which jogging demands must make it a marketer's least favored form of recreation.

Some scout-masterish philosophers argue that the appeal of 6 jogging and other body-maintenance programs is the discipline they afford. We live in a world in which individuals have fewer and fewer obligations. The work week has shrunk. Weekend worship is less compulsory. Technology gives us more free time. Satisfactorily filling free time requires imagination and effort. Freedom is a wide and risky river; it can drown the person who does not know how to swim across it. The more obligations one takes on, the more time one occupies, the less threat freedom poses. Jogging can become an instant obligation. For a portion of his day, the jogger is not his own man; he is obedient to a regimen he has accepted.

Theologists may take the argument one step further. It is 7 our modern irreligion, our lack of confidence in any hereafter, that makes us anxious to stretch our mortal stay as long as possible. We run, as the saying goes, for our lives, hounded by the suspicion that these are the only lives we are likely to enjoy.

All of these theorists seem to me more or less right. As the 8 growth of cults and charismatic religions and the resurgence of enthusiasm for the military draft suggest, we do crave commitment. And who can doubt, watching so many middle-aged and older persons torturing themselves in the name of fitness, that we are unreconciled to death, more so perhaps than any generation in modern memory?

But I have a hunch there's a further explanation of our ob- 9 session with exercise. I suspect that what motivates us even more than a fear of death is a fear of dearth. Our era is the first to anticipate the eventual depletion of all natural resources. We see wilderness shrinking; rivers losing their capacity to sustain life; the air, even the stratosphere, being loaded with potentially deadly junk. We see the irreplaceable being squandered, and in the depths of our consciousness we are fearful that we are creating an uninhabitable world. We feel more or less helpless and yet, at the same time, desirous to protect what resources we can. We recycle soda bottles and restore old buildings and protect our nearest natural resource—our physical health—in the almost superstitious hope that such small gestures will help save an earth that we are blighting. Jogging becomes a sort of penance for our sins of gluttony, greed, and waste. Like a hairshirt or a bed of nails, the more one hates it, the more virtuous it makes one feel.

That is why *we* jog. Why *I* jog is to win at tennis.   10

Vocabulary

tedious (1), conducive (1), monotony (1), contemplation (1), diverting (2), infinite (2), array (2), participants (3), realization (3), disparate (4), obsession (4), distinguishes (4), zany (5), myopia (5), compulsory (6), regimen (6), irreligion (7), hounded (7), charismatic (8), resurgence (8), unreconciled (8), dearth (9), anticipate (9), depletion (9), irreplaceable (9), squandered (9), uninhabitable (9), blighting (9)

Questions

1. What is the pun implied in the title?
2. What is the purpose of the first two paragraphs?
3. How does the topic of each paragraph relate to the controlling idea?
4. Does the conclusion relate to the introduction?
5. Discuss the figurative language of paragraph 3.
6. Is this essay convincing? Which arguments make the most sense to you?
7. What is the most outstanding feature of the writing?
8. Is the first sentence in paragraph 3 correct? An exaggeration?

Suggestions for Writing

1. This is an excellent model for an effect/cause essay. Like Tucker,
   start with the effect and then write your own explanations for why
   you and/or other people do what they do—become intoxicated,
   attend sports events, disco dance, join clubs, travel, or search
   out "roots," for example. Some research may well add strength to
   this essay.
2. What activity do you continue in spite of the fact that "Bill-
   paying would be as diverting"? Why?

E. M. FORSTER

My Wood

Born in London and educated at Cambridge University, E. M. Forster (1879–1970) lived in Greece, Italy, India, and Egypt as well as in England. His works include short stories; novels such as A Room with a View *(1908),* Howard's End *(1910),* A Passage to India *(1924), and* Maurice *(1971); critical works like* Aspects of the Novel *(1927),* The Development of English Prose between 1918– 1939 *(1945); and collections of essays,* Two Cheers for Democracy *(1951), and* Abinger Harvest *(1936), from which "My Wood" is taken. Like Tucker in "Fear of Dearth," Forster asks a question and then provides an answer in the body of his essay, but although Tucker focuses on causes, Forster bases his essay on effects. Notice how fully he develops each paragraph, allowing his imagination to roam in an effort to understand the effects on him of owning a piece of property.*

A few years ago I wrote a book which dealt in part with the difficulties of the English in India.[1] Feeling that they would have had no difficulties in India themselves, the Americans read the book freely. The more they read it the better it made them feel, and a cheque to the author was the result. I bought a wood with the cheque. It is not a large wood—it contains scarcely any trees, and it is intersected, blast it, by a public footpath. Still, it is the first property that I have owned, so it is right that other people should participate in my shame, and should ask themselves, in accents that will vary in horror, this very important question: What is the effect of property

[1] *A Passage to India* (1924).

upon the character? Don't let's touch economics; the effect of
private ownership upon the community as a whole is another
question—a more important question, perhaps, but another
one. Let's keep to psychology. If you own things, what's their
effect on you? What's the effect on me of my wood?

In the first place, it makes me feel heavy. Property does have 2
this effect. Property produces men of weight, and it was a man
of weight who failed to get into the Kingdom of Heaven.[2] He
was not wicked, that unfortunate millionaire in the parable, he
was only stout; he stuck out in front, not to mention behind,
and as he wedged himself this way and that in the crystalline
entrance and bruised his well-fed flanks, he saw beneath him
a comparatively slim camel passing through the eye of a needle
and being woven into the robe of God. The Gospels all through
couple stoutness and slowness. They point out what is perfectly
obvious, yet seldom realized: that if you have a lot of things
you cannot move about a lot, that furniture requires dusting,
dusters require servants, servants require insurance stamps,
and the whole tangle of them makes you think twice before you
accept an invitation to dinner or go for a bathe in the Jordan.
Sometimes the Gospels proceed further and say with Tolstoy
that property is sinful;[3] they approach the difficult ground of
asceticism here, where I cannot follow them. But as to the immediate effects of property on people, they just show straightforward logic. It produces men of weight. Men of weight cannot, by definition, move like the lightning from the East unto
the West,[4] and the ascent of a fourteen-stone bishop into a pul-
pit is thus the exact antithesis of the coming of the Son of Man.
My wood makes me feel heavy.

In the second place, it makes me feel it ought to be larger. 3

The other day I heard a twig snap in it. I was annoyed at 4
first, for I thought that someone was blackberrying, and depreciating the value of the undergrowth. On coming nearer, I saw
it was not a man who had trodden on the twig and snapped it,
but a bird, and I felt pleased. My bird. The bird was not equally

---

[2] Matthew 19:24.

[3] Tolstoy (1828–1910): Russian novelist, author of *War and Peace* and
Anna Karenina.

[4] Matthew 24:27.

pleased. Ignoring the relation between us, it took fright as soon as it saw the shape of my face, and flew straight over the boundary hedge into a field, the property of Mrs. Henessy, where it sat down with a loud squawk. It had become Mrs. Henessy's bird. Something seemed grossly amiss here, something that would not have occurred had the wood been larger. I could not afford to buy Mrs. Henessy out, I dared not murder her, and limitations of this sort beset me on every side. Ahab [5] did not want that vineyard—he only needed it to round off his property; preparatory to plotting a new curve—and all the land around my wood has become necessary to me in order to round off the wood. A boundary protects. But—poor little thing—the boundary ought in its turn to be protected. Noises on the edge of it. Children throw stones. A little more, and then a little more, until we reach the sea. Happy Canute! Happier Alexander. [6] And after all, why should even the world be the limit of possession? A rocket containing a Union Jack, [7] will, it is hoped, be shortly fired at the moon. Mars. Sirius. Beyond which . . . But these immensities ended by saddening me. I could not suppose that my wood was the destined nucleus of universal dominion—it is so very small and contains no mineral wealth beyond the blackberries. Nor was I comforted when Mrs. Henessy's bird took alarm for the second time and flew clean away from us all, under the belief that it belonged to itself.

In the third place, property makes its owner feel that he ought to do something to it. Yet he isn't sure what. A restlessness comes over him, a vague sense that he has a personality to express—the same sense which, without any vagueness, leads the artist to an act of creation. Sometimes I think I will cut down such trees as remain in the wood, at other times I want to fill up the gaps between them with new trees. Both impulses are pretentious and empty. They are not honest movements towards money-making or beauty. They spring from a foolish desire to express myself and from an inability to enjoy what I

5

---

[5] I Kings 21.

[6] Canute (994–1035): conqueror of England, Denmark, and Norway; Alexander (356–23 B.C.) conquered most of the Eastern Mediterranean and a large part of Asia.

[7] The British flag.

have got. Creation, property, enjoyment form a sinister trinity
in the human mind. Creation and enjoyment are both very
very good, yet they are often unattainable without a material
basis, and at such moments property pushes itself in as a substitute, saying, "Accept me instead—I'm good enough for all
three." It is not enough. It is, as Shakespeare said of lust, "The
expense of spirit in a waste of shame": [8] it is "Before, a joy
proposed: behind, a dream." Yet we don't know how to shun it.
It is forced on us by our economic system as the alternative to
starvation. It is also forced on us by an internal defect in the
soul, by the feeling that in property may lie the germs of self-
development and of exquisite or heroic deeds. Our life on
earth is, and ought to be, material and carnal. But we have not
yet learned to manage our materialism and carnality properly;
they are still entangled with the desire for ownership, where (in
the words of Dante) "Possession is one with loss." [9]

And this brings us to our fourth and final point: the black- 6
berries.

Blackberries are not plentiful in this meagre grove, but they 7
are easily seen from the public footpath which traverses it,
and all too easily gathered. Foxgloves, too—people will pull up
the foxgloves, and ladies of an educational tendency even grub
for toad stools to show them on the Monday in class. Other
ladies, less educated, roll down the bracken in the arms of their
gentlemen friends. There is paper, there are tins. Pray, does
my wood belong to me or doesn't it? And, if it does, should I
not own it best by allowing no one else to walk there? There is
a wood near Lyme Regis,[10] also cursed by a public footpath,
where the owner has not hesitated on this point. He has built
high stone walls each side of the path, and has spanned it by
bridges, so that the public circulate like termites while he
gorges on the blackberries unseen. He really does own his wood,
this able chap. Dives in Hell did pretty well, but the gulf
dividing him from Lazarus could be traversed by vision,[11] and
nothing traverses it here. And perhaps I shall come to this in
time. I shall wall in and fence out until I really taste the sweets

---

[8] Sonnet 129.
[9] Possibly *Convivio,* IV, X–XII.
[10] Small fishing town in southern England.
[11] Luke 16:19–31.

of property. Enormously stout, endlessly avaricious, pseudo-creative, intensely selfish, I shall weave upon my forehead the quadruple crown of possession until those nasty Bolshies come and take it off again and thrust me aside into the outer darkness.[12]

Vocabulary

intersected (1), wedged (2), crystalline (2), flanks (2), asceticism (2), antithesis (2), depreciating (4), grossly (4), impulses (5), pretentious (5), sinister (5), unattainable (5), exquisite (5), carnal (5), entangled (5), meagre (7), traverses (7), foxgloves (7), bracken (7), spanned (7), gorges (7), traversed (7), avaricious (7)

Questions

1. Why does Forster say about Mrs. Henessy, "I dared not murder her"?
2. Why does he devote so much attention to the bird of paragraph 4?
3. Why does the property speak in its own words in paragraph 5?
4. What attitude does Forster really have toward his property?
5. What is the purpose of the allusions to the Bible?
6. What is the purpose of paragraphs 3 and 6?
7. Do you see any significance to the "difficulties of the English in India" in the first sentence? Why does he refer to America?
8. Look up the parable in Matthew 19:24 and discuss its relevance to the essay.
9. A "stone" equals fourteen pounds. Why did Forster mention the weight of the bishop?
10. How does Forster suggest that the essay is over, even without a separate concluding paragraph?
11. What are the connections between Forster's experience and that of the British Empire? What does he think about imperialism?

Suggestions for Writing

1. Write an essay in which you consider the effects of a new possession in your life—possibly a new car, a stereo, a dog, a book. Look at the methods Forster uses for developing his paragraphs.

---

[12] Bolshies: short for Bolsheviks, Russian revolutionary party under Lenin, eventually the Communist party.

2. Critic Lawrence Brander has said of Forster, "He watches himself with genial amusement, it is all great fun." Do you see any evidence of this attitude in Forster's essay?

3. Read Robert Browning's "My Last Duchess" on the following page and compare the attitudes of the speakers in "My Wood" and in the poem.

ROBERT BROWNING

My Last Duchess

Ferrara [1]

That's my last Duchess painted on the wall,
Looking as if she were alive. I call
That piece a wonder, now: Frà Pandolf's hands [2]
Worked busily a day, and there she stands.
Will't please you sit and look at her? I said   5
"Frà Pandolf" by design, for never read
Strangers like you that pictured countenance,
The depth and passion of its earnest glance,
But to myself they turned (since none puts by
The curtain I have drawn for you, but I)   10
And seemed as they would ask me, if they durst,
How such a glance came there; so, not the first
Are you to turn and ask thus. Sir, 'twas not
Her husband's presence only, called that spot
Of joy into the Duchess' cheek: perhaps   15
Frà Pandolf chanced to say "Her mantle laps
Over my lady's wrist too much," or "Paint
Must never hope to reproduce the faint
Half-flush that dies along her throat": such stuff
Was courtesy, she thought, and cause enough   20
For calling up that spot of joy. She had
A heart — how shall I say? — too soon made glad,
Too easily impressed; she liked whate'er
She looked on, and her looks went everywhere.
Sir, 'twas all one! My favor at her breast,   25
The dropping of the daylight in the West,
The bough of cherries some officious fool
Broke in the orchard for her, the white mule

---

[1] Possibly Alfonso II, sixteenth-century Duke of Ferrara in Italy.

[2] A fictitious name for the painter as is "Claus of Innsbruck," the sculptor, later.

She rode with round the terrace — all and each
Would draw from her alike the approving speech,   30
Or blush, at least. She thanked men, — good! but thanked
Somehow — I know not how — as if she ranked
My gift of a nine-hundred-years-old name
With anybody's gift. Who'd stoop to blame
This sort of trifling? Even had you skill   35
In speech —which I have not — to make your will
Quite clear to such an one, and say, "Just this
Or that in you disgusts me; here you miss,
Or there exceed the mark" — and if she let
Herself be lessoned so, nor plainly set   40
Her wits to yours, forsooth, and made excuse,
— E'en then would be some stooping; and I choose
Never to stoop. Oh sir, she smiled, no doubt,
Whene'er I passed her; but who passed without
Much the same smile? This grew; I gave commands;   45
Then all smiles stopped together. There she stands
As if alive. Will't please you rise? We'll meet
The company below, then. I repeat,
The Count your master's known munificence
Is ample warrant that no just pretense   50
Of mine for dowry will be disallowed;
Though his fair daughter's self, as I avowed
At starting, is my object. Nay, we'll go
Together down, sir. Notice Neptune, though,
Taming a sea-horse, thought a rarity,   55
Which Claus of Innsbruck cast in bronze for me!

IV · Combinations

And yet the significance of a writer is in the unpre-dictable pattern made by the opposing pull and tug; the pull of established practice and the tug of wayward impulse. . . . Sidney Cox

The essays in Part IV have much in common with those of earlier parts, but they move still further from the most basic pattern. In fact, with the exception of dividing an essay into two parts—thesis and "subthesis" —all of the variations have been encountered before.

What distinguishes these essays is the extent of the variation and the combination of several kinds of break from the simple structure. In this part, a writer may make an extended digression rather than a brief departure, or an essay might contain, for example, an implied thesis, several interruptions, and an absorbed conclusion.

Notice, however, that no matter how elaborate the break from the central thought, or how complex the adaptations, the purpose is always clear and the relationship to the thesis is never in doubt.

K. W. CARTER

I Remember . . . My Little *White* Schoolhouse

K. W. Carter, born in 1913, grew up on the family farm in rural Maine, an experience that "led to the belief that there must be some easier way to make a living." Before retiring at age sixty to devote time to writing, he worked as a retail salesman of bread and pastry, a welder at the Bath Iron Works, a restaurant cook, and a supervisor for a life insurance company. He has published some fiction, political and social commentary, and articles, often nostalgic, in a variety of newspapers and magazines. This piece is a recollection of Carter's elementary school. Notice how he chooses details that turn the "little white schoolhouse" into my "little white schoolhouse." Also notice the dominant impression created by the details.

The little red schoolhouse in my community was white. In 1 fact, I do not recall ever seeing red schoolhouses in rural Maine in the old days; usually they were white or, more commonly, the color of weather-beaten shingles. It must be remembered that the reputation of town officials was measured by their reluctance to spend money on education.

I have before me a copy of the 1935 Town Report for Mont- 2 ville. Three grade schools operated there at the time, and the entire budget for schools, including money from state funds, was $6,170. Of this amount $2,736.26 was allotted to other towns for high school tuition, Montville having no high school of its own. There was an unexpected balance of $408.51 at the end of that year. From this it can be seen that the town operated three grammar schools for a total of $3,025.23.

The outlay for textbooks was $23.95, and for other supplies, 3

From *Down East* Magazine, April 1979. Reprinted by permission.

$6.08. And this in an era when rural taxpayers were emitting anguished cries about the high cost of education! The total budget for teachers was $1,572.50. Out of these handsome salaries, teachers who didn't live within commuting distance of the school paid their board to a local resident.

Since the low salaries in rural schools kept the profession 4 from being attractive to men, the teacher was invariably a woman. Prior to the 1920s, when teachers were paid even less, they boarded "around," living a week or two at a time with one family and then moving on to the nearest or most desirable place they could find. If some of the living conditions were less than satisfactory, at least they were free, for it was then a public duty for townspeople to take turns "boarding the teacher." After two or three years of this rather nomadic way of life, most school mistresses were ready to marry anyone who asked their hand, in order to escape. If a teacher was fortunate enough to live near the school, she might make a lifetime career of instructing the young, thereby becoming what was always called "an old maid schoolteacher."

The schoolhouse I attended consisted of one room, roughly 5 thirty feet square, with a large entryway where outdoor clothing, rubbers, and dinner pails could be left during the day. There was a woodshed large enough to store a supply of kindling and five or six split cords of wood, cut in two-and-one-half-foot lengths. At the back of the woodshed were two three-holers, a stout board between them rigorously segregating the sexes.

The interior of the schoolroom was finished in matched soft- 6 wood boards which may have been painted a generation before. The floor was of unpainted softwood and so worn that every knot was a good half-inch higher than the rest of the board. Since the building had no basement, winter winds whistled under it and up through cracks in the floor; chill breezes also invaded the room through the walls and around windows and doors; and sometimes fine snow, driven by a northeast wind, filtered in. The room was heated by a pot-bellied, black-iron barrel stove, stoked with dry hardwood billets from the woodshed. Sometimes a bit of exuberant horseplay at recess or lunchtime might lead to one of the stove's three legs being kicked askew, tipping the whole thing, fire and all, onto the floor. To keep the small building from going up in smoke required swift, heroic work on the part of the larger boys, and they always managed to avoid disaster.

Some twenty young scholars attended this school, although   7
there were desks for thirty. Books, stored in old, glass-fronted bookcases, were used until they were so dogeared and defaced as to be almost unreadable. On the rare occasions when new books were available, they were distributed reluctantly, usually, it was believed, to the teacher's favorites. On a table at the back of the room was a well-worn dictionary, a flyspecked globe (word had crept into the community that the world was round), paper, pencils, erasers, and chalk.

Of course, there was no piano nor any musical instruction.   8
The teacher would open "morning exercises" by having us sing a hymn, but more often any ceremony was limited to a recital of the Lord's Prayer and a salute to the flag, mumbling rites now outlawed by the wisdom of the Supreme Court.

The curriculum included the three Rs, geography, and   9
American history. Penmanship was taught by the Palmer Method, standard procedure in all Maine schools. Whether there was something wrong with the system of the immortal Palmer or whether I had no talent for calligraphy must remain a moot question, since I never learned to write well enough to read my own handwriting an hour after it was put on paper.

Social affairs and extracurricular activities at the little "red"   10
schoolhouse were almost nonexistent. The town fathers felt it unnecessary to spend money on such frivolity, and the poorly paid teachers could not generate enough enthusiasm for any fun and games. Yes, at Christmas time we would have a tree and the children would exchange presents of fudge, little note-books, or small bags of candy tied up with ribbon. To wind up the festivities we would sing "Jingle Bells" or "Come All Ye Faithful." Then, liberated for two weeks, we would go home for sliding, and for flu and runny noses.

Vocabulary

reluctance (1), outlay (3), emitting (3), invariably (4), nomadic (4), kindling (5), cords (5), rigorously (5), billets (6), exuberant (6), askew (6), dogeared (7), defaced (7), calligraphy (9), moot (9), generate (10)

Questions

1. What is the thesis?
2. What is the purpose of paragraphs 2 and 3? Could they be eliminated? How does this essay vary from the basic pattern?
3. How are the subsequent paragraphs divided? Which paragraph is the most effective?
4. Select three details that give you the most vivid picture of the schoolhouse.
5. What is the purpose of the essay?
6. What is the dominant impression of the school? What led you to this conclusion?
7. Did it remind you of your own elementary school? Why or why not?
8. Does this essay have anything in common with "A Long Road Ago" on p. 89.

Suggestions for Writing

1. Write an essay in which you recall your own "little schoolhouse," whether or not it was actually little, big, red, or white. If you attended several elementary schools, focus on one of them, preferably the one that made the strongest impression on you. Who taught there? What were the students like? What were the building and its environs like? Try not to be random in your selection of details; attempt to give a dominant impression. Was it poor, palatial, prison-like? (You may not have appropriate statistics, so the "financial" interruption may well be eliminated.)
2. According to the *Oxford English Dictionary,* the word "nostalgia" comes from two Greek words, "nostos" (return home) and "algos" (pain). Nostalgia, then, is at base a "home-pain" or homesickness. Do you see any evidence for nostalgia in this essay or in the one by Charles Doss (p. 89)? Or do you see any evidence for it in our society? What are its possible causes? Do advertisers ever make use of this yearning for "the good old days"?

CARLL TUCKER

Disconnection

(See introduction to the writer, p. 125.)
*Here Tucker gives a personal reaction to a discotheque
in New York, Studio 54. Making no pretense to objectivity, he announces his disappointment in the first paragraph. Not only does he find the club objectionable,
he finds the attitude that it represents—disconnection—
also objectionable. Notice the techniques he uses to persuade the reader of his "aversion."*

*The apparition of these faces in the crowd—petals on a wet,
black bough.*—Ezra Pound [1]

Quick, before I forget, let me limn New York's famous dis- 1
cotheque, Studio 54—because if I do not do it now, I never
will. Barring the worst luck, I will never pass through its
portals again.

According to "the media," Studio 54 is the *in* night spot in 2
New York. Mikhail Baryshnikov goes there. Vitas Gerulaitis
goes there. Truman Capote makes the scene. Vladimir Horowitz went there for his 74th birthday.[2] So glittering is the clientele that it makes everyone who goes to Studio 54 seem famous,
whether they are or not.

One of the attractions of Studio 54 is the much-bruited fact 3
that its management turns away customers—not just customers

[1] From a poem by Ezra Pound (1885–1972), "In a Station of the Metro."

[2] Baryshnikov (b. 1948): Russian-born ballet dancer; Gerulaitis (b. 1954):
American tennis player; Capote (b. 1924): American writer, author of *In
Cold Blood;* Horowitz (b. 1924): Russian born, now American, concert
pianist.

they can't accommodate, but customers they don't cotton to. No reasons are given—and the pattern of rejections is sufficiently fickle to frustrate anyone who wants either to be assured of admission or to sue the disco's proprietors for unlawful discrimination. To emphasize this deliberately outrageous policy. the entrance on 54th Street, west of Broadway, is cordoned off; a constant throng (most of whom, I'd wager, are employed by the management) presses against the barriers, affording those admitted a delicious sense of superiority.

No fool I. To avoid the risk of rejection, I waited until I had   4
in hand a card that read "This invitation admits two." The display of the card caused the cordon to be momentarily parted, then quickly rejoined like the Red Sea after Moses.

Inside, the light is murky, lurid, unreal. Although it is not   5
difficult to see where you are going, it is impossible to identify faces until they are upon you, like emergent ghosts. A shape approaches—you squint—until you make the disconcerting discovery that you've been staring at the fair bare chest of an androgynous cigarette-butt-sweeper clad in nothing but running shorts, socks, and sneakers. Such shocks heighten one's curiosity about the participants, while also forcing one's glances to become furtive. One must take care not to end up peering at some part of the anatomy one would prefer not to be peering at.

The light *feels* decadent. Purplish, artificial, unreal, unlike   6
any natural hue, it makes the large spaces seem out of this world, like a dream. Decadence in any era is characterized by a rejection of *what is* (the ordinary, the familiar, the popular) in favor of fantastic distortions of reality appreciated by cognoscenti only. Rome's painted, baubled grostesques that Fellini depicted in *Satyricon,* the fantasticoes of English Restoration comedy, the wild excesses of Rococo architecture, the drugged dreams of a Baudelaire, the perverse visions of an Aubrey Beardsley [3]—all testify to a boredom or disgust with life that historically typifies decadence.

---

[3] Fellini (b. 1920): Italian film director; Restoration comedy: plays written after the restoration of Charles II to the English throne (1660); Rococo architecture: ornate and intricate style especially of the eighteenth century; Baudelaire (1821–67); French poet; Beardsley (1872–98), English illustrator.

The glorification of drugs in Studio 54—against one wall is 7
a large cutout of the man-in-the-moon sniffing cocaine—em-
phasizes the discotheque's deliberate, one might even say desperate, striving to escape the reality outdoors. Likewise the
relentless decibel level of the music (one begins to feel a throb-
bing in the thorax, as if a bass player was strumming one's
vocal chords) defeats all but the most determined attempts at
conversation, isolating each individual in his or her sense-bom-
barded cocoon.

I confess: I do not like dancing, especially dancing that pre- 8
cludes conversation. If I danced better, I might enjoy Studio 54
more. Nonetheless, I believe that my aversion to Studio 54 has
deeper wellsprings.

Solipsism is the sickness of our age. Every periodical, talk 9
show, advertisement harps on how to increase satisfaction and
gratification. Slimmer thighs, whiter teeth, plusher pleasures,
sexier sex—contentment is discussed as if it were heat: to
raise it, to turn the thermostat up a couple of degrees, just
spend a few extra dollars.

The hoary truth is that contentment depends on none of 10
these accouterments. Contentment depends on feeling needed,
and to be needed one must give another something uniquely
one's own, be it love, advice, support, wisdom, solace, entertainment, education, leadership, or care. Contentment depends, in
short, on *connection,* and the more connected, the more cohesive, a society is, the more likely it will be to work together
for the benefit of all.

In Studio 54, only the eyes connect. Every dancer, partnered 11
or not, dances alone. Even if one could converse, one's partner
might not even be there, his or her brain abducted by cocaine.
The only unique contributions an individual can make there
are beauty and dancing, but few are beauteous enough or
dance well enough to make such contributions in any way
noteworthy.

Fantasy is necessary. Escape is necessary. Revelry is an in- 12
dispensable social steam valve. But this sort of revelry, the kind
that isolates individuals and encourages self-absorption, can
finally only exacerbate loneliness and despair.

Fleeing that lurid light, I resisted telling the two dozen ex- 13
cluded from the discotheque how lucky they were.

Vocabulary

limn (1), bruited (3), cordoned (3), murkey (5), lurid (5), emergent (5), disconcerting (5), androgynous (5), furtive (5), decadent (6), cognoscenti (6), fantasticoes (6), thorax (7), precludes (8), aversion (8), wellsprings (8), solipsism (9), hoary (10), accouterments (10), cohesive (10), abducted (11), indispensable (12), exacerbate (12)

Questions

1. What is implied by the comparison to the "Red Sea after Moses"?
2. Paragraph 6 opens with an example of synaesthesia, the transference of a word that is appropriate to one sense to the description of another sense — sweet sound, for example, or loud color. What is the effect of this mixture of the sense impressions at this point in the essay?
3. Why does Tucker compare the clientele to "emergent ghosts" in paragraph 5?
4. What is the purpose of the epigraph by Ezra Pound?
5. What is the purpose of paragraphs 2 and 3?
6. How do paragraphs 4, 5, 6, and 7 relate to the thesis?
7. What is the "deeper wellspring" of Tucker's aversion?
8. What persuasive techniques does Tucker use?
9. What does the discussion of solipsism have to do with the main point?
10. What is the effect of the allusions in paragraph 6?
11. Why does he include two lists of references — paragraph 2 and paragraph 6? Is there any connection between them?

Suggestions for Writing

1. Write your own personal reaction to a club, restaurant, or other place of entertainment about which you have strong feelings. (You might also write about a concert or a show, but be sure to concentrate on the physical impression of the location and its effect on you.) Explain first what you like or do not like about the place and then attempt to explain your reaction to these things (actually, you are explaining your explanation). What are the "deeper wellsprings" of your reactions?
2. Do you agree that solipsism is "the sickness of our age"?

CYRA MCFADDEN

Wait — Perhaps Your Cause Is Already Lost

Cyra McFadden is a free-lance writer, often on media, and the author of The Serial. *In this essay, Cyra McFadden confesses a "fault" in her personality and then gives examples of several occasions when it shows up. Notice that she uses a variety of methods for developing each example and that much of the essay is devoted to frustrated efforts at dealing with her weakness.*

Somewhere in the pile of books, bills, papers and cats on my desk is an ad I clipped for a book about how to cure yourself of procrastination. 1

I desperately need this book, having long since modified the old adage "Never put off till tomorrow what you can do today" to "Never do anything you can avoid doing until your back is up against the wall." To make matters worse, I am married to a fellow procrastinator. This is like one heroin addict being married to another: we know we ought to kick the habit, but we have a sordid interdependence going and find it easier to believe that if we really wanted to, we could quit any time. Oh, sure. 2

Take the matter of the Christmas ornaments. Christmas is a nightmare for procrastinators because of the logistical problems it presents: buying and mailing cards and presents, lugging home and putting up a tree, planning the holiday party which, in our case, we are never sufficiently organized to give. (Any year now, we're actually going to follow through and give such a party. By that time, I figure, we'll be living in a nearby 3 "mobile home ranch" unhappily named "Trail's End," and we can use the community center.)

But I procrastinate. About the Christmas decorations. . . .   4

As I write, it is midsummer and still on the counter top in   5
the family room—the elephant's graveyard in our house for all domestic clutter with which nobody wants to cope—are two large cartons of Christmas lights and wrapping paper. The latter is unusuable the rest of the year because it's all relentlessly Christmas-oriented, and it seems a little tactless to wrap wedding presents in paper with a "HO-HO-HO" motif.

Obviously we ought to put this stuff up in the attic, al-   6
though, as my husband reasonably points out, it's only another four months until next Christmas and then we'll need it again. And the attic is full of such a depressing collection of things we'll never use again that when I climbed the ladder and poked around for the ornaments *last* December, I told myself that before I stashed them away again, I'd clean it out.

I intend to do it, too, but there's no sense rushing into things   7
and, anyway, God knows what's up there. I have to think about my physical safety. As for the Christmas cartons, we've arrived at an understanding. I don't bother them and they don't bother me.

Then there are the four pounds or so of unanswered cor-   8
respondence waiting in a boot box in what is all too accurately called my den. I love receiving mail and am upset on days when I don't get any—doesn't anybody love me?—but I am temperamentally incapable of answering it unless I'm being threatened. ("Dear Madam: Remit at once, or. . . .")

So the mail piles up. For a while I kept it in a shoebox, and   9
then, when the shoebox overflowed and it seemed I had no recourse but to sit down and take it from the top, I remembered the boot box and the crisis was averted.

Other problems don't lend themselves so easily to solution,   10
especially when one stalls at length about addressing them at all and when one is aided and abetted by a fellow procrastinator. A sample conversation at our house:

"We've got to paint this place—it's getting shabbier and   11
shabbier."

"I hate painting. You hate painting. Why don't we just have   12
a gin and tonic?"

"We could, but I didn't get around to buying gin."   13
"Maybe we have vodka. We could have a vodka and tonic."   14
"We could if you'd got around to filling the ice trays."   15
"I hate filling the ice trays."   16
Meanwhile, having clipped that ad for the self-help book on   17
how to stop procrastinating, I feel I've acted with nothing
short of dispatch and thereby made a start at turning our lives
around. Soon—perhaps in a week or ten days— I'm going to
call the bookstore and order a copy, and fairly soon after that
I'll make a point of reading it. It's on my list, right after working through the boot box full of mail, and the boot box comes
right after buying gin.

Right now, unfortunately, I'm too busy even to make the   18
phone call. We leave for a vacation in Spain in a couple of
weeks, and I haven't yet signed up for the conversational Spanish course I intended to take. There's probably no hurry. I
don't think my husband has got around to ordering the plane
tickets yet.

Vocabulary

procrastination (1), modified (2), adage (2), sordid (2), interdependence (2), logistical (3), relentlessly (5), tactless (5), motif (5), temperamentally (8), averted (9), abetted (10), dispatch (17)

Questions

1. What is the thesis?
2. Why does McFadden mention the proverb in paragraph 2?
3. What is the purpose of the parenthetical expression in paragraph 3?
4. Notice that McFadden devotes five paragraphs to the Christmas
   ornaments. Why? What makes each paragraph distinctive, even
   though the general topic is the same?
5. What is the tone of the essay?
6. Did you enjoy the essay? Explain.

Suggestions for Writing

1. Using McFadden as a model, write an essay on one of your own
   weaknesses. Are you an exaggerator, a compulsive eater, clutterer,
   a gossip, a borrower, a spendthrift? Are you too quick to anger,

too quick to get involved, too quick to judge others? Do you love danger? Rather than simply listing examples of this weakness, try to use various means as McFadden does, for illustrating and elaborating.

2. "Never put off till tomorrow what you can do today." Discuss.

3. Compare this essay with Lawrence Witchel's "A Pepsi Person in the Perrier Generation" (p. 45). What are the similarities and the differences?

4. Write an essay in which you illustrate or refute the truth (or falsehood) of a proverb — "Too many cooks spoil the broth"; "A stitch in time saves nine." (You might try to write this essay ironically, appearing to argue just the opposite of what you mean.)

5. Make up your own proverb and explain why you feel it is a good idea.

ROBIN ROBERTS

Strike Out Little League

Robin Roberts, born in Illinois in 1926, attended Michigan State University, playing baseball and basketball, and in 1946 was named Michigan's outstanding basketball player. He joined the Philadelphia Phillies in 1948 and played with them until 1962. In 1976, he was elected to the National Baseball Hall of Fame. In this essay, he argues strongly against the organization of young children into Little League teams and makes some suggestions of his own. Notice the clear plan of his essay and the obvious transition to the second part.

In 1939, Little League baseball was organized by Bert and 1
George Bebble and Carl Stotz of Williamsport, Pa. What they
had in mind in organizing this kids' baseball program, I'll
never know. But I'm sure they never visualized the monster it
would grow into.

At least 25,000 teams, in about 5,000 leagues, compete for a 2
chance to go to the Little League World Series in Williamsport
each summer. These leagues are in more than fifteen countries,
although recently the Little League organization has voted to
restrict the competition to teams in the United States. If you
judge the success of a program by the number of participants,
it would appear that Little League has been a tremendous success. More than 600,000 boys from 8 to 12 are involved. But I
say Little League is wrong—and I'll try to explain why.

If I told you and your family that I want you to help me 3
with a project from the middle of May until the end of July,
one that would totally disrupt your dinner schedule and pay

nothing, you would probably tell me to get lost. That's what Little League does. Mothers or fathers or both spend four or five nights a week taking children to Little League, watching the game, coming home around 8 or 8:30 and sitting down to a late dinner.

These games are played at this hour because the adults are   4
running the programs and this is the only time they have available. These same adults are in most cases unqualified as instructors and do not have the emotional stability to work with children of this age. The dedication and sincerity of these instructors cannot be questioned, but the purpose of this dedication should be. Youngsters eligible for Little League are of the age when their concentration lasts, at most, for five seconds —and without sustained concentration organized athletic programs are a farce.

Most instructors will never understand this. As a result   5
there is a lot of pressure on these young people to do something that is unnatural for their age—so there will always be hollering and tremendous disappointment for most of these players. For acting their age, they are made to feel incompetent. This is a basic fault of Little League.

If you watch a Little League game, in most cases the pitchers   6
are the most mature. They throw harder, and if they throw strikes very few batters can hit the ball. Consequently, it makes good baseball sense for most hitters to take the pitch. Don't swing. Hope for a walk. That could be a player's instruction for four years. The fun is in hitting the ball; the coach says don't swing. That may be sound baseball, but it does nothing to help a young player develop his hitting. What would seem like a basic training ground for baseball often turns out to be a program of negative thoughts that only retards a young player.

I believe more good young athletes are turned off by the   7
pressure of organized Little League than are helped. Little Leagues have no value as a training ground for baseball fundamentals. The instruction at that age, under the pressure of an organized league program, creates more doubt and eliminates the naturalness that is most important.

If I'm going to criticize such a popular program as Little   8
League, I'd better have some thoughts on what changes I would like to see.

First of all, I wouldn't start any programs until the school 9
year is over. Any young student has enough of a schedule
during the school year to keep busy.

These programs should be played in the afternoon—with a 10
softball. Kids have a natural fear of a baseball; it hurts when it
hits you. A softball is bigger, easier to see and easier to hit. You
get to run the bases more and there isn't as much danger of
injury if one gets hit with the ball. Boys and girls could play
together. Different teams would be chosen every day. The instructors would be young adults home from college, or high-
school graduates. The instructor could be the pitcher and the
umpire at the same time. These programs could be run on
public playgrounds or in schoolyards.

I guarantee that their dinner would be at the same time 11
every night. The fathers could come home after work and re-
lax; most of all, the kids would have a good time playing ball
in a program in which hitting the ball and running the bases
are the big things.

When you start talking about young people playing base- 12
ball at 13 to 15, you may have something. Organize them a
little, but be careful; they are still young. But from 16 and on,
work them really hard. Discipline them, organize the leagues,
strive to win championships, travel all over. Give this age all
the time and attention you can.

I believe Little League has done just the opposite. We've 13
worked hard with the 8- to 12-year-olds. We overorganize them,
put them under pressure they can't handle and make playing
baseball seem important. When our young people reach 16
they would appreciate the attention and help from the parents,
and that's when our present programs almost stop.

The whole idea of Little League baseball is wrong. There 14
are alternatives available for more sensible programs. With the
same dedication that has made the Little League such a major
part of many of our lives, I'm sure we'll find the answer.

I still don't know what those three gentlemen in Williams- 15
port had in mind when they organized Little League baseball.
I'm sure they didn't want parents arguing with their children
about kids' games. I'm sure they didn't want to have family
meals disrupted for three months every year. I'm sure they
didn't want young athletes hurting their arms pitching under

pressure at such a young age. I'm sure they didn't want young boys who don't have much athletic ability made to feel that something is wrong with them because they can't play baseball. I'm sure they didn't want a group of coaches drafting the players each year for different teams. I'm sure they didn't want unqualified men working with the young players. I'm sure they didn't realize how normal it is for an 8-year-old boy to be scared of a thrown or batted baseball.

For the life of me, I can't figure out what they had in mind. 16

Vocabulary

sustained (4), incompetent (5), retards (6), alternatives (14),

Questions

1. What objections does Roberts have to Little League?
2. What does he prefer?
3. Why was Little League organized?
4. What is the thesis of this argument?
5. What is implied in the title?
6. Why was the essay written?
7. Why does he end with, "For the life of me, I can't figure out what they had in mind."
8. Is the argument convincing? Why?
9. Does Roberts' style back up his point?
10. Do you see any way this essay might be improved?

Suggestions for Writing

1. Write an essay on a debated subject — spectator sports, IQ testing, SAT examinations — making your reason for opposing or approving the subjects for your paragraphs. If it seems appropriate, you might offer some solutions, as Roberts does, in the second part of your essay.
2. How do you think children of Little League age should spend their free time? Be specific.

HILAIRE BELLOC

On a Piece of Rope

*Hilaire Belloc (1870–1953), born in France, was an
English writer of light verse, essays, travel books, history,
and fiction. His works include* A Bad Child's Book of
Beasts *(1896), a series of essays,* On Nothing, On Everything, On Anything, On Something, On *(1908–11, 1923),
and biographies of Robespierre, Cardinal Wolsey, and
others. In "On a Piece of Rope," his mind wanders over
many thoughts stimulated by a piece of rope near him
on a boat trip. Notice, however, that even the seemingly
free association of ideas is not carelessly random. Look
for Belloc's organizing principles, which he uses to create
artistic order out of free thought.*

The other day as I was sailing down channel at dawn I con- 1
templated a piece of rope (which was my only companion) and
considered how many things attached to it, and of what sort
these were.

I considered in the first place (as it has become my unhappy 2
custom to do about most things) how mighty a theme this piece
of rope would be for the modern rubbish, for the modern
abandonment of common sense. I considered how many thousand people would, in connexion with that bit of rope, write
that man had developed it through countless ages of upward
striving from the first dim savage regions where some half-
apelike creature first twisted grass, to the modern factory of
Lord Ropemaker-in-chief, which adorns some Midland Hell
to-day. I considered how people made up history of that kind
entirely out of their heads and how it sold by the wagon-load.

From *Selected Essays of Hilaire Belloc*. Reprinted by permission of A D
Peters & Co. Ltd.

I considered how the other inventions which I had seen arise with my own eyes had always come suddenly, with a burst, unexpectedly, from the oddest quarters. I considered how not even this glaring experience was of the least use in preventing fools from talking folly.

Next I considered, as I watched that bit of rope, the curious [3] historical fact of anonymity. Someone first thought out the bowline knot. Who was it? He never left a record. It seems that he desired to leave none. There would appear to be only two kinds of men who care about leaving a record of themselves: artists and soldiers. Innumerable other creators since the world began are content, it would seem, with creation and despise fame. I have often wondered, for instance, who invented forming fours. I very much doubt his being a soldier. Certainly he was not a poet. If he had been a soldier he would not have let you forget him in a hurry—and as for poets, they are good for nothing and could no more invent a useful thing than fly.

Note you, that forming fours is something which must have [4] been invented at one go. There is no "Development" about it. It is a simple, immediate, and revolutionary trick. It was not— and then it was. Note you also that until the trick of forming fours was discovered, no conversion from line into column was possible, and therefore no quick handling of men. So with knots and so with splicing. There are, indeed, one or two knots that have names of men attached to them. There is Walker's knot, for instance. But Walker (if Walker it was who invented it) made no great effort to perpetuate his fame, and all the common useful knots without which civilization could not go on, and on which the State depends, were modestly given to mankind as a Christian man, now dead, used to give his charity! without advertisement.

And this consideration of knots led me to another, which [5] was of those things which had been done with ropes and which without ropes would never have happened. The sailing of the sea, the execution of countless innocent men, and now and then, by accident, of somebody who really deserved death: The tying up of bundles, which is the solid foundation of all trade: The lasso for the catching of beasts: The hobbling of horses: The strengthening of man through pulleys: The casting of bridges over chasms: The sending of great messages to belea-

guered cities: The escapes of kings and heroes. All these would
not have been but for ropes.

As I looked at the rope I further considered how strange it   6
was that ropes had never been worshipped. Men have worshipped the wall, and the post, and the sun, and the house.
They have worshipped their food and their drink. They have,
you may say, ceremonially worshipped their clothes; they have
worshipped their headgear especially, crowns, mitres, ta-ra-ras; [1]
and they have worshipped the music which they have created.
But I never heard of anyone worshipping a rope. Nor have I
ever heard of a rope being made a symbol. I can recollect but
one case in which it appears in a coat-of-arms, and that is, I
think, in the case of the County or City of Chester,[2] where, as I
seem to remember, the Chester knot is emblazoned. But no one
used it that I can remember in the Crusades, when all coats-of-
arms were developing. And this is odd, for they used every
other conceivable thing—windmills, spurs, boots, roses, staffs,
waves of the sea, the crescent moon, lions and leopards and
even the elephant, and black men's heads, birds, horses, unicorns, griffons, jolly little dogs, chess boards, eagles—every conceivable thing human or imaginary they pressed into service;
but no ropes.

One would have thought that the rope would have been   7
a basis of measurement, but there are only two ways in which
it comes in for so obvious a purpose, and one of these is lost.
There was the old Norman *hrap*, which was vague enough, and
there is the cable, the tenth of a sea mile. But the rope does not
come into any other measurement; for you cannot count the
knots on a log line as a form of measurement with ropes. The
measurement itself is not drawn from the rope but from geographical degrees.

Further, I considered the rope (as it lay there) on its literary   8
side. No one has written verses to ropes. There is one verse
about ropes, or mainly about ropes in a chaunty, but I do not
think there is any poem dedicated to ropes and dealing mainly
with ropes. They are about the only thing upon which verse
has not been accumulated—bad verse—for centuries.

Yet the rope has one very important place in literature   9

---

[1] Perhaps tiaras.
[2] County town of Cheshire in northern England.

which is not recognized. It is this: that ropes more than any other subject are, I think, a test of a man's power of exposition in prose. If you can describe clearly without a diagram the proper way of making this or that knot, then you are a master of the English tongue. You are not only a master—you are a sign, a portent, a new discoverer, an exception among your fellow men, a unique fellow. For no one yet in this world surely has attained to lucidity in this most difficult branch of all expression. I find over and over again in the passages of those special books which talk of ropes, such language as: "This is a very useful knot and is made as follows:—a bight is taken in the standing apart and is then run over right handedly, that is with the sun or, again, the hands of a watch (only backward), and then under the running part and so through both times and hauled tight by the free end." But if any man should seek to save his life on a dark night in a sudden gust of wind by this description he would fail: he would drown.

Take the simplest of them. Take the Clove-Hitch. Write 10 a sentence in English which will explain (without a picture) how to cast a Clove-Hitch. I do not think you will succeed.

Talking of this literary side of ropes, see how the rope has 11 accumulated, like everything else, a vast army of technical terms, a whole regiment of words which are its family and of which it is very jealous. People who write of ropes are hardly able to keep off these words although they mean nothing to the reader and are but a darkening and a confusion. There is stranding and half-stranding, and there is parcelling, serving and whipping, and crowning and all the rest of it. How came such words there? Who thought them to the point? On what possible metaphors were they founded? In nearly all other groups of technical words you can trace the origin, but here you cannot. Nor can you find the origin of the names for all the hundred things that are made of ropes. Why is a gasket called a gasket? Why is a grommet called a grommet? Why is a true lover's-knot called a true lover's-knot? or a tack a tack? Now and then there is a glimmering of sense. Halyard is obvious and sheet is explicable. Outhaul and downhaul might be Greek or German so plainly do they reveal their make-up. But what are you to make of bobstay, parrel, runner, and shroud? Why are ratlines ratlines? What possible use could they be to a rat? They are no good for *leaving* a sinking ship, though excellent

for running up out of the rising water. "Springs" I half understand, but whence in the name of Chelsea came "painter"? Reef
points might pass. That is if you admit reef—which, I suppose,
is the same as "reave" and "rove"—but, great heavens, where
did they get "ear-rings"—and why do you "mouse" hooks, and
what have cats to do with anchors?

A ship is a little world, a little universe, and it has a lan- 12
guage of its own, which disdains the land and its reasons.

Vocabulary

contemplated (1), anonymity (3), bowline (3), innumerable (3),
splicing (4), perpetuate (4), hobbling (5), chasms (5), beleaguered
(5), ceremonially (6), crescent (6), griffons (6), unicorns (6), chaunty
(8), exposition (9), portent (9), attained (9), lucidity (9), bight (9),
accumulated (11), glimmering (11), halyard (11), explicable (11)

Questions

1. Why does Belloc begin thinking about the rope?
2. What are the various things "attached" to the rope as Belloc
   thinks about it?
3. Why does he spend so much time on the literary aspect of the
   rope?
4. Does this essay have anything in common with Highet's "Go and
   Catch a Falling Remark" (p. 61)?
5. Can you see any reason for writing an essay like this?
6. Why does Belloc call attention to his transitions?
7. Is the essay only about rope or does it move on to a larger discussion?
8. What is the meaning of the conclusion?
9. What is the purpose of the many technical terms?
10. How would you describe his feeling about the rope?

Suggestion for Writing

Write an essay in which you discuss the thoughts that occur to you as
you contemplate a seemingly insignificant object right in front of you
— the pencil on your desk, the spider's web in the corner. Select three
or four of these ideas and develop them in separate paragraphs.

JOHN J. O'CONNOR

The Wide World on a Small Screen

John J. O'Connor, television and radio critic for The
New York Times, *considers the question of "reality" in
our perception of the world as experienced through television. Notice how he discriminates among types of programs in order to draw his conclusions. In fact, his thesis
is merely suggested by the question at the end of paragraph 2 and, finally, stated in the conclusion.*

If it's Sunday, this must be the Bunker household in New 1
York City. Or so it might seem to the tens of millions of television viewers tuning in to *All in the Family.* The furniture has
become so much a part of our nation's image of the borough of
Queens that Archie's favorite armchair has been installed in
the Smithsonian Institution. But, of course, Archie and Edith
are really doing their familiar turns in a California studio. The
rest is pure illusion.

Accepting the premise, admittedly slippery, that television 2
can provide a mirror image of the world, we are left with several delicate questions. How valid are our perceptions of this
planet and beyond when most or all of our knowledge has been
gained through electronic images on a small screen in our
living rooms?

Clearly, there are accepted conventions in television enter- 3
tainment. A majority of viewers probably guessed that *The
Mary Tyler Moore Show* was not actually being broadcast from
Minneapolis, despite those lovely pictures of Mary bubbling
her way through the streets of that city. Most episodes of *Kojak*,
starring Telly Savalas as the ultimate in New York detectives,

used stock exterior footage filmed in the city to dress up scenes performed in the studios of Burbank. The inevitable distortions, however subtle, are real.

In television news, the problem of defining reality becomes 4 crucial. The textbook illustration of potential manipulation is the small protest demonstration staged for the six o'clock news. Bring the cameras in close, and the viewer gets the impression that the city is going berserk. Pull back for a long shot, and it becomes evident that this is a noisy but isolated incident surrounded by quite ordinary calm. On the level of national network news, a world panorama is whipped up in the space of a half-hour (or, minus commercials, about twenty-two minutes). As a result, the tendency is to resort to visual shorthand. With a Washington story, the reporter stands in front of the White House. The favorite British backdrop is Parliament. Information is reduced to the level of picture postcards.

Needless to say, the electronic image cannot compete with 5 the real thing. The experience of an expresso bar in Rome or a bread shop in Paris demands the senses of taste and smell for delicious fulfillment. But television can be extraordinarily satisfying: the proper formula seems to consist of time, talent and imagination.

The British appear to have a special knack of evoking 6 authenticity. On-location shooting has been used to marvelous advantage in such lofty series as Kenneth Clark's *Civilization* or Alistair Cooke's *America. The Mayor of Casterbridge* was filmed beautifully in and around Dorset, the heart of Thomas Hardy country. *Poldark* captured some of the special beauty of Cornwall. Compare these with the American production of Irwin Shaw's *Evening in Byzantium,* in which shots of the French Riviera could have been taken on any snazzy stretch of beachfront.

Public television's *World* documentary series has at least 7 two exquisite essays to its credit. *Bogotá: One Day* offered a detailed tour of the capital of Colombia, wandering from the wealth of suburbs to the poverty of the inner city. And in a portrait of an elderly uncle, the writer Ved Mehta distilled the unique social, economic and political aspects of life in India.[1]

---

[1] Ved Mehta (b. 1934 in Lahore, India): author of *Portrait of India* (1970) and many other works.

Perhaps, production intentions count for everything. A re- 8
cent, valuable NBC documentary on China explained new developments in education. Visual content, however, was limited
largely to closeups of faces. China as a place remained curiously
hazy. Yet, several years ago, when China was considerably less
open, Italy's Michelangelo Antonioni compiled, with almost
no narration, a startingly vivid portrait.[2]

The question of image and reality is hardly new. Robert 9
Flaherty's *Man of Aran,* made in the early Thirties, is considered one of the best "documentaries" ever made. Yet, when
George Stoney, an NYU professor, recently returned to the islands off the coast of Ireland, he found many of the residents
still insisting that Flaherty had, quite intentionally, distorted
both the land and their lives. The documentary, it seems, was
really more of a poetic statement, a personal vision.

And so television scatters before us everything from the 10
cliché of enormous waves in Hawaii to the absorbing contemporary reconstruction of a Medieval pilgrimage in Spain. The
message is clear: let the viewer beware—and, not infrequently,
enjoy.

Vocabulary

borough (1), premise (2), valid (2), inevitable (3), distortions (3),
subtle (3), crucial (4), potential (4), manipulation (4), berserk (4),
authenticity (6), documentary (7), exquisite (7), cliché (10)

Questions

1. Dicuss the introduction.
2. Where was "Kojak" filmed?
3. What is implied by the title?
4. When does the problem of defining reality become crucial?
5. Who seems to have a special knack for "evoking authenticity"?
6. What does the intention of the program have to do with the issue
   of accuracy?
7. What does O'Connor mean by "let the viewer beware" in the
   conclusion?

---

[2] Antonioni (b. 1912): Italian film director.

8. Why does he include so many specific references to specific programs?
9. What is the purpose of the reference to the film done by Robert Flaherty?
10. Were you convinced by this essay? If so, what points did you find most effective? If you were not convinced, explain why.

Suggestions for Writing

1. This essay can be carried still further — into an analysis of other types of television programs and their relationship to the "real" world. How valid a picture do television programs — police, detective, soap opera, western, sports, talk, hospital, children's or even news — present? You might focus on a single program and discuss its validity (or possibly you could compare two programs of the same type, two doctor shows, for example.) Try to make subtle distinctions as O'Connor does, pointing out detailed strengths or weaknesses or both in the television program that you are evaluating.
2. In a recent article in *The Christian Science Monitor,* John Gould suggests that media — TV, radio, print — sometimes favor certain political candidates and subtly adapt their reports to reflect this favoritism. Do you see any evidence for this kind of slanted reporting (about any subjects, not just candidates)?

H. ALLEN SMITH

It Must Be War on a Dudelsack with the Hi-Fi

H. Allen Smith (1907–76), American humorist, news-man, editor, and essayist, frequently wrote about the lighter side of his many subjects. His books include People Named Smith *(1950), and* The Compleat Practical Joker *(1953). In this piece, Smith reveals strong feelings about his subject, the bagpipe. Notice the tone, however, and the use of background information to add interest to his personal prejudice.*

Long ago when the Lower Cambrian fossils were young and lively, I, Smith of Illinois, arrived at a judgment concerning the most hideous noise ever contrived by the human race. It was not the yelping of a female yodeler, nor yet the screech of chalk against a blackboard. It was the sound of a bagpipe. 1

We had there in Illinois a neighbor who laid claim to Scottish blood strains and who had a Highland bagpipe. He played only one selection on it, a tender folk ballad titled *The Sow Got the Measles and Died in the Spring*. He played it every day of his life; worse, he sang along with it. We tried to get him arrested and, failing that, formed up a conspiracy to kill him. He got wind of this and fled to the town of Mattoon. Even today I slit his throat in my dreams. 2

Let it be understood, the prejudice is not against the Scots. They did not invent the bagpipe. That crime was probably perpetrated in the Near East. There is evidence that the first of these instruments, once known as The Cow's Complaint, appeared on Earth in the Sumerian Plain and spread westward 3 to Turkey and Greece and then all of Europe. History first mentions the bagpipe as playing for the Roman legions, and some historians suggest that Nero played it—not the fiddle— while Rome burned.

As a lay musicologist I have a theory that the bagpipe scourge started in China and was brought home to Italy by Marco Polo,[1] who also may have brought back spaghetti flour, which was used for thousands of years in Asia. In Italy to this day the bagpipe is called a *cornamusa,* as it should be. In Germany it is a *Dudelsack* and the man who plays upon it is a *Dudelsackpfeifer.* That is a fine title, but I still think he should be fed from a bowl outside the kitchen door.

My musician friend Will Fowler, asked to name the most important feature of the bagpipe, responded: "It is the only instrument that can get out of tune in four different directions at the same time."

He had in mind that gaggle of pipes appended to the greased leathern bag. Pipers call the blowpipe the insufflation tube; they sufflate air through it to an underarm reservoir bag which is kept under a squeezing pressure. There is a big tube called a chanter, which is the melody pipe, as rueful a misnomer as was ever bestowed. The chanter has six or seven holes so that the piper can render those compositions said to be most suited to bagpipe treatment, such as reels, laments, barcaroles, pibrochs, strathspeys, and country and western. All of these sound, to my ear, like *The Sow Got the Measles and Died in the Spring.*

Among the Scots and the Irish the bagpipe has long been a military weapon, employed against heavily armored English men-at-arms in the same way that the Confederates used the rebel yell presumably to paralyze the Yankees. And there is the lore that at Kimlochmoidart (either a town or a Grampian hiring-hall for shepherds) there is preserved a bagpipe which was played at the battle of Bannockburn.[2] Caledonian poppycock. The bonny lads under Robert the Bruce insufflated into no bags that famous day—they drove off the English by beating on haggis pots and howling verses writ by Thomas of Ercel-

---

[1] Marco Polo (1254?–1324?): Venetian traveler and adventurer.

[2] Site of the 1314 defeat of the English King, Edward II, by Robert Bruce, a Scottish national hero who had become king in 1306.

doune.[3] They wore no kilt, either. As a matter of fact they were apt to attack with nothing on at all below the waist.

Why this sudden concern over bagpipes in the Era of the 8 Amplified Guitar? Just recently I witnessed a telecast from a town in upstate New York where some people have established a school for teaching the bagpipe. The man said they couldn't begin to cope with the pile of applications coming in. He said the electronic *Dudelsack* might be upon us soon.

I take oath. If those Nashville folks discard their git-fiddles 9 and embrace the hi-fi *Dudelsack,* I shall study the Inquisition techniques of Torquemada.[4] If my war on the *Dudelsack* should fail, I intend to contract the measles and die in the spring.

Vocabulary

perpetrated (3), musicologist (4), insufflation (6), rueful (6), misnomer (6), bestowed (6), barcaroles (6), pibrochs (6), strathspeys (6), lore (7), poppycock (7), haggis (7)

Questions

1. Why does Smith call the bagpipe a "dudelsack" in the title?
2. What is the reference in the last line?
3. What is the purpose of paragraph 2?
4. Why does he refer to historical figures — some obscure?
5. What do you think of Smith's interpretation of history?
6. Notice the hyperbole (deliberate use of exaggeration) in this essay. Choose two examples and discuss their effect. Why does he exaggerate?
7. Why does Smith delay the more detailed description of the bagpipes?
8. What is "country and western" doing in the list in paragraph 6?

Suggestions for Writing

1. Write an essay on the musical instrument you like least (or most). Like Smith, do some research on its background, but be sure

---

[3] Thirteenth-century Scottish poet.

[4] Torquemada (1421?–98): Spanish Dominican monk, known for cruelty, eventually became Grand Inquisitor under Innocent VIII.

to make your reaction to the sound of the instrument the focus of the essay. Try to persuade the reader of how strong your feeling is.

2. Write an essay on something in your life that you would like to see outlawed, or at least absent from your life — a television, a car, a hair dryer, mathematics tests, a day of the week, for example. Why would you be better off without it? Keep Smith's tone in mind and do some research on the origins and history of your subject, if it will add to the reader's interest.

3. Which sound stirs a strong reaction in you? The German philosopher, Schopenhauer (1788–1860) said, "The most inexcusable and disgraceful of all noises is the cracking of whips — a truly infernal thing when it is done in the narrow resounding streets of a town." What is the sound you like least, what is your reaction to it, and what do you think are the reasons for your disliking it?

J. FRANK DOBIE

My Horse Buck

*J. Frank Dobie (1888–1964), born in Texas and edu-
cated there, has been a high school teacher, a professor of
English at the University of Texas, head of the English
Department at Oklahoma A and M and a visiting professor of American Literature at Cambridge University. In
spite of his career in education, he once commented, "The
land on which I was reared and the brush growing on the
land taught me more than school teachers have ever
taught." His books are often about Texas and the Southwest—*Mustangs *(1952), and* Guide to Life and Literature
in the Southwest *(1952), for example. He has contributed
essays to* Atlantic Monthly, Harper's, Saturday Evening
Post, Holiday, *and* Yale Review. *"My Horse Buck" is a
personal reminiscence on a favorite animal; it might
easily be described as a "character sketch," in this case,
the character of a horse. Notice that Dobie focuses on the
distinctive characteristics, good and bad, that made this
horse different from all others. Also notice how heavily
this essay relies on narrative and on detailed description.*

All the old-time range men of validity whom I have known 1
remember horses with affection and respect as a part of the
best of themselves. After their knees have begun to stiffen, most
men realize that they have been disappointed in themselves, in
other men, in achievement, in love, in most of whatever they expected out of life; but a man who has had a good horse in his
life—a horse beyond the play world—will remember him as a
certitude, like a calm mother, a lovely lake, or a gracious tree,
amid all the flickering vanishments.

I remember Buck. He was raised on our ranch and was about   2
half Spanish. He was a bright bay with a blaze in his face and
stockings on his forefeet. He could hardly have weighed when
fat over 850 pounds and was about 14 hands high. A Mexican
broke him when he was three years old. From then on, nobody
but me rode him, even after I left for college. He had a fine
barrel and chest and was very fast for short distances but did
not have the endurance of some other horses, straight Spaniards, in our remuda.[1] What he lacked in toughness, he made up
in intelligence, especially cow sense, loyalty, understanding,
and generosity.

As a colt he had been bitten by a rattlesnake on the right   3
ankle just above the hoof; a hard, hairless scab marked the
place as long as he lived. He traveled through the world listening for the warning rattle. A kind of weed in the Southwest
bears seeds that when ripe rattle in their pods a good deal like
the sound made by a rattlesnake. Many a time when my spur
or stirrup set these seeds a-rattling, Buck's suddenness in jumping all but left me seated in the air. I don't recall his smelling
rattlesnakes, but he could smell afar off the rotten flesh of a
yearling or any other cow brute afflicted with screwworms. He
understood that I was hunting these animals in order to drive
them to a pen and doctor them. In hot weather they take refuge
in high weeds and thick brush. When he smelled one, he would
point to it with his ears and turn towards it. A dog trained for
hunting out wormy cases could not have been more helpful.

Once a sullen cow that had been roped raked him in the   4
breast with the tip of a horn. After that experience, he was
wariness personified around anything roped, but he never, like
some horses that have been hooked, shied away from an animal
he was after. He knew and loved his business too well for that.
He did not love it when, at the rate of less than a mile an hour,
he was driving the thirsty, hot, tired, slobbering drag end of a
herd, animals stopping behind every bush or without any bush,
turning aside the moment they were free of a driver. When
sufficiently exasperated, Buck would go for a halting cow with
mouth open and grab her just forward of the tail bone if she
did not move on. Work like this may be humiliating to a gal-

---

[1] Remuda: relay of horses, spares.

lant young cowboy and an eager cow horse; it is never pictured
as a part of the romance of the range, but it is very necessary.
It helps a cowboy to graduate into a cowman. A too highstrung horse without cow sense, which includes cow patience,
will go to pieces at it just as he will go to pieces in running
or cutting cattle.

Buck had the rein to make the proverbial "turn on a two-   5
bit piece and give back fifteen cents in change." One hot summer while we were gathering steers on leased grass about
twelve miles from home, I galled his side with a tight cinch. I
hated to keep on riding him with the galled side, but was
obliged to on account of a shortage of horses. As I saddled up in
camp one day after dinner, I left the cinch so loose that a hand
might have been laid between it and Buck's belly. We had to
ride about a mile before going through a wire gap into the
pasture where some snaky steers ran. As we rode along, a
vaquero [2] called my attention to the loose cinch.

"I will tighten it when we get to the gap," I said.   6

"*Cuidado* (have care) and don't forget," he said.   7

At the gap, which he got down to open, I saw him look at   8
me. I decided to wait until we struck something before tight-
ening the girth. Two minutes later my father yelled and we saw
a little bunch of steers high-tailing it through scattered mesquites for a thicket along a creek beyond. I forgot all about the
cinch. Buck was easily the fastest horse ridden by the four or
five men in our "cow crowd." He left like a cry of joy to get
around the steers.

As we headed them, they turned to the left at an acute angle,   9
and Buck turned at an angle considerably more acute. Sometimes he turned so quickly that the *tapadera* (toe-fender) of my
stirrup raked the ground on the inside of the turn. This time
when he doubled back, running full speed, the loose saddle
naturally turned on him. As my left hip hit the ground, I saw
stars. One foot was still in a stirrup and the saddle was under
Buck's belly. I suppose that I instinctively pulled on the reins,
but I believe that Buck would have stopped had he not been
bridled. His stop was instantaneous; he did not drag me on the
ground at all. He had provocation to go on, too, for in coming

---

[2] Vaquero: cowboy.

over his side and back, the spur on my right foot had raked
him. He never needed spurs. I wore them on him just to be in
fashion.

Sometimes in running through brush, Buck seemed to read   10
my mind—or maybe I was reading his. He was better in the
brush than I was. In brush work, man and horse must dodge,
turn, go over bushes and under limbs, absolutely in accord,
rider yielding to the instinct and judgment of the horse as
much as horse yields to his.

Buck did not have to be staked. If I left a dragrope on him,   11
he would stay close to camp, at noon or through the night. He
was no paragon. Many men have ridden and remembered
hardier horses. He was not proud, but carried himself in a very
trim manner. He did the best he could, willingly and gen-
erously, and he had a good heart. His chemistry mixed with
mine. He was good company. I loved to hear him drink water,
he was so hearty in swallowing, and then, after he was full, to
watch him lip the water's surface and drip big drops back into
it.

Sometimes after we had watered and, passing on, had come   12
to good grass near shade, I'd unsaddle and turn him loose to
graze. Then I'd lie down on the saddle and, while the blanket
dried, listen to his energetic cropping and watch the buzzards
sail and the Gulf clouds float. Buck would blow out his breath
once in a while, presumably to clear his nostrils but also, it
seemed to me, to express contentment.

He never asked me to stop, unless it was to stale, and never,   13
like some gentle saddle horses, interrupted his step to grab a
mouthful of grass; but if I stopped with slackened rein to
watch cattle, or maybe just to gaze over the flow of hills to the
horizon, he'd reach down and begin cutting grass. He knew
that was all right with me, though a person's seat on a grazing
horse is not nearly so comfortable as on one with upright head.
Occasionally I washed the sweat off his back and favored him
in other ways, but nobody in our part of the country pampered
cow horses with sugar or other delicacy.

While riding Buck in boyhood and early youth, I fell in love   14
with four or five girls but told only one. She was right in considering the matter a joke and thereby did me one of the biggest favors of my life. All those rose-lipped maidens and all

the light-foot lads [3] with whom I ran in those days have little meaning for me now. They never had much in comparison with numerous people I have known since. Buck, however, always in association with the plot of earth over which I rode him, increases in meaning. To remember him is a joy and a tonic.

Vocabulary

validity (1), certitude (1), vanishments (1), refuge (3), exasperated (4), galled (5), cinch (5), mesquites (8), instantaneous (9), provocation (9), paragon (11), cropping (12), stale (13)

Questions

1. What is the purpose of this essay (the larger and smaller purpose)?
2. What is the tone? Where does the evidence seem the strongest?
3. Do you get a sense of "local color"? Where?
4. Notice the sentences in paragraph 4. Discuss their type and length.
5. What does the proverb in paragraph 5 contribute to the essay?
6. Why does Dobie use so many Spanish vocabulary words?
7. What is the purpose of paragraphs 5–9?
8. Why are paragraphs 11 and 12 included?
9. Discuss the conclusion. Rewrite it, attempting to destroy Dobie's effect.
10. Which passage in the essay do you like best? Why?
11. Is the essay sentimental?

Suggestions for Writing

1. Write an essay on either a person or an animal you can remember "as a certitude . . . amid all the flickering vanishments." Attempt to make the characteristic traits the subjects of each paragraph and, like Dobie, bring them to life with carefully selected, distinguishing detail. (If appropriate, include a narrative passage. Re-

---

[3] From a poem beginning "With rue my heart is laden," by the English poet A. E. Housman (1859–1936), he laments the passing away of the maidens and the lads.

member, however, that you are writing an essay, not a short story. Make the narrative *part* of your essay, not the dominant element.)

2. When Dobie used to write at his typewriter, he used to leave his hat on his head and read aloud, "tinkering" with sentences until "they [sang] like a fiddle." Do you have a ritual for writing? a special location, a series of steps, or specific requirements for comfort, before you can write?

3. Compare the sketch of Dobie's horse to Lawrence Durrell's characterization of "Smartie." What do they have in common? What are the major differences? Consider structure and method as well as subject.

CHARLES DARWIN

The Conclusion to
The Voyage of the Beagle

*Charles Darwin (1809–82) is the most famous name in
modern biology. He is primarily known as the exponent of
natural selection and evolution.* His Origin of Species
*(1859) shocked the Victorians and changed our picture of
nature and ourselves. Darwin was also a powerful writer,
writing detailed scientific treatises as well as popular general explications of his work. His works include* The Descent of Man *(1874) and* The Voyage of the Beagle *(1845).
The last is an account of his almost five-year voyage
around the world as the naturalist for HMS* Beagle *(1832–
37). The concluding paragraphs are excerpted here and
form an essay on the value of travel.*

Our Voyage having come to an end, I will take a short retro- 1
spect of the advantages and disadvantages, the pains and pleasures, of our circumnavigation of the world. If a person asked
my advice, before undertaking a long voyage, my answer would
depend upon his possessing a decided taste for some branch of
knowledge, which could by this means be advanced. No doubt
it is a high satisfaction to behold various countries and the many
races of mankind, but the pleasures gained at the time do not
counterbalance the evils. It is necessary to look forward to a
harvest, however distant that may be, when some fruit will be
reaped, some good effected.

Many of the losses which must be experienced are obvious; 2
such as that of the society of every old friend, and of the sight
of those places with which every dearest remembrance is so
intimately connected. These losses, however, are at the time
partly relieved by the exhaustless delight of anticipating the
long wished-for day of return. If, as poets say, life is a dream,

I am sure in a voyage these are the visions which best serve to pass away the long night. Other losses, although not at first felt, tell heavily after a period: these are the want of room, of seclusion, of rest; the jading feeling of constant hurry; the privation of small luxuries, the loss of domestic society, and even of music and the other pleasures of imagination. When such trifles are mentioned, it is evident that the real grievances, excepting from accidents, of a sea-life are at an end. The short space of sixty years has made an astonishing difference in the facility of distant navigation. Even in the time of Cook,[1] a man who left his fireside for such expeditions underwent severe privations. A yacht now, with every luxury of life, can circumnavigate the globe. Besides the vast improvements in ships and naval resources, the whole western shores of America are thrown open, and Australia has become the capital of a rising continent. How different are the circumstances to a man shipwrecked at the present day in the Pacific, to what they were in the time of Cook! Since his voyage a hemisphere has been added to the civilized world.

If a person suffer much from sea-sickness, let him weigh it [3] heavily in the balance. I speak from experience: it is no trifling evil, cured in a week. If, on the other hand, he take pleasure in naval tactics, he will assuredly have full scope for his taste. But it must be borne in mind, how large a proportion of the time, during a long voyage, is spent on the water, as compared with the days in harbour. And what are the boasted glories of the illimitable ocean? A tedious waste, a desert of water, as the Arabian calls it. No doubt there are some delightful scenes. A moonlight night, with the clear heavens and the dark glittering sea, and the white sails filled by the soft air of a gently-blowing trade-wind; a dead calm, with the heaving surface polished like a mirror, and all still except the occasional flapping of the canvas. It is well once to behold a squall with its rising arch and coming fury, or the heavy gale of wind and mountainous waves. I confess, however, my imagination had painted something more grand, more terrific in the full-grown storm. It is an incomparably finer spectacle when beheld on shore, where the waving trees, the wild flight of the birds, the dark

---

[1] James Cook (1728–79): celebrated English navigator, killed in Hawaii.

shadows and bright lights, the rushing of the torrents, all proclaim the strife of the unloosed elements. At sea the albatross
and little petrel fly as if the storm were their proper sphere,
the water rises and sinks as if fulfilling its usual task, the ship
alone and its inhabitants seem the objects of wrath. On a forlorn and weather-beaten coast, the scene is indeed different, but
the feelings partake more of horror than of wild delight.

Let us now look at the brighter side of the past time. The 4
pleasure derived from beholding the scenery and the general
aspect of the various countries we have visited, has decidedly
been the most constant and highest source of enjoyment. It is
probable that the picturesque beauty of many parts of Europe
exceeds anything which we beheld. But there is a growing
pleasure in comparing the character of the scenery in different
countries, which to a certain degree is distinct from merely
admiring its beauty. It depends chiefly on an acquaintance with
the individual parts of each view: I am strongly induced to
believe that, as in music, the person who understands every
note will, if he also possesses a proper taste, more thoroughly
enjoy the whole, so he who examines each part of a fine view,
may also thoroughly comprehend the full and combined effect.
Hence, a traveller should be a botanist, for in all views plants
form the chief embellishment. Group masses of naked rock
even in the wildest forms, and they may for a time afford a
sublime spectacle, but they will soon grow monotonous. Paint
them with bright and varied colours, as in Northern Chile, they
will become fantastic; clothe them with vegetation, they must
form a decent, if not a beautiful picture.

When I say that the scenery of parts of Europe is probably 5
superior to anything which we beheld, I except, as a class by
itself, that of the intertropical zones. The two classes cannot be
compared together; but I have already often enlarged on the
grandeur of those regions. As the force of impressions generally depends on preconceived ideas, I may add, that mine were
taken from the vivid descriptions in the Personal Narrative of
Humboldt,[2] which far exceed in merit anything else which I
have read. Yet with these high-wrought ideas, my feelings were

---

[2] Friedrich Alexander von Humboldt (1769–1859): scientist and travel
writer.

far from partaking of a tinge of disappointment on my first and final landing on the shores of Brazil.

Among the scenes which are deeply impressed on my mind, 6 none exceed in sublimity the primeval forests undefaced by the hand of man; whether those of Brazil, where the powers of Life are predominant, or those of Tierra del Fuego, [3] where Death and Decay prevail. Both are temples filled with the varied productions of the God of Nature:—no one can stand in these solitudes unmoved, and not feel that there is more in man than the mere breath of his body. In calling up images of the past, I find that the plains of Patagonia [4] frequently cross before my eyes; yet these plains are pronounced by all wretched and useless. They can be described only by negative characters; without habitations, without water, without trees, without mountains, they support merely a few dwarf plants. Why then, and the case is not peculiar to myself, have these arid wastes taken so firm a hold on my memory? Why have not the still more level, the greener and more fertile Pampas, which are serviceable to mankind, produced an equal impression? I can scarcely analyze these feelings: but it must be partly owing to the free scope given to the imagination. The plains of Patagonia are boundless, for they are scarcely passable, and hence unknown: they bear the stamp of having lasted, as they are now, for ages, and there appears no limit to their duration through future time. If, as the ancients supposed, the flat earth was surrounded by an impassable breadth of water, or by deserts heated to an intolerable excess, who would not look at these last boundaries to man's knowledge with deep but ill-defined sensations?

Lastly, of natural scenery, the views from lofty mountains, 7 though certainly in one sense not beautiful, are very memorable. When looking down from the highest crest of the Cordillera, [5] the mind, undisturbed by minute details, was filled with the stupendous dimensions of the surrounding masses.

Of individual objects, perhaps nothing is more certain to create astonishment than the first sight in his native haunt of a 8

---

[3] Tierra del Fuego: island at the top of South America.
[4] Patagonia: area of southern Chile and Argentina.
[5] Cordillera: the Andes.

barbarian,—of man in his lowest and most savage state. One's mind hurries back over past centuries, and then asks, could our progenitors have been men like these?—men, whose very signs and expressions are less intelligible to us than those of the domesticated animals; men, who do not possess the instinct of those animals, nor yet appear to boast of human reason, or at least of arts consequent on that reason. I do not believe it is possible to describe or paint the difference between savage and civilized man. It is the difference between a wild and tame animal: and part of the interest in beholding a savage, is the same which would lead every one to desire to see the lion in his desert, the tiger tearing his prey in the jungle, or the rhinoceros wandering over the wild plains of Africa.

Among the other most remarkable spectacles which we have 9 beheld, may be ranked the Southern Cross, the cloud of Magellan, and the other constellations of the southern hemisphere— the water-spout—the glacier leading its blue stream of ice, over-hanging the sea in a bold precipice—a lagoon-island raised by the reef-building corals—an active volcano—and the over-whelming effects of a violent earthquake. These latter phenomena, perhaps, possess for me a peculiar interest, from their intimate connexion with the geological structure of the world. The earthquake, however, must be to every one a most impressive event: the earth, considered from our earliest childhood as the type of solidity, has oscillated like a thin crust beneath our feet; and in seeing the laboured works of man in a moment overthrown, we feel the insignificance of his boasted power.

It has been said, that the love of the chase is an inherent 10 delight in man—a relic of an instinctive passion. If so, I am sure the pleasure of living in the open air, with the sky for a roof and the ground for a table, is part of the same feeling; it is the savage returning to his wild and native habits. I always look back to our boat cruises, and my land journeys, when through unfrequented countries, with an extreme delight, which no scenes of civilization could have created. I do not doubt that every traveller must remember the glowing sense of happiness which he experienced, when he first breathed in a foreign clime, where the civilized man had seldom or never trod.

There are several other sources of enjoyment in a long voy- 11

age, which are of a more reasonable nature. The map of the
world ceases to be a blank; it becomes a picture full of the
most varied and animated figures. Each part assumes its proper
dimensions: continents are not looked at in the light of islands,
or islands considered as mere specks, which are, in truth, larger
than many kingdoms of Europe. Africa, or North and South
America, are well-sounding names, and easily pronounced; but
it is not until having sailed for weeks along small portions of
their shores, that one is thoroughly convinced what vast spaces
on our immense world these names imply.

From seeing the present state, it is impossible not to look   12
forward with high expectations to the future progress of nearly
an entire hemisphere. The march of improvement, consequent
on the introduction of Christianity throughout the South Sea,
probably stands by itself in the records of history. It is the more
striking when we remember that only sixty years since, Cook,
whose excellent judgment none will dispute, could foresee no
prospect of a change. Yet these changes have now been effected by the philanthropic spirit of the British nation.

In the same quarter of the globe Australia is rising, or in-   13
deed may be said to have risen, into a grand centre of civilization, which, at some not very remote period, will rule as empress over the southern hemisphere. It is impossible for an
Englishman to behold these distant colonies, with a high
pride and satisfaction. To hoist the British flag, seems to draw
with it as a certain consequence, wealth, prosperity, and civilization.

In conclusion, it appears to me that nothing can be more   14
improving to a young naturalist, than a journey in distant
countries. It both sharpens, and partly allays that want and
craving, which, as Sir J. Herschel [6] remarks, a man experiences
although every corporeal sense be fully satisfied. The excitement from the novelty of objects, and the chance of success,
stimulate him to increased activity. Moreover, as a number of
isolated facts soon become uninteresting, the habit of comparison leads to generalization. On the other hand, as the
traveller stays but a short time in each place, his descriptions

---

[6] Herschel (1792–1871): astronomer and physicist, was the son of Sir
William Herschel, the astronomer.

must generally consist of mere sketches, instead of detailed observations. Hence arises, as I have found to my cost, a constant tendency to fill up the wide gaps of knowledge, by inaccurate and superficial hypotheses.

But I have too deeply enjoyed the voyage, not to recom- 15 mend any naturalist, although he must not expect to be so fortunate in his companions as I have been, to take all chances, and to start, on travels by land if possible, if otherwise on a long voyage. He may feel assured, he will meet with no difficulties or dangers, excepting in rare cases, nearly so bad as he beforehand anticipates. In a moral point of view, the effect ought to be, to teach him good-humoured patience, freedom from selfishness, the habit of acting for himself, and of making the best of every occurrence. In short, he ought to partake of the characteristic qualities of most sailors. Travelling ought also to teach him distrust; but at the same time he will discover, how many truly kind-hearted people there are, with whom he never before had, or ever again will have any further communication, who yet are ready to offer him the most disinterested assistance.

Vocabulary

circumnavigation (1), effected (1), privations (2), illimitable (3), albatross (3), petrel (3), forlorn (3), embellishment (4), sublime (4), spectacle (4), primeval (6), habitations (6), duration (6), progenitors (8), intelligible (8), consequent (8), hemisphere (9), oscillated (8), inherent (10), clime (10), philanthropic (13), corporeal (14), hypotheses (14), disinterested (15)

Questions

1. What is Darwin's purpose in writing this section of his book?
2. For what audience is it written?
3. How does he allow himself to be influenced by the broader pattern of nature?
4. What is the purpose of paragraph 3?
5. How does he relate his scientific knowledge to the enjoyment of travel?

6. What does Darwin think about the civilized man and the savage?
7. What do you think of Darwin's nationalism?
8. Why does he mention "distrust" so late in his essay?
9. What character traits of Darwin emerge from the passage?
10. What special characteristics make his writing strong?

Suggestions for Writing

1. Write an essay trying to convince a stubborn friend to take a trip with you. Include in your essay both the vices and the virtues of travel.
2. Write an essay on the value of never leaving your hometown.

CASKIE STINNETT

One-Day Castaway

*Caskie Stinnett, born in Virginia in 1911, graduated
from William and Mary College, was hired by Curtis Publishing Company, in 1946.* He has written for The Saturday Evening Post *and has been editor-in-chief of* Holiday
and Travel and Leisure; *now he is a regular contributor
to* Atlantic Monthly. *When he is not traveling, he writes
on his own island off the coast of Maine. When asked how
he set his writing standards, Stinnett replied, "I went to
the great novelists for their standards and patterns and got
so accustomed to them that when I did a book myself I
had excruciating standards that I'd imposed on myself."
Among his books are* Will Not Run February 22nd *(1954),*
Back to Abnormal *(1963), and* Grand and Private Pleasures *(1966), from which this essay is taken. Here Stinnett
describes the fulfillment of a dream—to go alone to a
desert island. Notice that the awareness of the dream is always part of the action and that the time sequence is ad-
justed to concentrate on the important events and to
compress others.*

Cherished dreams die lingering deaths: the fantasy of an un- 1
inhabited South Pacific island has always haunted me. In my
mind's eye I could see myself walking a deserted beach at sundown searching for driftwood and coconuts or netting fish in a
blue lagoon or whiling away the hot, languid hours by pad-
dling about naked in the freshwater pool under the waterfall.

In French Polynesia, I asked a friend who worked for the 2
government if he could arrange to have me put ashore for a

day on an uninhabited island near Bora-Bora. "You will go
crazy if you aren't already," he replied. "Make it a couple of
hours instead." I insisted. It must be a full day. I wanted an
island with shade, some coconut palms, a beach, and if possible,
fresh water. I wanted to wade ashore at first light in the morning, and I wanted to be picked up at sundown. For twelve
hours I wanted to be forgotten, a castaway. He shook his head
in bewilderment and went away, saying he would inquire
around and find out what would be the best island for the adventure.

Later that evening he came to my hotel at Bora-Bora. I was   3
on the verandah drinking a gin and tonic. "I've found an island
for you," he said, "but it doesn't have fresh water. At least
no one knows whether it has fresh water or not. No one has
been very far inland and I doubt if you will go either because
there are wild pigs there. But if there are pigs, there must be
drinking water. However, don't be foolish. Take food and
water." He clapped his hands for service and pointed toward
my drink and said something in Polynesian. In a moment he
was raising his glass to me. "Good luck," he said. "I wouldn't
spend a whole day on that island alone for a full week's salary."
I asked him the name of the island. "It doesn't have a name
that I know of," he said. "Who wants to name a clump of
coconut palms?"

I got up at four o'clock the next morning. It was still dark   4
as I walked along the gravel walk from my bungalow to the
main hotel building. The jasmine was still open and the early
morning air was filled with the scent of the blossoms. The
aroma of jasmine travels in tantalizing waves; one smells it one
moment, and in the next it is gone. I went into the kitchen and
found a boy sweeping the floor. He pointed to my food and
water basket—a pathetically small package, it struck me at the
time—and set about to prepare a cup of coffee. I ate a banana,
drank the coffee, and carrying the basket, I went out on the
porch to await the car that was to take me to the dock. The
driver was punctual. He told me in French that he would pick
me up that night at the dock about eight o'clock. The dawn began to break as we drove along the coast road to Vaitape, the
village where I was to take the boat. It was cool, but I knew
enough about the islands to know that in a couple of hours it

would be hot. We drove past the tiny, white church, and through the village's single street. At the dock we both got out of the car and he carried my basket to the boat, which was bobbing in the gentle swell. The boatman smiled and said something in Polynesian, which I assume was a greeting. I said, "Bon jour," and jumped into the boat. The driver handed me the basket and untied the line. The boatman started the motor, and in a few minutes the village and Pofai Bay were falling behind us. We had been going about forty-five minutes when the boatman said something and pointed ahead. There seemed to be a half-dozen islands on the horizon and I couldn't tell which one he was pointing to. When I pointed at one, he shook his head vigorously and began to flap his arms like wings. I gathered that was a bird sanctuary. As I pointed to the various islands he flapped at them all except one. That was my island.

He came in as close as he could without going aground, then 5 jumped into water about waist-deep and steadied the boat for me. I took off my wristwatch and put it in a shirt pocket and buttoned the flap. Then I jumped into the water, and reached under the seat and retrieved my basket. The water was cool but not unpleasantly so. The boatman smiled and said, *"A sept heures."* I said, *"D'accord,"* [1] and turned and started wading toward land.

My first disappointment was that I had been put ashore 6 not on a beach but on a coral strand. Since I had kept on my shoes, I was able to walk on the coral but it was uneven and I had to walk with caution. Land, when I reached it, was also coral, which is beautiful underwater but about as exciting and inert as lava when exposed. When I looked back at the boat, it was rapidly becoming a small object on the horizon. I was alone.

I don't know what I had imagined I would do first if I were 7 ever put ashore on a deserted island, but I'm sure I didn't do it. What I actually did was place the basket of food and water in the shade of some pandanus plants, and then I came back to the open space by the water's edge, removed my trousers, wrung the seawater from them, and placed them on the coral

---

[1] "At seven o'clock"; "Agreed."

rocks to dry. I couldn't tell if the tide was rising or falling, and while it probably didn't matter much, I decided it was the sort of thing a man should know. I placed a stone that I would recognize at the point where the last wave had touched, and I figured to use that to determine tidal action. Then I took out my watch and strapped it to my wrist. It was 6:40.

About two hundred feet from where I had waded ashore, 8 the coral rose to a high promontory and I decided to start my exploration there. I climbed carefully to the top of the ledge, and looked around. Only a narrow strait, about the length of a football field, separated me from the nearest island, which I assumed was one of the bird sanctuaries. A submerged reef seemed to join the two islands together. On the other side of the rock ledge was more coral and no sign of sand. As far as I could see, which was no more than a few hundred feet since the island curved sharply, there was nothing but a forest of coconut palms, coral and the sea. I turned and went back to my arrival point. My government friend had told me there was a sand beach on the island; I decided the best way to find it would be to go inland and come out on the other side.

If the romance of the adventure had not already started to 9 fall apart, it did at that moment. A flock of frigate birds came out of the trees and began dive-bombing me with the most raucous screams I have ever heard from a bird, and when I retreated to cover I saw two enormous land crabs crawling across the top of my food basket, searching for an entry point. The crabs scampered back into their holes when I struck at them with a stick, but from the way the ground was pocked with holes I knew there were others that were awaiting their chance. Obviously, wherever I went I would have to carry the basket with me. The birds flew in a tight circle over my head, ready to resume their attack when I came out in the open again. I moved the basket as far from the crab holes as I could get, and sat on a fallen palm log. I was off to a bad start.

It was obvious that I was too close to the birds' nesting area, 10 so I made a quick run into the open to get my trousers, then picked up the basket, and started moving cautiously through the underbrush around the edge of the coral. I felt foolish being frightened by a flock of birds, but their initial bombing run had seemed completely businesslike and I didn't care to see what they had in mind for me if I reappeared in the open. The growth was much denser than I had imagined it would be, and there were crabholes everywhere, including one monstrous one at least six inches in diameter. Moreover, the sun was moving higher in the sky and I was beginning to feel the heat. Where was the freshwater pool and the waterfall, the white beach, the blue lagoon, the trade winds?

It took a half-hour or more to get to a point where I could 11 no longer see or hear the birds and, still carrying the basket and my trousers, I stepped out into the open and walked to the water's edge. There was still no sign of sand, but I knew I had covered only a very small part of the island's circumference. Again, I spread my trousers out on the rocks and decided to use them as my guidepost on the island. The boatman would pick me up that night where he had put me ashore, and I needed some point of orientation. Already, everything on the island had begun to look alike.

I realized I was thirsty, and I opened the basket and took out 12 the water bottle. It was smaller than I expected. I removed the cap and took a couple of swallows. I would have to conserve water unless I could open some coconuts and so far the only coconuts I had seen were waterlogged ones floating partly submerged in the surf. It was getting steadily warmer, and I had grown tired of the sharp coral. I wanted to get to a beach where I could swim, and stretch out in the sand. I decided to head inland and get across to the other side.

Stepping into the palm forest was like stepping into a cathe- 13 dral. The sun was suddenly gone, and the air was totally still. The undergrowth—mostly pandanus—was much thicker than I had thought it would be, and the ground was covered with guano and rotting vegetation. My foot sank in this about six inches with every step I took. Sometimes the pandanus grew in such dense clumps that I had to circle them. I had the feeling that everything in that suffocating jungle forest was hostile, and I grew jumpy at mysterious rustlings in the fallen fronds. I wondered if it were possible that the island was big enough for me to get lost on, but I looked back and saw that my tracks were well marked and could guide me back to the sea with no trouble. I discovered very soon that I had made a major mistake in leaving my trousers, as the pandanus fronds were sharp and in places they grew so profusely it was impossible to skirt them. The air was heavy and I began to sweat profusely.

I don't know when it was that I became aware of a noise 14 ahead of me; it was one of those minor sounds that one hears for a while before it penetrates the conscious mind. I stopped in my tracks and listened. It was audible now: things were moving—some distance away—in the forest. Then I heard a high-pitched squeal, followed by more scampering. Of course, the wild pigs. They seemed dead ahead, so I veered slightly toward the left. I doubted that they were dangerous, but I preferred to avoid them if possible. I stopped for another drink from the bottle—it was almost half empty now—and then pushed on. My shirt was soaked with perspiration, and my feet were covered with jungle filth halfway to my knees.

And then suddenly I stepped out of the forest. In front of 15 me was the sea, with gentle rollers coming up on a beach that seemed to slope hardly at all. I was momentarily dazzled by the brilliance of the sun and the water, and then I dropped the basket, unbuttoned my shirt and threw it in the sand, and ran into the water. I swam, I dived, I floated, and once I remember, I stood on my head. It was wonderful, and for at least an hour I gloried in the splendor of it. Then I came out and, naked, flopped in the sand. I think I slept.

The sun was almost directly overhead when the heat drove 16 me back into the shade but not back into the forest. I found a small clump of palms very close to the water's edge, and I settled there. Opening the food basket, I was pleased to find half a roast chicken, a ripe mango, several slices of bread, and a paper napkin. I recoiled slightly at the latter; it seemed incongruous on a desert island. I dug a hole in the sand and buried it. Later I interred the chicken bones and the mango seed beside the napkin; if civilization was coming to the island it would not be in the form of littering.

It was perhaps an hour later that out of the blue came a 17 strange realization: I was bored. I went back into the sea and repeated my water sports, but the original zest was lacking. I gazed at the next island in the chain—it was about a quarter of a mile away—and pondered whether or not I would swim to it if I saw a native girl on the beach there. I decided I would. But like my own island, it showed no sign of life. I got up and decided to walk around the other side of the island as far as I

could, but once away from the beach there was the same lifeless coral that had driven me away from my first landing spot.
I wished I had brought something to read. It was 2:49; almost
five hours to go.

I went back to the shade of the palm trees and slumped 18
down in the sand. Suppose the boatman forgot to come back
for me, or suppose some accident befell him and no one would
know that he had even brought me here. My water was down
to a few swallows; my food was gone. What would I do? I would
stalk a wild pig, I decided, and spear it with a sharp stick,
after tracing it to its watering hole. But my friend in the government knew where I was and when I failed to show up at the
hotel, he would send someone for me. There was no danger.

During the next couple of hours, I tried to climb a palm 19
tree, and failed; I tried to drive an ugly-looking fish into a tiny
pool behind a sandbar, and failed; and I tried to start a fire by
reflecting the sun from my watch crystal. That didn't work
either, but the three efforts brought me to five o'clock. I felt
better, but thirsty; all of my water was gone.

I took one more swim, dried off in the sun, put on my shirt 20
and shoes, and plunged again into the jungle forest. It was easy
to follow my trail, but it was even hotter and more oppressive
than it had been earlier that morning. When I came out of the
forest, I saw my trousers spread out on the coral and they
seemed like an old friend. I put them on; the sun was dropping
low and I could expect my boatman to appear any time. It was
nearly seven o'clock.

The mosquitoes arrived before the boatman; at first just a 21
few and then they began to swarm. I turned up my shirt collar
and sought to protect my head and hands. This wasn't altogether successful, and I was about to wade into the water when
I heard the sound of a motor. It was the boat, still some distance away but it signaled the arrival of a civilization I had
so happily discarded twelve hours earlier. I slapped at the mosquitoes, and waited.

Vocabulary

cherished (1), lagoon (1), languid (1), jasmine (4), tantalizing (4),
pathetically (4), sanctuary (4), pandanus (7), promontory (8),

strait (8), reef (8), frigate birds (9), raucous (9), orientation (11), guano (13), fronds (13), profusely (13), mango (16), recoiled (16), interred (16)

Questions

1. What has long been Stinnett's dream?
2. What did he expect?
3. What contributed to his disillusionment?
4. Why is the friend who works for the government included in the essay?
5. How does the introduction work?
6. What is the tone? What is his attitude toward himself as castaway — heroic? ironic? self-mocking? pathetic?
7. Select the paragraph you find most effective and write an analysis of sentence types and lengths.
8. Choose three details that you feel contribute effectively to the meaning of the essay and discuss their purposes.
9. What is the effect of the simile, "Stepping into the palm forest was like stepping into a cathedral"?
10. How does the description of the external world help the reader to appreciate the feelings of the writer? Choose a specific descriptive passage and explain this interrelationship.
11. Is the conclusion appropriate to the rest of the essay?
12. What aspects of stories of castaways does Stinnett use, and why?
13. How does he give life to this worn-out theme?

Suggestions for Writing

1. Consider a cherished dream of yours that you have had occasion to experience. Write an essay on the actual experience of this "dream." Did it work out as you had hoped or did it "die a lingering death" when you finally lived it out?
2. Write a "desert island" essay. If you were to be exiled alone on a desert island for *one year,* what would you be sure to take with you? What records, books, possessions, supplies, etc. would you be sure to pack? Give detailed reasons for each of them. Like Stinnett, try to give new life to this old subject.
3. Compare Stinnett's experience with that of Darwin in "The Conclusion to *The Voyage of the Beagle*" (p. 173).
4. Write an essay on what you would be sure to leave behind if you were to spend a year on a desert island.
5. What is your conception of a desert island? Do you have the same fantasies that Stinnett had before he finally visited one?

v · Elaborations

When the shoe fits, the foot is forgotten. . . .
Chuang Tzu

Although they still provide some good models for your own essays, the selections in this part are, for the most part, longer and more complex than the earlier ones. Many of them are classics of the art of essay writing and will reward any close attention you may give to them.

Pay particular attention to the highly skilled use of dialogue, details, figurative language, interruptions, transitions, allusions, sentence variety and rhythm, and individual words, for a combination of purposes—describing, arguing, persuading, narrating, explaining and most importantly, for moving the personal experience to a greater, more universal level of significance.

Make some effort to identify the basic pattern in these essays and to appreciate the complex adaptation to the writer's purposes. What is traditional and what is individual in each essay? What makes each writer unique? In their hands, the possibilities for the essay become infinite.

HELEN KELLER

Days of Discovery

Helen Keller (1880–1968), American author, translator, and lecturer, became blind and deaf through scarlet fever at the age of nineteen months (she later learned to speak). In her famous autobiography, Story of My Life *(1903), she tells of her experiences before, during, and after she discovered language, assisted by her patient teacher, Anne Sullivan. She received a B.A. from Radcliffe, memorizing the lectures that Anne tapped on her hand. After Anne's death in 1936, she wrote* Helen Keller's Journal 1936–1937 *(1938), describing her life without her closest companion. Just before his death, Mark Twain said, "The two most interesting characters of the nineteenth century are Napoleon and Helen Keller." In "Days of Discovery," she discusses the important days on which she broke through the restriction of her handicap. As you can tell from the quality of her writing, she went far beyond minimal communication to a very fine writing style. Notice her exceptional ability to bring an experience to life.*

The most important day I remember in all my life is the one 1
on which my teacher, Anne Mansfield Sullivan, came to me. I am filled with wonder when I consider the immeasurable contrast between the two lives which it connects. It was the third of March, 1887, three months before I was seven years old.

On the afternoon of that eventful day, I stood on the porch, 2
dumb, expectant. I guessed vaguely from my mother's signs and from the hurrying to and fro in the house that something unusual was about to happen, so I went to the door and waited

"Days of Discovery" from *The Story of My Life* by Helen Keller. Reprinted by permission of Doubleday & Company, Inc.

on the steps. The afternoon sun penetrated the mass of honeysuckle that covered the porch, and fell on my upturned face.
My fingers lingered almost unconsciously on the familiar leaves
and blossoms which had just come forth to greet the sweet
southern spring. I did not know what the future held of marvel
or surprise for me. Anger and bitterness had preyed upon me
continually for weeks and a deep languor had succeeded this
passionate struggle.

Have you ever been at sea in a dense fog, when it seemed as 3
if a tangible white darkness shut you in, and the great ship,
tense and anxious, groped her way toward the shore with plum-
met and sounding-line, and you waited with beating heart for
something to happen? I was like that ship before my education
began, only I was without compass or sounding-line, and had
no way of knowing how near the harbour was. "Light! give me
light!" was the wordless cry of my soul, and the light of love
shone on me in that very hour.

I felt approaching footsteps. I stretched out my hand as I 4
supposed to my mother. Some one took it, and I was caught up
and held close in the arms of her who had come to reveal all
things to me, and, more than all things else, to love me.

The morning after my teacher came she led me into her 5
room and gave me a doll. The little blind children at the Per-
kins Institution had sent it and Laura Bridgman had dressed
it; but I did not know this until afterward. When I had played
with it a little while, Miss Sullivan slowly spelled into my hand
the word "d-o-l-l." I was at once interested in this finger play
and tried to imitate it. When I finally succeeded in making the
letters correctly I was flushed with childish pleasure and pride.
Running downstairs to my mother I held up my hand and
made the letters for *doll*. I did not know that I was spelling a
word or even that words existed; I was simply making my fingers go in monkey-like imitation. In the days that followed
I learned to spell in this uncomprehending way a great many
words, among them *pin, hat, cup* and a few verbs like *sit, stand,*
and *walk*. But my teacher had been with me several weeks before I understood that everything has a name.

One day, while I was playing with my new doll, Miss Sulli- 6
van put my big rag doll into my lap also, spelled "d-o-l-l" and
tried to make me understand that "d-o-l-l" applied to both.

Earlier in the day we had had a tussle over the words "m-u-g" and "w-a-t-e-r." Miss Sullivan had tried to impress it upon me that "m-u-g" is *mug* and that "w-a-t-e-r" is *water,* but I persisted in confounding the two. In despair she had dropped the subject for the time, only to renew it at the first opportunity. I became impatient at her repeated attempts and, seizing the new doll, I dashed it upon the floor. I was keenly delighted when I felt the fragments of the broken doll at my feet. Neither sorrow nor regret followed my passionate outburst. I had not loved the doll. In the still, dark world in which I lived there was no strong sentiment or tenderness. I felt my teacher sweep the fragments to one side of the hearth, and I had a sense of satisfaction that the cause of my discomfort was removed. She brought me my hat, and I knew I was going out into the warm sunshine. This thought, if a wordless sensation may be called a thought, made me hop and skip with pleasure.

We walked down the path to the well-house, attracted by 7 the fragrance of the honeysuckle with which it was covered. Some one was drawing water and my teacher placed my hand under the spout. As the cool stream gushed over one hand she spelled into the other the word *water* first slowly, then rapidly. I stood still, my whole attention fixed upon the motions of her fingers. Suddenly I felt a misty consciousness as of something forgotten—a thrill of returning thought; and somehow the mystery of language was revealed to me. I knew then that "w-a-t-e-r" meant that wonderful cool something that was flowing over my hand. That living word awakened my soul, gave it light, hope, joy, set it free! There were barriers still, it is true, but barriers that could in time be swept away.

I left the well-house eager to learn. Everything had a name, 8 and each name gave birth to a new thought. As we returned to the house every object which I touched seemed to quiver with life. That was because I saw everything with the strange, new sight that had come to me. On entering the door I remembered the doll I had broken. I felt my way to the hearth and picked up the pieces. I tried vainly to put them together. Then my eyes filled with tears; for I realized what I had done, and for the first time I felt repentance and sorrow.

I learned a great many new words that day. . . . It would 9 have been difficult to find a happier child than I was as I lay in my crib at the close of that eventful day and lived over the joys it had brought me, and for the first time longed for a new day to come.

Suggestions for Writing

1. Consider what has been the most important day of your life so far. When was it? Why was it important? Whether you discuss a sequence of days as Keller does or just one important day, be sure to give the reader a sense not only of the experiences but also of the quality of those experiences. Were you jubilant as Keller was? or disappointed, shocked, angry, etc.?

2. Write an essay on the greatest discovery you have made so far in your life. What was the "discovery?" How did it come about? How did you react to it?

3. What is the greatest handicap you have had to overcome in your life so far? What strategies have you developed for handling it?

4. Compare the experience of the child in this essay with that of the boy in "Salvation" by Langston Hughes, p. 121.

GILBERT HIGHET

Pictures of War

(See introduction to the writer on page 61.) This is a more serious essay by Highet, author of the short piece, "Go and Catch a Falling Remark." Here he writes an extended comparison of pictures of war, discussing the distinguishing characteristics of each one. Notice that his description of what is in each picture is so carefully detailed that it is not necessary to have the picture before you in order to understand his discussion.

Did you ever try to compare the different ways in which 1
artists, living at different times or in different countries, handle
the same subject? It is well worth doing. Usually it tells us
something new about each of the artists, and the ages they lived
in—something we might have suspected, but never realized
with such vividness.

Take one powerful subject, which has been much in all our 2
minds in these last years: the sufferings of the civilian population during a war. In wartime—always, from the beginning of
history—soldiers and sailors have been able to fight and defend themselves: they can act as well as endure. But the non-
combatants must only suffer in a world which seems to have
gone mad. As soon as I think of this, there leaps into my mind's
eye a photograph taken during the Japanese invasion of China.
It showed a street, or a highroad, or possibly even a railroad
station, partly ruined and apparently still under bombard-
ment. The background contained several dim figures running
for shelter. The air was dark with smoke and dust. In the foreground was one human being which epitomized the whole mad-

ness and cruelty of war. It was a baby of about two, deserted and alone, its face blackened with earth from shell-bursts, its limbs too small to carry it more than a few yards away, its mind too tormented to understand anything of what was happening, its parents perhaps killed a few moments before. There it sat, with its eyes closed on the universe, weeping bitterly.

Now, the same subject—the horrors of war as felt by defenseless civilians—has interested a number of the world's finest painters. 3

The most eminent painter of our generation, Pablo Picasso,[1] made it the subject of his most famous picture: *Guernica*. This was done in 1937, just after the Nazi air force, working for Franco,[2] had carried out, as a tactical experiment, the first saturation bombing raid in history, and had virtually destroyed the ancient Basque city of Guernica. Picasso does not attempt to show us the flaming and exploding city, nor the raiding airplanes. The whole picture, although it is enormous in size, contains only five human beings and two animals. 4

On the extreme right is a man with his mouth gaping in a hideous shriek, and his head thrown back at an angle so impossible that only an ultimate agony could produce it. He stretches two ugly and helpless hands to the black sky; and around him are triangular forms which look like stylized flames. On the extreme left is a woman, also screaming madly in a long endless scream, with a dead baby in her arms. In the foreground are three figures. One is a woman, rushing wildly across the scene—but such a woman as we have never seen except in a nightmare (and such events as this are nightmares, which have become facts). Every one of her limbs is distorted with speed and effort; she seems to be trying to escape from everything, even from her body. Opposite her is the corpse of a man, still clutching the fragment of a weapon, but dead—not only dead, but dismembered. Between the two is a gigantic horse, wounded, and screaming in agony, as though it were calling for death. Near it are the impassive head and forequarter of a fighting bull. (These are the two symbols of death best known to the Spaniards: the helpless horse, and the ruth- 5

---

[1] Pablo Picasso (1881–1973): Spanish painter and sculptor.

[2] Francisco Franco (1892–1975): Spanish general and dictatorial ruler.

less bull which attacks and destroys it, long before it is itself sacrificed.) Above this entire picture there is one face, not calm, but at least sane: the idealized face of a spirit, holding a lamp at the center of the scene and gazing on it with grief-stricken amazement. The entire picture is executed in gloomy colors: black, glaring white, many shades of gray. Instead of looking like a normal three-dimensional scene taken from reality and transferred to two-dimensional canvas, it seems to vibrate, to stagger, to jerk abruptly into harsh projections which strike our horrified eyes with something like a physical shock.

Look back now for more than a century. Look back to the 6
Napoleonic wars. Spain suffered in them also, and a Spanish artist recorded her sufferings then too. This was Goya.[3] His finest painting on this subject is *The Executions of May Third 1808*. Picasso's *Guernica* is all distortion and symbolism. Goya's *Executions of May Third* is all realism.

The scene is a little valley outside a Spanish city. There are 7
stately buildings in the background. On the left stand four or five defenseless men in civilian clothes, with expressions of terror in their rough Spanish faces. One of them, all in white, waves his hands as though appealing for mercy. On the right, only a few feet away, is a line of uniformed French soldiers, aiming their muskets at the hearts of the condemned men. In one minute, in one second, they will fire a volley. The line of muskets is steady and efficient, appearing all the more ruthless because all the bayonets are fixed; if the bullets fail, the soldiers will stab the men to death. The soldiers themselves are quite impersonal: resolute efficient figures in uniforms and heavy shakos, their faces almost invisible behind arms raised to fire. (Their steady line, contrasted with the broken group of civilians, reminds us of another essential horror of war—that the forces of destruction always seem to be more efficient and better organized than the forces which build civilization.) In the center of the picture, behind the bayonets, is a group of condemned men waiting for their turn to die; they are kneeling, and hiding their faces, or perhaps weeping. A few corpses are already lying on the ground.

---

[3] Francisco Goya (1746–1828): Spanish painter, often of war subjects.

Now turn back further yet, another two hundred years, to the 8
age which we know best as the age of the Pilgrim Fathers. Just
about the time the Pilgrims were building their earliest settlement, a young man in France was completing a set of pictures which he named *The Miseries and Misfortunes of War*.
This was Jacques Callot.[4] He was one of the greatest etchers
who ever lived, and probably the first man to turn etching into
an independent art. He was born about 1592 (a generation after
Shakespeare). His father was (of all things) a herald; and he
himself was intended for the church. But he ran away from
home twice, because he wanted to be an artist. At last he was
sent to Italy for training. It was there that he learned his astounding technique and formed his style. For years he served
the Medici in Florence.[5] Then he returned to France, and
worked for Louis XIII and other potentates. He himself was
not a Frenchman, strictly speaking, but a Burgundian from
Lorraine; there is a story that he made a wonderful etching of
King Louis's siege of La Rochelle, but refused point-blank to
make another picture of the same king's armies besieging his
own native city of Nancy.

Now, consider one of Callot's etchings of *The Miseries and* 9
Misfortunes of War. When we look at it, our first impression is
not of destruction and disintegration, but of order, balance,
symmetry, and even grace. It is quite a small picture. Picasso's
Guernica is an enormous mural, covering many square yards.
Goya's *Executions* is eight feet by eleven. Callot's etching is
not much bigger than a man's hand. It looks rather like an
episode from a picturesque ballet, seen from a distant part of
the theater. Then we look more closely into it. We examine the
various groups which make up this neat symmetrical composition. We see that, though they are all carefully disposed, and
form an over-all pattern which is both pleasing and intricate,
they are not merely posed—like lay figures. There is a good
deal of action in their arrangement, and there is a sinister logic.

The scene is a small village. In the foreground there is a 10
cottage of two or maybe three rooms, only one story high.

---

[4] Jacques Callot (1594–1635): French engraver.
[5] Medici: an Italian family, powerful in Florence and Tuscany from the
fourteenth to the sixteenth century.

There are three or four more cottages visible at the right. Opposite them a large old tree frames the picture gracefully. In the background is a little church, which when full might hold sixty people: the whole population of the village and the surrounding farms. It is an elegiac scene. Immediately in front of us as we look at it, an old cart has stopped, and the horse is hanging its head as though in exhaustion. And then we begin to see that the village has been transformed by a life which is not its own. Figures are climbing all over the cart, figures with gay feathers on their heads, and swords sticking out prominently from their left sides; they are unloading the wine casks and whatever else the cart was carrying. Two groups of what might be dancers, at right and left, prove to contain more of these befeathered and sworded figures. One has grasped a woman by the hair as she runs from him; the other is running rapidly after a terrified girl with his sword in the air. The cottages are smoking, with smoke which does not come from their peaceful hearths. They are burning. And the church itself, the church as we look more closely is seen to be on fire; the steeple is already pouring out smoke which will soon change to flames. On the extreme left a purposeful group of soldiers has discharged a volley of shots from muskets at the church. Apparently the villagers have gathered on its steps and in its churchyard to make a concerted stand. Some of them have guns, and are firing back.

But the issue is not in doubt. There is a vicious energy   11
about the organized soldiers which convinces us that they will take this village and loot it as they have taken many more already; they are experienced in this kind of amateur fighting. Some of them have already started looting and raping. Meanwhile, how long will the villagers continue to resist, with the church burning over their heads?

This is not a mere atrocity picture. Such events were com-   12
mon during the terrible wars of the seventeenth century—especially in the religious conflicts, when men fought more savagely over religious dogmas than they have ever done over politics. Still, its effect is supremely harrowing. And yet there is a paradox. As an artistic composition, the picture is graceful and harmonious. The lines are deft and delicate, the figures of both murderers and victims are skilfully and not grotesquely posed,

the bitter conflicts of emotion are offset by the control and the balance of the design.

Powerful, these contrasts between artists—powerful and sig- 13 nificant. Working in our own time and using many of the new devices of twentieth-century art, Picasso conveyed the effect of an air raid by using figures which were anatomically (though not spiritually) impossible; which were less real than symbolic. In the early nineteenth century, Goya combined realism with romance; his picture of the execution looks like an eye-witness sketch, but it is in fact a collection of carefully composed and heightened contrasts, meant to play on our emotions. Callot, working in the period when the aim of art was symmetry and control, produced something comparable to a Bach fugue,[6] combining heart-rending pathos with supreme intellectual and aesthetic detachment. Callot lived in the era of authority; Goya in the era of passion and rebellion; Picasso in—what can we call it?—the era of disintegration?

Suggestions for Writing

1. Study the three representations of death (on the following pages) and then compare them to one another. Like Highet, notice details that distinguish one from the other and attempt to characterize the attitude toward death in each one. Remember, the reader should be able to visualize the important aspects of your examples, even without the benefit of the printed illustrations.

2. In addition to Picasso's paintings, do you see any other evidence that we may be living in an "era of disintegration"?

3. Read W. H. Auden's poem, "Musée des Beaux Arts," (p. 202) and discuss his poetic interpretation of the Brueghel painting, "Landscape with the Fall of Icarus."

4. Discuss the interpretation of Brueghel's painting in William Carlos Williams' "Landscape with the Fall of Icarus." Compare to Auden's poem, if it will make your discussion more interesting.

---

[6] Johann Sebastian Bach (1685–1750): German composer.

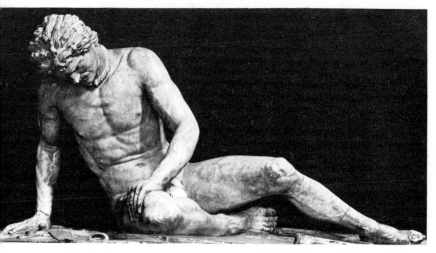

Dying Gaul. About 240–200 B.C., Roman copy of original sculpture. Capitoline Museum, Rome. Courtesy of Alinari-Scala.

Albert Pinkham Ryder. *Death on a Pale Horse (The Race Track).* c. 1910. The Cleveland Museum of Art. Purchase, J. H. Wade Fund.

Pieter Brueghel the Elder. *Landscape with the Fall of Icarus* (1525–1569). Museum of Fine Arts, Brussels. Courtesy of Alinari-Scala. (See discussion of the myth of Daedalus & Icarus on p. 202.)

W. H. AUDEN [1]

Musée des Beaux Arts [2]

About suffering they were never wrong,
The Old Masters: how well they understood
Its human position; how it takes place
While someone else is eating or opening a window or just walking
    dully along;
How, when the aged are reverently, passionately waiting   5
For the miraculous birth, there always must be
Children who did not specially want it to happen, skating
On a pond at the edge of the wood:
They never forgot
That even the dreadful martyrdom must run its course   10
Anyhow in a corner, some untidy spot
Where the dogs go on with their doggy life and the torturer's horse
Scratches its innocent behind on a tree.

In Brueghel's *Icarus*,[3] for instance: how everything turns away
Quite leisurely from the disaster; the plowman may   15
Have heard the splash, the forsaken cry,
But for him it was not an important failure; the sun shone
As it had to on the white legs disappearing into the green
Water; and the expensive delicate ship that must have seen
Something amazing, a boy falling out of the sky,   20
Had somewhere to get to and sailed calmly on.

---

[1] Auden (1907–73): English poet.

[2] The Museum of Fine Arts, Brussels, where the painting, "Landscape with the Fall of Icarus," by Pieter Brueghel the Elder is located.

[3] In the Greek myth, the artificer, Daedalus, for an escape from Crete, makes wings for himself and his son, Icarus, and attaches them with wax. Against his father's advice, Icarus flies too close to the sun causing the wax to melt, and he drowns.

WILLIAM CARLOS WILLIAMS[1]

Landscape with the Fall of Icarus

According to Brueghel
when Icarus fell
it was spring

a farmer was plowing
his field   5
the whole pageantry

of the year was
awake tingling
near

the edge of the sea   10
concerned
with itself

sweating in the sun
that melted
the wing's wax   15

unsignificantly
off the coast
there was

a splash quite unnoticed
this was   20
Icarus drowning

[1] Williams (1883–1963): American poet.

BRUNO BETTELHEIM

The Three Little Pigs

Bruno Bettelheim, born in Vienna in 1903, received his doctorate at the University of Vienna and was later imprisoned at the concentration camps of Dachau and Buchenwald for a year. About this experience he wrote The Informed Heart *(1964). After moving to the United States he became a professor of education, behavioral science, and psychology, specializing in the psychology of children, at the University of Chicago where he is now director emeritus of the Orthogenic School. Other books include* Dynamics of Prejudice *(1950),* The Children of the Dream *(1969),* A Home for the Heart *(1974), and* The Uses of Enchantment *(1976), from which this discussion is taken. Here Bettelheim gives a psychoanalytic explication of the meaning contained in the famous fairy tale. In order to make his point that it teaches a lesson in favor of the "reality principle" over the "pleasure principle," he refers in detail to the action of the story and compares it to a fable.*

The myth of Hercules deals with the choice between following the pleasure principle or the reality principle in life. So, likewise, does the fairy story of "The Three Little Pigs." 1

Stories like "The Three Little Pigs" are much favored by children over all "realistic" tales, particularly if they are presented with feeling by the storyteller. Children are enraptured when the huffing and puffing of the wolf at the pig's door is acted out for them. "The Three Little Pigs" teaches the nursery-age child in a most enjoyable and dramatic form that we 2 must not be lazy and take things easy, for if we do, we may perish. Intelligent planning and foresight combined with hard labor will make us victorious over even our most ferocious enemy—the wolf! The story also shows the advantages of growing up, since the third and wisest pig is usually depicted as the biggest and oldest.

The houses the three pigs build are symbolic of man's progress in history: from a lean-to shack to a wooden house, finally to a house of solid brick. Internally, the pigs' actions show progress from the id-dominated personality to the superego-influenced but essentially ego-controlled personality. 3

The littlest pig builds his house with the least care out of straw; the second uses sticks; both throw their shelters together as quickly and effortlessly as they can, so they can play for the rest of the day. Living in accordance with the pleasure principle, the younger pigs seek immediate gratification, without a thought for the future and the dangers of reality, although the middle pig shows some growth in trying to build a somewhat more substantial house than the youngest. 4

Only the third and oldest pig has learned to behave in accordance with the reality principle: he is able to postpone his desire to play, and instead acts in line with his ability to foresee what may happen in the future. He is even able to predict correctly the behavior of the wolf—the enemy, or stranger within, which tries to seduce and trap us; and therefore the third pig is able to defeat powers both stronger and more ferocious than he is. The wild and destructive wolf stands for all asocial, unconscious, devouring powers against which one must learn to protect oneself, and which one can defeat through the strength of one's ego. 5

"The Three Little Pigs" makes a much greater impression on children than Aesop's parallel but overtly moralistic fable of "The Ant and the Grasshopper." In this fable a grasshopper, starving in winter, begs an ant to give it some of the food which the ant had busily collected all summer. The ant asks what the grasshopper was doing during the summer. Learning that the grasshopper sang and did not work, the ant rejects his plea by saying, "Since you could sing all summer, you may dance all winter." 6

This ending is typical for fables, which are also folk tales 7 handed down from generation to generation. "A fable seems to be, in its genuine state, a narrative in which beings irrational, and sometimes inanimate, are, for the purpose of moral instruction, feigned to act and speak with human interests and passions" (Samuel Johnson). Often sanctimonious, sometimes amusing, the fable always explicitly states a moral truth; there is no hidden meaning, nothing is left to our imagination.

The fairy tale, in contrast, leaves all decisions up to us, including whether we wish to make any at all. It is up to us whether we wish to make any application to our life from a fairy tale, or simply enjoy the fantastic events it tells about. Our enjoyment is what induces us to respond in our own good time to the hidden meanings, as they may relate to our life experience and present state of personal development.   8

A comparison of "The Three Little Pigs" with "The Ant and the Grasshopper" accentuates the difference between a fairy tale and a fable. The grasshopper, much like the little pigs and the child himself, is bent on playing, with little concern for the future. In both stories the child identifies with the animals (although only a hypocritical prig can identify with the nasty ant, and only a mentally sick child with the wolf); but after having identified with the grasshopper, there is no hope left for the child, according to the fable. For the grasshopper beholden to the pleasure principle, nothing but doom awaits; it is an "either/or" situation, where having made a choice once settles things forever.   9

But identification with the little pigs of the fairy tale teaches that there are developments—possibilities of progress from the pleasure principle to the reality principle, which, after all, is nothing but a modification of the former. The story of the three pigs suggests a transformation in which much pleasure is retained, because now satisfaction is sought with true respect for the demands of reality. The clever and playful third pig outwits the wolf several times: first, when the wolf tries three times to lure the pig away from the safety of home by appealing to his oral greed, proposing expeditions to where the two would get delicious food. The wolf tries to tempt the pig with turnips which may be stolen, then with apples, and finally with a visit to a fair.   10

Only after these efforts have come to naught does the wolf   11 move in for the kill. But he has to enter the pig's house to get him, and once more the pig wins out, for the wolf falls down the chimney into the boiling water and ends up as cooked meat for the pig. Retributive justice is done: the wolf, which has devoured the other two pigs and wished to devour the third, ends up as food for the pig.

The child, who throughout the story has been invited to 12 identify with one of its protagonists, is not only given hope, but is told that through developing his intelligence he can be victorious over even a much stronger opponent.

Since according to the primitive (and a child's) sense of jus- 13 tice only those who have done something really bad get destroyed, the fable seems to teach that it is wrong to enjoy life when it is good, as in summer. Even worse, the ant in this fable is a nasty animal, without any compassion for the suffering of the grasshopper—and this is the figure the child is asked to take for his example.

The wolf, on the contrary, is obviously a bad animal, be- 14 cause it wants to destroy. The wolf's badness is something the young child recognizes within himself: his wish to devour, and its consequence—the anxiety about possibly suffering such a fate himself. So the wolf is an externalization, a projection of the child's badness—and the story tells how this can be dealt with constructively.

The various excursions in which the oldest pig gets food in 15 good ways are an easily neglected but significant part of the story, because they show that there is a world of difference between eating and devouring. The child subconsciously understands it as the difference between the pleasure principle uncontrolled, when one wants to devour all at once, ignoring the consequences, and the reality principle, in line with which one goes about intelligently foraging for food. The mature pig gets up in good time to bring the goodies home before the wolf appears on the scene. What better demonstration of the value of acting on the basis of the reality principle, and what it consists of, than the pig's rising very early in the morning to secure the delicious food and, in so doing, foiling the wolf's evil designs?

In fairy tales it is typically the youngest child who, although 16 at first thought little of or scorned, turns out to be victorious in the end. "The Three Little Pigs" deviates from this pattern, since it is the oldest pig who is superior to the two little pigs all along. An explanation can be found in the fact that all three pigs are "little," thus immature, as is the child himself. The child identifies with each of them in turn and recognizes the progression of identity. "The Three Little Pigs" is a fairy tale because of its happy ending, and because the wolf gets what he deserves.

While the child's sense of justice is offended by the poor **17** grasshopper having to starve although it did nothing bad, his feeling of fairness is satisfied by the punishment of the wolf. Since the three little pigs represent stages in the development of man, the disappearance of the first two little pigs is not traumatic; the child understands subconsciously that we have to shed earlier forms of existence if we wish to move on to higher ones. In talking to young children about "The Three Little Pigs," one encounters only rejoicing about the deserved punishment of the wolf and the clever victory of the oldest pig—not grief over the fate of the two little ones. Even a young child seems to understand that all three are really one and the same in different stages—which is suggested by their answering the wolf in exactly the same words: "No, no, not by the hair of my chinni-chin-chin!" If we survive in only the higher form of our identity, this is as it should be.

"The Three Little Pigs" directs the child's thinking about **18** his own development without ever telling what it ought to be, permitting the child to draw his own conclusions. This process alone makes for true maturing, while telling the child what to do just replaces the bondage of his own immaturity with a bondage of servitude to the dicta of adults.

Suggestions for Writing

1. In *The Uses of Enchantment* (New York: Vintage Books, 1977, p. 5), Bettelheim says:

> Just because his life is often bewildering to him, the child needs even more to be given the chance to understand himself in this complex world with which he must learn to cope. . . . The child finds this kind of meaning through fairy tales.

Select a fairy tale about which you have a strong feeling, possibly one remembered from childhood, and write an explication of the possible lessons contained there for the child.

2. In an essay called "Nursery Crimes" (from *One Hundred and Nineteen Years of the Atlantic,* Boston: Little, Brown and Company, 1971, pp. 344–349), Bergen Evans charges:

> That the older generation is what it is surprises no one with any knowledge of psychology who has examined the pabulum upon which its members were nourished in their most impressionable years, In fact, it redounds to our credit that we are not more abandoned than we are when we consider that at a formative age we are taught to admire such things as Jack's murderous requital of the giant's hospitality, little Goldilocks' atrocious greediness, and the unscrupulous mendacity of little Hans!

With reference to specific tales with which you are familiar or in detail to one of them, evaluate Evans' criticism. Do you agree that the tales may be placed among the "dangerous influences" on the young? Or, may it be, as Bettelheim says, that "when unconscious material *is* to some degree permitted to come to awareness and worked through in imagination, its potential for causing harm — to ourselves or others — is much reduced" (*The Uses of Enchantment,* p. 7)?

H. L. MENCKEN

Larval Stage of a Bookworm

H. L. Mencken (1880–1956), was an American journal-
ist, editor, essayist, and philologist. Disturbed by the
values of what he called the "booboisie," he edited the
controversial journal, American Mercury, *from 1924–1933*
and published a variety of books including, George Bernard Shaw: His Plays *(1905),* The Philosophy of Friedrich
Nietzsche *(1908),* Prejudices *(1919, '20, '22, '24, '26, '27),*
The American Language *(1919), plus* Supplement One
(1945) and Supplement Two *(1948). He also wrote auto-*
biographical works: Happy Days *(1940),* Newspaper Days
(1941), and Heathen Days *(1943). In this essay from*
Happy Days, *Mencken discusses the books most important*
to him in his early experience with reading. Notice how
he breaks up the simple sequence of the essay with digres-
sions on activities other than reading, on his father, and
on Germany. Also notice that he returns to the central
plan.

The first long story I ever read was "The Moose Hunters," a 1
tale of the adventures of four half-grown boys in the woods of
Maine, published in *Chatterbox* for 1887. *Chatterbox,* which
now seems to be pretty well forgotten, was an English annual
that had a large sale, in those days, in the American colonies,
and "The Moose Hunters" seems to have been printed as a sort
of sop or compliment to that trade, just as an English novelist
of today lards his narrative with such cheery native bait as
"waal, pardner," "you betcha" and "geminy-crickets." The

rest of the 1887 issue was made up of intensely English stuff; indeed, it was so English that, reading it and looking at the woodcuts, I sucked in an immense mass of useless information about English history and the English scene, so that to this day I know more about Henry VIII and Lincoln Cathedral than I know about Millard Fillmore or the Mormon Temple at Salt Lake City.

"The Moose Hunters," which ran to the length of a full-length juvenile, was not printed in one gob, but spread through *Chatterbox* in instalments. This was an excellent device, for literary fans in the youngest brackets do their reading slowly and painfully, and like to come up frequently for air. But writing down to them is something else again, and that error the anonymous author of "The Moose Hunters" avoided diligently. Instead, he wrote in the best journalese of the era, and treated his sixteen-year-old heroes precisely as if they were grown men. So I liked his story very much, and stuck to it until, in a series of perhaps twenty sessions, I had got it down.

This was in the Summer of 1888 and during hot weather, for I remember sitting with the volume on the high marble front steps of our house in Hollins street, in the quiet of approaching dusk, and hearing my mother's warnings that reading by failing light would ruin my eyes. The neighborhood apprentices to gang life went howling up and down the sidewalk, trying to lure me into their games of follow-your-leader and run-sheep-run, but I was not to be lured, for I had discovered a new realm of being and a new and powerful enchantment. What was follow-your-leader to fighting savage Canucks on the Little Magalloway river, and what was chasing imaginary sheep to shooting real meese? I was near the end of the story, with the Canucks all beaten off and two carcasses of gigantic meese hanging to trees, before the author made it clear to me that the word *moose* had no plural, but remained unchanged *ad infinitum*.

Such discoveries give a boy a considerable thrill, and augment his sense of dignity. It is no light matter, at eight, to penetrate suddenly to the difference between *to, two* and *too,* or to that between *run* in baseball and *run* in topographical science, or *cats* and *Katz.* The effect is massive and profound, and at least comparable to that which flows, in later life, out of filling a royal flush or debauching the wife of a major-general of cavalry. I must have made some effort to read *Chatterbox* at the time my Grandmother Mencken gave it to me, which was at Christmas, 1887, but for a while it was no go. I could spell out the shorter pieces at the bottoms of columns, but the longer stories were only jumbles of strange and baffling words. But then, as if by miracle, I found suddenly that I could read them, so I tackled "The Moose Hunters" at once, and stuck to it to the end. There were still, of course, many hard words, but they were no longer insurmountable obstacles. If I staggered and stumbled somewhat, I nevertheless hung on, and by the Fourth of July, 1888, I had blooded my first book.

An interval of rough hunting followed in Hollins street and 5 the adjacent alleys, with imaginary Indians, robbers and sheep and very real tomcats as the quarry. Also, I was introduced to chewing tobacco by the garbageman, who passed me his plug as I lay on the roof of the ash-shed at the end of the backyard, watching him at his public-spirited work. If he expected me to roll off the roof, clutching at my midriff, he was fooled, for I managed to hold on until he was out of sight, and I was only faintly dizzy even then. Again, I applied myself diligently to practising leap-frog with my brother Charlie, and to mastering the rules of top-spinning, catty and one-two-three. I recall well how it impressed me to learn that, by boys' law, every new top had to have a license burned into it with a red-hot nail, and that no strange boy on the prowl for loot, however black-hearted, would venture to grab a top so marked. That discovery gave me a sense of the majesty of the law which still sustains me, and I always take off my hat when I meet a judge—if, of course, it is in any place where a judge is not afraid to have his office known.

But pretty soon I was again feeling the powerful suction of 6 beautiful letters—so strange, so thrilling, and so curiously suggestive of the later suction of amour—, and before Christmas I was sweating through the translation of Grimms' Fairy Tales that had been bestowed upon me, "for industry and good deportment," at the closing exercises of F. Knapp's Institute on June 28. This volume had been put into lame, almost pathological English by a lady translator, and my struggles with it awoke in me the first faint gutterings of the critical faculty.

Just what was wrong with it I couldn't, of course, make out, for my gifts had not yet flowered, but I was acutely and unhappily conscious that it was much harder going than "The Moose Hunters," and after a month or so of unpleasantly wrestling with it I put it on the shelf. There it remained for more than fifty years. Indeed, it was not until the appearance of "Snow White" as a movie that I took it down and tried it again, and gagged at it again.

That second experiment convinced me that the fault, back 7
in 1888, must have been that of either the brothers Grimm or their lady translator, but I should add that there was also some apparent resistant within my own psyche. I was born, in truth, without any natural taste for fairy tales, or, indeed, for any other writing of a fanciful and unearthly character. The fact explains, I suppose, my lifelong distrust of poetry, and may help to account for my inability to memorize even a few stanzas of it at school. It probably failed to stick in my mind simply because my mind rejected it as nonsense—sometimes, to be sure, very jingly and juicy nonsense, but still only nonsense. No doubt the same infirmity was responsible for the feebleness of my appetite for the hortatory and incredible juvenile fiction fashionable in my nonage—the endless works of Oliver Optic, Horatio Alger, Harry Castlemon and so on. I tried this fiction more than once, for some of the boys I knew admired it vastly, but I always ran aground in it. So far as I can recall, I never read a single volume of it to the end, and most of it finished me in a few pages.

What I disliked about it I couldn't have told you then, and 8
I can account for my aversion even now only on the theory that I appear to have come into the world with a highly literal mind, geared well enough to take in overt (and usually unpleasant) facts, but very ill adapted to engulfing the pearls of the imagination. All such pearls tend to get entangled in my mental *vibrissae,* and the effort to engulf them is as disagreeable to me as listening to a sermon or reading an editorial in a second-rate (or even first-rate) newspaper. I was a grown man, and far gone in sin, before I ever brought myself to tackle "Alice in Wonderland," and even then I made some big skips, and wondered sadly how and why such feeble jocosity had got so high a reputation. I am willing to grant that it must be a

masterpiece, as my betters allege—but not to *my* taste, not for *me*. To the present moment I can't tell you what is in any of the other juvenile best-sellers of my youth, of moral and socio-logical hallucination all compact, just as I can't tell you what is in the Bhagavad-Gita (which Will Levington Comfort urged me to read in 1912 or thereabout), or in the works of Martin Tupper, or in the report of Vassar Female College for 1865. I tried dime-novels once, encouraged by a boy who aspired to be a train-robber, but they only made me laugh. At a later time, discovering the pseudo-scientific marvels of Jules Verne, I read his whole canon, and I recall also sweating through a serial in a boys' weekly called *Golden Days,* but this last dealt like-wise with *savants* and their prodigies, and was no more a juve-nile, as juveniles were then understood, than "Ten Thousand Leagues Under the Sea."

But before you set me down a prig, let me tell you the rest   9 of it. That rest of it is my discovery of "Huckleberry Finn," probably the most stupendous event of my whole life. The time was the early part of 1889, and I wandered into Paradise by a kind of accident. Itching to exercise my newly acquired art of reading, and with "The Moose Hunters" exhausted and Grimms Fairy Tales playing me false, I began exploring the house for print. The Baltimore *Sunpaper* and *Evening News,* which came in daily, stumped me sadly, for they were full of political diatribes in the fashion of the time, and I knew no more about politics than a chimpanzee. My mother's long file of *Godey's Lady's Book* and her new but growing file of the *Ladies' Home Journal* were worse, for they dealt gloomily with cooking, etiquette, the policing of children, and the design and construction of millinery, all of them sciences that still baffle me. Nor was there any pabulum for me in the hired girl's dog's-eared files of *Bow Bells* and the *Fireside Companion,* the first with its ghastly woodcuts of English milkmaids in bustles ske-daddling from concupiscent baronets in frock-coats and cork-screw mustaches. So I gradually oscillated, almost in despair, toward the old-fashioned secretary in the sitting-room, the up-per works of which were full of dismal volumes in the black cloth and gilt stamping of the era. I had often eyed them from afar, wondering how long it would be before I would be ripe enough to explore them. Now I climbed up on a chair, and began to take them down.

They had been assembled by my father, whose taste for 10 literature in its purer states was of a generally low order of visibility. Had he lived into the days of my practice as a literary critic, I daresay he would have been affected almost as unpleasantly as if I had turned out a clergyman, or a circus clown, or a labor leader. He read every evening after dinner, but it was chiefly newspapers that he read, for the era was one of red-hot politics, and he was convinced that the country was going to Hell. Now and then he took up a book, but I found out long afterward that it was usually some pamphlet on the insoluble issues of the hour, say "Looking Backward," or "If Christ Came to Chicago," or "Life Among the Mormons." These works disquieted him, and he naturally withheld them from his innocent first-born. Moreover, he was still unaware that I could read—that is, fluently, glibly, as a pleasure rather than a chore, in the manner of grown-ups.

Nevertheless, he had managed somehow to bring together a 11 far from contemptible collection of books, ranging from a set of Chambers' Encyclopedia in five volumes, bound in leather like the Revised Statutes, down to "Atlantis: the Antediluvian World," by Ignatius Donnelly, and "Around the World in the Yacht *Sunbeam*." It included a two-volume folio of Shakespeare in embossed morocco, with fifty-odd steel plates, that had been taken to the field in the Civil War by "William H. Abercrombie, 1st Lieut. Company H, 6th Regiment, Md. Vol. Inftr.," and showed a corresponding dilapidation. Who this gallant officer was I don't know, or whether he survived the carnage, or how his cherished text of the Bard ever fell into my father's hands. Also, there were Dickens in three thick volumes, George Eliot in three more, and William Carleton's Irish novels in a third three. Again, there were "Our Living World," by the Rev. J. G. Wood; "A History of the War For the Union," by E. A. Duyckinck; "Our Country," by Benson J. Lossing, LL.D., and "A Pictorial History of the World's Great Nations From the Earliest Dates to the Present Time," by Charlotte M. Yonge—all of them likewise in threes, folio, with lavish illustrations on steel, stone and wood, and smelling heavily of the book-agent. Finally, there were forty or fifty miscellaneous books, among them, as I recall, "Peculiarities of American Cities," by Captain Willard Glazier; "Our Native Land," by George T. Ferris; "A Compendium of Forms," by one Glaskell; "Adventures Among Cannibals" (with horrible pictures of missionaries being roasted, boiled and fried), "Uncle Remus," "Ben Hur," "Peck's Bad Boy," "The Adventures of Baron Münchhausen," "One Thousand Proofs That the Earth Is Not a Globe" (by a forgotten Baltimore advanced thinker named Carpenter), and a deadly-looking "History of Freemasonry in Maryland," by Brother Edward T. Schultz, 32°, in five coal-black volumes.

I leave the best to the last. All of the above, on my first ex- 12
ploration, repelled and alarmed me; indeed, I have never read some of them to this day. But among them, thumbing round, I found a series of eight or ten volumes cheek by jowl, and it appeared on investigation that the whole lot had been written by a man named Mark Twain. I had heard my father mention this gentleman once or twice in talking to my mother, but I had no idea who he was or what he had done: he might have been, for all I knew, a bartender, a baseball-player, or one of the boozy politicoes my father was always meeting in Washington. But here was evidence that he was a man who wrote books, and I noted at once that the pictures in those books were not of the usual funereal character, but light, loose and lively. So I proceeded with my inquiry, and in a little while I had taken down one of them, a green quarto, sneaked it to my bedroom, and stretched out on my bed to look into it. It was, as smarties will have guessed by now, "Huckleberry Finn."

If I undertook to tell you the effect it had upon me my talk 13
would sound frantic, and even delirious. Its impact was genuinely terrific. I had not gone further than the first incomparable chapter before I realized, child though I was, that I had entered a domain of new and gorgeous wonders, and thereafter I pressed on steadily to the last word. My gait, of course, was still slow, but it became steadily faster as I proceeded. As the blurbs on the slip-covers of murder mysteries say, I simply couldn't put the book down. After dinner that evening, braving a possible uproar, I took it into the family sitting-room, and

resumed it while my father searched the *Evening News* hopefully for reports of the arrest, clubbing and hanging of labor leaders. Anon, he noticed what I was at, and demanded to know the name of the book I was reading. When I held up the green volume his comment was "Well, I'll be durned!"

I sensed instantly that there was no reproof in this, but a [14] kind of shy rejoicing. Then he told me that he had once been a great reader of Mark Twain himself—in his younger days. He had got hold of all the volumes as they came out—"The Innocents" in 1869, when he was still a boy himself; "Roughing It" in 1872, "The Gilded Age" in 1873, "Tom Sawyer" in 1876, "A Tramp Abroad" in 1880, the year of my birth, and so on down to date. (All these far from pristine firsts are still in the Biblioteca Menckeniana in Hollis street, minus a few that were lent to neighbor boys and never returned, and had to be replaced.) My father read them in the halcyon days before children, labor troubles and Grover Cleveland had begun to frazzle him, and he still got them down from the shelf on quiet evenings, after the first-named were packed off to bed. But a man of advancing years and cares had to consider also the sorrows of the world, and so he read in Mark less than aforetime.

As for me, I proceeded to take the whole canon at a gulp— [15] and presently gagged distressfully. "Huckleberry Finn," of course, was as transparent to a boy of eight as to a man of eighty, and almost as pungent and exhilarating, but there were passages in "A Tramp Abroad" that baffled me, and many more in "The Innocents," and a whole swarm in "The Gilded Age." I well recall wrestling with the woodcut by W. F. Brown on page 113 of the "Tramp." It shows five little German girls swinging on a heavy chain stretched between two stone posts on a street in Heilbronn,[1] and the legend under it is "Generations of Bare Feet." That legend is silly, for all the girls have shoes on, but what puzzled me about it was something quite different. It was a confusion between the word *generation* and the word

---

[1] Heilbronn: town on the Neckar River where Twain saw a "party of barefooted children" swinging on chains surrounding a public building, "and having a noisy good time." Twain saw evidence for "generations of swinging children" in the worn flagstones, but the illustrator put shoes on his "barefooted children."

federation, which latter was often in my father's speech in
those days, for the American Federation of Labor had got
under way only a few years before, and was just beginning in
earnest to harass and alarm employees. Why I didn't consult
the dictionary (or my mother, or my father himself) I simply
can't tell you. At eight or nine, I suppose, intelligence is no
more than a small spot of light on the floor of a large and
murky room. So instead of seeking help I passed on, wondering
idiotically what possible relation there could be between a gang
of little girls in pigtails and the Haymarket anarchists, and it
was six or seven years later before the "Tramp" became clear
to me, and began to delight me.

It then had the curious effect of generating in me both a   16
great interest in Germany and a vast contempt for the German
language. I was already aware, of course, that the Mencken
family was of German origin, for my Grandfather Mencken, in
his care for me as *Stammhalter,*[2] did not neglect to describe
eloquently its past glories at the German universities, and to
expound its connections to the most remote degrees. But my
father, who was only half German, had no apparent interest in
either the German land or its people, and when he spoke of the
latter at all, which was not often, it was usually in sniffish
terms. He never visited Germany, and never signified any desire
to do so, though I recall my mother suggesting, more than
once, that a trip there would be swell. It was "A Tramp
Abroad" that made me German-conscious, and I still believe
that it is the best guide-book to Germany ever written. Today,
of course, it is archaic, but it was still reliable down to 1910,
when I made my own first trip. The uproarious essay on "The
Awful German Language," which appears at the end of it as an
appendix, worked the other way. That is to say, it confirmed
my growing feeling, born of my struggles with the conjuga-
tions and declensions taught at F. Knapp's Institute, that German was an irrational and even insane tongue, and not worth
the sufferings of a freeborn American. These diverse impressions have continued with me ever since. I am still convinced
that Germany, in the intervals of peace, is the most pleasant
country to travel in ever heard of, and I am still convinced that

---

[2] Eldest son of the family: heir.

the German language is of a generally preposterous and malignant character.

"Huck," of course, was my favorite, and I read it over and   17
over. In fact, I read it regularly not less than annually down to
my forties, and only a few months ago I hauled it out and read
it once more—and found it as magnificent as ever. Only one
other book, down to the beginning of my teens, ever beset me
with a force even remotely comparable to its smash, and that
was a volume called "Boys' Useful Pastimes," by "Prof. Robert
Griffith, A.M., principal of Newton High School." This was
given to me by my Grandmother Mencken at Christmas, 1889,
and it remained my constant companion for at least six years.
The sub-title describes its contents: "Pleasant and profitable
amusement for spare hours, comprising chapters on the use and
care of tools, and detailed instructions by means of which boys
can make with their own hands a large number of toys, household ornaments, scientific appliances, and many pretty, amusing and necessary articles for the playground, the house and
out-of-doors." Manual training was still a novelty in those days,
and I suspect that the professor was no master of it, for many
of his plans and specifications were completely unintelligible
to me, and also to all the neighborhood boys who dropped in
to help and advise. I doubt, indeed, that any human being on
earth, short of an astrophysicist, could have made anything of
his directions for building boat models. But in other cases he
was relatively explicit and understandable, and my brother
Charlie and I, after long efforts, managed to make a steam-
engine (or, more accurately, a steam-mill) according to his
recipe. The boiler was a baking-powder tin, and the steam, is-
suing out of a small hole in the top, operated a sort of fan or
mill-wheel. How we provided heat to make steam I forget, but I
remember clearly that my mother considered the process dangerous, and ordered us to take the engine out of the cellar and
keep it in the backyard.

I had no more mechanical skill than a cow, but I also man-   18
aged to make various other things that the professor described,
including a what-not for the parlor (my mother professed to
admire it, but never put it into service), a rabbit-trap (set in the
backyard, it never caught anything, not even a cat), and a fancy
table ornamented with twigs from the pear tree arranged in

more or less geometrical designs. "Boys' Useful Pastimes" was printed by A. L. Burt on stout paper, and remains extant to this day—a rather remarkable fact, for other boys often borrowed it, and sometimes they kept it on their work-benches for a long while, and thumbed it diligently. One of those boys was Johnnie Sponsler, whose father kept a store in the Frederick road, very near Hollins street. Johnnie was vastly interested in electricity, as indeed were most other boys of the time, for such things as electric lights, motors, telephones and doorbells were just coming in. He thus made hard use of Professor Griffith's Part VII, which was headed "Scientific Apparatus and Experiments," and included directions for making a static machine, and for electroplating door-keys. He later abandoned the sciences for the postal service, and is now, I believe, retired. "Boys' Useful Pastimes," and my apparent interest in it, may have been responsible for my father's decision to transfer me from F. Knapp's Institute to the Baltimore Polytechnic in 1892. If so, it did me an evil service in the end, for my native incapacity for mechanics made my studies at the Polytechnic a sheer waste of time, though I managed somehow to pass the examinations, even in such abysmal subjects as steam engineering.

The influence of "Huck Finn" was immensely more powerful and durable. It not only reinforced my native aversion to the common run of boys' books; it also set me upon a systematic exploration of all the volumes in the old secretary, and before I finished with them I had looked into every one of them, including even Brother Schultz's sombre history of Freemasonry in Maryland. How many were actually intelligible to a boy of eight, nine, ten? I should say about a fourth. I managed to get through most of Dickens, but only by dint of hard labor, and it was not until I discovered Thackeray, at fourteen, that the English novel really began to lift me. George Eliot floored me as effectively as a test in Hittite,[3] and to the present day I have never read "Adam Bede" or "Daniel Deronda" or "The Mill on the Floss," or developed any desire to do so. So far as I am concerned, they will remain mere names to the end of the

19

---

[3] An ancient language of Asia Minor.

chapter, and as hollow and insignificant as the names of Gog and Magog.[4]

But I plowed through Chambers' Encyclopedia relentlessly, [20] beginning with the shortest articles and gradually working my way into the longer ones. The kitchen-midden of irrelevant and incredible information that still burdens me had its origins in those pages, and I almost wore them out acquiring it. I read, too, the whole of Lossing, nearly all of Charlotte M. Yonge, and even some of Duyckinck, perhaps the dullest historian ever catalogued by faunal naturalists on this or any other earth. My brother Charlie and I enjoyed "Our Living World" chiefly because of the colored pictures, but I also read long stretches of it, and astonished my father by calling off the names of nearly all the wild beasts when the circus visited Baltimore in 1889. Finally, I recall reading both "Life Among the Mormons" and "One Thousand Proofs That the Earth Is Not a Globe."

Thus launched upon the career of a bookworm, I presently [21] began to reach out right and left for more fodder. When the Enoch Pratt Free Library of Baltimore opened a branch in Hollins street, in March, 1886, I was still a shade too young to be excited, but I had a card before I was nine, and began an almost daily harrying of the virgins at the delivery desk. In 1888 my father subscribed to *Once-a-Week,* the predecessor of *Collier's,* and a little while later there began to come with it a long series of cheap reprints of contemporary classics, running from Tennyson's poems to Justin M'Carthy's "History of Our Own Times"; and simultaneously there appeared from parts unknown a similar series of cheap reprints of scientific papers, including some of Herbert Spencer.[5] I read them all, sometimes with shivers of puzzlement and sometimes with delight, but always calling for more. I began to inhabit a world that was two-thirds letterpress and only one-third trees, fields, streets and people. I acquired round shoulders, spindly shanks, and a despondent view of humanity. I read everything that I could find in English, taking in some of it but boggling most of it.

---

[4] In British legend, gigantic descendants of the daughters of Diocletian, made to do service as porters at the royal palace.

[5] Herbert Spencer (1820–1903): English philosopher and social scientist.

This madness ran on until I reached adolescence, and began   22
to distinguish between one necktie and another, and to notice
the curiously divergent shapes, dispositions and aromas of girls.
Then, gradually, I began to let up.

But to this day I am still what might be called a reader, and   23
have a high regard for authors.

Suggestions for Writing

1. Like Mencken, write an essay on books that you recall from your
   "larval stage" with either pleasure or pain. Your discussion will
   probably not be as long as Mencken's, but make an effort to
   recall and evaluate at least four early experiences from your early
   reading.
2. In an essay called, "Odd Volumes," Robert Lynd comments on
   the books that he has not yet read, "Perhaps a book means even
   more to me on account of my not having read it. At present it is
   not an achievement, but a hope, a perpetual promise." Do you have
   any books that might fall into this category? Write an essay on
   them, perhaps explaining how and why you got them in the first
   place, why you haven't gotten to them yet, or what you expect
   from them if you ever do.
3. As Mencken does with *Huckleberry Finn,* discuss the "most stupendous event" in your early experience with books. Why was it
   so stupendous?

KATHERINE ANNE PORTER

The Fiesta of Guadalupe

Katherine Anne Porter (1890–1980) was a distant
relative of Daniel Boone and of the short story writer,
O. Henry. She was educated at a small southern convent
school and spent many of her early years writing and then
destroying manuscripts, "literally by the trunkful." Later,
she published essays, short stories, translations, travel
articles, and novels. Among her works are Flowering
Judas *(1930),* The Leaning Tower *(1944),* Pale Horse, Pale
Rider *(1939), and* Ship of Fools *(1962). About her profes-*
sion as a writer, she says, "I did not choose this vocation
and if I had any say in the matter, I would not have
chosen it." In "The Fiesta of Guadalupe," Porter de-
scribes a religious procession she witnessed in Mexico. It
is a fine example of sophisticated travel-writing that gives
the reader a clear sense of the place and more, not just an
account of plane schedules and hotel rates. Notice her
selection of details, which make the Guadalupe festival
distinctive.

I followed the crowd of tired burdened pilgrims, bowed un- 1
der their loads of potteries and food and babies and baskets,
their clothes dusty and their faces a little streaked with long-
borne fatigue. Indians all over Mexico had gathered at the feet
of Mary Guadalupe for this greatest *fiesta* of the year, which
celebrates the initiation of Mexico into the mystic company of
the Church, with a saint and a miracle all her own, not trans-
planted from Spain. Juan Diego's long-ago vision of Mary on

the bare hillside made her Queen of Mexico where before she
had been Empress.

Members of all tribes were there in their distinctive cos- 2
tumes. Women wearing skirts of one piece of cloth wrapped
around their sturdy bodies and women wearing gaily embroi-
dered blouses with very short puffed sleeves. Women wearing
their gathered skirts of green and red, with blue *rebosos*
wrapped tightly around their shoulders. And men in great hats
with peaked crowns, wide flat hats with almost no crown.
Blankets, and *serapes,* and thonged sandals. And a strange-
appearing group whose men all wore a large square of fiber
cloth as a cloak, brought under one arm and knotted on the
opposite shoulder exactly in the style depicted in the old
drawings of Montezuma.

A clutter of babies and dolls and jars and strange-looking 3
people lined the sidewalks, intermingled with booths, red cur-
tained and hung with paper streamers, where sweets and food
and drinks were sold and where we found their astonishing
crafts—manlike potteries and jars and wooden pails bound
with hard wrought clasps of iron, and gentle lacework immac-
ulately white and unbelievably cheap of price.

I picked my way through the crowd looking for the dancers, 4
that curious survival of the ancient Dionysian rites, which in
turn were brought over from an unknown time. The dance and
blood sacrifice were inextricably tangled in the worship of men,
and the sight of men dancing in a religious ecstasy links one's
imagination, for the moment, with all the lives that have been.

A woven, moving arch of brilliant-colored paper flowers 5
gleaming over the heads of the crowd drew me near the gate
of the cathedral as the great bells high up began to ring—
sharply, with shocking clamor, they began to sway and ring,
their ancient tongues shouting notes of joy a little out of tune.
The arches began to leap and flutter. I managed to draw near
enough to see, over the fuzzy poll of sleeping baby on his
mother's back. A group of Indians, fantastically dressed, each
carrying an arch of flowers, were stepping it briskly to the smart
jangle of the bells. They wore tinsel crowns over red bandanas
which hung down their necks in Arab fashion. Their costumes
were of varicolored bits of cloth, roughly fashioned into short
skirts and blouses. Their muscular brown legs were disfigured

with cerise and blue cotton stockings. They danced a short, monotonous step, facing each other, advancing, retreating, holding the arches over their crowns, turning and bowing, in a stolid sarabande. The utter solemnity of their faces made it a moving sight. Under their bandanas, their foreheads were knitted in the effort to keep time and watch the figures of the dance. Not a smile and not a sound save the mad hysteria of the old bells awakened from their sleep, shrieking praise to the queen of Heaven and the Lord of Life.

Then the bells stopped, and a man with a mandolin stood 6 near by, and began a quiet rhythmic tune. The master of ceremonies, wearing around his neck a stuffed rabbit clothed in a pink satin jacket, waved the flagging dancers in to line, helped the less agile to catch step, and the dancing went on. A jammed and breathless crowd and pilgrims inside the churchyard peered through the iron fence, while the youths and boys scrambled up, over the heads of the others, and watched from a precarious vantage. They reminded one irresistibly of a menagerie cage lined with young monkeys. They spraddled and sprawled, caught toeholds and fell, gathered themselves up and shinned up the railings again. They were almost as busy as the dancers themselves.

Past stalls of fruits and babies crawling underfoot away from 7 their engrossed mothers, and the vendors of images, scapulars and rosaries, I walked to the church of the well, where is guarded the holy spring of water that gushed from beneath Mary's feet at her last appearance to Juan Diego, December twelve, in the year of grace fifteen and thirty-one.

It is a small darkened place, the well covered over with a 8 handsomely wrought iron grating, through which the magic waters are brought up in a copper pail with a heavy handle. The people gather here and drink reverently, passing the pail from mouth to mouth, praying the while to be delivered of their infirmities and sins.

A girl weeps as she drinks, her chin quivering. A man, sweating and dusty drinks and drinks and drinks again, with a great sigh of satisfaction, wipes his mouth and crosses himself devoutly. 9

My pilgrimage leads me back to the great cathedral, intent 10 on seeing the miraculous Tilma of Juan Diego, whereon the queen of Heaven deigned to stamp her lovely image. Great is the power of that faded virgin curving like a new moon in her bright blue cloak, dim and remote and immobile in her frame above the soaring altar columns.

From above, the drone of priests' voices in endless prayers, 11 answered by the shrill treble of boy singers. Under the overwhelming arches and the cold magnificence of the white altar, their faces lighted palely by the glimmer of candles, kneel the Indians. Some of them have walked for days for the privilege of kneeling on these flagged floors and raising their eyes to the Holy Tilma.

There is a rapt stillness, a terrible reasonless faith in their 12 dark faces. They sigh, turn toward the picture of their beloved Lady, printed on the garment of Juan Diego only ten years after Cortes had brought the new God, with fire and sword, into Mexico. Only ten years ago, but it is probable that Juan Diego knew nothing about the fire and sword which have been so often the weapons of the faithful servants of our Lady. Maybe he had learned religion happily, from some old gentle priest, and his thoughts of the Virgin, ineffably mysterious and radiant and kind must have haunted him by day and by night for a long time; until one day, oh, miracle of miracles, his kindled eyes beheld her, standing, softly robed in blue, her pale hands clasped, a message of devotion on her lips, on a little hill in his own country, the very spot where his childhood had been passed.

Ah well—why not? And I passed on to the steep winding 13 ascent to the chapel of the little hill, once a Teocalli, called the Hill of Tepeyac, and a scene of other faiths and other pilgrimages. I think, as I follow the path, of those early victims of Faith who went up (mighty slowly and mighty heavily, let the old Gods themselves tell you) to give up their beating hearts in order that the sun might rise again on their people. Now there is a great crucifix set up with the transfixed and bleeding heart of one Man nailed upon it—one magnificent Egoist who dreamed that his great heart could redeem from death all the other hearts of earth destined to be born. He has taken the old hill by storm with his mother, Mary Guadalupe, and their shrine brings the Indians climbing up, in silent groups, pursued by the prayers of the blind and the halt and

the lame who have gathered to reap a little share of the blessings being rained upon the children of faith. Theirs is a dole-
ful litany: "In the name of our Lady, Pity, a little charity for
the poor—for the blind, for the little servants of God, for the
humble in heart!" The cries waver to you on the winds as the
slope rises, and comes in faintly to the small chapel where is the
reclining potent image of Guadalupe, second in power only to
the Holy Tilma itself.

It is a more recent image, copied from the original picture 14
but now she is lying down, hands clasped, supported by a company of saints. There is a voluptuous softness in her face and
pose—a later virgin, grown accustomed to homage and from
the meek maiden receiving the announcement of the Angel
Gabriel on her knees, she has progressed to the role of Powerful
Intercessor. Her eyes are vague and a little indifferent, and she
does not glance at the devout adorer who passionately clasps
her knees and bows his head upon them.

A sheet of glass protects her, or she would be literally wiped 15
away by the touches of her devotees. They crowd up to the case,
and rub their hands on it, and cross themselves, then rub the
afflicted parts of their bodies, hoping for a cure. A man reached
up and rubbed the glass, then gently stroked the head of his
sick and pallid wife, who could not get near enough to touch
for herself. He rubbed his own forehead, knees, then stroked
the woman's chest. A mother brought her baby and leaned his
little toes against the glass for a long time, the tears rolling
down her cheeks.

Twenty brown and work-stained hands are stretched up to 16
touch the magic glass—they obscure the still face of the adored
Lady, they blot out with their insistent supplications her remote eyes. They have parted a carved bit of wood and plaster,
I see the awful hands of faith, the credulous and worn hands of
believers; the humble and beseeching hands of the millions and
millions who have only the anodyne of credulity. In my dreams
I shall see those groping insatiable hands reaching, reaching,
reaching, the eyes turned blinded away from the good earth
which should fill then, to the vast and empty sky.

Cut upon the downward road again, I stop and look over the 17
dark and brooding land, with its rim of mountains swathed in
layer upon layer of filmy blue and gray and purple mists, the

low empty valleys blackened with clumps of trees. The flat-topped houses of adobe drift away casting no shadows on the flooding blue, I seem to walk in a heavy, dolorous dream.

It is not Mary Guadalupe nor her son that touches me. It is 18 Juan Diego I remember, and his people I see, kneeling in scattered ranks on the flagged floor of their church, fixing their eyes on mystic, speechless things. It is their ragged hands I see, and their wounded hearts that I feel beating under their work-stained clothes like a great volcano under the earth and I think to myself, hopefully, that men do not live in a deathly dream forever.

Suggestions for Writing

1. Write an essay in which you describe a particular event in time sequence — a procession, a parade, a rock concert, or a picket line, for example. Be sure to elaborate not only on the visual details, but on the sounds, sights, tastes, and smells, if they contribute to your sense of the experience. Focus on the dominant impression and, like Porter, try to explain the significance.
2. Write a "travel essay" in which you describe a place or an event experienced away from home. It might be only a company picnic, but try to make the reader feel a part of the scene.
3. In an essay called, "It Don't Mean a Thing If It Ain't Got That Sting," Caskie Stinnett says that good travel writing can "capture the essential spirit of a place . . . its sounds, its smells, its tempo, its historical perspective, the rhythm and life-style of its people," and includes Porter among the writers who are able to do this. Does "The Fiesta of Guadalupe" live up to Stinnett's description of good travel writing? How?

ARTHUR L. CAMPA

Anglo vs. Chicano: Why?

Arthur L. Campa (1905–78) was born in Mexico of American missionary parents. Educated at the University of New Mexico and Columbia University, he chaired the Department of Modern Languages at the University of Denver and directed the Center of Latin American Studies in Denver from 1946 until his death. He also served in the United States Air Force, worked as a cultural affairs officer in foreign embassies, and directed training projects for the Peace Corps. His books include Spanish Folk Poetry in New Mexico *(1946),* Treasure of the Sangres des Christos *(1963), and* Hispanic Culture in the Southwest *(1978). In this essay he draws on his wide knowledge of Hispanic culture and writes an analysis of the major differences between Anglo-Americans and Chicanos. He does not simply list differences, however; he also attempts to account for them.*

The cultural differences between Hispanic and Anglo-American people have been dwelt upon by so many writers that we should all be well informed about the values of both. But audiences are usually of the same persuasion as the speakers, and those who consult published works are for the most part specialists looking for affirmation of what they believe. So, let us consider the same subject, exploring briefly some of the basic cultural differences that cause conflict in the Southwest, where Hispanic and Anglo-American cultures meet. 1

Cultural differences are implicit in the conceptual content of the languages of these two civilizations, and their value sys- 2

Reprinted by permission of Lucille Campa from *Intellectual Digest* (January 1973). First published in *Western Review,* vol. IX (Spring 1972).

tems stem from a long series of historical circumstances. Therefore, it may be well to consider some of the English and
Spanish cultural configurations before these Europeans set foot
on American soil. English culture was basically insular, geo-
graphically and ideologically; was more integrated on the
whole, except for some strong theological differences; and was
particularly zealous of its racial purity. Spanish culture was
peninsular, a geographical circumstance that made it a catch-
all of Mediterranean, central European and north African
peoples. The composite nature of the population produced a
market regionalism that prevented close integration, except for
religion, and led to a strong sense of individualism. These differences were reflected in the colonizing enterprise of the two
cultures. The English isolated themselves from the Indians
physically and culturally; the Spanish, who had strong notions
about *pureza de sangre* [purity of blood] among the nobility,
were not collectively averse to adding one more strain to their
racial cocktail. Cortés led the way by siring the first *mestizo*
in North America, and the rest of the conquistadores followed
suit. The ultimate products of these two orientations meet today in the Southwest.

Anglo-American culture was absolutist at the onset; that is, 3
all the dominant values were considered identical for all, re-
gardless of time and place. Such values as justice, charity,
honesty were considered the superior social order for all men
and were later embodied in the American Constitution. The
Spaniard brought with him a relativistic viewpoint and saw
fewer moral implications in man's actions. Values were looked
upon as the result of social and economic conditions.

The motives that brought Spaniards and Englishmen to 4
America also differed. The former came on an enterprise of
discovery, searching for a new route to India initially, and
later for new lands to conquer, the fountain of youth, minerals,
the Seven Cities of Cíbola and, in the case of the missionaries,
new souls to win for the Kingdom of Heaven. The English came
to escape religious persecution, and once having found a haven,
they settled down to cultivate the soil and establish their
homes. Since the Spaniards were not seeking a refuge or running away from anything, they continued their explorations

and circled the globe 25 years after the discovery of the New World.

This peripatetic tendency of the Spaniard may be accounted 5 for in part by the fact that he was the product of an equestrian culture. Men on foot do not venture far into the unknown. It was almost a century after the landing on Plymouth Rock that Governor Alexander Spotswood of Virginia crossed the Blue Ridge Mountains, and it was not until the nineteenth century that the Anglo-Americans began to move west of the Mississippi.

The Spaniard's equestrian role meant that he was not close 6 to the soil, as was the Anglo-American pioneer, who tilled the land and built the greatest agricultural industry in history. The Spaniard cultivated the land only when he had Indians available to do it for him. The uses to which the horse was put also varied. The Spanish horse was essentially a mount, while the more robust English horse was used in cultivating the soil. It is therefore not surprising that the viewpoints of these two cultures should differ when we consider that the pioneer is looking at the world at the level of his eyes while the *caballero* [horseman] is looking beyond and down at the rest of the world.

One of the most commonly quoted, and often misinter- 7 preted, characteristics of Hispanic peoples is the deeply ingrained individualism in all walks of life. Hispanic individualism is a revolt against the incursion of collectivity, strongly asserted when it is felt that the ego is being fenced in. This attitude leads to a deficiency in those social qualities based on collective standards, an attitude that Hispanos do not consider negative because it manifests a measure of resistance to standardization in order to achieve a measure of individual freedom. Naturally, such an attitude has no *reglas fijas* [fixed rules].

Anglo-Americans who achieve a measure of success and se- 8 curity through institutional guidance not only do not mind a few fixed rules but demand them. The lack of a concerted plan of action, whether in business or in politics, appears unreasonable to Anglo-Americans. They have a sense of individualism, but they achieve it through action and self-determination.

Spanish individualism is based on feeling, on something that is the result not of rules and collective standards but of a person's momentary, emotional reaction. And it is subject to change when the mood changes. In contrast to Spanish emotional in-dividualism, the Anglo-American strives for objectivity when choosing a course of action or making a decision.

The Southwestern Hispanos voiced strong objections to the 9 lack of courtesy of the Anglo-Americans when they first met them in the early days of the Sante Fe trade. The same accusa-tion is leveled at the *Americanos* today in many quarters of the Hispanic world. Some of this results from their different con-ceptions of polite behavior. Here too one can say that the Span-ish have no *reglas fijas* because for them courtesy is simply an expression of the way one person feels toward another. To some they extend the hand, to some they bow and for the more *intimos* there is the well-known *abrazo*. The concepts of "good or bad" or "right and wrong" in polite behavior are moral con-siderations of an absolutist culture.

Another cultural contrast appears in the way both cultures 10 share part of their material substance with others. The prag-matic Anglo-American contributes regularly to such institu-tions as the Red Cross, the United Fund and a myriad of asso-ciations. He also establishes foundations and quite often leaves millions to such institutions. The Hispano prefers to give his contribution directly to the recipient so he can see the person he is helping.

A century of association has inevitably acculturated both 11 Hispanos and Anglo-Americans to some extent, but there still persist a number of culture traits that neither group has relin-quished altogether. Nothing is more disquieting to an Anglo-American who believes that time is money than the time per-spective of Hispanos. They usually refer to this attitude as the "*mañana* psychology." Actually, it is more of a "today psychol-ogy," because Hispanos cultivate the present to the exclusion of the future; because the latter has not arrived yet, it is not a reality. They are reluctant to relinquish the present, so they hold on to it until it becomes the past. To an Hispano, nine is nine until it is ten, so when he arrives at nine-thirty, he jubi-lantly exclaims: "*¡Justo!*" [right on time]. This may by why the clock is slowed down to a walk in Spanish while in English it runs. In the United States, our future-oriented civilization plans our lives so far in advance that the present loses its meaning. January magazine issues [including ID's] are out in December; 1973 cars have been out since October; cemetery plots and even funeral arrangements are bought on the installment plan. To a person engrossed in living today the very idea of planing his funeral sounds like the tolling of the bells.

It is a natural corollary that a person who is present oriented   12 should be compensated by being good at improvising. An Anglo-American is told in advance to prepare for an "impromptu speech," but an Hispano usually can improvise a speech because *"Nosotros lo improvisamos todo"* [we improvise everything].

Another source of cultural conflict arises from the difference   13 between *being* and *doing*. Even when trying to be individualistic, the Anglo-American achieves it by what he does. Today's young generation decided to be themselves, to get away from standardization, so they let their hair grow, wore ragged clothes and even went barefoot in order to be different from the Establishment. As a result they all ended up doing the same things and created another stereotype. The freedom enjoyed by the individuality of *being* makes it unnecessary for Hispanos to strive to be different.

In 1963 a team of psychologists from the University of Gua-   14 dalajara in Mexico and the University of Michigan compared 74 upper-middle-class students from each university. Individualism and personalism were found to be central values for the Mexican students. This was explained by saying that a Mexican's value as a person lies in his *being* rather than, as is the case of the Anglo-Americans, in concrete accomplishments. Efficiency and accomplishments are derived characteristics that do not affect worthiness in the Mexican, whereas in the American it is equated with success, a value of highest priority in the American culture. Hispanic people disassociate themselves from material things or from actions that may impugn a person's sense of being, but the Anglo-American shows great concern for material things and assumes responsibility for his actions. This is expressed in the language of each culture. In Spanish one says, *"Se me cayó la taza"* [the cup fell away from me] instead of "I dropped the cup."

In English, one speaks of money, cash and all related trans- 15
actions with frankness because material things of this high
order do not trouble Anglo-Americans. In Spanish such mate-
rialistic concepts are circumvented by referring to cash as
efectivo [effective] and when buying or selling as something
al contado [counted out], and when without it by saying *No
tengo fondos* [I have no funds]. This disassociation from material things is what produces *sobriedad* [sobriety] in the Spaniard according to Miguel de Unamuno, but in the Southwest
the disassociation from materialism leads to *dejadez* [lassitude]
and *desprendimiento* [disinterestedness]. A man may lose his
life defending his honor but is unconcerned about the lack of
material things. *Desprendimiento* causes a man to spend his
last cent on a friend, which when added to lack of concern for
the future may mean that tomorrow he will eat beans as a result of today's binge.

The implicit differences in words that appear to be identical 16
in meaning are astonishing. Versatile is a compliment in English and an insult in Spanish. An Hispano student who is told
to apologize cannot do it, because the word doesn't exist in
Spanish. *Apología* means words in praise of a person. The
Anglo-American either apologizes, which is a form of retraction
abhorrent in Spanish, or compromises, another concept foreign
to Hispanic culture. *Compromiso* means a date, not a compromise. In colonial Mexico City, two hidalgos once entered a narrow street from opposite sides, and when they could not go
around, they sat in their coaches for three days until the viceroy
ordered them to back out. All this because they could not work
out a compromise.

It was that way then and to some extent now. Many of to- 17
day's conflicts in the Southwest have their roots in polarized
cultural differences, which need not be irreconcilable when
approached with mutual respect and understanding.

Suggestions for Writing

1. Discuss the characteristics of your own cultural or ethnic background, focusing on the major traits and illustrating with concrete
   details. Or, if you feel qualified to discuss another group, broaden

the assignment to a comparison of two cultural or ethnic groups with which you are familiar. Attempt to identify the differences in values, motives, customs, and approaches to life. (You might also compare yourself with a friend of a different background.)

2. In *The Outline of History,* H. G. Wells said, "Our true nationality is mankind." Write an essay on those characteristics which seem to be part of our common humanity — the major similarities among us all. Is "mankind" a more important concept than "nationality"? Explain your response.

E. B. WHITE

Once More to the Lake

E. B. White, born in Mt. Vernon, N.Y. in 1899, is thought by many to be the finest essayist in the United States. In 1926, after graduating from Cornell University, White joined the staff of the New Yorker *and also wrote a column, "One Man's Meat" for* Harper's. *His great variety of books include* The Sub-Treasury of American Humor *(1941) written with his wife, Katharine S. White, children's books:* Stuart Little *(1945),* Charlotte's Web *(1952), and* The Trumpet of the Swan *(1970), the well-known revision of William Strunk's* Elements of Style *(1959),* The Points of My Compass *(1962),* The Letters of E. B. White *(1976), and* Essays of E. B. White *(1977). This essay, originally published in* Harper's *and then in a volume,* One Man's Meat *(1942), is an account of a personal experience and a reflection on the passage of time.*

One summer, along about 1904, my father rented a camp on a lake in Maine and took us all there for the month of August. We all got ringworm from some kittens and had to rub Pond's Extract on our arms and legs night and morning, and my father rolled over in a canoe with all his clothes on; but outside of that the vacation was a success and from then on none of us ever thought there was any place in the world like that lake in Maine. We returned summer after summer—always on August 1 for one month. I have since become a salt-water man, but sometimes in summer there are days when the restlessness of the tides and the fearful cold of the sea water and the incessant wind that blows across the afternoon and into the evening make me wish for the placidity of a lake in the woods. A few weeks ago this feeling got so strong I bought myself a couple of bass hooks and a spinner and returned to the lake where we used to go, for a week's fishing and to revisit old haunts.

I took along my son, who had never had any fresh water up 2 his nose and who had seen lily pads only from train windows. On the journey over to the lake I began to wonder what it would be like. I wondered how the time would have marred this unique, this holy spot—the coves and streams, the hills that the sun set behind, the camps and the paths behind the camps. I was sure that the tarred road would have found it out, and I wondered in what other ways it would be desolated. It is strange how much you can remember about places like that once you allow your mind to return into the grooves that lead back. You remember one thing, and that suddenly reminds you of another thing. I guess I remembered clearest of all the early mornings, when the lake was cool and motionless, remembered how the bedroom smelled of the lumber it was made of and of the wet woods whose scent entered through the screen. The partitions in the camp were thin and did not extend clear to the top of the rooms, and as I was always the first up I would dress softly so as not to wake the others, and sneak out into the sweet outdoors and start out in the canoe, keeping close along the shore in the long shadows of the pines. I remembered being very careful never to rub my paddle against the gunwale for fear of disturbing the stillness of the cathedral.

The lake had never been what you would call a wild lake. 3 There were cottages sprinkled around the shores, and it was in farming country although the shores of the lake were quite heavily wooded. Some of the cottages were owned by nearby farmers, and you would live at the shore and eat your meals at the farmhouse. That's what our family did. But although it wasn't wild, it was a fairly large and undisturbed lake and there were places in it that, to a child at least, seemed infinitely remote and primeval.

I was right about the tar: it led to within half a mile of the 4 shore. But when I got back there, with my boy, and we settled

into a camp near a farmhouse and into the kind of summertime
I had known, I could tell that it was going to be pretty much
the same as it had been before—I knew it, lying in bed the first
morning, smelling the bedroom and hearing the boy sneak
quietly out and go off along the shore in a boat. I began to sustain the illusion that he was I, and therefore, by simple trans-
position, that I was my father. This sensation persisted, kept
cropping up all the time we were there. It was not an entirely
new feeling, but in this setting, it grew much stronger. I seemed
to be living a dual existence. I would be in the middle of some
simple act, I would be picking up a bait box or laying down a
table fork, or I would be saying something, and suddenly it
would be not I but my father who was saying the words or
making the gesture. It gave me a creepy sensation.

We went fishing the first morning. I felt the same damp moss   5
covering the worms in the bait can, and saw the dragonfly
alight on the tip of my rod as it hovered a few inches from the
surface of the water. It was the arrival of this fly that convinced
me beyond any doubt that everything was as it always had
been, that the years were a mirage and that there had been no
years. The small waves were the same, chucking the rowboat under the chin as we fished at anchor, and the boat was the same
boat, the same color green and the ribs broken in the same places,
and under the floorboards the same fresh-water leavings and dé-
bris—the dead helgramite, the wisps of moss, the rusty discarded
fishhook, the dried blood from yesterday's catch. We stared
silently at the tips of our rods, at the dragonflies that came and
went. I lowered the tip of mine into the water, tentatively, pen-
sively dislodging the fly, which darted two feet away, poised,
darted two feet back, and came to rest again a little farther
up the rod. There had been no years between the ducking of
this dragonfly and the other one—the one that was part of
memory. I looked at the boy, who was silently watching his fly,
and it was my hands that held his rod, my eyes watching. I felt
dizzy and didn't know which rod I was at the end of.

We caught two bass, hauling them in briskly as though they   6
were mackerel, pulling them over the side of the boat in a businesslike manner without any landing net, and stunning them
with a blow on the back of the head. When we got back for a
swim before lunch, the lake was exactly where we had left it,

the same number of inches from the dock, and there was only the merest suggestion of a breeze. This seemed an utterly enchanted sea, this lake you could leave to its own devices for a few hours and come back to, and find that it had not stirred, this constant and trustworthy body of water. In the shallows, the dark, water-soaked sticks and twigs, smooth and old, were undulating in clusters on the bottom against the clean ribbed sand, and the track of the mussel was plain. A school of minnows swam by, each minnow with its small individual shadow, doubling the attendance, so clear and sharp in the sunlight. Some of the other campers were in swimming, along the shore, one of them with a cake of soap, and the water felt thin and clear and unsubstantial. Over the years there had been this person with the cake of soap, this cultist, and here he was. There had been no years.

Up to the farmhouse to dinner through the teeming, dusty 7 field, the road under our sneakers was only a two-track road. The middle track was missing, the one with the marks of the hooves and the splotches of dried, flaky manure. There had always been three tracks to choose from in choosing which track to walk in; now the choice was narrowed down to two. For a moment I missed terribly the middle alternative. But the way led past the tennis court, and something about the way it lay there in the sun reassured me; the tape had loosened along the backline, the alleys were green with plantains and other weeds, and the net (installed in June and removed in September) sagged in the dry noon, and the whole place steamed with midday heat and hunger and emptiness. There was a choice of pie for dessert, and one was blueberry and one was apple, and the waitresses were the same country girls, there having been no passage of time, only the illusion of it as in a dropped curtain— the waitresses were still fifteen; their hair had been washed, that was the only difference—they had been to the movies and seen the pretty girls with the clean hair.

Summertime, oh, summertime, pattern of life indelible, the 8 fade-proof lake, the woods unshatterable, the pasture with the sweetfern and the juniper forever and ever, summer without end; this was the background, and the life along the shore was the design, the cottages with their innocent and tranquil design, their tiny docks with the flagpole and the American flag

floating against the white clouds in the blue sky, the little paths
over the roots of the trees leading from camp to camp and the
paths leading back to the outhouses and the can of lime for
sprinkling, and at the souvenir counters at the store the miniature birch-bark canoes and the postcards that showed things
looking a little better than they looked. This was the American family at play, escaping the city heat, wondering whether
the newcomers in the camp at the head of the cove were "common" or "nice," wondering whether it was true that the people
who drove up for Sunday dinner at the farmhouse were turned
away because there wasn't enough chicken.

It seemed to me, as I kept remembering all this, that those 9
times and those summers had been infinitely precious and
worth saving. There had been jollity and peace and goodness.
The arriving (at the beginning of August) had been so big a
business in itself, at the railway station the farm wagon drawn
up, the first smell of the pine-laden air, the first glimpse of the
smiling farmer, and the great importance of the trunks and
your father's enormous authority in such matters, and the feel
of the wagon under you for the long ten-mile haul, and at the
top of the last long hill catching the first view of the lake after
eleven months of not seeing this cherished body of water. The
shouts and cries of the other campers when they saw you, and
the trunks to be unpacked, to give up their rich burden.
(Arriving was less exciting nowadays, when you sneaked up in
your car and parked it under a tree near the camp and took out
the bags and in five minutes it was all over, no fuss, no loud
wonderful fuss about trunks.)

Peace and goodness and jollity. The only thing that was 10
wrong now, really, was the sound of the place, an unfamiliar
nervous sound of the outboard motors. This was the note that
jarred, the one thing that would sometimes break the illusion
and set the years moving. In those other summertimes all
motors were inboard; and when they were at a little distance,
the noise they made was a sedative, an ingredient of summer
sleep. They were one-cylinder and two-cylinder engines, and
some were make-and-break and some were jump-spark, but they
all made a sleepy sound across the lake. The one-lungers
throbbed and fluttered, and the twin-cylinder ones purred and
purred, and that was a quiet sound, too. But now the campers

all had outboards. In the daytime, in the hot mornings, these motors made a petulant, irritable sound; at night, in the still evening when the afterglow lit the water, they whined about one's ears like mosquitoes. My boy loved our rented outboard, and his great desire was to achieve single-handed mastery over it, and authority, and he soon learned the trick of choking it a little (but not too much), and the adjustment of the needle valve. Watching him I would remember the things you could do with the old one-cylinder engine with the heavy flywheel, how you could have it eating out of your hand if you got really close to it spiritually. Motorboats in those days didn't have clutches, and you would make a landing by shutting off the motor at the proper time and coasting in with a dead rudder. But there was a way of reversing them, if you learned the trick, by cutting the switch and putting it on again exactly on the final dying revolution of the flywheel, so that it would kick back against compression and begin reversing. Approaching a dock in a strong following breeze, it was difficult to slow up sufficiently by the ordinary coasting method, and if a boy felt he had complete mastery over his motor, he was tempted to keep it running beyond its time and then reverse it a few feet from the dock. It took a cool nerve, because if you threw the switch a twentieth of a second too soon you would catch the flywheel when it still had speed enough to go up past center, and the boat would leap ahead, charging bull-fashion at the dock.

We had a good week at the camp. The bass were biting well 11
and the sun shone endlessly, day after day. We would be tired at night and lie down in the accumulated heat of the little bedrooms after the long hot day and the breeze would stir almost imperceptibly outside and the smell of the swamp drift in through the rusty screens. Sleep would come easily and in the morning the red squirrel would be on the roof, tapping out his gay routine. I kept remembering everything, lying in bed in the mornings — the small steamboat that had a long rounded stern like the lip of a Ubangi, and how quietly she ran on the moonlight sails, when the older boys played their mandolins and the girls sang and we ate doughnuts dipped in sugar, and how sweet the music was on the water in the shining night, and what it had felt like to think about girls then. After breakfast we would go up to the store and the things were in the same

place — the minnows in a bottle, the plugs and spinners dis-
arranged and pawed over by the youngsters from the boys'
camp, the Fig Newtons and the Beeman's gum. Outside, the
road was tarred and cars stood in front of the store. Inside, all
was just as it had always been, except there was more Coca-Cola
and not so much Moxie [1] and root beer and birch beer and
sarsaparilla. We would walk out with the bottle of pop apiece
and sometimes the pop would backfire up our noses and hurt.
We explored the streams, quietly, where the turtles slid off logs
and dug their way into the soft bottom; and we lay on the town
wharf and fed worms to the tame bass. Everywhere we went I
had trouble making out which was I, the one walking at my
side, the one walking in my pants.

One afternoon while we were there at the lake a thunder-   12
storm came up. It was like the revival of an old melodrama that
I had seen long ago with childish awe. The second-act climax of
the drama of the electrical disturbance over a lake in America
has not changed in any important respect. This was the big
scene, still the big scene. The whole thing was so familiar, the
first feeling of oppression and heat and a general air around
camp of not wanting to go very far away. In midafternoon (it
was all the same) a curious darkening of the sky, and a lull in
everything that had made life tick; and then the way the boats
suddenly swung the other way at their moorings with the
coming of a breeze out of the new quarter, and the premonitory
rumble. Then the kettle drum, then the snare, then the bass
drum and cymbals, then crackling light against the dark, and
the gods grinning and licking their chops in the hills. Afterward
the calm, the rain steadily rustling in the calm lake, the return
of light and hope and spirits, and the campers running out in
joy and relief to go swimming in the rain, their bright cries
perpetuating the deathless joke about how they were getting
simply drenched, and the children screaming with delight at
the new sensation of bathing in the rain, and the joke about
getting drenched linking the generations in a strong indestructi-
ble chain. And the comedian who waded in carrying an
umbrella.

When the others went swimming, my son said he was going   13

---

[1] Brand name of a soft drink.

in, too. He pulled his dripping trunks from the line where they had hung all through the shower and wrung them out. Languidly, and with no thought of going in, I watched him, his hard little body, skinny and bare, saw him wince slightly as he pulled up around his vitals the small, soggy, icy garment. As he buckled the swollen belt, suddenly my groin felt the chill of death.

Suggestions for Writing

1. Write an account of a place at two points in time — in your past and now. You might, for example, focus on the changes that have occurred in your neighborhood or hometown since your childhood or compare two visits to a vacation spot as White does. Notice that White moves far beyond the simple comparison to a reflection on the meaning of the experience for him, and ultimately, for all of us. Consider your own reaction when you reflect on these changes (or on the absence of them, if this happens to be the case).

2. Caskie Stinnett says, "Of all the writers in the world my favorite is E. B. White . . . you can take any paragraph of White's and try to rewrite it and improve it, and you find out in the end that you can't change a word." Try to rewrite one of White's paragraphs. Did it come out any better? Why or why not?

3. Based on this essay and possibly on additional ones, write an analysis of White's style. Consider such matters as tone, diction, sentence forms and variety, rhythm, use of detail, and figurative language.

4. In his essay, "The Years of Wonder," E. B. White says about his early writing, "I operated, generally, on too high a level for routine reporting, and had not yet discovered the eloquence of facts." Do you see any evidence of the "eloquence of facts" in "Once More to the Lake"?

MARTIN LUTHER KING, JR.

I Have a Dream

Martin Luther King, Jr. (1929–68), president of the Southern Christian Leadership Conference, winner of the Nobel Peace Prize, and author of Stride Toward Freedom *and* Why We Can't Wait, *was one of the most active and influential of the civil rights leaders until his assassination. He actively opposed all forms of racial segregation while also preaching the virtues of nonviolence and brotherhood. In his famous speech, "I Have a Dream," delivered at the March on Washington on August 28, 1963, he calls for a new commitment to the cause of freedom. Notice the persuasiveness of the appeal — the repetitions, the short phrases, the figurative language, the crescendo of the message.*

Five score years ago, a great American, in whose symbolic 1
shadow we stand, signed the Emancipation Proclamation. This momentous decree came as a great beacon light of hope to millions of Negro slaves who had been seared in the flames of withering injustice. It came as a joyous daybreak to end the long night of captivity.

But one hundred years later, we must face the tragic fact 2
that the Negro is still not free. One hundred years later, the life of the Negro is still sadly crippled by the manacles of segregation and the chains of discrimination. One hundred years later, the Negro lives on a lonely island of poverty in the midst of a vast ocean of material prosperity. One hundred years later, the Negro is still languished in the corners of American society and finds himself an exile in his own land. So we have come here today to dramatize an appalling condition.

In a sense we have come to our nation's Capital to cash a 3
check. When the architects of our republic wrote the magnificent words of the Constitution and the Declaration of Indepen-
dence, they were signing a promissory note to which every Ameri-
ican was to fall heir. This note was a promise that all men
would be guaranteed the unalienable rights of life, liberty, and
the pursuit of happiness.

It is obvious today that America has defaulted on this 4
promissory note insofar as her citizens of color are concerned.
Instead of honoring this sacred obligation, America has given
the Negro people a bad check; a check which has come back
marked "insufficient funds." But we refuse to believe that the
bank of justice is bankrupt. We refuse to believe that there are
insufficient funds in the great vaults of opportunity of this nation. So we have come to cash this check — a check that will
give us upon demand the riches of freedom and the security of
justice. We have also come to this hallowed spot to remind
America of the fierce urgency of *now*. This is no time to engage
in the luxury of cooling off or to take the tranquilizing drug
of gradualism. *Now* is the time to make real the promises of
Democracy. *Now* is the time to rise from the dark and desolate
valley of segregation to the sunlit path of racial justice. *Now* is
the time to open the doors of opportunity to all of God's children. *Now* is the time to lift our nation from the quicksands
of racial injustice to the solid rock of brotherhood.

It would be fatal for the nation to overlook the urgency of 5
the moment and to underestimate the determination of the
Negro. This sweltering summer of the Negro's legitimate discontent will not pass until there is an invigorating autumn of
freedom and equality. 1963 is not an end, but a beginning.
Those who hope that the Negro needed to blow off steam and
will now be content will have a rude awakening if the nation
returns to business as usual. There will be neither rest nor
tranquility in America until the Negro is granted his citizen-
ship rights. The whirlwinds of revolt will continue to shake the
foundations of our nation until the bright day of justice
emerges.

But there is something that I must say to my people who 6
stand on the warm threshold which leads into the palace of
justice. In the process of gaining our rightful place we must not
be guilty of wrongful deeds. Let us not seek to satisfy our

thirst for freedom by drinking from the cup of bitterness and hatred. We must forever conduct our struggle on the high plane of dignity and discipline. We must not allow our creative protest to degenerate into physical violence. Again and again we must rise to the majestic heights of meeting physical force with soul force. The marvelous new militancy which has engulfed the Negro community must not lead us to a distrust of all white people, for many of our white brothers, as evidenced by their presence here today, have come to realize that their destiny is tied up with our destiny and their freedom is inextricably bound to our freedom. We cannot walk alone.

And as we walk, we must make the pledge that we shall 7 march ahead. We cannot turn back. There are those who are asking the devotees of civil rights, "When will you be satisfied?" We can never be satisfied as long as the Negro is the victim of the unspeakable horrors of police brutality. We can never be satisfied as long as our bodies, heavy with the fatigue of travel, cannot gain lodging in the motels of the highways and the hotels of the cities. We cannot be satisfied as long as the Negro's basic mobility is from a smaller ghetto to a larger one. We can never be satisfied as long as a Negro in Mississippi cannot vote and a Negro in New York believes he has nothing for which to vote. No, no, we are not satisfied, and we will not be satisfied until justice rolls down like waters and righteousness like a mighty stream.

I am not unmindful that some of you have come here out of 8 great trials and tribulations. Some of you have come fresh from narrow jail cells. Some of you have come from areas where your quest for freedom left you battered by the storms of persecution and staggered by the winds of police brutality. You have been the veterans of creative suffering. Continue to work with the faith that unearned suffering is redemptive.

Go back to Mississippi, go back to Alabama, go back to 9 South Carolina, go back to Georgia, go back to Louisiana, go back to the slums and ghettos of our northern cities, knowing that somehow this situation can and will be changed. Let us not wallow in the valley of despair.

I say to you today, my friends, that in spite of the difficulties 10 and frustrations of the moment I still have a dream. It is a dream deeply rooted in the American dream.

I have a dream that one day this nation will rise up and 11

live out the true meaning of its creed: "We hold these truths to be self-evident; that all men are created equal."

I have a dream that one day on the red hills of Georgia the 12 sons of former slaves and the sons of former slaveowners will be able to sit down together at the table of brotherhood.

I have a dream that one day even the state of Mississippi, a 13 desert state sweltering with the heat of injustice and oppression, will be transformed into an oasis of freedom and justice.

I have a dream that my four little children will one day live 14 in a nation where they will not be judged by the color of their skin but by the content of their character.

I have a dream today. 15

I have a dream that one day the state of Alabama, whose gov- 16 ernor's lips are presently dripping with the words of interposition and nullification, will be transformed into a situation where little black boys and black girls will be able to join hands with little white boys and white girls and walk together as sisters and brothers.

I have a dream today. 17

I have a dream that one day every valley shall be exalted, 18 every hill and mountain shall be made low, the rough places will be made plains, and the crooked places will be made straight, and the glory of the Lord shall be revealed, and all flesh shall see it together.

This is our hope. This is the faith with which I return to 19 the South. With this faith we will be able to hew out of the mountain of despair a stone of hope. With this faith we will be able to transform the jangling discords of our nation into a beautiful symphony of brotherhood. With this faith we will be able to work together, to pray together, to struggle together, to go to jail together, to stand up for freedom together, knowing that we will be free one day.

This will be the day when all of God's children will be able 20 to sing with new meaning

> My country, 'tis of thee,
> Sweet land of liberty,
>   Of thee I sing:
> Land where my fathers died,
> Land of the pilgrims' pride
> From every mountain-side
>   Let freedom ring.

And if America is to be a great nation this must become true. 21
So let freedom ring from the prodigious hilltops of New Hampshire. Let freedom ring from the mighty mountains of New York. Let freedom ring from the heightening Alleghenies of Pennsylvania!

Let freedom ring from the snowcapped Rockies of Colorado! 22
Let freedom ring from the curvacious peaks of California! 23
But not only that; let freedom ring from Stone Mountain of 24
Georgia!

Let freedom ring from Lookout Mountain of Tennessee! 25
Let freedom ring from every hill and molehill of Mississippi. 26
From every mountainside, let freedom ring.

When we let freedom ring, when we let it ring from every 27
village and every hamlet, from every state and every city, we will be able to speed up that day when all of God's children, black men and white men, Jews and Gentiles, Protestants and Catholics, will be able to join hands and sing in the words of the old Negro spiritual, "Free at last! free at last! thank God almighty, we are free at last!"

Suggestions for Writing

1. What is your most compelling "dream" at this point in your life? Write a personal essay in which you attempt to lead others to share your feelings about it.
2. In persuasive speaking, "The rational and non-rational elements of proof combine to influence audience response. Indeed, they are so closely intermingled in any persuasive speech that only the critic who is consciously looking for them can isolate one aspect of the proof from another." * In the light of this comment on persuasive speaking, discuss King's speech.
3. Write an essay in which you analyze the qualities of a speech you have heard. Identify and illustrate what contributed to the speaker's effectiveness or lack of it.

---

* Charles S. Mudd and Malcolm O. Sillars, *Speech: Context and Communication* (San Francisco: Chandler Publishing Company, 1969), p. 319.

CLARENCE DARROW

Why I Am an Agnostic

Clarence Darrow (1857–1938), probably the most famous of American criminal lawyers, was born in Ohio, attended one year of law school at the University of Michigan, worked in an attorney's office for one year, and was admitted at age twenty-one to the Ohio bar. He successfully defended Eugene V. Debs in the American Railway Union Strike (1894) and argued against William Jennings Bryan in the famous Scopes Trial (1925), where he defended the right of a high school science teacher, John Scopes, to teach the subject of evolution. His works include Crime: Its Cause and Treatment *(1922) and* The Story of My Life *(1932). "Why I Am an Agnostic" (1929) was originally written as part of a formal discussion about religion with a Protestant bishop, a Catholic judge, and a rabbi. It has been printed in* Verdicts Out of Court *(1963). Here he discusses the reasons for his being an agnostic; notice the many rhetorical questions and the confident answers.*

An agnostic is a doubter. The word is generally applied to 1
those who doubt the verity of accepted religious creeds or faiths.
Everyone is an agnostic as to the beliefs or creeds they do not
accept. Catholics are agnostic to the Protestant creeds, and the
Protestants are agnostic to the Catholic creed. Anyone who
thinks is an agnostic about something, otherwise he must believe that he is possessed of all knowledge. And the proper place
for such a person is in the madhouse or the home for the feeble-
minded. In a popular way, in the western world, an agnostic

From *Verdicts Out of Court* (New York: Quadrangle, 1963). Reprinted by permission of the Darrow family.

is one who doubts or disbelieves the main tenets of the Christian faith.

I would say that belief in at least three tenets is necessary 2 to the faith of a Christian: a belief in God, a belief in immortality, and a belief in a supernatural book. Various Christian sects require much more, but it is difficult to imagine that one could be a Christian, under any intelligent meaning of the word, with less. Yet there are some people who claim to be Christians who do not accept the literal interpretation of all the Bible, and who give more credence to some portions of the book than to others.

I am an agnostic as to the question of God. I think that it is 3 impossible for the human mind to believe in an object or thing unless it can form a mental picture of such object or thing. Since man ceased to worship openly an anthropomorphic God and talked vaguely and not intelligently about some force in the universe, higher than man, that is responsible for the eixstence of man and the universe, he cannot be said to believe in God. One cannot believe in a force excepting as a force that pervades matter and is not an individual entity. To believe in a thing, an image of the thing must be stamped on the mind. If one is asked if he believes in such an animal as a camel, there immediately arises in his mind an image of the camel. This image has come from experience or knowledge of the animal gathered in some way or other. No such image comes, or can come, with the idea of a God who is described as a force.

Man has always speculated upon the origin of the universe, 4 including himself. I feel, with Herbert Spencer,[1] that whether the universe had an origin—and if it had—what the origin is will never be known by man. The Christian says that the universe could not make itself; that there must have been some higher power to call it into being. Christians have been obsessed for many years by Paley's[2] argument that if a person passing through a desert should find a watch and examine its spring, its hands, its case and its crystal, he would at once be

---

[1] Herbert Spencer: see note, p. 221.

[2] William Paley (1743–1805): English theologian and philosopher; author of *View of the Evidences of Christianity* (1794).

satisfied that some intelligent being capable of design had made the watch. No doubt this is true. No civilized man would question that someone made the watch. The reason he would not doubt it is because he is familiar with watches and other appliances made by man. The savage was once unfamiliar with a watch and would have had no idea upon the subject. There are plenty of crystals and rocks of natural formation that are as intricate as a watch, but even to intelligent man they carry no implication that some intelligent power must have made them. They carry no such implication because no one has any knowledge or experience of someone having made these natural objects which everywhere abound.

To say that God made the universe gives no explanation 5 of the beginning of things. If we are told that God made the universe, the question immediately arises: Who made God? Did he always exist, or was there some power back of that? Did he create matter out of nothing, or is his existence co-extensive with matter? The problem is still there. What is the origin of it all? If, on the other hand, one says that the universe was not made by God, that it always existed, he has the same difficulty to confront. To say that the universe was here last year, or millions of years ago, does not explain its origin. This is still a mystery. As to the question of the origin of things, man can only wonder and doubt and guess.

As to the existence of the soul, all people may either believe 6 or disbelieve. Everyone knows the origin of the human being. They know that it came from a single cell in the body of the mother, and that the cell was one out of ten thousand in the mother's body. Before gestation the cell must have been fertilized by a spermatozoön from the body of the father. This was one out of perhaps a billion spermatozoa that was the capacity of the father. When the cell is fertilized a chemical process begins. The cell divides and multiplies and increases into millions of cells, and finally a child is born. Cells die and are born during the life of the individual until they finally drop apart, and this is death.

If there is a soul, what is it, and where did it come from, 7 and where does it go? Can anyone who is guided by his reason possibly imagine a soul independent of a body, or the place of its residence, or the character of it, or anything concerning it? If man is justified in any belief or disbelief on any subject, he is warranted in the disbelief in a soul. Not one scrap of evidence exists to prove any such impossible thing.

Many Christians base the belief of a soul and God upon the   8
Bible. Strictly speaking, there is no such book. To make the
Bible, sixty-six books are bound into one volume. These books
were written by many people at different times, and no one
knows the time or the identity of any author. Some of the books
were written by several authors at various times. These books
contain all sorts of contradictory concepts of life and morals
and the origin of things. Between the first and the last nearly
a thousand years intervened, a longer time than has passed
since the discovery of America by Columbus.

When I was a boy the theologicans used to assert that the   9
proof of the divine inspiration of the Bible rested on miracles
and prophecies. But a miracle means a violation of a natural
law, and there can be no proof imagined that could be sufficient to show the violation of a natural law; even though
proof seemed to show violation, it would only show that we
were not acquainted with all natural laws. One believes in the
truthfulness of a man because of his long experience with the
man, and because the man has always told a consistent story.
But no man has told so consistent a story as nature.

If one should say that the sun did not rise, to use the ordi-   10
nary expression, on the day before, his hearer would not believe it, even though he had slept all day and knew that his
informant was a man of the strictest veracity. He would not believe it because the story is inconsistent with the conduct of
the sun in all the ages past.

Primitive and even civilized people have grown so accus-   11
tomed to believing in miracles that they often attribute the
simplest manifestations of nature to agencies of which they
know nothing. They do this when the belief is utterly inconsistent with knowledge and logic. They believe in old miracles
and new ones. Preachers pray for rain, knowing full well that
no such prayer was ever answered. When a politician is sick,
they pray for God to cure him, and the politician almost invariably dies. The modern clergyman who prays for rain and
for the health of the politician is no more intelligent in this
matter than the primitive man who saw a separate miracle in

the rising and setting of the sun, in the birth of an individual, in the growth of a plant, in the stroke of lightning, in the flood, in every manifestation of nature and life.

As to prophecies, intelligent writers gave them up long ago. 12 In all prophecies facts are made to suit the prophecy, or the prophecy was made after the facts, or the events have no relation to the prophecy. Weird and strange and unreasonable interpretations are used to explain simple statements, that a prophecy may be claimed.

Can any rational person believe that the Bible is anything 13 but a human document? We now know pretty well where the various books came from, and about when they were written. We know that they were written by human beings who had no knowledge of science, little knowledge of life, and were influenced by the barbarous morality of primitive times, and were grossly ignorant of most things that men know today. For instance, Genesis says that God made the earth, and he made the sun to light the day and the moon to light the night, and in one clause disposes of the stars by saying that "he made the stars also." This was plainly written by someone who had no conception of the stars. Man, by the aid of his telescope, has looked out into the heavens and found stars whose diameter is as great as the distance between the earth and the sun. We now know that the universe is filled with stars and suns and planets and systems. Every new telescope looking further into the heavens only discovers more and more worlds and suns and systems in the endless reaches of space. The men who wrote Genesis believed, of course, that this tiny speck of mud that we call the earth was the center of the universe, the only world in space, and made for man, who was the only being worth considering. These men believed that the stars were only a little way above the earth, and were set in the firmament for man to look at, and for nothing else. Everyone today knows that this conception is not true.

The origin of the human race is not as blind a subject as it 14 once was. Let alone God creating Adam out of hand, from the dust of the earth, does anyone believe that Eve was made from Adam's rib—that the snake walked and spoke in the Garden of Eden—that he tempted Eve to persuade Adam to eat an apple, and that it is on that account that the whole human race was doomed to hell—that for four thousand years there was no chance for any human to be saved, though none of them had anything whatever to do with temptation; and that finally men were saved only through God's son dying for them, and that unless human beings believed this silly, impossible and wicked story they were doomed to hell? Can anyone with intelligence really believe that a child born today should be doomed because the snake tempted Eve and Eve tempted Adam? To believe that is not God-worship; it is devil-worship.

Can anyone call this scheme of creation and damnation 15 moral? It defies every principle of morality, as man conceives morality. Can anyone believe today that the whole world was destroyed by flood, save only Noah and his family and a male and female of each species of animal that entered the Ark? There are almost a millon species of insects alone. How did Noah match these up and make sure of getting male and female to reproduce life in the world after the flood had spent its force? And why should all the lower animals have been destroyed? Were they included in the sinning of man? This is a story which could not beguile a fairly bright child of five years of age today.

Do intelligent people believe that the various languages 16 spoken by man on earth came from the confusion of tongues at the Tower of Babel, some four thousand years ago? Human languages were dispersed all over the face of the earth long before that time. Evidences of civilizations are in existence now that were old long before the date claimed for the flood.

Do Christians believe that Joshua made the sun stand still, 17 so that the day could be lengthened, that a battle might be finished? What kind of person wrote that story, and what did he know about astronomy? It is perfectly plain that the author thought that the earth was the center of the universe and stood still in the heavens, and that the sun either went around it or was pulled across its path each day, and that the stopping of the sun would lengthen the day. We know now that had the sun stopped when Joshua commanded it, and had it stood still until now, it would not have lengthened the day. We know that the day is determined by the rotation of the earth upon its axis, and not by the movement of the sun. Everyone knows that this story simply is not true, and not many even pretend to believe the childish fable.

What of the tale of Balaam's ass speaking to him, probably [18] in Hebrew? Is it true, or is it a fable? Many asses have spoken, and doubtless some in Hebrew, but they have not been that breed of asses. Is salvation to depend on a belief in a monstrosity like this?

Above all the rest, would any human being today believe [19] that a child was born without a father? Yet this story was not at all unreasonable in the ancient world; at least three or four miraculous births are recorded in the Bible, including John the Baptist and Samson. Immaculate conceptions were common in the Roman world at the time and at the place where Christianity really had its nativity. Women were taken to the temples to be inoculated of God so that their sons might be heroes, which meant, generally, wholesale butchers. Julius Caesar was a miraculous conception—indeed, they were common all over the world. How many miraculous-birth stories is a Christian now expected to believe?

In the days of the formation of the Christian religion, dis- [20] ease meant the possession of human beings by devils. Christ cured a sick man by casting out the devils, who ran into the swine, and the swine ran into the sea. Is there any question but what that was simply the attitude and belief of a primitive people? Does anyone believe that sickness means the possession of the body by devils, and that the devils must be cast out of the human being that he may be cured? Does anyone believe that a dead person can come to life? The miracles recorded in the Bible are not the only instances of dead men coming to life. All over the world one finds testimony of such miracles; miracles which no person is expected to believe, unless it is his kind of a miracle. Still at Lourdes today, and all over the present world, from New York to Los Angeles and up and down the lands, people believe in miraculous occurrences, and even in the return of the dead. Superstition is everywhere prevalent in the world. It has been so from the beginning, and most likely will be so unto the end.

The reasons for agnosticism are abundant and compelling. [21] Fantastic and foolish and impossible consequences are freely claimed for the belief in religion. All the civilization of any period is put down as a result of religion. All the cruelty and error and ignorance of the period has no relation to religion.

The truth is that the origin of what we call civilization is not due to religion but to skepticism. So long as men accepted miracles without question, so long as they believed in original sin and the road to salvation, so long as they believed in a hell where man would be kept for eternity on account of Eve, there was no reason whatever for civilization: life was short, and eternity was long, and the business of life was preparation for eternity.

When every event was a miracle, when there was no order   22 or system or law, there was no occasion for studying any subject, or being interested in anything excepting a religion which took care of the soul. As man doubted the primitive conceptions about religion, and no longer accepted the literal, miraculous teachings of ancient books, he set himself to understand nature. We no longer cure disease by casting out devils. Since that time, men have studied the human body, have built hospitals and treated illness in a scientific way. Science is responsible for the building of railroads and bridges, of steamships, of telegraph lines, of cities, towns, large buildings and small, plumbing and sanitation, of the food supply, and the countless thousands of useful things that we now deem necessary to life. Without skepticism and doubt, none of these things could have been given to the world.

The fear of God is not the beginning of wisdom. The fear of   23 God is the death of wisdom. Skepticism and doubt lead to study and investigation, and investigation is the beginning of wisdom.

The modern world is the child of doubt and inquiry, as the   24 ancient world was the child of fear and faith.

Suggestions for Writing

1. Consider why you hold a very strong belief in something and then write an essay on "Why I am . . ." (a Protestant, a Democrat, a member of the 4-H, a student, etc.).
2. If you disagree with Darrow, write a rebuttal of his argument.
3. Write a definition of "Believer," or of a specific kind of believer.
4. Can you give any interpretations of the Bible other than Darrow's to substantiate its claims?

JOAN DIDION

The Women's Movement

*Joan Didion, born in 1934, has been described by poet
James Dickey as "the finest woman prose stylist writing
in English today." Always interested in reading, by the
age of thirteen she was typing out pages from Hemingway
and Conrad, "just to see how the sentences worked." She
now lives in Los Angeles with her husband, writer John
Gregory Dunne, and their daughter. She has described
herself as a person "whose most absorbed and passionate
hours are spent arranging words on pieces of paper." Her
novels include* Run River *(1961),* Play It as It Lays *(1970),
and* A Book of Common Prayer *(1977), and she has published two well-known collections of essays,* Slouching
Towards Bethlehem *(1968) and the recent* White Album
*(1979) from which this essay is taken. Here Didion at-
tempts to assess the progress of the "movement" after several years of existence. Notice the use of concrete illustrative detail and the constant evaluation of what she sees
as outstanding characteristics of this movement.*

To make an omelette you need not only those broken eggs 1
but someone "oppressed" to break them: every revolutionist is
presumed to understand that, and also every woman, which
either does or does not make fifty-one per cent of the population of the United States a potentially revolutionary class. The
creation of this revolutionary "class" was from the virtual beginning the "idea" of the women's movement, and the tendency
for popular discussion of the movement to center for so long
around day-care centers is yet another instance of that studied

resistance to political ideas which characterizes our national life.

"The new feminism is not just the revival of a serious politi- 2 cal movement for social equality," the feminist theorist Shulamith Firestone announced flatly in 1970. "It is the second wave of the most important revolution in history." This was scarcely a statement of purpose anyone could find cryptic, and it was scarcely the only statement of its kind in the literature of the movement. Nonetheless, in 1972, in a "special issue" on women, *Time* was still musing genially that the movement might well succeed in bringing about "fewer diapers and more Dante."

That was a very pretty image, the idle ladies sitting in the 3 gazebo and murmuring *lasciate ogni speranza*,[1] but it depended entirely upon the popular view of the movement as some kind of collective inchoate yearning for "fulfillment," or "self-expression," a yearning absolutely devoid of ideas and capable of engendering only the most *pro forma* benevolent interest. In fact there was an idea, and the idea was Marxist, and it was precisely to the extent that there was this Marxist idea that the curious historical anomaly known as the women's movement would have seemed to have any interest at all. Marxism in this country had ever been an eccentric and quixotic passion.[2] One oppressed class after another had seemed finally to miss the point. The have-nots, it turned out, aspired mainly to having. The minorities seemed to promise more, but finally disappointed: it developed that they actually cared about the issues, that they tended to see the integration of the luncheonette and the seat in t' e front of the bus as real goals, and only rarely as ploys, counters in a larger game. They resisted that essential inductive leap from the immediate reform to the social ideal, and, just as disappointingly, they failed to perceive their common cause with other minorities, continued to exhibit a self-interest disconcerting in the extreme to organizers steeped in the rhetoric of "brotherhood."

And then, at that exact dispirited moment when there 4

---

[1] Lasciate ogni speranza: "Abandon all hope"—is the opening of Canto III of Dante's (1265–1321) *Inferno*, at the entrance to the underworld.

[2] Marxism: socialistic doctrine of Karl Marx (1818–83), German political theorist.

seemed no one at all willing to play the proletariat, along came the women's movement, and the invention of women as a "class." One could not help admiring the radical simplicity of this instant transfiguration. The notion that, in the absence of a cooperative proletariat, a revolutionary class might simply be invented, made up, "named" and so brought into existence, seemed at once so pragmatic and so visionary, so precisely Emersonian,[3] that it took the breath away, exactly confirmed one's idea of where nineteenth-century transcendental instincts, crossed with a late reading of Engels and Marx, might lead.[4] To read the theorists of the women's movement was to think not of Mary Wollstonecraft but of Margaret Fuller at her most high-minded,[5] of rushing position papers off to mimeo and drinking tea from paper cups in lieu of eating lunch; of thin raincoats on bitter nights. If the family was the last fortress of capitalism, then let us abolish the family. If the necessity for conventionl reproduction of the species seemed unfair to women, then let us transcend, via technology, "the very organization of nature," the oppression, as Shulamith Firestone saw it, "that goes back through recorded history to the animal kingdom itself." *I accept the universe,* Margaret Fuller had finally allowed: Shulamith Firestone did not.

It seemed very New England, this febrile and cerebral passion. The solemn *a priori* idealism in the guise of radical materialism somehow bespoke old-fashioned self-reliance and prudent sacrifice. The clumsy torrent of words became a principle, a renunciation of style as unserious. The rhetorical willingness to break eggs became, in practice, only a thrifty capacity for finding the sermon in every stone. Burn the literature, Ti-Grace Atkinson said in effect when it was suggested that, even come the revolution, there would still remain the whole body of "sexist" Western literature. But of course no books would be burned: the women of this movement were perfectly capable

---

[3] Emersonian: after Ralph Waldo Emerson (1803–82), American essayist and poet; he believed in the importance of phenomena that transcend the experience of the senses.

[4] Friedrich Engels (1820–95): German socialist.

[5] Mary Wollstonecraft (1759–97): English writer, known for her *Vindication of the rights of Women* (1792). Margaret Fuller (1810–50): American writer and feminist, influenced by transcendentalism.

of crafting didactic revisions of whatever apparently intractable
material came to hand. "As a parent you should become an in-
terpreter of myths," advised Letty Cottin Pogrebin in the preview issue of *Ms.* "Portions of any fairy tale or children's story
can be salvaged during a critique session with your child."
Other literary analysts devised ways to salvage other books:
Isabel Archer in *The Portrait of a Lady* need no longer be the
victim of her own idealism.[6] She could be, instead, the victim
of a sexist society, a woman who had "internalized the conven-
tional definition of wife." The narrator of Mary McCarthy's
The Company She Keeps could be seen as "enslaved because
she persists in looking for her identity in a man." Similarly,
Miss McCarthy's *The Group* could serve to illustrate "what
happens to women who have been educated at first-rate
women's colleges—taught philosophy and history—and then
are consigned to breast-feeding and gourmet cooking." [7]

The idea that fiction has certain irreducible ambiguities   6
seemed never to occur to these women, nor should it have, for
fiction is in most ways hostile to ideology. They have invented
a class; now they had only to make that class conscious. They
seized as a political technique a kind of shared testimony at
first called a "rap session," then called "consciousness-raising,"
and in any case a therapeutically oriented American reinterpre-
tation, according to the British feminist Juliet Mitchell, of a
Chinese revolutionary practice known as "speaking bitterness."
They purged and regrouped and purged again, worried out one
another's errors and deviations, the "elitism" here, the "career-
ism" there. It would have been merely sententious to call some
of their thinking Stalinist: of course it was. It would have been
pointless even to speak of whether one considered these women
"right" or "wrong," meaningless to dwell upon the obvious,
upon the coarsening of moral imagination to which such social
idealism so often leads. To believe in "the greater good" is to
operate, necessarily, in a certain ethical suspension. Ask anyone
committed to Marxist analysis how many angels on the head of

---

[6] Isabel Archer: romantic character in a novel by Henry James (1843-
1916), who foolishly marries an impoverished gentleman who is after her
money.

[7] Mary McCarthy (b. 1912): American essayist, travel writer, novelist;
wrote *The Company She Keeps* (1942), *The Group* (1954).

a pin, and you will be asked in return to never mind the angels, tell me who controls the production of pins.

To those of us who remain committed mainly to the exploration of moral distinctions and ambiguities, the feminist analysis may have seemed a particularly narrow and cracked determinism. Nonetheless it was serious, and for these highstrung idealists to find themselves out of the mimeo room and onto the Cavett show must have been in certain ways more unsettling to them than it ever was to the viewers. They were being heard, and yet not really. Attention was finally being paid, and yet that attention was mired in the trivial. Even the brightest movement women found themselves engaged in sullen public colloquies about the inequities of dishwashing and the intolerable humiliations of being observed by construction workers on Sixth Avenue. (This grievance was not atypic in that discussion of it seemed always to take on unexplored Ms. Scarlett overtones,[8] suggestions of fragile cultivated flowers being "spoken to," and therefore violated, by uppity proles.) They totted up the pans scoured, the towels picked off the bathroom floor, the loads of laundry done in a lifetime. Cooking a meal could only be "dogwork," and to claim any pleasure from it was evidence of craven acquiescence in one's own forced labor. Small children could only be odious mechanisms for the spilling and digesting of food, for robbing women of their "freedom." It was a long way from Simone de Beauvoir's [9] grave and awesome recognition of woman's role as "the Other" to the notion that the first step in changing that role was Alix Kates Shulman's marriage contract ("wife strips beds, husband remakes them"), a document reproduced in *Ms.*, but it was toward just such trivialization that the women's movement seemed to be heading.

Of course this litany of trivia was crucial to the movement in the beginning, a key technique in the politicizing of women who had perhaps been conditioned to obscure their resentments even from themselves. Mrs. Shulman's discovery that she

7

8

---

[8] Scarlett O'Hara: heroine of Margaret Mitchell's novel, *Gone with the Wind* (1936).

[9] Simone de Beauvoir (b. 1908): French writer, known for her studies of the feminine condition—*The Second Sex* (1949), for example.

had less time than her husband seemed to have was precisely the kind of chord the movement had hoped to strike in all women (the "click! of recognition," as Jane O'Reilly described it), but such discoveries could be of no use at all if one refused to perceive the larger point, failed to make that inductive leap from the personal to the political. Splitting up the week into hours during which the children were directed to address their "personal questions" to either one parent or another might or might not have improved the quality of Mr. and Mrs. Shulman's marriage, but the improvement of marriages would not a revolution make. It could be very useful to call housework, as Lenin did, "the most unproductive, the most barbarous and the most arduous work a woman can do," but it could be useful only as the first step in a political process, only in the "awakening" of a class to its position, useful only as a metaphor: to believe, during the late Sixties and early Seventies in the United States of America, that the words had literal meaning was not only to stall the movement in the personal but to seriously delude oneself.

More and more, as the literature of the movement began to reflect the thinking of women who did not really understand the movement's ideological base, one had the sense of this stall, this delusion, the sense that the drilling of the theorists had struck only some psychic hardpan dense with superstitions and little sophistries, wish fulfillment, self-loathing and bitter fancies. To read even desultorily in this literature was to recognize instantly a certain dolorous phantasm, an imagined Everywoman with whom the authors seemed to identify all too entirely. This ubiquitous construct was everyone's victim but her own. She was persecuted even by her gynecologist, who made her beg in vain for contraceptives. She particularly needed contraceptives because she was raped on every date, raped by her husband, and raped finally on the abortionist's table. During the fashion for shoes with pointed toes, she, like "many women," had her toes amputated. She was so intimidated by cosmetics advertising that she would sleep "huge portions" of her day in order to forestall wrinkling, and when awake she was enslaved by detergent commercials on television. She sent her child to a nursery school where the little girls huddled in a "doll corner," and were forcibly restrained from playing with

building blocks. Should she work she was paid "three to ten
times less" than an (always) unqualified man holding the same
job, was prevented from attending business lunches because
she would be "embarrassed" to appear in public with a man
not her husband, and, when she traveled alone, faced a choice
between humiliation in a restaurant and "eating a doughnut"
in her hotel room.

The half-truths, repeated, authenticated themselves. The 10
bitter fancies assumed their own logic. To ask the obvious—
why she did not get herself another gynecologist, another job,
why she did not get out of bed and turn off the television set,
or why, the most eccentric detail, she stayed in hotels where
only doughnuts could be obtained from room service—was to
join this argument at its own spooky level, a level which had
only the most tenuous and unfortunate relationship to the actual
condition of being a woman. That many women are victims of
condescension and exploitation and sex-role stereotyping was
scarcely news, but neither was it news that other women are
not: nobody forces women to buy the package.

But of course something other than an objection to being 11
"discriminated against" was at work here, something other than
an aversion to being, "stereotyped" in one's sex role. Increasingly it seemed that the aversion was to adult sexual life itself:
how much cleaner to stay forever children. One is constantly
struck, in the accounts of lesbian relationships which appear
from time to time in movement literature, by the emphasis on
the superior "tenderness" of the relationship, the "gentleness"
of the sexual connection, as if the participants were wounded
birds. The derogation of assertiveness as "machismo" has
achieved such currency that one imagines several million
women too delicate to deal at any level with an overtly hetero-
sexual man. Just as one had gotten the unintended but ines-
capable suggestion, when told about the "terror and revulsion"
experienced by women in the vicinity of construction sites, of
creatures too "tender" for the abrasiveness of daily life, too
fragile for the streets, so now one was getting, in the later literature of the movement, the impression of women too "sensitive"
for the difficulties of adult life, women unequipped for reality
and grasping at the movement as a rationale for denying that
reality. The transient stab of dread and loss which accompanies

menstruation simply never happens: we only thought it happened, because a male-chauvinist psychiatrist told us so. No
woman need have bad dreams after an abortion: she has only
been told she should. The power of sex is just an oppressive
myth, no longer to be feared, because what the sexual connection really amounts to, we learn in one woman's account of a
postmarital affair presented as liberated and liberating, is
"wisecracking and laughing" and "lying together and then
leaping up to play and sing the entire *Sesame Street Song-
book.*" All one's actual apprehension of what it is like to be a
woman, the irreconcilable difference of it—that sense of living
one's deepest life underwater, that dark involvement with
blood and birth and death—could now be declared invalid,
unnecessary, *one never felt it at all.*

One was only told it, and now one is to be reprogrammed,   12
fixed up, rendered again as inviolate and unstained as the
"modern" little girls in the Tampax advertisements. More and
more we have been hearing the wishful voices of just such perpetual adolescents, the voices of women scarred not by their
class position as women but by the failure of their childhood
expectations and misapprehensions. "Nobody ever so much as
mentioned" to Susan Edmiston "that when you say 'I do,' what
you are doing is not, as you thought, vowing your eternal love,
but rather subscribing to a whole system of rights, obligations
and responsibilities that may well be anathema to your most
cherished beliefs." To Ellen Peck "the birth of children too
often means the dissolution of romance, the loss of freedom,
the abandonment of ideals to economics." A young woman described on the cover of *New York* as "The Suburban Housewife
Who Bought the Promises of Women's Lib and Came to the
City to Live Them" tells us what promises she bought: "The
chance to respond to the bright lights and civilization of the
Big Apple, yes. The chance to compete, yes. But most of all,
the chance to have some fun. Fun is what's been missing."

Eternal love, romance, fun. The Big Apple.[10] These are   13
relatively rare expectations in the arrangements of consenting
adults, although not in those of children, and it wrenches the
heart to read about these women in their brave new lives. An

---

[10] The Big Apple: New York City.

ex-wife and mother of three speaks of her plan to "play out my college girl's dream. I am going to New York to become this famous writer. Or this working writer. Failing that, I will get a job in publishing." She mentions a friend, another young woman who "had never had any other life than as a daughter or wife or mother" but who is "just discovering herself to be a gifted potter." The childlike resourcefulness — to get a job in publishing, to become a gifted potter! — bewilders the imagination. The astral discontent with actual lives, actual men, the denial of the real generative possibilities of adult sexual life, somehow touches beyond words. "It is the right of the oppressed to organize around their oppression *as they see and define it*," the movement theorists insist doggedly in an effort to solve the question of these women, to convince themselves that what is going on is still a political process, but the handwriting is already on the wall. These are converts who want not a revolution but "romance," who believe not in the oppression of women but in their own chances for a new life in exactly the mold of their old life. In certain ways they tell us sadder things about what the culture has done to them than the theorists ever did, and they also tell us, I suspect, that the movement is no longer a cause but a symptom.

Suggestions for Writing

1. Write your own evaluation of a recent "movement" — women's, antinuclear, consumer, for example. What are its major characteristics (use sources for this information) and what do you think about its effectiveness?
2. Do you agree about the women's movement that "the movement is no longer a cause but a symptom"?

GEORGE ORWELL

Politics and the English Language

George Orwell (1903–50) was born in India and attended Eton in England where he felt lonely and uncomfortable among his more wealthy classmates. Later, he became a member of the Indian Imperial Police and in 1927 went to Paris where he worked part of the time as a dishwasher. He also held jobs as a tutor, a classroom teacher, a bookshop assistant, and a keeper of a pub. In 1936 he was wounded fighting in the Spanish Civil War. Because of tuberculosis, he was hospitalized at the end of his life, completing his well-known novel, Nineteen Eighty-Four, *at University Hospital, London. Other works include* Animal Farm *(1945),* Shooting an Elephant *(1950), and* Such, Such Were the Joys *(1953). This essay is one of his most famous, reflecting his deep concern for the welfare of language as one of civilization's main weapons against tyranny. Notice how clearly he writes his own argument against lack of clarity in writing.*

Most people who bother with the matter at all would admit that the English language is in a bad way, but it is generally assumed that we cannot by conscious action do anything about it. Our civilization is decadent and our language — so the argument runs — must inevitably share in the general collapse. It follows that any struggle against the abuse of language is a sentimental archaism, like preferring candles to electric light or hansom cabs to aeroplanes. Underneath this lies the half-conscious belief that language is a natural growth and not an instrument which we shape for our own purposes.

Now, it is clear that the decline of a language must ulti- 2
mately have political and economic causes: it is not due simply to the bad influence of this or that individual writer. But an effect can become a cause, reinforcing the original cause and producing the same effect in an intensified form, and so on indefinitely. A man may take to drink because he feels himself to be a failure, and then fail all the more completely because he drinks. It is rather the same thing that is happening to the English language. It becomes ugly and inaccurate because our thoughts are foolish, but the slovenliness of our language makes it easier for us to have foolish thoughts. The point is that the process is reversible. Modern English, especially written English, is full of bad habits which spread by imitation and which can be avoided if one is willing to take the necessary trouble. If one gets rid of these habits one can think more clearly, and to think clearly is a necessary first step towards political regeneration: so that the fight against bad English is not frivolous and is not the exclusive concern of professional writers. I will come back to this presently, and I hope that by that time the meaning of what I have said here will have become clearer. Meanwhile, here are five specimens of the English language as it is now habitually written.

These five passages have not been picked out because they 3
are especially bad — I could have quoted far worse if I had chosen — but because they illustrate various of the mental vices from which we now suffer. They are a little below the average, but are fairly representative samples. I number them so that I can refer back to them when necessary:

> (1) I am not, indeed, sure whether it is not true to say that the Milton who once seemed not unlike a seventeenth-century Shelley had not become, out of an experience ever more bitter in each year, more alien [*sic*] to the founder of that Jesuit sect which nothing could induce him to tolerate.
>
> Professor Harold Laski
(Essay in *Freedom of Expression*)

> (2) Above all, we cannot play ducks and drakes with a native battery of idioms which prescribes such egregious collocations of

vocables as the Basic *put up with* for *tolerate* or *put at a loss* for
bewilder.

> Professor Lancelot Hogben *(Interglossa)*

(3) On the one side we have the free personality: by definition
it is not neurotic, for it has neither conflict nor dream. Its desires,
such as they are, are transparent, for they are just what institutional approval keeps in the forefront of consciousness; another
institutional pattern would alter their number and intensity;
there is little in them that is natural, irreducible, or culturally
dangerous. But *on the other side,* the social bond itself is nothing
but the mutual reflection of these self-secure integrities. Recall
the definition of love. Is not this the very picture of a small
academic? Where is there a place in this hall of mirrors for either
personality or fraternity?

> Essay on psychology in *Politics* (New York)

(4) All the "best people" from the gentlemen's clubs, and all
the frantic fascist captains, united in common hatred of Socialism
and bestial horror of the rising tide of the mass revolutionary
movement, have turned to acts of provocation, to foul incendiarism,
to medieval legends of poisoned wells, to legalize their own destruction of proletarian organizations, and rouse the agitated
petty-bourgeoisie to chauvinistic fervour on behalf of the fight
against the revolutionary way out of the crisis.

> Communist pamphlet

(5) If a new spirit *is* to be infused into this old country, there
is one thorny and contentious reform which must be tackled, and
that is the humanization and galvanization of the B.B.C. Timidity
here will bespeak canker and atrophy of the soul. The heart of
Britain may be sound and of strong beat, for instance, but the
British lion's roar at present is like that of Bottom in Shakespeare's
Midsummer Night's Dream — as gentle as any sucking dove. A
virile new Britain cannot continue indefinitely to be traduced in
the eyes or rather ears, of the world by the effete languors of
Langham Place, brazenly masquerading as "standard English."
When the Voice of Britain is heard at nine o'clock, better far and
infinitely less ludicrous to hear aitches honestly dropped than
the present priggish, inflated, inhibited, school-ma'amish arch
braying of blameless bashful mewing maidens!

> Letter in *Tribune*

Each of these passages has faults of its own, but, quite apart   4
from avoidable ugliness, two qualities are common to all of

them. The first is staleness of imagery; the other is lack of precision. The writer either has a meaning and cannot express it, or he inadvertently says something else, or he is almost indifferent as to whether his words mean anything or not. This mixture of vagueness and sheer incompetence is the most marked characteristic of modern English prose, and especially of any kind of political writing. As soon as certain topics are raised, the concrete melts into the abstract and no one seems able to think of turns of speech that are not hackneyed: prose consists less and less of *words* chosen for the sake of their meaning, and more and more of *phrases* tacked together like the sections of a prefabricated hen-house. I list below, with notes and examples, various of the tricks by means of which the work of prose-construction is habitually dodged:

Dying metaphors. A newly invented metaphor assists thought 5 by evoking a visual image, while on the other hand a metaphor which is technically "dead" (e.g. *iron resolution*) has in effect reverted to being an ordinary word and can generally be used without loss of vividness. But in between these two classes there is a huge dump of worn-out metaphors which have lost all evocative power and are merely used because they save people the trouble of inventing phrases for themselves. Examples are: *Ring the changes on, take up the cudgels for, toe the line, ride roughshod over, stand shoulder to shoulder with, play into the hands of, no axe to grind, grist to the mill, fishing in troubled waters, on the order of the day, Achilles' heel, swan song, hotbed.* Many of these are used without knowledge of their meaning (what is a "rift," for instance?), and incompatible metaphors are frequently mixed, a sure sign that the writer is not interested in what he is saying. Some metaphors now current have been twisted out of their original meaning without those who use them even being aware of the fact. For example, *toe the line* is sometimes written *tow the line*. Another example is *the hammer and the anvil,* now always used with the implication that the anvil gets the worst of it. In real life it is always the anvil that breaks the hammer, never the other way about: a writer who stopped to think what he was saying would be aware of this, and would avoid perverting the original phrase.

Operators or *verbal false limbs.* These save the trouble of 6
picking out appropriate verbs and nouns, and at the same time
pad each sentence with extra syllables which give it an appearance of symmetry. Characteristic phrases are *render inopera-
tive, militate against, make contact with, be subjected to, give
rise to, give grounds for, have the effect of, play a leading part
(role) in, make itself felt, take effect, exhibit a tendency to,
serve the purpose of,* etc., etc. The keynote is the elimination of
simple verbs. Instead of being a single word, such as *break,
stop, spoil, mend, kill,* a verb becomes a *phrase,* made up of a
noun or adjective tacked on to some general-purposes verb such
as *prove, serve, form, play, render.* In addition, the passive
voice is wherever possible used in preference to the active, and
noun constructions are used instead of gerunds (*by examination of* instead of *by examining*). The range of verbs is further
cut down by means of the *-ize* and *de-* formations, and the
banal statements are given an appearance of profundity by
means of the *not un-* formation. Simple conjunctions and prep-
ositions are replaced by such phrases as *with respect to, having
regard to, the fact that, by dint of, in view of, in the interests
of, on the hypothesis that;* and the ends of sentences are saved
from anticlimax by such resounding common-places as *greatly
to be desired, cannot be left out of account, a development to
be expected in the near future, deserving of serious consideration, brought to a satisfactory conclusion,* and so on and so forth.

Pretentious diction. Words like *phenomenon, element, in-* 7
dividual (as noun), *objective, categorical, effective, virtual, basic,
primary, promote, constitute, exhibit, exploit, utilize, elimi-
nate, liquidate,* are used to dress up simple statements and give
an air of scientific impartiality to biased judgments. Adjectives
like *epoch-making, epic, historic, unforgettable, triumphant,
age-old, inevitable, inexorable, veritable,* are used to dignify the
sordid processes of international politics, while writing that
aims at glorifying war usually takes on an archaic colour, its
characteristic words being: *realm, throne, chariot, mailed fist,
trident, sword, shield, buckler, banner, jackboot, clarion.* Foreign words and expressions such as *cul de sac, ancien régime,
deus ex machina, mutatis mutandis, status quo, gleichschaltung,
weltanschauung,* are used to give an air of culture and elegance.

Except for the useful abbreviations *i.e., e.g.,* and *etc.,* there is no real need for any of the hundreds of foreign phrases now current in English. Bad writers, and especially scientific, political and sociological writers, are nearly always haunted by the notion that Latin or Greek words are grander than Saxon ones, and unnecessary words like *expedite, ameliorate, predict, extraneous, deracinated, clandestine, subaqueous* and hundreds of others constantly gain ground from their Anglo-Saxon opposite numbers.[1] The jargon peculiar to Marxist writing (*hyena, hangman, cannibal, petty bourgeois, these gentry, lacquey, flunkey, mad dog, White Guard,* etc.) consists largely of words and phrases translated from Russian, German or French; but the normal way of coining a new word is to use a Latin or Greek root with the appropriate affix and, where necessary, the -ize formation. It is often easier to make up words of this kind (*deregionalize, impermissible, extramarital, non-fragmentary,* and so forth) than to think up the English words that will cover one's meaning. The result, in general, is an increase in slovenliness and vagueness.

Meaningless words. In certain kinds of writing, particularly 8 in art criticism and literary criticism, it is normal to come across long passages which are almost completely lacking in meaning.[2] Words like *romantic, plastic, values, human, dead, sentimental, natural, vitality,* as used in art criticism, are strictly meaningless, in the sense that they not only do not point to any discoverable object, but are hardly ever expected to do so by the reader. When one critic writes, "The outstanding fea-

---

[1] An interesting illustration of this is the way in which the English flower names which were in use till very recently are being ousted by Greek ones, *snapdragon* becoming *antirrhinum, forget-me-not* becoming *myosotis,* etc. It is hard to see any practical reason for this change of fashion: it is probably due to an instinctive turning-away from the more homely word and a vague feeling that the Greek word is scientific.

[2] Example: "Comfort's catholicity of perception and image, strangely Whitmanesque in range, almost the exact opposite in aesthetic compulsion, continues to evoke that trembling atmospheric accumulative hinting at a cruel, an inexorably serene timelessness. . . . Wrey Gardiner scores by aiming at simple bull's-eyes with precision. Only they are not so simple, and through this contended sadness runs more than the surface bitter-sweet of resignation." (*Poetry Quarterly.*)

ture of Mr. X's work is its living quality," while another writes,
"The immediately striking thing about Mr. X's work is its peculiar deadness," the reader accepts this as a simple difference
of opinion. If words like *black* and *white* were involved, instead
of the jargon words *dead* and *living,* he would see at once that
language was being used in an improper way. Many political
words are similarly abused. The word *Fascism* has now no
meaning except in so far as it signifies "something not desirable." The words *democracy, socialism, freedom, patriotic,*
realistic, justice, have each of them several different meanings
which cannot be reconciled with one another. In the case
of a word like *democracy,* not only is there no agreed definition,
but the attempt to make one is resisted from all sides. It is almost universally felt that when we call a country democratic
we are praising it: consequently the defenders of every kind of
régime claim that it is a democracy, and fear that they might
have to stop using the word if it were tied down to any one
meaning. Words of this kind are often used in a consciously
dishonest way. That is, the person who uses them has his own
private definition, but allows his hearer to think he means
something quite different. Statements like *Marshal Pétain was*
a true patriot, The Soviet Press is the freest in the world, The
Catholic Church is opposed to persecution, are almost always
made with intent to deceive. Other words used in variable
meanings, in most cases more or less dishonestly, are: *class,*
totalitarian, science, progressive, reactionary, bourgeois, equal-
ity.

Now that I have made this catalogue of swindles and per- 9
versions, let me give another example of the kind of writing
that they lead to. This time it must of its nature be an imaginary one. I am going to translate a passage of good English into
modern English of the worst sort. Here is a well-known verse
from *Ecclesiastes:*

> I returned and saw under the sun, that the race is not to the
> swift, nor the battle to the strong, neither yet bread to the wise,
> nor yet riches to men of understanding, nor yet favour to men of
> skill; but time and chance happeneth to them all.

Here it is in modern English: 10

> Objective consideration of contemporary phenomena compels the
> conclusion that success or failure in competitive activities
> exhibits no tendency to be commensurate with innate capacity,
> but that a considerable element of the unpredictable must
> invariably be taken into account.

This is a parody, but not a very gross one. Exhibit (3), above, 11
for instance, contains several patches of the same kind of English. It will be seen that I have not made a full translation.
The beginning and ending of the sentence follow the original
meaning fairly closely, but in the middle the concrete illustrations—race, battle, bread—dissolve into the vague phrase "success or failure in competitive activities." This had to be so,
because no modern writer of the kind I am discussing—no one
capable of using phrases like "objective consideration of contemporary phenomena"—would ever tabulate his thoughts in
that precise and detailed way. The whole tendency of modern
prose is away from concreteness. Now analyze these two sentences a little more closely. The first contains forty-nine words
but only sixty syllables, and all its words are those of everyday life. The second contains thirty-eight words of ninety syllables: eighteen of its words are from Latin roots, and one
from Greek. The first sentence contains six vivid images, and
only one phrase ("time and chance") that could be called
vague. The second contains not a single fresh, arresting phrase,
and in spite of its ninety syllables it gives only a shortened version of the meaning contained in the first. Yet without a doubt
it is the second kind of sentence that is gaining ground in modern English. I do not want to exaggerate. This kind of writing
is not yet universal, and outcrops of simplicity will occur here
and there in the worst-written page. Still, if you or I were told
to write a few lines on the uncertainty of human fortunes, we
should probably come much nearer to my imaginary sentence
than to the one from *Ecclesiastes.*

As I have tried to show, modern writing at its worst does 12
not consist in picking out words for the sake of their meaning
and inventing images in order to make the meaning clearer. It
consists in gumming together long strips of words which have
already been set in order by someone else, and making the results presentable by sheer humbug. The attraction of this way
of writing is that it is easy. It is easier—even quicker, once

you have the habit—to say *In my opinion it is not an unjustifiable assumption that* than to say *I think*. If you use ready-
made phrases, you not only don't have to hunt about for
words; you also don't have to bother with the rhythms of your
sentences, since these phrases are generally so arranged as to be
more or less euphonious. When you are composing in a hurry
—when you are dictating to a stenographer, for instance, or
making a public speech—it is natural to fall into a pretentious,
Latinized style. Tags like *a consideration which we should do
well to bear in mind* or *a conclusion to which all of us would
readily assent* will save many a sentence from coming down
with a bump. By using stale metaphors, similes and idioms, you
save much mental effort, at the cost of leaving your meaning
vague, not only for your reader but for yourself. This is the
significance of mixed metaphors. The sole aim of a metaphor is
to call up a visual image. When these images clash—as in *The
Fascist octopus has sung its swan song, the jackboot is thrown
into the melting pot*—it can be taken as certain that the writer
is not seeing a mental image of the objects he is naming; in
other words he is not really thinking. Look again at the examples I gave at the beginning of this essay. Professor Laski (1)
uses five negatives in fifty-three words. One of these is superflu-
ous, making nonsense of the whole passage, and in addition
there is the slip *alien* for akin, making further nonsense, and
several avoidable pieces of clumsiness which increase the general vagueness. Professor Hogben (2) plays ducks and drakes
with a battery which is able to write prescriptions, and, while
disapproving of the everyday phrase *put up with,* is unwilling
to look *egregious* up in the dictionary and see what it means;
(3), if one takes an uncharitable attitude towards it, is simply
meaningless: probably one could work out its intended meaning by reading the whole of the article in which it occurs. In
(4), the writer knows more or less what he wants to say, but
an accumulation of stale phrases chokes him like tea leaves
blocking a sink. In (5), words and meaning have almost parted
company. People who write in this manner usually have a general emotional meaning—they dislike one thing and want to
express solidarity with another—but they are not interested in
the detail of what they are saying. A scrupulous writer, in every
sentence that he writes, will ask himself at least four questions,

thus: What am I trying to say? What words will express it? What image or idiom will make it clearer? Is this image fresh enough to have an effect? And he will probably ask himself two more: Could I put it more shortly? Have I said anything that is avoidably ugly? But you are not obliged to go to all this trouble. You can shirk it by simply throwing your mind open and letting the ready-made phrases come crowding in. They will construct your sentences for you—even think your thoughts for you, to a certain extent—and at need they will perform the important service of partially concealing your meaning even from yourself. It is at this point that the special connection between politics and the debasement of language becomes clear.

In our time it is broadly true that political writing is bad 13 writing. Where it is not true, it will generally be found that the writer is some kind of rebel, expressing his private opinions and not a "party line." Orthodoxy, of whatever color, seems to demand a lifeless, imitative style. The political dialects to be found in pamphlets, leading articles, manifestos, White Papers and the speeches of undersecretaries do, of course, vary from party to party, but they are all alike in that one almost never finds in them a fresh, vivid, homemade turn of speech. When one watches some tired hack on the platform mechanically repeating the familiar phrases—*bestial atrocities, iron heel, bloodstained tyranny, free peoples of the world, stand shoulder to shoulder*—one often has a curious feeling that one is not watching a live human being but some kind of dummy: a feeling which suddenly becomes stronger at moments when the light catches the speaker's spectacles and turns them into blank discs which seem to have no eyes behind them. And this is not altogether fanciful. A speaker who uses that kind of phraseology has gone some distance towards turning himself into a machine. The appropriate noises are coming out of his larynx, but his brain is not involved as it would be if he were choosing his words for himself. If the speech he is making is one that he is accustomed to make over and over again, he may be almost unconscious of what he is saying, as one is when one utters the responses in church. And this reduced state of consciousness, if not indispensable, is at any rate favorable to political conformity.

In our time, political speech and writing are largely the 14 defense of the indefensible. Things like the continuance of British rule in India, the Russian purges and deportations, the dropping of the atom bombs on Japan, can indeed be defended, but only by arguments which are too brutal for most people to face, and which do not square with the professed aims of political parties. Thus political language has to consist largely of euphemism, question-begging and sheer cloudy vagueness. Defenseless villages are bombarded from the air, the inhabitants driven out into the countryside, the cattle machine-gunned, the huts set on fire with incendiary bullets: this is called *pacification*. Millions of peasants are robbed of their farms and sent trudging along the roads with no more than they can carry: this is called *transfer of population* or *rectification of frontiers*. People are imprisoned for years without trial, or shot in the back of the neck or sent to die of scurvy in Arctic lumber camps: this is called *elimination of unreliable elements*. Such phraseology is needed if one wants to name things without calling up mental pictures of them. Consider for instance some comfortable English professor defending Russian totalitarianism. He cannot say outright, "I believe in killing off your opponents when you can get good results by doing so." Probably, therefore, he will say something like this:

> While freely conceding that the Soviet régime exhibits certain
> features which the humanitarian may be inclined to deplore, we
> must, I think, agree that a certain curtailment of the right
> to political opposition is an unavoidable concomitant of transitional
> periods, and that the rigours which the Russian people have been
> called upon to undergo have been amply justified in the sphere
> of concrete achievement.

The inflated style is itself a kind of euphemism. A mass of 15 Latin words falls upon the facts like soft snow, blurring the outlines and covering up all the details. The great enemy of clear language is insincerity. When there is a gap between one's real and one's declared aims, one turns as it were instinctively to long words and exhausted idioms, like a cuttlefish squirting out ink. In our age there is no such thing as "keeping out of politics." All issues are political issues, and politics itself is a mass of lies, evasions, folly, hatred and schizophrenia. When the general atmosphere is bad, language must suffer. I should

expect to find—this is a guess which I have not sufficient knowledge to verify—that the German, Russian and Italian languages
have all deteriorated in the last ten or fifteen years, as a result
of dictatorship.

But if thought corrupts language, language can also corrupt   16
thought. A bad usage can spread by tradition and imitation,
even among people who should and do know better. The de-
based language that I have been discussing is in some ways very
convenient. Phrases like *a not unjustifiable assumption, leaves
much to be desired, would serve no good purpose, a consideration which we should do well to bear in mind,* are a continuous
temptation, a packet of aspirins always at one's elbow. Look
back through this essay, and for certain you will find that I
have again and again committed the very faults I am protesting
against. By this morning's post I have received a pamphlet
dealing with conditions in Germany. The author tells me that
he "felt impelled" to write it. I open it at random, and here
is almost the first sentence that I see: "[The Allies] have an opportunity not only of achieving a radical transformation of
Germany's social and political structure in such a way as to
avoid a nationalistic reaction in Germany itself, but at the same
time of laying the foundations of a co-operative and unified
Europe." You see, he "feels impelled" to write—feels, presumably, that he has something new to say—and yet his words,
like cavalry horses answering the bugle, group themselves automatically into the familiar dreary pattern. This invasion of
one's mind by ready-made phrases (*lay the foundations, achieve
a radical transformation*) can only be prevented if one is constantly on guard against them, and every such phrase anaesthe-
tizes a portion of one's brain.

I said earlier that the decadence of our language is probably   17
curable. Those who deny this would argue, if they produced
an argument at all, that language merely reflects existing social
conditions, and that we cannot influence its development by
any direct tinkering with words and constructions. So far as the
general tone or spirit of a language goes, this may be true, but
it is not true in detail. Silly words and expressions have often
disappeared, not through any evolutionary process but owing
to the conscious action of a minority. Two recent examples
were *explore every avenue* and *leave no stone unturned,* which

were killed by the jeers of a few journalists. There is a long list of flyblown metaphors which could similarly be got rid of if enough people would interest themselves in the job; and it should also be possible to laugh the *not un-* formation out of existence,[3] to reduce the amount of Latin and Greek in the average sentence, to drive out foreign phrases and strayed scientific words, and, in general, to make pretentiousness unfashionable. But all these are minor points. The defense of the English language implies more than this, and perhaps it is best to start by saying what it does *not* imply.

To begin with it has nothing to do with archaism, with the   18 salvaging of obsolete words and turns of speech, or with the setting up of a "standard English" which must never be departed from. On the contrary, it is especially concerned with the scrapping of every word or idiom which has outworn its usefulness. It has nothing to do with correct grammar and syntax, which are of no importance so long as one makes one's meaning clear, or with the avoidance of Americanisms, or with having what is called a "good prose style." On the other hand it is not concerned with fake simplicity and the attempt to make written English colloquial. Nor does it even imply in every case preferring the Saxon word to the Latin one, though it does imply using the fewest and shortest words that will cover one's meaning. What is above all needed is to let the meaning choose the word, and not the other way about. In prose, the worst thing one can do with words is to surrender to them. When you think of a concrete object, you think wordlessly, and then, if you want to describe the thing you have been visualizing you probably hunt about till you find the exact words that seem to fit it. When you think of something abstract you are more inclined to use words from the start, and unless you make a conscious effort to prevent it, the existing dialect will come rushing in and do the job for you, at the expense of blurring or even changing your meaning. Probably it is better to put off using words as long as possible and get one's meaning as clear as one can through pictures or sensations. Afterwards

---

[3] One can cure oneself of the *not un-* formation by memorizing this sentence: *A not unblack dog was chasing a not unsmall rabbit across a not ungreen field.*

one can choose—not simply *accept*—the phrases that will best cover the meaning, and then switch round and decide what impression one's words are likely to make on another person. This last effort of the mind cuts out all stale or mixed images, all prefabricated phrases, needless repetitions, and humbug and vagueness generally. But one can often be in doubt about the effect of a word or a phrase, and one needs rules that one can rely on when instinct fails. I think the following rules will cover most cases:

(i)   Never use a metaphor, simile or other figure of speech which you are used to seeing in print.

(ii) Never use a long word where a short one will do.

(iii) If it is possible to cut a word out, always cut it out.

(iv) Never use the passive where you can use the active.

(v)   Never use a foreign phrase, a scientific word or a jargon word if you can think of an everyday English equivalent.

(vi) Break any of these rules sooner than say anything outright barbarous.

These rules sound elementary, and so they are, but they demand a deep change of attitude in anyone who has grown used to writing in the style now fashionable. One could keep all of them and still write bad English, but one could not write the kind of stuff that I quoted in those five specimens at the beginning of this article.

I have not here been considering the literary use of language, but merely language as an instrument for expressing and not for concealing or preventing thought. Stuart Chase and others have come near to claiming that all abstract words are meaningless, and have used this as a pretext for advocating a kind of political quietism. Since you don't know what Fascism is, how can you struggle against Fascism? One need not swallow such absurdities as this, but one ought to recognize that the present political chaos is connected with the decay of language, and that one can probably bring about some improvement by starting at the verbal end. If you simplify your English, you are freed from the worst follies of orthodoxy. You cannot speak any of the necessary dialects, and when you make a stupid remark its stupidity will be obvious, even to yourself. Political language—and with variations this is true of all political parties, from Conservatives to Anarchists—is designed to make lies sound truthful and murder respectable, and to give an appearance of solidity to pure wind. One cannot change this all in a moment, but one can at least change one's own habits, and from time to time one can even, if one jeers loudly enough, send some worn-out and useless phrase—some *jackboot, Achilles' heel, hotbed, melting pot, acid test, veritable inferno* or other lump of verbal refuse—into the dustbin where it belongs.

Suggestions for Writing

1. Find and duplicate a recent political speech, then analyze and evaluate it according to the principles of Orwell's essay. Include the speech with your analysis.
2. Choose several examples of what you consider bad writing of the present and discuss their major faults. Be sure to quote the original passages.
3. What is the connection between politics and the language? Is there any special reason to argue for the clarity of political language? Why does Orwell think it is so important?

JONATHAN SWIFT

A Modest Proposal

Jonathan Swift (1667–1745) was born of an English family in Dublin where he eventually became Dean of St. Patrick's Cathedral. A great satirist, Swift raged at social injustices and man's abuse of reason. His best known works are The Battle of the Books *(1704),* The Tale of a Tub *(1704),* Gulliver's Travels *(1726), and the essay included here, "A Modest Proposal" (1729). In this famous attack on the greedy and insensitive English landlords, Swift argues in favor of exactly what he does not want. Pay careful attention to the character of the speaker in the essay and see if you can discover what Swift actually does favor. Also, notice the tone he maintains in order to appear perfectly reasonable.*

It is a melancholy object to those who walk through this 1
great town or travel in the country, when they see the streets, the roads, and cabin-doors, crowded with beggars of the female sex, followed by three, four, or six children, all in rags, and importuning every passenger for an alms. These mothers, instead of being able to work for their honest livelihood, are forced to employ all their time in strolling to beg sustenance for their helpless infants; who, as they grow up, either turn thieves for want of work, or leave their dear native country to fight for the Pretender in Spain, or sell themselves to the Barbadoes.

I think it is agreed by all parties, that the prodigious number 2
of children in the arms, or on the backs, or at the heels of their mothers, and frequently of their fathers, is, in the present deplorable state of the kingdom, a very great additional grievance; and, therefore, whoever could find out a fair, cheap, and easy method of making these children sound, useful members

of the commonwealth, would deserve so well of the public, as to have his statue set up for a preserver of the nation.

But my intention is very far from being confined to provide 3 only for the children of professed beggars; it is of a much greater extent, and shall take in the whole number of infants at a certain age, who are born of parents in effect as little able to support them, as those who demand our charity in the streets.

As to my own part, having turned my thoughts for many 4 years upon this important subject, and maturely weighed the several schemes of our projectors, I have always found them grossly mistaken in their computation. It is true, a child, just dropped from its dam, may be supported by her milk for a solar year, with little other nourishment; at most, not above the value of two shillings, which the mother may certainly get, or the value in scraps, by her lawful occupation of begging; and it is exactly, at one year old that I propose to provide for them in such a manner, as, instead of being a charge upon their parents, or the parish, or wanting food and raiment for the rest of their lives, they shall, on the contrary, contribute to the feeding and partly to the clothing, of many thousands.

There is likewise another great advantage in my scheme, 5 that it will prevent those voluntary abortions, and that horrid practice of women murdering their bastard children, alas, too frequent among us! sacrificing the poor innocent babes, I doubt more to avoid the expense than the shame, which would move tears and pity in the most savage and inhuman breast.

The number of souls in this kingdom being usually reckoned 6 one million and a half, of these I calculate there may be about two hundred thousand couple whose wives are breeders; from which number I subtract thirty thousand couple, who are able to maintain their own children (although I apprehend there cannot be so many, under the present distresses of the kingdom); but this being granted, there will remain a hundred and seventy thousand breeders. I again substract fifty thousand, for those women who miscarry, or whose children die by accident or disease within the year. There only remain a hundred and twenty thousand children of poor parents annually born. The question therefore is, How this number shall be reared and provided for? which, as I have already said, under the present situation of affairs, is utterly impossible by all the methods hitherto proposed. For we can neither employ them in handicraft or agriculture; we neither build houses (I mean in the country), nor cultivate land: they can very seldom pick up a livelihood by stealing, till they arrive at six years old, except where they are of towardly parts; although I confess they learn the rudiments much earlier; during which time they can, however, be properly looked upon only as probationers; as I have been informed by a principal gentleman in the county of Cavan, who protested to me, that he never knew above one or two instances under the age of six, even in a part of the kingdom so renowned for the quickest proficiency in that art.

I am assured by our merchants, that a boy or a girl before 7 twelve years old is no saleable commodity; and even when they come to this age they will not yield above three pounds, or three pounds and half-a-crown at most, on the exchange; which cannot turn to account either to the parents or kingdom, the charge of nutriment and rags having been at least four times that value.

I shall now, therefore, humbly propose my own thoughts, 8 which I hope will not be liable to the least objection.

I have been assured by a very knowing American of my 9 acquaintance in London, that a young healthy child, well nursed, is, at a year old, a most delicious, nourishing, and wholesome food, whether stewed, roasted, baked, or boiled; and I make no doubt that it will equally serve in a fricassee or a ragout.

I do therefore humbly offer it to public consideration, that 10 of the hundred and twenty thousand children already computed, twenty thousand may be reserved for breed, whereof only one-fourth part to be males; which is more than we allow to sheep, black-cattle, or swine; and my reason is, that these children are seldom the fruits of marriage, a circumstance not much regarded by our savages, therefore one male will be sufficient to serve four females. That the remaining hundred thousand may, at a year old, be offered in sale to the persons of quality and fortune through the kingdom; always advising the mother to let them suck plentifully in the last month, so as to render them plump and fat for a good table. A child will make two dishes at an entertainment for friends; and when the family dines alone, the fore or hind quarter will make a reasonable dish, and, seasoned with a little pepper or salt, will be very good boiled on the fourth day, especially in winter.

I have reckoned, upon a medium, that a child just born will 11 weigh twelve pounds, and in a solar year, if tolerably nursed, will increase to twenty-eight pounds.

I grant this food will be somewhat dear, and therefore very 12 proper for landlords, who, as they have already devoured most of the parents, seem to have the best title to the children.

Infant's flesh will be in season throughout the year, but more 13 plentifully in March, and a little before and after: for we are told by a grave author, an eminent French physician, that fish being a prolific diet, there are more children born in Roman Catholic countries about nine months after Lent, than at any other season; therefore, reckoning a year after Lent, the markets will be more glutted than usual, because the number of Popish infants is at least three to one in this kingdom; and therefore it will have one other collateral advantage, by lessening the Papists among us.

I have already computed the charge of nursing a beggar's 14 child (in which list I reckon all cottagers, labourers, and four-fifths of the farmers) to be about two shillings per annum, rags included; and I believe no gentleman would repine to give ten shillings for the carcass of a good fat child, which, as I have said, will make four dishes of excellent nutritive meat, when he has only some particular friend, or his own family, to dine with him. Thus the squire will learn to be a good landlord, and grow popular among his tenants; the mother will have eight shillings net profit, and be fit for work till she produces another child.

Those who are more thrifty (as I must confess the times re- 15 quire) may flay the carcass; the skin of which, artificially dressed, will make admirable gloves for ladies, and summer-boots for fine gentlemen.

As to our city of Dublin, shambles may be appointed for this 16 purpose in the most convenient parts of it, and butchers, we may be assured, will not be wanting; although I rather recommend buying the children alive, then dressing them hot from the knife, as we do roasting pigs.

A very worthy person, a true lover of his country, and whose 17 virtues I highly esteem, was lately pleased, in discoursing on this matter, to offer a refinement upon my scheme. He said, that many gentlemen of this kingdom, having of late destroyed their deer, he conceived that the want of venison might be well supplied by the bodies of young lads and maidens, not exceeding fourteen years of age, nor under twelve; so great a number of both sexes in every country being now ready to starve for want of work and service; and these to be disposed of by their parents, if alive, or otherwise by their nearest relations. But, with due deference to so excellent a friend, and so deserving a patriot, I cannot be altogether in his sentiments; for as to the males, my American acquaintance assured me, from frequent experience, that their flesh was generally tough and lean, like that of our schoolboys, by continual exercise, and their taste disagreeable; and to fatten them would not answer the charge. Then as to the females, it would, I think, with humble submission, be a loss to the public, because they soon would become breeders themselves: and besides, it is not improbable that some scrupulous people might be apt to censure such a practice (although indeed very unjustly), as a little bordering upon cruelty; which, I confess, has always been with me the strongest objection against any project, how well soever intended.

But in order to justify my friend, he confessed that this expedient was put into his head by the famous Psalmanazar, a native of the island Formosa, who came from thence to London above twenty years ago; and in conversation told my friend, that in his country, when any young person happened to be put to death, the executioner sold the carcass to persons of quality as a prime dainty; and that in his time the body of a plump girl of fifteen, who was crucified for an attempt to poison the emperor, was sold to his imperial majesty's prime minister of state, and other great mandarins of the court, in joints from the gibbet, at four hundred crowns. Neither indeed can I deny, that, if the same use were made of several plump young girls in this town, who, without one single groat to their fortunes, cannot stir abroad without a chair, and appear at playhouse and assemblies in foreign fineries which they never will pay for, the kingdom would not be the worse. 18

Some persons of a desponding spirit are in great concern 19

about that vast number of poor people, who are aged, diseased, or maimed; and I have been desired to employ my thoughts, what course may be taken to ease the nation of so grievous an encumbrance. But I am not in the least pain upon that matter, because it is very well known, that they are every day dying, and rotting, by cold and famine, and filth and vermin, as fast as can be reasonably expected. And as to the young labourers, they are now in almost as hopeful a condition: they cannot get work, and consequently pine away for want of nourishment, to a degree, that if at any time they are accidentally hired to common labour, they have not strength to perform it; and thus the country and themselves are happily delivered from the evils to come.

I have too long digressed, and therefore shall return to my subject. I think the advantages by the proposal which I have made are obvious and many, as well as of the highest importance.   20

For first, as I have already observed, it would greatly lessen the number of Papists, with whom we are yearly over-run, being the principal breeders of the nation, as well as our most dangerous enemies; and who stay at home on purpose to deliver the kingdom to the Pretender, hoping to take their advantage by the absence of so many good Protestants, who have chosen rather to leave their country than stay at home and pay tithes against their conscience to an Episcopal curate.   21

Secondly, The poorer tenants will have something valuable of their own, which by law may be made liable to distress, and help to pay their landlord's rent; their corn and cattle being already seized, and money a thing unknown.   22

Thirdly, Whereas the maintenance of a hundred thousand children, from two years old and upwards, cannot be computed at less than ten shillings a piece per annum, the nation's stock will be thereby increased fifty thousand pounds per annum, beside the profit of a new dish introduced to the tables of all gentlemen of fortune in the kingdom, who have any refinement in taste. And the money will circulate among ourselves, the goods being entirely of our own growth and manufacture.   23

Fourthly, The constant breeders, beside the gain of eight shillings sterling per annum by the sale of their children, will be rid of the charge of maintaining them after the first year.   24

Fifthly, This food would likewise bring great custom to 25 taverns; where the vintners will certainly be so prudent as to procure the best receipts for dressing it to perfection, and, consequently, have their houses frequented by all the fine gentlemen, who justly value themselves upon their knowledge in good eating: and a skillful cook, who understands how to oblige his guests, will contrive to make it as expensive as they please.

Sixthly, This would be a great inducement to marriage, 26 which all wise nations have either encouraged by rewards, or enforced by laws and penalties. It would increase the care and tenderness of mothers toward their children, when they were sure of a settlement for life to the poor babes, provided in some sort by the public, to their annual profit or expense. We should see an honest emulation among the married women, which of them could bring the fattest child to the market. Men would become as fond of their wives during the time of their pregnancy as they are now of their mares in foal, their cows in calf, their sows when they are ready to farrow; nor offer to beat or kick them (as is too frequent a practice) for fear of a miscarriage.

Many other advantages might be enumerated. For instance, 27 the addition of some thousand carcasses in our exportation of barrelled beef; the propagation of swine's flesh, and improvement in the art of making good bacon, so much wanted among us by the great destruction of pigs, too frequent at our table; which are no way comparable in taste or magnificence to a well-grown, fat, yearling child, which, roasted whole, will make a considerable figure at a lord mayor's feast, or any other public entertainment. But this, and many others, I omit, being studious of brevity.

Supposing that one thousand families in this city would be 28 constant customers for infants' flesh, beside others who might have it at merry-meetings, particularly at weddings and christenings, I compute that Dublin would take off annually about twenty thousand carcasses; and the rest of the kingdom (where probably they will be sold somewhat cheaper) the remaining eighty thousand.

I can think of no one objection, that will possibly be raised 29 against this proposal, unless it should be urged, that the number of people will be thereby much lessened in the kingdom.

This I freely own, and it was indeed one principal design in offering it to the world. I desire the reader will observe, that I calculate my remedy for this one individual kingdom of Ireland, and for no other that ever was, is, or I think ever can be, upon earth. Therefore let no man talk to me of other expedients: of taxing our absentees at five shillings a pound: of using neither clothes, nor household furniture, except what is our own growth and manufacture: of utterly rejecting the materials and instruments that promote foreign luxury: of curing the expensiveness of pride, vanity, idleness, and gaming in our women: of introducing a vein of parsimony, prudence, and temperance: of learning to love our country, in the want of which we differ even from LAPLANDERS, and the inhabitants of TOPINAMBOO: of quitting our animosities and factions, nor acting any longer like the Jews, who were murdering one another at the very moment their city was taken: of being a little cautious not to sell our country and conscience for nothing: of teaching landlords to have at least one degree of mercy toward their tenants: lastly, of putting a spirit of honesty, industry, and skill into our shopkeepers; who, if a resolution could now be taken to buy only our native goods, would immediately unite to cheat and exact upon us in the price, the measure, and the goodness, nor could ever yet be brought to make one fair proposal of just dealing, though often and earnestly invited to it.

Therefore I repeat, let no man talk to me of these and the like expedients, till he has at least some glimpse of hope, that there will be ever some hearty and sincere attempt to put them in practice.

But, as to myself, having been wearied out for many years with offering vain, idle, visionary thoughts, and at length utterly despairing of success, I fortunately fell upon this proposal; which, as it is wholly new, so it has something solid and real, of no expense and little trouble, full in our own power, and whereby we can incur no danger in disobliging ENGLAND. For this kind of commodity will not bear exportation, the flesh being of too tender a consistence to admit a long continuance in salt, although perhaps I could name a country, which would be glad to eat up our whole nation without it.

After all, I am not so violently bent upon my own opinion as to reject any offer proposed by wise men, which shall be found equally innocent, cheap, easy, and effectual. But before something of that kind shall be advanced in contradiction to my scheme, and offering a better, I desire the author, or authors, will be pleased maturely to consider two points. First, as things now stand, how they will be able to find food and raiment for a hundred thousand useless mouths and backs. And, secondly, there being a round million of creatures in human figure throughout this kingdom, whose whole subsistence put into a common stock would leave them in debt two million of pounds sterling, adding those who are beggars by profession, to the bulk of farmers, cottagers, and labourers, with the wives and children who are beggars in effect; I desire those politicians who dislike my overture, and may perhaps be so bold as to attempt an answer, that they will first ask the parents of these mortals, whether they would not at this day think it a great happiness to have been sold for food at a year old, in the manner I prescribe, and thereby have avoided such a perpetual scene of misfortunes, as they have since gone through, by the oppression of landlords, the impossibility of paying rent without money or trade, the want of common sustenance, with neither house nor clothes to cover them from the inclemencies of the weather, and the most inevitable prospect of entailing the like, or greater miseries, upon their breed for ever.

I profess, in the sincerity of my heart, that I have not the 33 least personal interest in endeavouring to promote this necessary work, having no other motive than the public good of my country, by advancing our trade, providing for infants, relieving the poor, and giving some pleasure to the rich. I have no children by which I can propose to get a single penny; the youngest being nine years old, and my wife past child-bearing.

Suggestions for Writing

1. Try writing your own ironic essay in which, for the sake of argument, you pretend to favor something which you do not approve or enjoy — buying term papers, sunbathing, driving into potholes, breathing smog, etc. Remember to control the tone so that you

appear reasonable and so that the reader will be able to recognize what you really believe.

2. Satire is a criticism of people, their habits, and their customs ultimately for the purpose of exposing some flaw and thereby encouraging improvement. It can range in mood from the good-natured prodding of the Latin satirist, Horace, to the harsh assaults of his successor, Juvenal. Based on your reading of "A Modest Proposal" (and possibly other works by Swift), how would you characterize his satire? What are its essential qualities?

VI · Applications

The essay is the most elastic of prose forms. . . .
Elinor Parker

The techniques necessary for writing good compositions are readily transferrable to other types of prose. Don't forget what you have already learned when it comes time to write a review of a book or a film, a literary analysis, an essay examination answer, or a research paper.

Although *book reviews* vary greatly in scope, detail, quality, and point of view, their main purpose is to inform a potential reader about a book, calling attention to its contents and its strengths and weaknesses, and possibly helping the reader to decide whether or not to read it. Ideally, a book review would be objective in its presentation of content and in its evaluation of quality.

Writing a *film review* has much in common with reviewing a book, except that the writer needs to be informed about such aspects of film-making as the actors, the director, the setting, the music, the technical qualities (lighting, camera work, etc.), and other aspects relevant to film. As in the book review, an understanding of the film's intention is important for making an evaluation that might influence a reader and potential member of the audience.

Literary papers are very common college writing assignments. The small analyses are often not based on research, but on your own thoughts and feelings about a character, a scene, a symbol, etc. in the text. Unlike the review, they do not usually focus on the overall quality of the book as a whole (although this may be a good topic for discussion), but on smaller critical issues within the text which may be handled in a shorter study. No matter what the assignment, be sure that your analysis is not pure speculation but an informed judgment based firmly in the source. Quote lines and refer to passages that back up your ideas. The reader wants to know "What makes you think so?"

The skills necessary for writing any essay are extremely valuable for composing *essay examinations*. Too often students see these as two different things, and choppy, chaotic, and vague answers are the result. The major differences between a formal, typed essay and an essay written for an examination are time and pressure, but the techniques for composing are the same.

Each essay question contains hints about what the instructor is after. Notice such key verbs as "compare," "discuss," "explain," "describe," "define," and the implied subdivision of the topics. "Give the causes for the Civil War and discuss the one you find most important," means to write an essay in two major parts—the first a series of causes, the second a personal evaluation. If the essay question itself is vague, you should still plan a clear approach, responding as specifically as possible to the elements of the question and including as much illustrative detail as it takes to prove your point. Of course, no good essay answer can be written without studying.

The major difference between *a research paper* and a personal essay or literary explication is the use of outside sources. The major pitfall is becoming lost in the thoughts and even the words of others, thus slipping into tedium or, worse, plagiarism. You can avoid such problems if you have a clear sense of your own intention at the outset. You should control your research; it should not control you. The reader must be constantly aware of a "guiding intelligence," of a thoughtful writer leading the way through the judgments, statistics, quotations, charts, etc. of others.

"Having lost sight of my objectives, I have redoubled my efforts" is not the way to approach any of these prose assignments. Always take time to determine your main purpose and your audience, and only then redouble your efforts. Be sure you know exactly what is expected of you in the assignment.

The Book Review

Three Reviews of Orwell's *Nineteen Eighty-Four*

Written in 1949, Orwell's Nineteen Eighty-Four *is a satirical novel about society in the year of the future, 1984, when everyone is ruled by the Thought Police and supervised by the omnipresent telescreen of Big Brother. (See note on Orwell on p. 266.) For a time, the hero, Winston Smith, thinks his own thoughts and experiences human love with another rebel, Julia. Notice the conviction each reviewer holds about the novel and the details each chooses as the basis for evaluation. Also pay attention to the varying approaches of each reviewer, and to the emphasis on content, on evaluation, or on both.*

MARGUERITE PACE CORCORAN

Review of *Nineteen Eighty-Four*

The essential core of this terrifying fantasy-novel is the exposition of Power; power not as a means but as an end in itself. The world of 1984 is divided into three great super-states, Eurasia, Eastasia, and Oceania, ruled over by a deified, invisible person, called Big Brother. 1

Inner Party, Outer Party and the Proles (proletariat) constitute the divisions of society and the two Parties govern the various Ministries. The Ministry of Truth (Minitru) falsifies all past records, because in Ignorance is Strength; Minilove strips sex of romance and emotion, because all emotion must be expended on war-frenzy and leader-worship. And, because 2

From *Catholic World*, August 1949 (169: 393). Reprinted by permission.

War is Peace, the three powers are engaged in continuous warfare, two against one with never a decisive victory or defeat.
Negotiations among the leaders are secret, the people being
kept in complete ignorance — a generation of automatons.

An all-seeing eye, through the medium of telescreen, observes 3
every act of the population, even the most intimate; food and
living conditions are vile, language is telescoped into a jargon
requiring less time and a minimum of thought. Thought becomes Double-think, a process whereby one can believe two
contradictory things at once — black is white, hate is a virtue.

Into this world of horror, the author introduces a compara- 4
tively normal young man, Winston Smith, thirty-nine years of
age, who concretely and most effectively demonstrates the thesis
of how this new world of 1984 with its fear, hatred, corruption
and regimentation can destroy the individual. You will be
greatly moved by Smith's longing for a home (he lives in a
government owned slum building called Victory Mansions,
London, Airstrip one); you will be emotionally stirred by his
tragic love affair with Julia; you will be overwhelmed mentally
and physically after reading what happens to Smith in Room
101, when his rebellion against Big Brother is discovered by the
Gestapo-Thought-Police.

Above all, the discerning reader will fearsomely observe in 5
this great novel the development of certain recognizable germs
of our present civilization. Mr. Orwell wastes no time in describing possible gadgets of the new era, nor in being satirical
or funny or purely fantastic. His is a rapt concern for the plight
of the human race, and in calm prose of high excellence, he
directs his diatribes chiefly at Soviet Communism and English
Socialism, but also, for the rest of us, living perhaps too smugly
under the aegis of Democracy, he sounds a liberal and rational
note of warning that we examine our motives and study the
meaning of our shibboleths.

SAMUEL SILLEN

Maggot-of-the-Month

Like his previous diatribe against the human race, *Animal* 1
Farm, George Orwell's new book has received an ovation in the
capitalist press. The gush of comparisons with Swift and Dos-
toyevsky has washed away the few remaining pebbles of literary
probity. Not even the robots of Orwell's dyspeptic vision of the
world in 1984 seem as solidly regimented as the freedom-
shouters who chose it for the Book of the Month Club, seri-
alized it in *Reader's Digest,* illustrated it in eight pages of *Life,*
and wrote pious homilies on it in *Partisan Review* and the New
York *Times.* Indeed the response is far more significant than
the book itself; it demonstrates that Orwell's sickness is epi-
demic.

The premise of the fable is that capitalism has ceased to 2
exist in 1984; and the moral is that if capitalism departs the
world will go to pot. The earth is divided into three "socialist"
areas, Oceania, Eurasia, and Eastasia, which unlike the good
old days of free enterprise are in perpetual warfare. The hero
Winston Smith, lives on Airstrip One (England) and balks at
the power-crazed regime. He is nabbed by the Thought Police,
tortured with fiendish devices, and finally he wins the privilege
of being shot when he learns to love the invisible dictator.

Orwell's nightmare is also inhabited by the "proles," who 3
constitute a mere 85 per cent of Oceania and who are described
with fear and loathing as ignorant, servile, brutish. A critic of
Orwell's earlier novel in the *Saturday Review of Literature*
expressed a profound insight when he noted: "The message of
Animal Farm seems to be . . . *that people are no damn
good."*

"People are no damn good" — that is precisely the message 4
of this plodding tale as well. For Orwell, life is a dunghill, and
after a while the "animals" look "from pig to man, and from
man to pig, and from pig to man again; but already it was
impossible to say which was which."

From *Masses and Mainstream,* Vol. II, Issue 8, August 1949. Reprinted
by permission of Janet Sillen.

As a piece of fiction this is threadbare stuff with a tasteless 5
sex angle which has been rhapsodically interpreted by Mark
Schorer in the New York *Times* as a "new discovery of the
beauty of love between man and woman." This new discovery
is well illustrated by the following scene in which Winston
Smith makes love to Julia, a fellow-rebel against the dictatorial
regime:

> "Listen. The more men you've had, the more I love you. Do
> you understand that?"
> "Yes, perfectly."
> "I hate purity, I hate goodness. I don't want any virtue to exist
> anywhere. I want everyone to be corrupt to the bones."
> "Well, then, I ought to suit you, dear. I'm corrupt to the bones."
> "You like doing this? I don't mean simply me; I mean the thing
> in itself?"
> "I adore it."
> That was above all what he wanted to hear. Not merely the love
> of one person, but the animal instinct, the simple undifferentiated
> desire: that was the force that would tear the Party to pieces.

According to *Life* magazine this is "one of the most furtive 6
and pathetic little love affairs in all literature."

Or consider this: Orwell's hero, who is supposed to awaken 7
what the reviewers call "compassion," is interviewed by a man
whom he believes to be the leader of the underground resistance
to the tyrannical regime:

> "You are prepared to cheat, to forge, to blackmail, to corrupt
> the minds of children, to distribute habit-forming drugs, to encour-
> age prostitution, to disseminate venereal diseases — to do anything
> which is likely to cause demoralization and weaken the power
> of the Party?
> "Yes."
> "If, for example, it would somehow serve our interests to
> throw sulphuric acid in a child's face — are you prepared to do
> that?"
> "Yes."

The author of this cynical rot is quite a hero himself. He 8
served for five years in the Indian Imperial Police, an excellent
training center for dealing with the "proles." He was later asso-

ciated with the Trotskyites in Spain, serving in the P.O.U.M.
and he freely concedes that when this organization of treason
to the Spanish Republic was "accused of pro-fascist activities I
defended them to the best of my ability." During World War II
he busied himself with defamation of the Soviet Union.

And now, as Lionel Trilling approvingly notes in *The New* 9
Yorker, Orwell "marks a turn in thought." What is the significance of this turn? The literary mouthpieces of imperialism
have discovered that the crude anti-Sovietism of a Kravchenko [1]
is not enough; the system of class oppression must be directly
upheld and *any* belief in change and progress must be frightened out of people.

Like Trilling, the editorial writers of *Life* have shrewdly 10
seized upon Orwell's generalized attack on the "welfare state"
to attack not only the Soviet Union but [Henry] Wallace and
the British Laborites. "Many readers in England," says *Life,*
"will find that his book reinforces a growing suspicion that
some of the British Laborites revel in austerity and would love
to preserve it—just as the more fervent New Dealers in the
U.S. often seemed to have the secret hope that the depression
mentality of the '30's, source of their power and excuse for their
experiments, would never end."

In short, Orwell's novel coincides perfectly with the propo- 11
ganda of the National Association of Manufacturers, and it is
being greeted for exactly the same reasons that Frederick
Hayek's *The Road to Serfdom* was hailed a few years back.

The bourgeoisie, in its younger days, could find spokesmen 12
who painted rosy visions of the future. In its decay, surrounded
by burgeoning socialism, it is capable only of hate-filled, de-
humanized anti-Utopias. Confidence has given way to the nihi-
listic literature of the graveyard. Now that Ezra Pound [2] has
been given a government award and George Orwell has become
a best-seller we would seem to have reached bottom. But there
is a hideous ingenuity in the perversions of a dying capitalism,

---

[1] Member of the Russian government who defected to the West in opposition to Stalin.

[2] E. Pound (1885–1972): American poet and scholar who supported Fascism during World War II; later tried for high treason, but judged insane.

and it will keep probing for new depths of rottenness which the maggots will find "brilliant and morally invigorating."

ROBERT KEE

Review of *Nineteen Eighty-Four*

When you put down *Tess of the D'Urbervilles* [1] your feel-   1
ings are not, in spite of the last sentence, directed primarily against the President of the Immortals. They are not in fact directed against anyone. They are too big for that, and too simple, amounting only to an overwhelming conviction of the tragedy of Tess. When the rubber truncheons, the electric torturing machines and the horrifying mysteries of Room 101 have finished their sport with Winston Smith, hero of Mr. Orwell's fascinating new book, you may conceivably feel bitter against Big Brother (mythical dictator of Oceania and London in 1984), more probably you will have an overwhelming sense of the tragedy of civilization, but you could hardly care less about Winston Smith. This is because Mr. Orwell has been interested in Smith not as a personality but as an instrument for analyzing totalitarianism. Certainly he has his moments of humanity, though these are not often to be found in the rather flat love affair with his co-rebel, Julia. His touching discovery of significance in the "lost" nursery rhyme is more convincing. But although *Nineteen Eighty-Four* is a parable of humanism, strangely it is not the human beings in it who count. And for this reason, strictly as a novel, it must be classed as a failure.

But it is not "strictly a novel." Regard it, then, as satire.   2
Mr. Orwell's ingenuity in devising details for this totalitarian society of the future has been remarkable. The ever-present telescreens which watch and blare propaganda simultaneously, and which can pick up an increase in your heart-beats and use what you say in your sleep in evidence against you; the all too probable official language, Newspeak; the fatuous slogans

From *Spectator,* June 17, 1949. Reprinted by permission of the publisher.
[1] *Tess of the D'Urbervilles:* novel by Thomas Hardy (1891).

("War is Peace," "Orthodoxy is Unconsciousness"); the "face-
crime," which would mean immediate vaporising for so many
of us—all this invention is in a class with *Gulliver, Erewhon*
and *Brave New World.* And yet even as satire there is a weakness. For the real power of satire lies in its ability to shock and
surprise. The material dealt with may be familiar, but it is the
new twist that makes us see it differently which counts. There
is no intellectual surprise in 1984. We knew all this before:
that totalitarian parties are interested only in power, that they
are capable of unpleasantness to an infinite degree, indifferent
to the sufferings of "the proles," and conducive to the total
extinction of the human spirit. "Stale news" is the last response
that one expects a good satire to evoke. And yet it rises continually to the mind on reading *Nineteen Eighty-Four.*

Again the book has many qualities as a thriller. The first   3
half is as exciting as one could wish. But there is a flaw here,
too. Just at the point where the excitement becomes excruciating
and Winston and Julia launch out into their revolt against the
Party, Mr. Orwell maddeningly reminds us that all he's really
interested in is the political implication of his story. He sus-
pends the plot for thirty pages of Trotsky-Goldstein-Orwell
analysis of contemporary political trends. And for the rest of
the book he is concerned only with establishing the fact that no
refinement of horror is beyond the Party's reach, not even that
of making a man wholly love and believe in something which
he knows is false and hateful.

Compounded of novel, satire and thriller, and unsatisfac-   4
tory as all three, *Nineteen Eighty-Four* is nevertheless a remarkable book. You may put it down, shaken, intrigued, or merely
disappointed; but one thing will have made its impact on you,
and that is the passionate force of Mr. Orwell's own feelings.
And passion is a rare thing in English writing today.

Suggestions for Writing

1. Write your own review of a book with which you are very
   familiar. Be sure to make every effort to understand the writer's
   purposes before judging its quality. Consider such matters as
   intention, presentation, organization, quality of thought, quality

of writing, special characteristics, technical quality, success in fulfilling the intention. Illustrate your judgments with specific examples from the text.

2. Read three reviews of a book with which you are very familiar and evaluate them as reviews. Which do you find most valuable and convincing? Why? (You might begin with the *Book Review Digest.*)

3. If you have read *Nineteen Eighty-Four,* evaluate the reviews presented here in the light of your own reaction to the novel.

4. Compare the approaches of these three reviewers. Which do you find most valuable? Why?

The Film Review

Two Reviews of the film, "Superman"

These two reviewers give personal reactions to the $35 million Warner Brothers film, "Superman." Before its release, the company distributed Superman bath towels, T shirts, dolls, lunch boxes, comic books, costumes, paperbacks, posters, and pogo sticks. But in spite of promotional paraphernalia, it is the reviewer's job to evaluate a film on its merits. Notice the selection of illustrative detail by each reviewer.

RICHARD A. BLAKE

Simply Super

Jackie Hudson had a broken front tooth that was the envy of the neighborhood. He also had a copy of the Superman comic book that traced the origins of the man of steel from the destruction of the planet Krypton to his discovery of his role in the fight for law and order. In a long and heated trading session, at the cost of several Green Hornets and Batmans, the prized Superman finally came into my possession. Few stories held such hypnotic fascination over my childhood imagination. 1

Superman has now leapt with a single bound into my adulthood, not as a 10-cent comic book but as a $35-million movie from Warners, with a script begun by Mario Puzo, father of "The Godfather," and cameo performances by Marlon Brando, Susannah York, Glenn Ford, Gene Hackman, Valerie Perrine and Jackie Cooper. A record album of the score by John Wil- 2

From *America* magazine, January 6–13, 1979. Reprinted by permission.

liams is an enthusiastic combination of the best of "Star Wars"
and Richard Strauss's "Death and Transfiguration." A paper-
back thriller, *Superman, The Last Son of Krypton,* by Elliott
S. Maggin is billed as "first in Warner's new serial of Superman novels." The Broadway revival of George Bernard Shaw's
"Man and Superman" [1] is apparently merely a coincidence,
but it does add to a general paranoia that the nation has been
taken over by the Superman industry.

Like most other big-budget movies intended to drag in 3
record audiences, "Superman" is aimed at young adults, who
were, of course, not even in sight when Superman first dropped
in from Krypton in 1938. The current version opens with a
small-screen image of an old comic book and, as the pages turn
and lumps of nostalgia rise in the throats of the pre-Beatles
generation, the screen grows wider and the sound rises for what
must be the longest and loudest set of credits in motion picture
history. The audience is whisked away from its old comic book
memories through the galaxies in a journey comparable to
"2001: A Space Odyssey." It turns out to be a joy ride from start
to finish.

Three stories, each with its own character, are folded in 4
upon another in this two-and-a-half-hour epic of good humor.
The first and most dominant story begins on the planet Krypton, as the wise and white-haired Jor-El (Marlon Brando) has
just finished his summation to the jury and must cast the deciding vote in the conviction of three traitors. The traitors are
condemned, compressed into a two-dimensional playing card
and whisked off to space in some kind of magical time warp.
They have nothing to do with the film, but the publicity grem-
lins at Warners have let out the word that this troublesome trio
will return to their villainous ways in "Superman II," now in
production.

After the distraction of this preview of things to come, 5
the real story begins. Krypton is coming apart at the seams.
This should be no surprise, even to the densest of Kryptonians,
since the whole place looks like a chandelier designed by one
of Queen Victoria's favorite artists gone mad. Jor-El fires his
son to Smallville, U.S.A., just as Krypton blows up. (It is a ter-

---

[1] Shaw (1856–1950), Irish essayist, critic and dramatist.

rible thing to do to a child, with Glenn Ford as a foster father, too!)

Aw, shucks, he can't even get to first base with the girls and 6
is making a gosh-darned mess out of his life, until that magic day when he travels to the North Pole, and there, amid the caves of ice, Jor-El appears as bard among the bergs and tells young Mr. Kent of his law-and-order destiny. The plot may seem a bit, shall we say, thin, but it does provide an excuse for the marvelous science-fiction special effects, and that is really what this Krypton story is all about anyway.

The second plot is cops-and-robbers comedy in the style of 7
the old Batman television series. Archvillain Lex Luthor steals a missile from the United States and plans to blast California into the Pacific by dropping a superbomb into the San Andreas fault. As a precaution, he uses a chunk of kryptonite from an old meteor to capture Superman and render him powerless in an apartment that is a replica of Grand Central Terminal in, not New York, but Metropolis. As the last possible minute . . . well, you know.

Superman's love life, the third plot, is centered on the 8
bumbling but nice Clark Kent, who has to put on his red cape and blue longjohns to have the courage to woo Lois Lane, a tough-talking but basically nice-once-you-get-to-know-her reporter for The Daily Planet.

Even though the three stories form an impossible mixture of 9
"Stars Wars," "Batman" and "The Front Page," the combination works. Most of the credit must go to the engaging performances of the two principals, Christopher Reeve in the title role and Margot Kidder as Lois. They seem to be enjoying themselves so much that an audience is swept right along by their enthusiasm. The director, Richard Donner, has left them enough humanity to make them believable and enough comic-book heroics to provide the laughs.

Analyses of "Superman" and the Superman phenomenon 10
are already rolling out of typewriters across the nation, much to my dread. Before long, there will no doubt be theological interpretations of the story: A father sends his son to earth to do good and save mankind from its evil ways, yet he is not to use his special powers to change the course of human history. Clark Kent must die, so that Superman may conquer evil. And so on and on and on.

The reason for this compulsion is obvious. This is a big, en- 11
joyable movie that is beautifully executed and competently
marketed during a holiday season. Not able to believe in the
skill of Hollywood fantasy makers and New York publicity
crafters, the critics and commentators will search the crevices of
their own imaginations to explain the enthusiasm.

Jackie Hudson knew the secret. He knew that his comic 12
book was a valuable piece of property and he made his customers pay for it. He did not have to speculate on America's
search for a hero or the age of cynicism that trivializes the
heroic. No, he knew a good comic book when he saw one.

LAWRENCE O'TOOLE

Superlunk

Proof of the pall that money can buy, *Superman,* heralded as 1
a kind of Second Coming with advanced aerodynamics to
match Christ's, is a passable entertainment. The long-awaited
flying sequences work (i.e. you can't see the wires), but they
aren't handled with much grace or rhythmic energy; when
Superman takes Lois Lane for an excursion over Metropolis it's
like a Cessna ride. The movie manages no magic. Richard Donner doesn't bring the imaginative vision to the material that a
director like Steven Spielberg [1] might have: the superkid's
arrival from Krypton in a meteor (the movie is a special effects
extravaganza, yet we don't see the meteor landing) has no wonder in it and Geoffrey Unsworth's images are big and be-
hemothic, not awesome. It's bigness that killed the beast.

Featuring the longest credit list ever unrolled, *Superman* 2
isn't a movie—it's a catalogue, mostly of disaster movies. Krypton exploding, Lois in a helicopter hanging off a skyscraper, a
train about to be derailed, an airliner losing an engine, and
the Boulder Dam bursting. The plot (sort of) pits Lex Luthor
(Gene Hackman) and his henchpeople (Valerie Perrine and
Ned Beatty) against the Man of Steel, with Luthor redirecting

---

From *Maclean's,* December 25, 1978. Reprinted by permission.
[1] Spielberg (b. 1947), director of "Jaws" and "Close Encounters of a
Third Kind."

nuclear warheads to land at the San Andreas Fault producing all the peril. Performances are little more than appearances: as the Kryptonians, Terence Stamp, Maria Schell, Trevor Howard and Susannah York are walk-ons. And then there's Marlon Brando as Jor-El, Superman's father, in a $3.7-million performance that is more like 10 cents a glance. John Barry's sets for Krypton are virtually the same as those he did for *Star Wars*, Luthor's underground lair little different from the villains' hideaways in TV's *Batman*.

Beyond and below everything else is the script, which nearly 3 everyone and his mother has worked on. A lot of the fun— and there is a lot of fun in the movie—is spoiled by the attitude taken to *Superman* by the movie-makers. He's not treated as a camp object and he's not played straight, either—he's an anachronism given to hip banter. "I never drink when I'm flying," he tells Lois. Lois, landed from her ride, says, "What a super man." Ah, hem. As Superman himself, Christopher Reeve is a gifted comedian and Margot Kidder's a saucy, sexy, wise-acre Lois. Only one scene has that unblemished eye for the newness and astonishment in things that draws us to movies: the big, lovable, dashing lunk orbiting around the earth at so supersonic a speed that he turns back time and saves Lois' life. Otherwise, there's no real flight. No supernal skies. Just small, technological sorceries. In a way, *Superman* never really leaves Smallville.

Suggestions for Writing

1. Write your own review of a film you have seen recently. Be sure to look up the necessary information on actors, etc. so that your discussion will be concrete. (It might be wise to attend a film for this purpose and to take notes while you are watching it.)

2. Find two or three reviews of a film about which you have strong feelings and clear recollection, summarize their judgments, and then evaluate them. (*The Reader's Guide to Periodical Literature* lists film reviews in the back of each volume.)

3. Compare these two reviews of "Superman." Which one do you find most convincing? Why? Do you see any weaknesses in either of them?

The Literary Paper

Writing on Scenes and Symbols

In the first paper, the writer studies the purpose of a particular scene in the novel Nineteen Eighty-Four *by George Orwell. It is written in response to the question, "Why does the writer include ———— in the novel?" The answers to the question eventually become the topics of the paragraphs. Notice that the basic pattern remains visible, even though the supporting information is drawn from the text rather than from personal experience.*

A literary symbol may be defined as something that represents something beyond itself. A red rose, for example, may symbolize a young, beautiful girl, or a lion may symbolize strength. In literature, a single person or object may represent meanings beyond itself that help us to understand the writer more fully. The second paper, on Frost's "Stopping by Woods on a Snowy Evening," discusses the possible meanings of a particular symbol in the poem—in this case, the woods. Notice how the close consideration of one small element in a literary work may broaden into larger issues of meaning.

EILEEN DRAGO (student)

The Meeting with the Old Proletarian in *Nineteen Eighty-Four*

In *Nineteen Eighty-Four,* Orwell's hero, Winston, an alien- 1 ated member of the Party, often wanders in the proletarian section of town for relief from the surveillance of the Thought

Police. In fact, he comes to place his hopes for the future in the eighty-five percent of society which makes up the lowest class, "But if there was hope, it lay in the proles." [1] During one of these excursions, he notices a man, nearly eighty years old, and tries to question him in an effort to discover the truth about life before the Revolution. But the old man answers none of his questions, only recalling random personal facts like the number of years since he has seen a top hat or the day he was pushed off the sidewalk by a drunken gentleman. Winston leaves in despair. Although this early encounter with the old proletarian is minor in comparison to later ones with Julia and O'Brien, Orwell includes it in his novel for a variety of reasons.

First, the meeting is evidence of Winston's desperate eager-   2
ness to discover the truth. All along he has been taking chances against the Party and its Thought Police, committing "thought-crime" by questioning the truth of their statements, secretly recording these anti-Party thoughts in an illicit diary and wandering in a section of town where Party members rarely go. Once he starts the search for the truth, however, these actions are not enough. He cannot stop his quest for information by which he may judge the statements of the party, so when he realizes that the old prole may remember pre-Revolutionary life, ". . . a lunatic response took hold of him" (p. 39). He knows that for taking actions like this he is "already dead" (p. 13), so he continues to take even more daring actions. Winston cannot give up.

The Party cannot satisfy his desire to learn about the past,   3
in spite of what he knows are the certain odds against him. He will be caught. It is this knowledge that makes the scene with the old man so frightening, another of its purposes in the novel. As in so many scenes before and after this one, the reader expects Winston to be arrested at any moment. Through him, we share the terror of living under the watchful and treacherous Thought Police and through him our fear increases as he

---

[1] George Orwell, *Nineteen Eighty-Four,* in *Orwell's Nineteen Eighty-Four: Text Sources, Criticism,* ed. Irving Howe (New York: Harcourt, Brace and World, Inc. 1963), p. 38. All further page references will be to this text.

slowly drags out useless answers from the tedious old pubber. Every pause in the octogenarian's speech, every drift of his thought adds to the reader's fright:

> "I was jest thinking, I ain't seen a top 'at in years. Gorn right out, they 'ave. The last time I wore one was at my sister-in-law's funeral. And that was — well, I couldn't give you the date, but it must 'a been fifty years ago. Of course it was only 'ired for the occasion, you understand" (p. 41).

It is one of the most frustrating and suspenseful encounters along the way to Winston's final capture.

And, seen in the larger context, it is a foreshadowing of his 4 ultimate defeat. By the end of the novel, the conversation with the old man takes its place among the many other pieces of evidence that Winston never could have won. Here, on a minor scale, Winston experiences the crushing of his hope, in this case the hope that he can uncover a fact inconsistent with the Party's presentation of its "fact" and thus prove his mind free from this control. He enters the pub full of hope, he eagerly buys a social drink for the old man, and he patiently quizzes him until he is forced to recognize the futility of his quest. As happens so often in the novel, most powerfully at the end, hope is destroyed, and the Party is the victor. In his intolerable ignorance, the old man deals a blow to Winston's search for a past and for freedom, driving him on to even more desperate and finally fatal chances.

In the old man himself we see living evidence of the total 5 success of the Thought Police. Members of the Party must think only as Members of the Party. Proletarians must not think at all. Any proletarian who does will be "vaporized" immediately. The fact of the old proletarian's existence at such an advanced age is sufficient evidence for his essential mindlessness, which he proves in every word he utters. He can make no judgments about the past or the present, he has no sense of the relative importance of facts and events, he has no ability to communicate coherently. In short, he cannot think. For all his potential value as a source of information, he might just as well have been "living in the treetops" (p. 40), as the barman says. If he were able to answer Winston's questions satisfactorily about the quality of life before the Revolution, he would not be alive in the first place. His longevity is a sign of his total ignorance, for the Thought Police would not have allowed real thought to thrive for so long.

Nor would they have allowed any accurate memory of the   6 historical past to linger even in one man's mind. The most important function of this encounter with the old proletarian is to show the effects of the loss of history. If accurate historical records are destroyed and if historical memory is entrusted to the mindless, history is essentially dead. Winston wants to know about poverty, capitalism, freedom, the relationship between the upper and the lower classes, so that he can compare his time with past time, and thus make an independent judgment, but he is forced to accept the fact that "the old man's memory was nothing but a rubbish heap of details" (p. 41). He is not one of the "last links" (p. 39) to the past, he is a missing link. In the prole's blundering and self-centered recollections, we see the past destroyed — one of Orwell's most sobering warnings in the novel. Once independent thought is gone and once all evidence of anything different from the present is obliterated, Big Brother has won. Later, when Winston finally consents to love Big Brother, he too has joined the old man in his loss of true self, in his mindlessness. He has only to die.

Thus, what at first might appear a minor scene, a mere   7 interlude in the long series of exploits for Winston, actually relates to many of the major ideas of the novel and contributes to their development. It helps in the characterization of Winston as an eager, if unwise, seeker after truth, it contributes to the fear and suspense of the novel, it warns of Winston's final defeat, it characterizes the perfect proletarian, giving evidence of the efficiency of the Thought Police, and most importantly, it displays the fatal danger of losing one's sense of the past. The question, "Was life better before the Revolution than it is now?" and all other questions like it are indeed unanswerable. Big Brother has *all* the answers.

Suggestion for Writing

Write an essay on a literary work in which you answer the question, "Why does the writer include ____ in the work?" Be careful not to get stuck in repeating the action of the story; assume your reader is already familiar with the text. Try to understand, from the writer's point of view, why a certain scene, object, character, or other element is part of the work.

ROBERT FROST

Stopping by Woods on a Snowy Evening

Whose woods these are I think I know.
His house is in the village, though;
He will not see me stopping here
To watch his woods fill up with snow.

My little horse must think it queer   5
To stop without a farmhouse near
Between the woods and frozen lake
The darkest evening of the year.

He gives his harness bells a shake
To ask if there is some mistake.   10
The only other sound's the sweep
Of easy wind and downy flake.

The woods are lovely, dark, and deep,
But I have promises to keep,
And miles to go before I sleep,   15
And miles to go before I sleep.

GUY O'BRIEN (student)

The Woods in "Stopping by Woods on a Snowy Evening"

In the four stanzas of the poem, "Stopping by Woods on a   1
Snowy Evening," the narrator describes a very small event of a

winter evening. In stanza one, he stops his horse-drawn carriage in order to watch someone's woods "fill up with snow"; then, in stanza two, he suggests that his horse must be wondering why he stopped in the first place, a concern which, in stanza three, causes the horse to give "his harness bells a shake." In the final stanza, the narrator praises the beauty of the snowy woods and acknowledges that he has "promises to keep" and "miles to go" before he sleeps. Clearly, the woods are important to the man in the wagon, causing him to stop without explanation, even though he has a long journey ahead of him. And the woods are important to the reader, for they suggest a variety of meanings in the poem.

First of all, the woods are literally someone's wooded property, a piece of land possibly owned by a man in the village. The narrator does not forget that there is an owner; in fact, his proprietorship intrudes on his immediate experience in the first stanza of the poem. But even though the woods are owned, the proprietor will not see the narrator watching them at the moment. So, for the time being, the woods are in a sense more the narrator's than the owner's who is not present to see, let alone claim, them. Once he is acknowledged, the owner is not mentioned again by the narrator. After all, he is in the village, not out near his woods on the cold road, "without a farmhouse near." 2

The woods are not simply the possession of either of them, however. They are a thing of beauty, appreciated by the narrator who was drawn to stop and watch them "fill up with snow." Peaceful and silent except for the "sweep / Of easy wind and downy flake," and even more explicitly, "lovely, dark, and deep," they are beautiful enough to overcome temporarily the practical need to travel. Seductive, like a lovely woman or a work of art, they make the narrator want to tarry in appreciation against the wishes of his horse and in spite of the long journey ahead. In fact, he seems willing to stay for a time, until the "woods fill up with snow." 3

And the woods suggest rest, another of their meanings in the poem. The words, "easy wind" and "downy flake," "lovely, dark, and deep," all suggest softness and peace, like a bed, a temporary respite not only from the journey home, but also from the responsibilities of life itself, from the duties of the village and from the recipients of those "promises" that must be 4 kept by the speaker. The snowy woods allow a peaceful pause in the evening, the day, and the life of the man who stops to rest with them; he may well be anticipating the comforts of bed, but the woods offer a rest of their own during the journey itself.

If the pause becomes more attractive to the narrator than the goal itself, the woods might also suggest a temporary desire for permanent rest, for the oblivion of being forever taken in by the "lovely, dark, and deep" woods. In his pausing, while the snow falls on him, his wagon, and his horse, as well as on the woods themselves, the narrator becomes, for a time, one with the natural world around him, sharing in the "sweep/Of easy wind and downy flake" on the "darkest evening of the year." If he chooses never to respond to the impatient shake of the harness bells, never to move on down the road, he will die there—finally a true part of the natural world. At this extreme, then, the woods might suggest a passing "death wish," a brief yearning to give up all effort to reach the village and to live out his own life.

But, apparently, this is not the resolution taken in this poem. He seems committed to go on, in spite of the attractions of stopping. Like a passing guest, he is merely "stopping by," not moving in. And he has responsibilities to others and a long trip ahead of him—"And miles to go before I sleep/And miles to go before I sleep"—possibly the miles of the road to the night's sleep in his bed and, by suggestion, the miles of his life before the long sleep in his grave. So, whether the woods be "borrowed" property of another, a vision of beauty, the attractions of temporary ease, or ultimately, a suggestion of the oblivion of death, the narrator feels compelled to move on and away from them. It is interesting to notice that at the end of the poem, he has not yet set out, but has simply stated some good reasons why he should. His resolve seems firm, however; neither he nor his horse seem ready to stop permanently.

Suggestions for Writing

1. Write an essay on another aspect of "Stopping by Woods on a Snowy Evening" — the horse, for example, or possibly the snow itself or the narrator.

2. Write an essay giving possible meanings for the road in the poem by Robert Frost, "The Road Not Taken," which follows these suggestions.
3. Consider the relationship between rhythm and meaning in either of these two poems.
4. Compare the narrators in these two poems by Frost. What kind of character emerges? What effect does the voice of the narrator have on each poem?

ROBERT FROST

The Road Not Taken

Two roads diverged in a yellow wood,
And sorry I could not travel both
And be one traveler, long I stood
And looked down one as far as I could
To where it bent in the undergrowth;

Then took the other, as just as fair,
And having perhaps the better claim,
Because it was grassy and wanted wear,
Though as for that the passing there
Had worn them really about the same,

And both that morning equally lay
In leaves no step had trodden black.
Oh, I kept the first for another day!
Yet knowing how way leads on to way,
I doubted if I should ever come back.

I shall be telling this with a sigh
Somewhere ages and ages hence:
Two roads diverged in a wood, and I —
I took the one less traveled by,
And that has made all the difference.

Essay Examination Answer:
Social Sciences–History

Question:
Compare and contrast Andrew Jackson's handling of the Nullification Controversy and James Buchanan's handling of the Secession Crisis. (45 min.)

Answer:
    Both Andrew Jackson and James Buchanan were involved [1] in important and complex issues which centered around the relationship between the power of the Federal Government and that of State Government. In the Nullification Controversy (1832–33), the state of South Carolina challenged the right of the Federal Government to levy a protective tariff. In the Secession Crisis, again spearheaded by South Carolina, states attempted to withdraw from the Union after the 1860 election of Lincoln. Although both of these issues required and received presidential responses, the kinds of actions taken by Jackson and Buchanan varied markedly from one another.

Andrew Jackson's reaction to South Carolina's attempts to 2 nullify the federal tariff was quick, forceful, and at the same time, conciliatory. He announced immediately that no state had the right to nullify a federal law or to secede from the Union. He induced Congress to pass a Force Act which allowed the use of military force against South Carolina, he sent reinforcements to the harbor of Charleston in order to insure compliance with the tariff law, and he announced that, if the need arose, he would personally lead forces against South Carolina. In conciliation, he assured the South Carolinians that the federal debt was being reduced thus promising tariff reduction, and he encouraged Congress to write a new bill which would provide for a gradual reduction in the tariff. This bill, the Compromise Tariff of 1833, was passed by Congress and finally accepted by South Carolina which then withdrew its previous ordinance of nullification.

Not to be placated entirely, however, South Carolina per- 3 sisted in its advocacy of States' Rights by gratuitously nullifying the Force Act itself, a bill which had already been rendered a dead letter by the acceptance of the 1833 Tariff. The basic issue of States' Rights was therefore left essentially unresolved and reared its head again in the Secession Crisis of 1860. Jackson's victory, although remarkable, was not total. His forceful approach did indeed lead to an acceptable resolution of a major controversy, but only for a time.

In the Secession Crisis of 1860, which followed on Lincoln's 4 election to the presidency, the less forceful and confident James Buchanan was required to respond. Possibly because of his own rather timid nature, his "lame duck" position until Lincoln's inauguration, his Democratic political leanings, and his pro-Southern sympathies, he failed to take strong action against the secessionist efforts of the south. He proclaimed, for example, that no state had the right to secede, but at the same time, he argued that no Constitutional power in the Federal Government could coerce a state to remain in the Union. Denying both secession and coercion, he remained essentially stalled, allowing secessionist members of his cabinet to remain for some time in power and hoping for a political compromise before any decisive actions had to be taken. When encouraged by the unionists in his cabinet, he finally determined to protect federal law and property in the south, he sent an unarmed ship, the "Star of the West," to Charleston harbor, but when the South Carolinians fired upon the ship, it fled without executing its mission. While Buchanan played for time and conducted ineffective operations against the south, all compromise efforts were rejected either by the south or by the Republicans, and he presided over the gradual secession of many of the states which would eventually form the Confederacy.

Granted, the issues were not identical, nor were the political 5 forces operating around each President identical—in 1832–33, South Carolina had the sympathy perhaps, but not the full support of the other southern states, while in 1860, she was supported by at least six states—but a comparison of their responses to two major States' Rights controversies nevertheless reveals a striking contrast in styles. Jackson was quick, forceful and yet conciliatory in reacting to the Nullification Controversy; Buchanan was hesitant, indecisive and ambiguous in responding to the Secession Crisis. A combination of character and circumstance contributed to the variations in approach to these important challenges to federal power.

Suggestions for Writing

1. For a subject with which you are familiar, make up your own "comparative" essay question and then answer it. (For example: "Compare and contrast Auden's and Williams' use of the Icarus myth in their poems on Brueghel's painting." Or "Compare the methods of Freudian with those of Jungian psychoanalysis.")
2. Write an answer to an essay question which you have received recently. Include the question with the answer. (You may use your books.)

Essay Examination Answer: Natural Sciences–Biology

Question:
Name three membranous organelles of eukaryotic cells and give the functions of each. (1 hour)

Answer:

Cells may be divided into two types, prokaryotic and eu- 1
karyotic, the major differences being the absence of a nuclear
membrane and of well-defined organelles in prokaryotic cells
and their consistent appearance in the eukaryote. All bacteria
are composed of prokaryotic cells; all other cells are eukaryotic,
whether they be found in the petal of a rose or the ear of an
elephant. Three of the membranous organelles of eukaryotic
cells are the mitochondria, chloroplasts and lysosomes, each one
with its own specific functions.

Mitochondria, found with very rare exceptions in all eu- 2
karyotic cells, contain the enzymes of cell respiration, the means
by which the cells make ATP. ATP, which may be described as
the energy currency of life, is required whenever work is done
by a cell—for muscle contraction (walking, breathing, writing,
speaking, digesting, etc.), for creation of nerve impulses (seeing,
hearing, tasting, learning, loving, hating, etc.), and for all other
functions demanding energy.

Chloroplasts, another of these membranous organelles, are 3
not distributed as widely as mitochondria, but are found only
in photosynthetic cells. Chloroplasts are responsible for carrying out the reactions of photosynthesis which involves the en-
trapment of light energy and its deposit into new kinds of
energy-rich organic molecules. Carbon dioxide and the energy
of the sun are combined to produce sugar, for example, itself a
source of further energy for the plant or for an animal that eats
the plant or one of its parts (an apple). Photosynthesis is, therefore, essential not only for the life of the plant, but indirectly
for the life of virtually every other organism living on the
earth. Without chloroplasts, life as it is presently represented
on earth could not exist.

Lysosomes, like mitochondria, are universally found organ- 4
elles in eukaryotic cells. They are membrane-bound sacks filled
with powerful digestive enzymes and are used for a great variety of puroposes. When, for example, a white blood cell phago-
cytizes a bacterium, a lysosome pours digestive enzymes into
the phagosome (the cellular cavity in which the bacterium is
trapped) and digests the vital components of the bacterium,
killing it. And, through a similar process, they may destroy
worn-out cell parts, a damaged mitochondrion in a liver cell,

for example; they also function in the selective destruction of worn-out cells, as many as several million red blood cells each second. Their important function in growth and development involves the shaping of body parts. In bones, for example, the lysosomes of special cells called "osteoclasts" work like sculptors, creating and shaping the marrow cavities as the bone grows. Lysosomes, by bursting and then digesting away the cells, are also responsible for the disappearance of the tadpole's tail as it undergoes metamorphosis into a frog. They are important also to the successive stages of development of the human fetus in preparation for birth. And they have recently been implicated in the process of aging and perhaps death itself, both of which seem to be programmed in DNA (genes) and can be looked upon as evolutionary strategies for survival, not of the individual, but of the species.

In summary, mitochondria are the sites of energy metabolism and the generation of ATP. Chloroplasts carry out photosynthesis, the reactions which link the energy metabolism of all organisms on earth to the radiant energy produced in the sun. Lysosomes, finally, have a wide range of functions, including protection against infection, selective destruction of worn-out cells and cell parts, the shaping of body parts which occurs during development and finally, aging and death. All three of these organelles are essential for life as we know it.

Suggestions for Writing

1. For a subject with which you are familiar, make up a sample essay question on function and then answer it. (For example: "What are the functions of the three branches of the Federal Government?" "What are some possible functions for the conclusion of an essay?")

2. Plan an approach for the following questions, whether or not you are familiar with the topic:
   a. Discuss the Norman Conquest of England in 1066. (25 pts., 30 min.)
   b. What evidence do you know that supports or fails to support Darwin's theory of evolution? (15 pts., 20 min.)
   c. In a letter to a popular magazine, a reader charged the general public with believing that "the killing of unborn babies is

thought a small price to pay for the pleasure of sex." How do you react to this opinion? (20 pts., 20 min.)

d. Describe and discuss the development of France under the Capetian kings — Hugh Capet (987) to Philip the Fair (1314). (50 pts., 45 min.)

e. Crane's "The Bride Comes to Yellow Sky" concerns change. Explain. (10 pts., 20 min.)

The Research Paper

*It is possible to write a paper in which you summarize
the opinions of others on a certain subject and then draw
a conclusion about them—the inductive method. Or it is
possible to follow a more traditional pattern, arguing a
thesis from the beginning and using the outside sources
in the service of the writer's argument—the deductive
method. This research paper, "Some Treatments for Alcoholism," is an example of the latter pattern.*

*You will probably do most of your research before you
start writing your own paper, but be sure you know
which kind of approach you are taking and make your intention clear to your reader very early. Documentation—
footnotes, bibliography, quotations, typing formalities—
must receive careful attention. The effect of a well-written
paper with original thought and excellent research can
be seriously harmed by careless errors in presentation.
Make neatness an indispensable requirement.*

CARL SANCHEZ (student)

Some Treatments for Alcoholism

Officially, alcoholism is a dependence on alcohol ". . . to such [1]
an extent that it shows noticeable interference with . . . bodily
or mental health, . . . interpersonal relations, and . . . satisfactory social and economic functioning." [1] After heart disease
and cancer, it is the third largest cause of death among those
between the ages of thirty-five and fifty-five.[2] In the United
States, there are approximately nine million alcoholics,[3] some
of whom cause thousands of dollars loss to the country's business [4] and all of whom reduce the quality of their own lives.

Usually a progressive disease, it moves gradually from over-drinking to chronic and uncontrolled addiction, affecting the liver, heart and nervous system of its victims, often isolating them from all society.[5] As the anthropologist, Margaret Mead, says, "The alcoholic is someone for whom alcohol is both irresistible and progressively poisonous."[6] To counteract these effects, much private and public money, time and attention has been given to discovering possible cures, to finding ways to check this almost certain slide to destruction. As a result, many treatments have been devised, some less successful than others, none perfect.

Among the least successful "treatments" are some of the stan- 2
dard reactions of those around the alcoholic: nagging, sermonizing on the virtues of temperance, guarding or protecting the drinker, and existing with long-suffering endurance.[7] The common denominator for failure in all of these "home remedies" for alcoholism is the acceptance of responsibility by those around the drinker rather than by the drinker him- or herself. Nagging creates an unpleasant atmosphere which the alcoholic feels all the more justified in escaping with drink. Sermonizing teaches what the alcoholic already knows—that excessive drinking is dangerous—or what is of no personal concern—that it is not virtuous. Guarding the drinker, searching for hidden bottles or checking for secret signs of drinking set up a futile competition between the guard and the guarded, while protecting the drinker from the consequences of alcohol sets the stage for further disaster by making the behavior seem less harmful than it actually is. Hurt endurance usually produces guilt in the alcoholic who recognizes the suffering but cannot stop the drinking and therefore sees further reason for escape by drinking.[8] None of these reactions places the responsibility on the alcoholic who chooses to drink or not to drink, yet only the drinker can stop drinking.

The central issue appears to be that the alcoholic feels that 3
drink is indispensable for survival, that there is no other way to cope with the daily stresses, that it is as necessary as breathing. As Dr. Ebbe Curtis Hoff, a specialist in the field of alcoholism, says, "He will surrender almost anything to support this way of life, and in this sense many an alcoholic has found in his alcoholism a kind of diabolical chemical religion."[9] In recognition

of the drinker's total commitment to drink, and the failure of "home remedies," other, more formal treatments have been devised.

A great variety of medicines have been tried in an attempt 4 to draw or to force the alcoholic away from drink. L.S.D., for example, (no longer commonly used) offers a pleasant and less destructive alternative to alcohol, but the obvious danger is that one serious addiction will be supplanted by another, also with disastrous consequences.[10] Other drugs, like valium and librium, are intended to calm the nerves of the alcoholic, making life feel less stressful and therefore making the retreat into alcoholism less necessary. But, again, there is a serious danger in the alcoholic's using the tranquilizing drugs as a supplement rather than as a substitute for alcohol. Reliance on both drugs and alcohol is doubly harmful.[11] In addition to these "positive" remedies, "aversive" medicines are also used. Pills, like "Antabuse" (the brand-name for the chemical, disulfiram), create headaches, irregular heartbeat, nausea and vomiting if a drink is taken.[12] The decision whether or not to take the pill, however, remains with the alcoholic, so the motivation for abstinence has to be present in the first place. "Aversive" drugs seem best as short-term deterrents while other treatments are being administered.[13]

Related to the medicinal aversion to alcohol is the psycho- 5 logical, through the use of conditioned responses. In this approach, the alcoholic learns to associate drinking with unpleasant sensations. When reaching for a drink, under controlled circumstances, the alcoholic may, for example, receive an electric shock, or immediately become nauseous because of a reaction to a substance injected before the drink.[14] The intention is that the alcoholic will be conditioned to associate these unpleasant responses with taking a drink and will therefore abstain, even in situations where the actual shock or sickness is no longer present. It is an effort to help the alcoholic "lose the taste" for alcohol by substituting unpleasant sensations for pleasant ones; none of the rewards associated with drink come with the drink. If the patient is susceptible to such conditioning and if the response carries over into actual situations where drink is available, this approach may encourage abstention in some cases.[15]

Some degree of success might also be experienced through 6
private therapy, using the traditional tools of psychoanalysis.
The idea behind this treatment is that, as in other cases of psychological disturbance, the problem will become more manage-
able as the causes become more apparent. The alcoholic who
examines such matters as childhood experiences and feelings,
the process of maturation, the reasons for the extreme response
to stress, the feelings for which drink seems the only answer,
and the motivation for resisting abstinence may well learn to
choose rather than be compelled to drink.[16] The most common
limitation here, however, seems to be the alcoholic's tendency
to make excuses for the habit and therefore an all-too-ready
agreement with the therapist that deeper problems are at the
root of the now-justified drinking problem. This attitude may
at worst lead to more drinking as the depth and extent of the
difficulties—past and present—become known.[17] For some, this
treatment is yet one more escape, as if to say, "The therapist
will cure me." As Jo Coudert, a writer on the problems of alcoholism, explains, ". . . but, having dumped the jigsaw pieces of
his life into the therapist's lap, he settles back and passively
awaits the return of the solved puzzle." [18]

  The most successful single approach to treatment seems to 7
be that which places responsibility for abstinence clearly on the
shoulders of the alcoholic and which offers support for the
habit of abstinence. This is the approach of Alcoholics Anonymous.[19] Through an unlimited number of group meetings
with other alcoholics at which the members share their experiences, through the repetition of key sayings: "First Things
First," "One Day at a Time," "Easy Does It," for example, and
through the network of round-the-clock telephone allies, many
alcoholics discover the emotional conditions which help them
to abstain from drink.[20] As one member said, "When you get
rid of the booze, you need something to take its place, and what
you have is AA." [21] By admitting the power of alcohol, the
drinker accepts responsibility for the drinking and then decides whether or not to stop. But here too there is a limitation.
Some alcoholics do not respond well to group meetings and,
although it is not associated with any religious organization,
the "piety" of AA's faith in a "higher power" may turn others

away.[22] For many, however, AA has been the only treatment that worked.[23]

And what of a combination of treatments—the so-called 8 "cafeteria" or "shot-gun" approach? This too has its advantages and disadvantages. It does attack the problem from a variety of angles—medicine, psychoanalysis, group therapy, support groups in or outside a hospital, etc.—and it allows the alcoholic a variety of options for achieving abstinence with which some drinkers might succeed.[24] But the very number of options may discourage or confuse others.[25] Unable to concentrate on any single treatment, an alcoholic resistant to this approach may reject all treatments and therefore choose the simple solution, drink, over the maze of cures.

As is apparent in this brief and selective survey, the prob- 9 lem of alcoholism remains a problem. Because of its severity and the disastrous effects on the drinker, the family and the society, much effort has been and will be spent on discovering a "cure." No perfect remedy has yet been found. Many treatments have something to offer some drinkers, but none is successful with all of the drinkers all of the time. The first step for all successful treatments, however, seems to be in the alcoholic's sincere desire to receive real help in achieving abstinence. As Dr. Frank Seixas, Medical Director of the National Council on Alcoholism, says, "Treating the alcoholic is like a recipe for rabbit stew: the first step is to catch the rabbit." [26] The steps after this first one vary with the pace and disposition of the drinker.

Notes

1. Pauline Cohen, *How to Help the Alcoholic* (New York: Public Affairs Committee, Inc., 1977), p. 2.
2. Geraldine Yoncha, *A Dangerous Pleasure* (New York: Hawthorne Books, Inc., 1978), p. 170.
3. Cohen, p. 1.
4. *Ibid.*, p. 17.
5. Henrik Wallgren and Herbert Barry, III, *Actions of Alcohol* (New York: Elsevier Publishing Co., 1970), Vol. II, pp. 574–582.

6. Margaret Mead. "How Women Can Help Other Women Who Drink," *Redbook,* Feb., 1975, p. 49.
7. Joseph L. Kellerman, *A Guide for the Family of the Alcoholic* (New York: Al-Anon Family Group Headquarters, 1979), p. 14.
8. *Ibid.,* pp. 5–12.
9. Ebbe Curtis Hoff, *Alcoholism: The Hidden Addiction* (New York: The Seabury Press, 1974), p. 66.
10. Yoncha, p. 180.
11. *Ibid.,* p. 173.
12. Vera Lindbeck, *The Woman Alcoholic* (New York: Public Affairs Committee, Inc., 1977), p. 21.
13. *Ibid.*
14. Wallgren, p. 758.
15. *Ibid.,* p. 759.
16. Jo Coudert, *The Alcoholic in Your Life* (New York: Warner Books, 1974), pp. 236–238.
17. Wallgren, p. 767.
18. Coudert, p. 238.
19. *Ibid.,* p. 230.
20. *What's Next? Asks the Husband of the Alcoholic* (New York: Al-Anon Family Group Headquarters, 1972), pp. 14-15.
21. Yoncha, p. 180.
22. Coudert, p. 229.
23. Yoncha, p. 181.
24. E. Mansell Pattison, Mark B. Sobell and Linda C. Sobell, *Emerging Concepts of Alcohol Dependence* (New York: Springer Publishing Co., 1977), p. 212.
25. *Ibid.*
26. Yoncha, p. 170.

Bibliography

Cohen, Pauline. *How to Help the Alcoholic.* New York: Public Affairs Committee, Inc., 1977.

Coudert, Jo. *The Alcoholic in Your Life.* New York: Warner Books, 1974.

Hoff, Ebbe Curtis. *Alcohol: The Hidden Addiction.* New York: The Seabury Press, 1974.

Kellermann, Joseph L. *A Guide for the Family of the Alcoholic.* New York: Al-Anon Family Group Headquarters, 1979.

Lindbeck, Vera. *The Woman Alcoholic.* New York: Public Affairs Committee, Inc., 1977.

Mead, Margaret. "How Women Can Help Other Women Who Drink." *Redbook,* February, 1975, pp. 49–50.

Pattison, E. Mansell, Mark B. Sobell and Linda C. Sobell. *Emerging Concepts of Alcohol Dependence.* New York: Springer Publishing Co., 1977.

Wallgren, Henrik, and Herbert Barry, III. *Actions of Alcohol.* Vol. II. New York: Elsevier Publishing Co., 1970.

What's Next? Asks the Husband of the Alcoholic. New York: Al-Anon Family Group Headquarters, 1972.

Suggestions for Writing

1. Investigate an aspect of a subject — such as the people who influenced John F. Kennedy, the causes of alcoholism, the types of modern rock music, the traits of a real or literary character, the steps to becoming a good golfer — and make a judgment or thesis based on what you have discovered in your research. As in your papers drawn from your own experiences, be sure to organize your thoughts around a controlling idea and stay on your central point. Think about your research and its meaning before you write.

2. Write a research paper in which you investigate a variety of opinions on a certain subject, making a summary of these opinions the major part of your paper. After giving a fair representation of the various arguments of others, evaluate their relative worth as far as you are able. Which seemed the most and least convincing to you? Why?

APPENDIX · A Checklist for Readers and Writers

The checklist presented in this appendix is designed to be a convenient reminder of important matters for reading and writing essays. As you will see in the first fifteen questions on the list, the issues to consider in someone else's writing are equally important in your own. Of course, the purposes of the questions vary slightly. Some are concerned with the product, others with the process of writing. For a reading assignment, the questions should help you to analyze and appreciate the writer's completed work. For your own writing assignment, the questions should help you to compose the paper as well as to evaluate the outcome. The five additional questions on the list—for the writer only—give still further attention to the writer actually composing the paper. The short essay by Kenneth Tynan and sample checklist with full discussions will help you see how the questions work in practice. After studying this essay and the checklist, you may want to do a checklist for a student essay, possibly for "Embarrassments at a Safe Distance" in the introduction to Part I.

A Checklist for Readers and Writers

The Whole Paper
1. What is the thesis?
2. What is the controlling idea?
3. For what readers is the essay written?
4. For what overall purpose is the essay written?
5. What is the basic method of development?
6. What is the tone?

Paragraphs
7. How does the introduction open the subject and prepare the readers for what follows?
8. How does the topic of each body paragraph relate to the controlling idea?
9. How do the paragraphs link to one another?
10. How does the conclusion relate to the body of the essay?

Smaller Components
11. Are sentences composed with variety and a sense of pace?
12. Are details carefully chosen?
13. Are there any examples of figurative language?
14. Are individual words chosen to advance the overall meaning of of the essay?

Evaluation
15. What do you think of the essay?

Further Evaluation: For the Writer Only
16. Have you corrected all mechanical errors?
17. Are outside sources fully acknowledged?
18. How would you describe your experience while writing this essay?
19. How would you compare this essay to others that you have written?
20. What aspect of your writing needs the most attention?

KENNETH TYNAN

The Difficulty of Being Dull

Kenneth Tynan (1927–1980) was born in Birmingham, England and educated at Oxford University. He was an art and drama critic for such journals as the Spectator *and the* Observer. *He has directed plays in London and written books, including,* Tynan Right and Left *(1967),* The Sound of Two Hands Clapping *(1975) and* Show People *(1980) and a play,* 'Carte Blanche' *(1976). In this short piece, Tynan drew on his experience as a drama critic for his discussion of the advantages enjoyed by filmmakers. Notice the conciseness of his discussion.*

Given a reasonable budget, it is hard to make an entirely 1 boring movie. This is one of the radical differences between cinema and the other narrative arts. Typeface and binding never redeemed a bad novel, and bad plays are very rarely saved by acting or direction; but even the worst movies employ so many expensive skills that they can seldom be totally dull. (Hence the cult of bad horror pictures; one can't imagine a cult of bad plays.)

Let the script, direction and star performances be never so 2 drab, they still cannot guarantee boredom. A brilliant camera-man, a master of editing or a couple of vivid supporting players can readily come to the rescue. Or a composer: much of con-temporary cinema is a musical art form, with illustrative pic-tures and dialogue interludes. Or a designer: we know what the Bond films owe to Ken Adam's decor.

If all else fails, there is always the cinema's ace of trumps: 3 mobility. Exciting locations are great saviours of drivel. When chopped into fragments, set against constantly changing back-grounds, and shot at varying distances from constantly shifting viewpoints, even the dullest writing and acting can hold one's attention. Seen from one angle in permanent long-shot against the same background—seen (in other words) as in the theatre—they would soon prove unbearably tedious. What theatre exposes, film can conceal.

Yet the cinema's advantage is also its pitfall. Where tedium 4
is so easily avoided, there is a terrible temptation to settle for the negative virtue of not being boring. The script may be flat and the star hung-over; but you've got Dmitri Tiomkin to write the score, Walter Matthau in a guest appearance, Oswald Morris behind the camera, and a location in Tahiti, so how can you lose?

Sample Checklist

The Whole Paper

1. What is the thesis?

The thesis is the central point or main idea of an essay, often expressed in a one-sentence declaration. Even if the thesis is implied rather than stated, the main idea should be clear to the reader. *In Tynan's essay, the thesis is " . . . even the worst movies employ so many expensive skills that they can seldom be totally dull."*

2. What is the controlling idea?

Within the thesis is an indication of what *aspect* of a subject the writer intends to develop—not, "I am going to write about off-campus housing," but "Off-campus housing has its advantages." "Advantages" is the controlling idea that must be developed. *Tynan's controlling idea is "expensive skills"; each body paragraph of his essay gives an example of such a skill.*

3. For what readers is the essay written?

All good writers compose with readers in mind. They must think of their readers' abilities, interests, prejudices, age, education, and potential reactions to the ideas in the essay. Otherwise they run the risk of "losing" them by being insulting, condescending, distant, simpleminded, or too scholarly. Here is one of the major areas of error for beginning writers. The reader is too often seen as a tricky "shape-shifter" who slips from one identity to another—from a generalized "other" much like the audience of popular television to a parent, professor, high school companion, or little sister—all in the course of a single essay. Decide who will be the audience of your essay and write consistently to that audience. In college essays, it is advisable to write for a knowledgeable readership made up of teachers, students, friends, and informed readers in and outside of school—not just the teacher who gave the assignment. *Tynan's readers are primarily those likely to be interested in film and theater; they may disagree with him.*

4. For what overall purpose is the essay written?

This question brings up the larger forms of discourse—description, narration, exposition, and argumentation. The writer must be aware of the overall rhetorical intention of the essay. Is it primarily to describe a person or a scene, to tell a story, to explain something, or to argue a case for or against something? Is there a combination of purposes? Does the essay tell a story as part of an argument, or describe something while giving an explanation? The writer must think of what kind of essay is being written. *Tynan's essay is primarily argumentative, trying to convince the reader of his opinion about the advantages of film.*

5. What is the basic method of development?

"Method of development" suggests the way in which the paper is constructed. Does it give a series of examples (exemplification); place things into categories (classification); or compare, contrast, or present causes and effects? Is the arrangement of material chronological? Do some paragraphs break away from the basic method? If so, why? If you work closely with the models, the method of development may already be set out for you. If you are trying a scheme of your own, be sure you know which method you are using and always follow through with what you suggest in your thesis. If you lead the reader to expect a comparison, live up to the expectation or change the thesis. *Tynan's essay is developed around examples of "expensive" skills—exemplification and division.*

6. What is the tone?

This question is concerned with attitude, with the feelings of the writer toward the subject and the audience. What is the writer's mood —amused, angry, serious, flippant, ironic, bitter? If the writer walked into the room, what would he or she be like? If the ideas of the essay were being spoken rather than written, what would be the tone of voice? Tone must be consistent with the writer's purpose and appropriate for the audience. *Tynan's tone, although argumentative, is good-tempered and essentially lighthearted.*

Paragraphs

7. How does the introduction open the subject and prepare the readers for what follows?

The introduction should perform two tasks—get the reader interested and set the scene for the essay to follow. The options are many. Writers may open with a story or an anecdote, a quotation, a question, a description, a surprising statement, or a broad discussion of a subject leading to the thesis. It should make the reader want to go on. *Tynan's brief essay opens abruptly, but he still prepares his readers by linking the issues of money and boredom in the first sentence, by comparing film to other forms of art, and by stating a clear thesis.*

8. How does the topic of each body paragraph relate to the controlling idea?

Every paragraph after the introduction looks in two directions—back to the thesis that controls the smaller topic (stated as a topic sentence or implied) and forward to the development of this thesis. It is important that the topic of the paragraph "echo" the main idea of the whole essay, and that it serve as a "mini-thesis" for its own smaller development of the main idea. The paragraph, a small unit of thought in itself, develops its own topic as the whole essay develops its thesis. It is in this development—with examples, concrete details, quotations, references, allusions, comparisons, etc.—that the interest of an essay lies. If a paragraph digresses from the main idea, its purpose should be obvious and it should be fully developed. Also, it is good to save the paragraph that most successfully proves the thesis for the climax of the essay. The most emphatic order of sentences within paragraphs should also be considered. *Paragraph 2 of Tynan's essay relates to the controlling idea with a discussion of an expensive advantage of film. The topic is developed with examples of "expensive" people. In Paragraph 3 is another expensive advantage of film. Tynan develops its topic by elaborating on the advantage of mobility and again comparing film to theater.*

9. How do the paragraphs link to one another?

This question calls attention to the flow of thoughts or the transitions from one paragraph to the next. The word "transition" comes from two Latin words—*trans,* meaning "across" and *ire,* "to go." A transition is basically a "going across," a link from one paragraph to another like a bridge stretched across a chasm. The reader should never be forced to dare a leap, but should feel secure when moving from one thought to the next. Transitions make reading smooth even when a new idea is difficult or quite different from the preceding one, because they make logical and linguistic connections that allow the reader to go on. Look for such signs as "and," "but," "however," "nevertheless," "on the other hand," "finally," "also," echoes of the final sentence in the previous paragraph, and even entire paragraphs devoted only to making a transition. Transitions are "acts of mercy," a relief from the tedious chore of thinking out connections that can be made best by the original writer. The reader should never feel deserted by the writer, especially between paragraphs. (It is also important for fluency to use transitions and logical connections among sentences within paragraphs.) *Tynan's transitions are clear. The first sentence in paragraph 2 echoes the idea of dullness by mentioning the word "drab," and paragraph 3 begins with "If all else fails," referring back to the list of paragraph 2. The conclusion refers to the cinema's "advantage," recalling the subjects of both paragraphs 2 and 3.*

10. How does the conclusion relate to the body of the essay?

Like the question on introductions that asks about the first impression, this one asks about the final effect on the reader. An essay should not simply stop as if the writer suddenly ran out of ink or inspiration. A conclusion can be long or very short; it can be a complex judgment, a further suggestion, a summary of the main points, a return to the thoughts of the introduction, or a personal note or question. As with introductions, the options are many. But whatever it is, the conclusion should leave the reader with a sense of "completeness," not with a futile search for the missing last page. *Tynan's conclusion opens with a "Yet," suggesting a contradiction, and then goes on to point out a danger inherent in simply "not being boring" —a precise link to the first sentence of paragraph 1.*

Smaller Components

11. Are sentences composed with variety and a sense of pace?

This question leads to the issue of prose rhythm, to the "sound" of the essay and its relationship to meaning. After a while, a long series of short sentences can begin to sound childish. A group of long, complex sentences, without the relief of a shorter statement, can become tedious. Good writing involves a sense of balance and an awareness of where the long and the short of it should be. Notice sentence length and rhythm; select at least two consecutive sentences that seem particularly effective, and explain why. *Tynan's sentences are varied. The short sentence, "Exciting locations are great saviours of drivel," is effective because it is a sharp statement of the "mobility" idea in the preceding sentence and a preparation for the longer sentence that follows.*

12. Are details carefully chosen?

Details are the life of an essay. They are the "thumbprints" that mark an experience, a description, an argument, even an objective discussion, as the writer's own and no one else's. A writer is always alert for the distinguishing details, the special facts that support the point, or the personal response to an experience or an idea. The automatic or expected response should be avoided. The best writer is one who is, as Henry James said, "the kind of person upon whom nothing is lost." Select at least two concrete details that seem to work well and explain why. *Tynan includes many details drawn from his wide experience as a critic (the James Bond films with sets designed by Ken Adams; the expensive talents of the musician, Dmitri Tiomkin, of the actor, Walter Matthau, and of a specific cameraman, Oswald Morris) to illustrate his point about the costly advantages of cinema.*

13. Are there any examples of figurative language?

Figurative language is a departure from the usual way of saying things—and often makes comparisons between two unlike subjects. Most common are the simile, as in Shakespeare's cloud which looked "very like a whale," the metaphor, as in his "All the world's a stage," or personification, as in Milton's "While the still morn went out with Sandals gray." The reader enjoys making the imaginative connections and is therefore inclined to continue reading. If there are any examples, choose at least one and explain how it works. *Tynan refers to " . . . the cinema's ace of trumps," a metaphor drawn from card playing which suggests that filmmaking shares something with a game of chance and that it always has a winning card—mobility—to save it from a total loss. The comparison joins the world of the professional gambler to the world of the filmmaker.*

14. Are individual words chosen to enhance the overall meaning of the essay?

The more we think about writing, the more time we spend trying to get the language to cooperate with our thoughts and the more concerned we become with vocabulary. No serious writer goes on for long without a good dictionary and perhaps a thesaurus. Vocabulary does not have to be learned or scholarly; it just has to be "right" for the writer's purpose. As thoughts become more sophisticated, vocabulary will be forced to grow to express these thoughts. Select at least two individual words that seem particularly well-chosen for meaning. *Tynan's use of the word "drivel," for example (defined as "spittle flowing from the mouth; slaver, dribblings"), is appropriate for describing a bad script. "Pitfall" (defined as a "concealed pit into which animals or men may fall and be captured) is more specific and powerful as a contrast to "advantage" than "disadvantage." It may contain a punning reference to the "pit" of an auditorium or theater into which actors have occasionally fallen.*

Evaluation

15. What do you think of the essay?

Now that you have looked at the essay from a variety of angles, it is important to pull it back together again. After one more reading, decide if it fulfills its original purpose and, most importantly, decide if you liked it as a piece of writing. Is it a well-written essay with which you disagree? Is it a poorly written essay with a convincing point? Do you like or accept only parts of it? What are its outstanding qualities? Its weaknesses? Would you read it again or look for a collection of essays by the same writer? Would you recommend it to a friend? Only after giving the writer a chance to speak are you capable of giving informed answers to these questions, but do not feel bound by the judgment of others once you have understood the essay.

When answering this question for your own paper, the question becomes much more personal. You may dislike an essay that was forced out of you between a history examination and a dormitory party, but you may, in fact, have succeeded under pressure. After you have finished the final draft, put it away for a few days and then read it again with a reader's critical eye. What seems to be its greatest virtue? Which is the best paragraph? The best sentence? If you read critically, you will probably be aware of places where the essay may be made better. If time allows, improve it. If you see a flaw but are unable to repair it, check a handbook, see your instructor, and try again until you are satisfied. Rewriting is as important as coming up with the original idea; it is here that most of the craft of writing is learned.

I enjoyed Tynan's short essay. It is a brief and forceful opinion about the costly cinematic weapons against dullness. I particularly enjoyed his comparisons between theater and film. I'm glad he said "seldom dull," because I have seen some films that I thought very dull in spite of great expense (Superman, for example). I got curious about which specific films the writer considers successful and which dull; maybe for that I will read more of his essays.

Further Evaluation: For the Writer Only

16. Have you corrected all mechanical errors?

A fast way to sabotage a good paper is to leave uncorrected errors in punctuation, capitalization, spelling, or typing. (Typing errors are ultimately your responsibility, not a typist's.) All of these errors suggest carelessness of thought, whether or not the thinking is actually careless. If necessary, use a handbook to check all possible mechanical problems.

17. Are outside sources fully acknowledged?

This question is intended as a "check" or discouragement to plagiarism, which is the presentation of someone else's material as if it
were your own. Take the trouble to footnote information (except for
generally known facts) that you have had to research. Any use of the
actual words of another should be placed in quotation marks and
identified.

18. How would you describe your experience while writing this essay?

This is a question that encourages you to think still further about
the process of writing. Did you change your thesis? If so, from what to
what? How many drafts did you write? What came easily to you—the
introduction, the details, the conclusion? What were the difficulties—
coming up with a thesis, making logical transitions, varying sentences?

19. How would you compare this essay to others that you have
written?

Whatever your response to this question, ask yourself why, so that
you will be learning about yourself and about your writing. It is also
instructive to compare your own evaluation to the comments, the cor-
rections, and the grade given by the instructor. You may not always
recognize your own strengths and weaknesses as accurately as an objective reader. Look carefully at all reactions.

20. What aspect of your writing needs the most attention?

Try to identify a single, important problem—one that you recognized as you composed the essay or one pointed out by the instructor.
Give it all the attention it needs before you write your next draft
or a completely new essay.